New York Times and *USA TODAY* bestselling author Gena Showalter has been praised for her "sizzling page-turners" and "utterly spellbinding" stories. The author of more than thirty novels and anthologies, Showalter has appeared in *Cosmopolitan* and *Seventeen* magazines, and has been nominated for the prestigious RITA® Award, as well as the National Reader's Choice Award. Visit her website at www.genashowalter.com.

GENA
SHOWALTER

LORD OF THE VAMPIRES

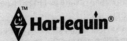

TORONTO NEW YORK LONDON
AMSTERDAM PARIS SYDNEY HAMBURG
STOCKHOLM ATHENS TOKYO MILAN MADRID
PRAGUE WARSAW BUDAPEST AUCKLAND

ISBN-13: 978-0-373-83772-4

LORD OF THE VAMPIRES
Copyright © 2011 by Gena Showalter

The publisher acknowledges the copyright holder
of the individual works as follows:

LORD OF THE VAMPIRES
Copyright © 2011 by Gena Showalter

THE DARKEST ANGEL
Copyright © 2010 by Gena Showalter

THE AMAZON'S CURSE
Copyright © 2009 by Gena Showalter

THE DARKEST PRISON
Copyright © 2009 by Gena Showalter

Recycling programs
for this product may
not exist in your area.

Dear Reader,

I'm so thrilled to bring you *Lord of the Vampires,* the first tale in the dark and sizzling Royal House of Shadows series.

Writing this book was such a blast! A world with vampires, werewolves, witches and monsters? Hell, yes! A prince known for his wicked ways and fearsome temper? Even better! A human woman who will either save or destroy him—bringing him to his knees in the process? Yes, yes, a thousand times yes.

Throw in upcoming stories by Jill Monroe *(Lord of Rage),* Jessica Andersen *(Lord of the Wolfyn)* and Nalini Singh *(Lord of the Abyss)* and I'm practically drooling about this series. Emailing these ladies about the different books was truly inspiring.

I hope you enjoy our modern takes on beloved fairy tales. We certainly had fun writing them.

All the best,

Gena Showalter

This one is for Jill Monroe, Jessica Andersen
and Nalini Singh.
Amazing ladies and talented authors.
I'd plot with you guys any day!

And to Tara Gavin, for her amazing support
and enthusiasm for the
Royal House of Shadows!

CONTENTS

LORD OF THE VAMPIRES

PROLOGUE

ONCE UPON A TIME, in a land of vampires, shape-shifters and witches, the Blood Sorcerer coveted the only power denied him: the right to rule. He and his monstrous army attacked the royal palace, slaughtered the beloved king and queen of Elden and sought to do the same to Nicolai, the crown prince, as well as his three siblings, Breena, Dayn and Micah.

The sorcerer succeeded in all but the latter. He had not counted on a king's hunger for retribution and a mother's love for her children.

Just before expelling his final breath, the king used his power to fill his offspring with an unbreakable need for vengeance, ensuring they would fight for eternity to claim their due. At the same time, the queen used her power to send them away, saving them. For the time being.

Only, the king and queen were weak, their minds fogged from pain, and their magic conflicting.

And so, the royals were now bound to destroy the man who had slain their parents, yet they were also cast out of the palace, each flung to different kingdoms within the realm with only one link to the Royal House of Elden: a timepiece, given to them by their parents.

Nicolai, the Dark Seducer as his people called him, had been in bed, but not alone. He was never alone. He was a man known for the violence of his temper as well as the deliciousness of his touch; and after his youngest brother's birthday celebration, he'd adjourned to his private chamber to sate himself on his newest conquest.

That's when the dual natures of the enchantments struck him.

When he next opened his eyes, he'd found himself in *another* bed—and not with his chosen partner. He was naked still, only now he was chained, a slave to the very desires he'd evoked in his lover. Desires that had mingled with the magic and sent him straight to the Sex Market, where he was quickly sold to a princess of Delfina, his will no longer his own, his pleasure no longer his own, his timepiece stolen and his memories wiped from his mind.

But two things could not be taken from him, no matter how fervently the princess tried. The cold rage in his chest and the blistering need for vengeance in his veins.

The first, he would unleash. The second, he would savor. First with the princess, and then with a sorcerer he could not quite remember, but a sorcerer he knew he despised all the same.

Soon.

He had only to escape....

CHAPTER ONE

"I NEED YOU, JANE."

Frowning, Jane Parker placed the note on her kitchen countertop. She studied the scarred, leather-bound book resting inside an unadorned box, surrounded by a sea of black velvet. A few minutes ago, she'd returned from her five-mile jog. This package had been waiting on her porch.

There'd been no return address. No explanation as to why the thing had been left for her, and no hint as to who "I" was. Or why Jane was needed. Why would anyone need *her?* She was twenty-seven years old and had only recently regained the use of her legs. She had no family, no friends, no job. Not anymore. Her little cabin in Smallest Town Ever, Oklahoma, was secluded, barely a blip in the neighboring expanse of lush green trees and wide-open, blue sky.

She should have tossed the thing. Of course, curiosity far outweighed caution. As always.

She carefully lifted the book. At the moment of contact, she saw her hands covered in blood and gasped, dropping the heavy tome on the counter. But when she lifted her hands to the light, they were scrubbed clean, her nails neat and painted a pretty morning rose.

You have an overactive imagination, and too much

oxygen pumping through your veins from the run. That's all.

Cold hard logic—her best and only friend.

The book's binding creaked as she opened to the middle, where a tattered pink ribbon rested. The scent of dust and musk wafted up, layered with something else. Something…mouthwatering and slightly familiar. Her frowned deepened.

She shifted in her seat, a twinge of pain shooting through her legs, and sniffed. Oh, yes. Her mouth definitely watered as she caught the slightest trace of sandalwood. Goose bumps broke out over her skin, her senses tingling, her blood heating. How embarrassing. And, okay, how interesting. Since the car accident that ruined her life eleven months ago, she had experienced arousal only at night, in her dreams. To react like this in daylight, because of a book…odd.

She didn't allow herself to ponder why. There wasn't an answer that would satisfy her. Instead, she concentrated on the pages in front of her. They were yellowed and brittle, delicate. And beaded with blood? Small dots of dried crimson marred the edges.

Gently she brushed her fingertips along the handwritten text, her gaze catching on several words. *Chains. Vampire. Belonged. Soul.* More goose bumps, more tingling.

Some blushing.

Her eyes narrowed. At last the sandalwood cologne made sense. For the past few months, she'd dreamed of a vampire male in chains and woken to the fragrance clinging to her skin. And yes, he's the one who had aroused her. She'd told no one. So, how had anyone known to give her this…journal?

She'd worked in quantum physics for years, as well as what was considered fringe science, sometimes studying creatures of "myth" and "legend." She'd conducted controlled interviews with actual blood drinkers and even dissected the corpses brought to her lab.

She knew that vampires, shape-shifters and other creatures of the night existed, even though her coworkers on the quantum physics side of the equation had not been privy to the truth. So, maybe someone had found out and this was a simple joke. Maybe her dreams had no connection. Except, forever had seemed to pass since she'd had any contact with those coworkers. And besides, who would do such a thing? None of them had cared enough about her to do *anything*.

Let this go, Parker. Before it's too late.

The command from her self-preservation instincts made no sense. *Too late for what?*

Her instincts offered no reply. Well, the scientist in her *needed* to know what was going on.

Jane cleared her throat. "I'm reading a few passages, and that's that." She'd been alone since leaving the hospital several months ago, and sometimes the sound of her voice was better than silence. "'Chains circled the vampire's neck, wrists and ankles. Because his shirt and pants had been stripped away, and a loincloth was his only apparel, there was nothing to protect his already savaged skin. The links cut him deeply, to the bone, before healing—and slicing open again. He did not care. What was pain when your will, your very soul, no longer belonged to you?'"

She pressed her lips together as a wave of dizziness crashed through her. A moment passed, then another, her heartbeat speeding up and hammering wildly against her ribs.

Raw images tore through her. This man—this vampire—bound, helpless. Hungry. His lush lips were pulled taut, his teeth sharp, white. He was surprisingly tanned, temptingly muscled, with dark, mussed hair and a face so eerily beautiful he would haunt her nighttime fantasies for years to come.

What she'd just read, she'd already seen. Many times. How? She didn't know. What she did know was that in her dreams, she felt compassion for this man, even anger. And yet, there was always that low simmer of arousal in the background. Now, the arousal took center stage.

The more she breathed, the more the sandalwood scent clung to her, and the more her reality altered, as if this, her home, was nothing more than a mirage. As if the vampire's cage was real. As if she needed to stand up and walk—no, *run*—until she reached him. Anything to be with him, now and forever.

Okay. Enough of that. She slapped the book closed, even though so many questions were left dangling, and strode away.

Such a strong reaction coupled with her dreams utterly nixed the idea of a joke. Not that she'd placed much hope in that direction. However, the remaining possibilities upset her, and she refused to contemplate them.

She showered, dressed in a T-shirt and jeans and ate a nutritious breakfast. Unbidden, she found her gaze returning to the leather binding, over and over again. She wondered if the enslaved vampire were real—and okay. If she could help him. A few times, she even opened to the middle of the book before she realized she'd moved. Always she darted off before the story could snare her.

And perhaps *that's* why the stupid thing had been given to her. To hook her, to send her racing back to work. Well, she didn't need to work. Money was not a problem for her. More than that, she no longer loved the sciences. Why would she? There was never a solution, only more problems.

Because when one puzzle piece slid into place, there were always twenty more needed. And in the end, nothing you did, nothing that had been solved or unraveled, would save the ones you loved. There would always be some dumb guy throwing back a few cold ones at the local bar, getting into his car and hitting yours. Or something equally tragic.

Life was random.

Jane craved monotony.

But when midnight rolled around, her mind still hadn't settled in regards to the vampire. Giving up, she returned to the kitchen, grabbed the book and stalked to bed. Just a few more passages, damn it, *then* she'd start craving monotony again.

Jane's oversize T-shirt bunched at her waist as she propped the book on her upraised legs, opened to the middle of the story, where the bookmark was still set, and returned her attention to the pages. For several seconds, the words appeared to be written in a language she did not understand. Then, a blink later, they were written in English again.

O-kay. Very weird, and surely—hopefully—an I-just-need-sleep mistake on her part.

She found her place. "'They called him Nicolai.'" Nicolai. A strong, luscious name. The syllables rolled through her mind, a caress. Her nipples beaded, aching for a hot, wet kiss, and every inch of her skin flushed. She thought back. She'd never interviewed a vampire named Nicolai, and the one in her dream had never spoken to her. He had never acknowledged her in any way. "'He did not know his past or if he had a future. He knew only his present. His hated, torturous present. He was a slave, locked away like an animal.'"

Just like before, a wave of dizziness slammed through her. This time, Jane pressed on, even as her chest constricted. "'He was kept clean and oiled. Always. Just in case Princess Laila had need of him in her bed. And the princess did have need of him. Often. Her cruel, twisted desires left him beaten and bruised. Not that he ever accepted defeat. The man was wild, nearly uncontrollable, and so filled with hate anyone who looked at him saw their death in his eyes.'"

The dizziness intensified. Hell, so did the desire. To tame a man like that, to have all of his vigor focused on you, pounding into you...his participation willing... Jane shivered.

Lose the ADD, Parker. She cleared her throat. "'He was hard, merciless. A warrior at heart. A man used to absolute control. At least, he thought he was. Even with his lack of memory, he was patently aware that every order directed his way scraped his nerves raw.'"

Another shiver rocked her. She grit her teeth. He needed her compassion, not her desire. *He's* that *real to you?* Yeah, he was. "'At least he would have a few days' reprieve,'" she read on, "'forgotten by one and all. The entire palace was frothing over Princess Odette's return from the grave and—'"

The rest of the page was blank. "And what?" Jane

flipped to the next, but quickly realized the story had ended on an unfinished cliff-hanger. Great.

Thankfully—or not—she discovered more writing toward the end and blinked, shook her head. The words didn't change. "'You, Jane Parker,'" she recited hollowly. "'You are Odette. Come to me, I command you. Save me, I beg you. Please, Jane. I need you.'"

Her name was in the book. How was her name in the book? And written by the same hand as the rest? On the same aged, stained pages, with the same smudged ink?

I need you.

Her attention returned to the part directed to her. She reread "You are Odette" until the urge to scream was at last overshadowed by curiosity. Her mind swirled. There were so many paths to take with this. Forged, genuine, dream, reality.

Come to me.

Save me.

Please.

I command you.

Something inside her responded to that command more than anything else in the book. The urge to run— here, there, anywhere—beat through her. As long as she found him, saved him, nothing else mattered. And she could save him, just as soon as she reached him.

I. Command. You.

Yes. She wanted to obey. So damn badly. She felt as if an invisible cord had been wound around her neck, and was now tugging at her.

Trembling, Jane closed the book. She wasn't searching for anyone. Not tonight. She needed to regroup. In the morning, after a few coffee IVs, her head would be clear and she could reason this out. She hoped.

After placing the tome on her nightstand, she flopped into her bed and closed her eyes, trying to force her brain to quiet. An unsuccessful endeavor. If Nicolai's story was true, he was as trapped by those chains as surely as she had once been trapped by her body's infirmities.

The compassion grew…spread…

While he was kept in a cage, she had been bound to a hospital bed, her bones broken, her muscles torn, her mind hazed by medication, all because a drunk driver had slammed into her car. And while she had been—was—tormented by the loss of her family, since her mother, father and sister had been in the car with her, Nicolai was tormented by a sadistic woman's unwanted touch. She felt a wave of regret, a crackle of fury.

I need you.

Jane inhaled deeply, exhaled slowly and shifted to her side, clutching her pillow close. As close as she suddenly wanted to clutch Nicolai, to comfort him. To be with him. *Uh, not going there.* She didn't know the man. Therefore, she wasn't going to imagine sleeping with him.

But that's exactly what she did. His plight was forgotten as she imagined him climbing on top of her, his silver eyes bright with desire, his pupils blown. His lips were plump and red from kissing her entire body, still moist with her flavor. She licked at him, tasting him, tasting herself, eager for anything and everything he would give her.

He growled his approval, flashing his fangs.

His big, muscled body surrounded her, his skin hot,

little beads of sweat forming, causing them to rub and glide together, straining toward release. God, he felt good. So damn good. Long and thick. A perfect fit, stretching her just right. Rocking, rocking, faster and faster, taking her to the edge of sensation before slowing…slowing…tormenting.

She clawed at him, her nails scouring his back. He groaned. She raised her knees, squeezing his hips. *Yes. Yes, more.* Faster, faster still. Never enough, almost enough. *More, please more.*

Nicolai's tongue thrust into her mouth, rolling with hers before he bit down, drawing blood, sucking. A sharp sting, and then, finally, oh, God, finally, she tumbled over.

Ripples of satisfaction swept through her entire body, little stars winking behind her eyes. Her inner muscles clenched and unclenched, liquid heat pooling between her legs. She rode the tide for endless seconds, minutes, before sagging against the mattress, boneless, unable to catch her breath.

An orgasm, she mused dazedly. A freaking orgasm from a fantasy man, and she hadn't even needed to touch herself.

"Nicolai…mine…" she whispered, and she was smiling as she at last drifted off to sleep.

CHAPTER TWO

"PRINCESS. PRINCESS, you must wake up."

Jane blinked open her eyes. Muted sunlight pushed into the bedroom—an unfamiliar bedroom, she realized with confusion. Her room was plain, with white walls and brown carpet, the only furniture an unadorned bed. Now, a lacy pink canopy was draped overhead. To her right was an intricately carved nightstand, a bejeweled goblet perched on top. Beyond that, a plush, glittery carpet led to arched double doors framing a spacious closet bursting with a rainbow of velvets, satins and silks.

This wasn't right.

She jolted upright. Dizziness hit her—familiar, but not comforting—and she moaned.

"Are you all right, princess?"

She forced herself to focus and take stock. A girl stood beside her bed. A girl she had never encountered before. Short, plump, with a freckled nose and frizzy red hair, wearing a coarse brown dress that appeared uncomfortably snug.

Jane scrambled backward, hitting the headboard. "Who are you? What are you doing here?" Even as she spoke, her eyes widened. She knew five different languages, but she wasn't speaking any of them. And yet, she understood every word that left her mouth.

No emotion crossed the girl's features, as if she were used to strange people yelling at her. "I am Rhoslyn, once personal servant to your mother but now personal servant to you. If you agree to keep me," she added, unsure now. She, too, spoke in that weird, lyrical language of flowing syllables. "The queen has bid me to rouse you and escort you to her study."

Servant? Mother? Jane's mother was dead, along with her father and her sister. The latter two had been killed on impact, the drunk driver having slammed his car into their side of the vehicle. Her mom, though…she had died right before Jane's eyes, her life dripping out of her and onto Jane, their car propped against a tree, their seat belts holding them in place, the metal doors and roof smashed so completely they'd had to be pried out. But, by then, it had been too late. She'd already taken her last, pained breath.

She'd died the very day she was told her cancer was gone.

"Don't you dare tease me about my mother," Jane growled, and Rhoslyn flinched.

"I'm sorry, princess, but I do not understand. I tease you not about your mother's summons." How frightened she sounded now. Tears even beaded in her dark eyes. "And I swear to you, I meant no offense. Please do not punish me."

Punish her? Was this some sort of joke?

The word *joke* was as familiar as the dizziness. But, really, *joke* still didn't fit. Nervous breakdown, perhaps? No, couldn't be. Breakdowns were a form of hysteria, and she was not hysterical. Plus, there was the language thing. *Come on. You're a scientist. You can reason this out.*

"Where am I? How did I get here?" Her last memory was of reading the book and—the book! Where was the book? Her heart thundered uncontrollably, a storm inside her chest, as she panned her surroundings once more. There! Her book rested on the vanity, so close, yet so far away.

Mine, every cell in her body screamed, surprising her. Equally surprising, the absolute rightness of the claim. But then, she'd practically made love to the thing. And, oh, damn. Her blood heated and her skin tingled, her body readying for absolute, utter possession.

I need you, Jane. The text. She remembered the text. *Come to me. Save me.*

Consider this logically. She'd fallen asleep, dreamed of a vampire's decadent touch and, like *Alice in Wonderland,* had woken up in a strange, new world. And she *was* awake. This was not a dream. So, where was she? How had she gotten here?

What if…?

She cut off the thought before it could veer into a direction she didn't like. There had to be a rational explanation. "Where am I?" she asked again.

As Jane scooted from the soft confines of the feather-lined mattress, the "servant" said, "You are in…Delfina." She spoke with a question in her tone, as if she couldn't quite grasp the fact that Jane didn't already know the answer. "A kingdom without time or age."

Delfina? She'd…heard of it, she realized with a start. Not the name, but the "kingdom without time." A few of the beings she'd interviewed had mentioned another realm, a magical realm, with differing kingdoms outside the notice of humans. At the time, she hadn't known whether to believe them or not. They'd been prisoners, locked away for the good of mankind. They would have said anything to gain their freedom. Even offer to escort her into their world.

What if...?

What if she'd crossed the threshold from her world and into the other? Jane finally allowed the thought to reach its conclusion, and her stomach churned with sickness.

Before the car accident changed her life so radically, she'd studied more than the creatures of myth. She'd studied the manipulation of macroscopic energy, attempting the "impossible" on a daily basis. Like the molecular transfer of an object from one location— one world—to another, and she had succeeded. Not with life-forms, of course, not yet, but with plastic and other materials. That's why she'd been deemed an acceptable risk for interacting with the captured beings, both dead and alive.

What if she'd somehow transferred *herself?* But how would she have done so, she wondered next, when the necessary tools were not in her cabin? Latent effects of her contact with the previously transferred materials, perhaps?

No. There were too many variables. Namely, her new, royal identity.

"Rhoslyn," she said, keeping her narrowed gaze on the girl as she settled her weight on her legs. Her knees knocked together, and her muscles knotted, but thankfully the dizziness did not return.

"Yes, princess?"

She gave herself a quick once-over, blinked with another dose of surprise and had to look again. She wore a lovely pink gown she hadn't purchased herself and had never before seen. The material bagged around her reed-thin body, dancing at her ankles.

Who the hell had dressed her?

Doesn't matter. She focused on the here and now. "What do I look like?"

Rhoslyn reached out, and Jane pursed her lips as she darted away. "Please, princess, you have been unwell. Allow me to assist you."

"Stay where you are," Jane told her. Until she figured out what was going on, she would trust no one. And without trust, there would be no touching.

The girl froze in place. "Wh-whatever you command, princess. Did you wish me to fetch something for you?"

"No, uh, I just want to grab something from over there." Jane lumbered forward. The carpet fibers were as soft as they appeared and caressed her bare feet, tickling the sensitive areas between her toes. She moved slowly, allowing the tension to drain from her abused legs. By the time she swiped up the book and turned, she felt normal. Still the girl had not moved, her arm extended toward the bed, shaking now. "At ease," she found herself saying.

With a sigh of relief, Rhoslyn dropped her arm to her side. "You asked what you look like. Beautiful, princess. As always." Said automatically, with no real feeling.

Half of Jane's attention remained on her while the other half focused on the book. She frowned. The dark leather was unmarred. She flipped to the middle. There was no bookmark, and the pages were new, fresh. Blank. "This isn't my book," she said. "Where's my book?"

"Princess Odette," Rhoslyn replied smoothly. "To

my knowledge, you did not arrive with a book. Now, would you like—?"

"Wait. What did you call me?"

"Pr-princess Odette? That is your title and name. Yes? Did you wish me to call you something else? Or, perhaps I can summon the healer, and have her—"

"No. No, that's okay." Princess Odette, returned from the grave. Jane had read those very words. She'd also read, "You, Jane Parker. You are Odette."

She twisted and leaned into the vanity, watching her reflection in the mirror. The moment she came into view, she stiffened. Light brown hair flowed over one shoulder. *Her* hair. Familiar. Her dark eyes were glassy, crescent-moon bruises underneath. Also familiar.

She reached out. Her fingertips pressed into the glass. Cool, solid. Real. If she lifted her gown, she would see the scars that marred her stomach and legs. She knew it.

She hadn't morphed into Princess Odette overnight, then. Or, hell, maybe she and the princess looked alike.

"How did I get here?" she croaked, swinging back around to face the girl.

I need you, Jane.

Nicolai. She sucked in a breath as his name suddenly filled her mind. Nicolai the enslaved vampire, chained, abused. Nicolai the lover, sliding into her body, her legs parting to welcome him, then squeezing to hold him captive.

Come to me.

Come to him, as if he knew her. As if she knew him. But she'd never met him. At least, not to her knowledge.

Such a thing *was* possible, she supposed. Paradox theory suggested—damn it. No. She wasn't going to hypothesize about paradox theory until she had more information. Otherwise, she'd be lost in her head for days.

Rhoslyn paled. "Yesterday evening a palace guard found you lying on the steps outside. He carried you here, to your bedchamber. You'll be happy to note it is in the same condition you left it."

Falling asleep at home, waking up...here. Princess Odette, returned from the grave, she thought again. Alice in her Wonderland.

"I hope you do not mind, but I bathed and changed you," Rhoslyn added.

White-hot heat in her cheeks. Plenty of strangers had bathed and changed her over the past eleven months, and she was relieved Rhoslyn had done so, rather than some sweating, panting guy. Still. *Mortifying.* "Where's my shirt?"

"It's being washed. I must admit, I have never seen its like. There was strange writing on it."

She closed the book and clutched it to her chest. "I want it back." Just then, it was her only link to home.

"Of course. After I escort you to your mother, I— oh, I'm sorry. I did not mean to mention her again. I will take you to...the study below and fetch the garment for you." Before Jane could comment, Rhoslyn added through gnashed teeth, "I am so happy—as are all your people—that you have come back to us. We missed you greatly."

A lie, no question. "Wh-where was I?"

"Your sister, Princess Laila, witnessed your fall from the cliffs what seems an eternity ago. After you were stabbed and drained by your new slave. Though your body was never found, it was assumed you were dead, as no one has ever survived such a drop before. We should have known that you, the darling of Delfina, would find a way." She flashed a stiff smile that lasted a single second, no more.

Princess Laila. That name, too, reverberated in Jane's head, followed on the heels of "cruel, twisted desires."

"Nicolai," she said. Was he here? Real?

The servant chewed on her bottom lip, suddenly nervous. "You wish me to bring the slave, Nicolai, to you?"

Jane's blood quickened and warmed, her skin tingling just as before. The girl knew who he was. That meant he *was* here, that he was as real as she was.

Her mind fizzed and crackled like her favorite candy. The book. The characters. The story, coming to life before her eyes…Jane now a part of it, deeply integrated, though she was someone other than herself. Finally. A puzzle piece slid into place.

The book could have been the catalyst. Maybe, when she'd read aloud, she'd somehow opened a doorway from her world into this one. Maybe Nicolai had somehow sent the book to her, and she was his only hope for freedom.

"Nicolai," she repeated. "I want you to take me to him." She had to see him, and was too impatient to wait. Would he know her? Was she right about the events that had unfolded?

Rhoslyn gulped. "But he's the one who stabbed you, and your moth—I mean, er, the queen does not like to be kept waiting. She visited you once already, but you were sound asleep and could not be roused. Her impatience grows, and as you know, her temper…" Her cheeks flushed as she realized what she was saying. "I'm sorry. I meant no disrespect to the queen."

Nicolai had stabbed Odette, the woman Jane was supposed to be? Talk about a plot twist Jane hadn't seen coming. Damn. What if he tried to do the same to Jane?

He won't, some deep, secret part of her said. *He needs you. He said so.*

"A few minutes more won't hurt the queen." Whoever the queen was, whatever she was supposed to mean to her, Jane didn't care. Although, the fact that the woman was in charge, her word law and she apparently had a temper, unsettled her.

"Your sister—"

"Doesn't matter." She, too, was dead. Although, according to the book, *Odette* might just have a sister. That other princess. But again, Jane didn't care. "Take me to Nicolai. Now." Time to find another puzzle piece.

A breath shuddered through the girl, the seconds ticking by in tension-filled silence. Then, "Whatever you wish, princess. This way."

CHAPTER THREE

THEY CALLED HIM NICOLAI. He didn't know if that was his real name. He didn't know anything about himself, really. Whenever he attempted to remember, his head throbbed with unbearable pain and his mind shut down. All he knew was that he was a vampire, and the females here were witches. That, and he despised this kingdom and its people—and he would destroy them. One day. Soon. Just as he'd destroyed one of their precious princesses.

Anticipation rushed through him. His captors thought him weak, ineffective. They kept him on the razor edge of hunger, giving him a drop of blood in the morning and a drop of blood at night. That was all. He was teased and tormented constantly. Especially by the Princess Laila. *So highborn, but look at you now. At my feet, mine to do with as I wish.*

Highborn? He would find out.

They assumed, just because he was chained and starved, he could not harm them. They had no idea of the power that swirled inside him. Power that was caged, like him, but still there, ready to burst free at any moment.

Soon, he thought again, grinning darkly.

They'd had their healer bind his powers, as well as wipe his memory, and they made no secret of those facts. Why they'd done the latter, however, they'd never said. What did they not want him to remember? Again, he would find out.

What *they* didn't know was that the witch had lacked Nicolai's inner strength, and already a few of his abilities had seeped through that mental cage, allowing him to summon a woman who could set him free.

A woman who had at last arrived. Urgency and relief rushed through him, driving him to pace, back and forth, back and forth, his bare feet pounding into the cold concrete, his chains rattling. Even his guards were shocked by the miracle of Princess Odette's appearance. Or rather, the girl they assumed was Princess Odette.

The real Odette was dead. He'd made sure of it. He had drained her, stabbed her, then shoved her over the cliffs outside this palace. Excessively violent, perhaps, but an enemy was an enemy, and his temper had been roused. And, as he'd known, not even the most powerful of witches could recover from that.

Hurry, female. I need you.

Nicolai had spent countless days, weeks, years—he wasn't sure—with Odette before he'd killed her. She was the one who had purchased him at the Sex Market, after all. She'd been a cruel girl, with a taste for delivering pain, unable to reach her climax until her unwilling partner screamed.

She had never climaxed with Nicolai.

Remaining silent had been a source of pride for him. No matter the instruments used on him, no matter how many males and females the bitch had allowed to touch and use him, he had only ever smiled.

When Odette took him outside the palace, threatening to throw *him* over the cliffs if he continued to defy her, he was finally given an opportunity to strike. She'd made the mistake of leaving his muzzle behind. She'd also made the mistake of stepping within his reach, chained though he'd been. He'd fallen on her, pinned her and sunk his fangs into her neck. Starved as he'd been, he'd drained her in minutes. And after that last, life-ending gulp, he'd stabbed her with her own dagger, just to be sure, and shoved her over the precipice.

Too late had the guard realized what had happened, and Nicolai had turned on him, ready for another snack. They'd fought like animals. More beastlike than most, Nicolai had won. The guard had never stood a chance, really. When provoked or hungry, vampires became frenzied and ravenous—unpredictable, uncontrollable predators who scented prey.

As he'd drained his second victim, Princess Laila had swooped in. Having coveted her older sister's right to the throne, as well as her possessions, including Nicolai himself, she had watched Odette, waiting for the perfect time to act.

Nicolai had inadvertently given it to her. She and her guards had moved faster than his gaze could track, unfettered magic giving them strength and speed, and though his first meal in weeks had rallied him, the chains had slowed him down. He'd been overpowered with embarrassing ease.

Footsteps suddenly sounded, followed by the waft of something sweet in the air, both catching his attention. Nicolai stiffened and stilled, his ears twitching, his mouth watering. Absolute hunger bathed him, his stomach twisting. *Must...taste...female...*

The desire did not spring from his mind, but from deep inside him. An instinct, a need.

Usually those footsteps heralded the arrival of Laila's servants, sent to drag him up the stairs and into her bedroom. This time, a plump redhead rounded the corner. He inhaled deeply, growled. Not her. She was not the source of that sweetness.

Nicolai stopped breathing, hoping his head would clear, if only for a moment. He was so damn hungry for the one responsible…had to see her. He rooted his feet in the center of his cage, his pallet behind him, thick bars in front of him, waiting. Who would next enter the dungeon?

And then, he saw her. The summoned female. His "Odette."

He sucked in another breath. Her. She was responsible. A second growl rose, this one straight from his soul. *Must taste female.*

She did not smell like the real Odette. To everyone else, she would. She would smell of too-strong floral perfume mixed with the raw ooze of a putrid wound— evidence of her rotting heart. But to him…oh, to him… He inhaled again, unable to stop himself. Mistake. The sweetness, thicker now, almost tangible, fogged his mind. *Must. Taste.* His fangs and gums actually ached with the need to sample her. *Must taste.*

He studied her, his blood practically on fire. Anyone who looked at her would see the mask his shifted glamour had created. The mystical illusion of being someone else. Hair as dark as the Abyss, eyes of vivid emerald, skin as pale as cream. But that was where the gift of her father's famed beauty ended, and the cruelty of her mother's ugliness revealed itself. Odette was tall yet thickly built, her cheeks puffed from excess, her jaw squared with jowls. Her dark brows were substantial, and nearly connected in the center. Her nose was long with a definite hook.

What Nicolai saw, however, was the woman his summoning had chosen. The one from his dreams. Dreams in which she stood off to the side, watching him, never speaking. Dreams he had not understood. Until now. All along, his magic had known what he needed.

She was just as tall as Odette, but reed slender, with hair the color of a honeycomb. Her eyes were seductively uptilted, a shade darker than her hair, and filled with haunting secrets. Her skin was slightly bronzed and radiant, as if the sun was hidden underneath. Her cheeks were perfectly sculpted, her chin stubborn and yet delicate.

Delicate, yes. That's what she was. Amorously delicate, utterly fragile and delightfully feminine. Almost… breakable. Would he kill her when he drank from her? And he *would* drink from her. He would not be able to resist that scent for long.

The protector in him rose up—a part of him he had not known existed, not for some stranger—demanding that he sweep her away from this and save her from the horror to come. Horror he would be responsible for. Not only from his dark embrace, but also from the evil of those around her. The people of Delfina wouldn't savor her blood if they learned the truth of her identity. They would spill it and kill her. Painfully.

Do you want your freedom or the girl out of harm's way? You can't have both.

He hardened his heart. He wanted his freedom.

Their gazes locked a second later, a shock of awareness blasting him. Perhaps she felt it, too, for she gasped, stumbled. She righted herself and stopped at the bars, her amber eyes wide, her lush, pink mouth open, revealing straight white teeth. She held a book.

Taste her...

He wished he could see her tongue. Wished he could capture that tongue with his own. His desire surprised him. How long since he'd experienced true, willing arousal?

"You're real," she whispered, gripping the metal with her free hand. She squeezed so tightly her knuckles bleached of color. "You're really here. And you look exactly as I dreamed."

He nodded stiffly—and that wasn't the only stiff thing about him. His cock filled, lengthening, thickening. "I am real, yes." She'd dreamed of him, as he'd dreamed of her? He liked the idea.

He motioned to the servant with a tilt of his chin. *Get rid of her.*

Her attention whipped to the girl, and she uttered another gasp, as though startled to find they weren't alone. "You may go, Rhoslyn. And thank you for bringing me here."

"Anything for you, princess." Expression softening with her relief, Rhoslyn curtsied. She raced around the corner and pounded up the stairs.

"You are confused," Nicolai said. How harsh his voice was, pushing through his teeth and slicing up his tone.

A shiver slid down her slight frame as she faced him. "Yes. One minute I was at home, reading a book—about you! The next I was here. How am I here? Where *is* here? At first, I thought I was hallucinating or that this was a joke, but that isn't right. I know that isn't right. I'm calm. I see, I feel."

"No hallucination, and no joke." His frown deepened, his fangs cutting into his bottom lip. Just a taste, one little taste. "You were reading a book about me? Is that it?"

Her gaze fell to his teeth, and she gulped. "Yes. Written by you, I think." Her voice was as soft and delicate as her features. "Or at least, part of it was. But no, this isn't it. This one is blank. Or maybe this *is* it, but the writing just hasn't happened yet."

To his knowledge, he had not written a book, and had not sent a book to anyone. That did not mean anything, however. The memory of doing so could be buried with all the rest of his past.

He closed his eyes for a moment, enjoying the scent of her—and felt the ache in his gums intensify. He was walking toward her, determined to grab her, bite her.

When he realized what he was doing, he forced himself to stop. He would scare her, and she would scream. Guards would rush inside to save her.

He could cover her mouth with one hand, of course, and tilt her back with the other, giving himself a wide playing field. He could lick…finally, blessedly taste…

Concentrate. "Do you know who I am?" Again, his tone was harsh, demanding. "Have you met me before? Besides in your dreams?"

"No."

Disappointing. "I will explain everything. Later," he lied. The less she knew, now and in the future, the better it would be for her. "Right now, we must hurry." Ever since he'd woken up in the slave market—weeks, months, *years* ago?—he'd been driven by more than a need to feed and escape. He'd been driven by an urge to reach the kingdom of Elden.

He must get there. And soon. More than that, he must slay the new king. He didn't know why, he just knew that even thinking of the man filled him with rage. And every day that this man lived, a piece of Nicolai died. The knowledge was separate from his memories, springing from the same place as his need to taste this woman.

Taste. How many times would he think the word?

Countless. Until he got what he wanted, he was sure.

"Give me your arm." He licked his lips at the thought of touching her, of knowing the texture of her skin. "I will mark you." A little nip of her wrist, and he would stop. He would make himself stop. For now.

She shook her head, honeycomb hair dancing over her shoulders. "No. Explain now. Afterward, we'll *talk* about the marking thing, whatever that is."

Surely the female was not as stubborn as she seemed. "We might be separated." Before she freed him. "I want to know where you are at all times."

"Uh, I'm not sure how I feel about someone knowing where I am at all times. But again, we'll discuss it. After."

All right, she was *more* stubborn than she seemed. "As you can see, I have been enslaved. Tortured." Uttering the words enraged him further. He should never have allowed himself to be placed in this situation. He should have been stronger. He *was* stronger. But he had no idea how he'd ended up in the Sex Market. "I don't even—"

"—know if your name is really Nicolai. Blah, blah, blah. *I know.* I told you, I read a few passages of the book. I just don't understand this." She motioned to the prison, to him, to her gown. "'Jane, I need you,' you said. How did you know to write to me when we've never met?" Desperation wafted from her. "Unless I came here before, but returned home to a time before we'd met, and my dreams were echoes of what was to be. That would mean history is now looping, but of course, that creates a paradox, and—"

"Enough." Jane. Her name was Jane. Somehow familiar, causing his arousal to ramp up…up. Maybe because the syllable was as soft and lyrical as her strange—though slight—accent. *Focus.* If she had asked anyone else these questions… "What have you mentioned to the others?"

"Nothing." She laughed without humor. "I don't know them."

"Good. That's good." But she knew him, even though they had only seen each other in their dreams? As he had claimed to know her in that book? Something more *was* going on here. "Where are you from, Jane?"

"Oklahoma."

Oklahoma was not part of this magical realm. "You are human, then? Not a witch?"

A sweep of dark lashes, momentarily hiding undiluted shock. And pride. "I was right. I crossed over, didn't I?"

"Jane. I asked you a question." And he was used to getting answers immediately. He felt it in his bones.

"Yes, I'm human, and no, I'm not a witch. But you, you're a vampire."

He nodded. He knew this realm coexisted alongside the mortal world—a world mostly ignorant of what surrounded them.

Crossing over, as she had mentioned, happened more often than it should. How and why, though, no one knew. One moment you would be talking to a shifter or fighting an ogre, and the next moment a human would be in his place. And if not a human, a useless, bendable object.

Disappointment nearly felled Nicolai. Why had his magic chosen this woman? What good was a human here? Even so luscious a human? If Jane were asked to perform a ritual, as Odette had often been asked, she would be unable. She would fail. Everyone would know she was not who she claimed to be, *before* he could get what he wanted.

He had to act faster than planned.

"Listen. I summoned you here, and I am the one who protects you." A small truth meant to pacify her. "Trust no one else. Only me." A lie meant to save him. For once she set him free, he truly planned to leave. This palace—and her. As unstable as his abilities were, he could not remove the mask that made her Odette while they were together without the possibility of sending her home. Plus, he needed her able to travel freely through this palace as only a princess could. What a princess *couldn't* do was travel unfettered outside these walls.

The moment she let him go, Jane would have nothing but her wits to shield her.

Guilt filled him. Before the emotion had time to settle, develop roots and grow, he ground it into powder and scattered every speck. He could not soften. No matter how desperately he craved this woman's blood.

"So, you wield some type of magic?" she said. "All right. I can roll with the idea of a magical vampire. But really, a lot of people assume science is magic, so are we talking about planar, natural, runic, divine or metaphysical, because I can—"

"Jane." She was a babbler. He found the trait… charming. He frowned. Charming? Truly? The need to taste her must be clouding his judgment.

Abashed, she smiled. "I'm sorry. Curiosity and puzzles are my downfall. At least, they used to be. I thought I'd come to hate them, but, well, as you can see, that's no longer the case."

That smile…had he ever seen so open and innocent a sight? Another spark of guilt ignited in his chest, but again, he quickly ground and scattered it. Easier done this time, as the force of his arousal intensified, becoming his sole focus.

No. Only escape mattered, he told himself.

"Why me?" she asked. "I mean, how did you know to summon *me?*"

He'd wanted a female susceptible to the lure of a vampire, one untainted by the evil of the Queen of Hearts, one who was not afraid of blood, who would understand his plight. He told her none of that. He knew women—or, at least, thought he did—and knew it would not please her. "Order my release. Now. Hurry."

Frustration suddenly radiated from her. "How?" she demanded.

"Summon the guard," he said. "Tell them to unchain me, that you wish to take me to your bedchamber. Then, tell them to bring the healer to us."

"The healer?" Her concerned gaze swept over him. "Are you hurt?"

No. But the healer had bound his memories and powers, and so the healer could easily free them. And, he mused darkly, he wanted to kill the bitch. "I do not hear you calling for the guard, Jane."

"Then your ears are working perfectly, Nicolai. So,

the guards will do what I tell them?" She snapped her fingers. "Just like that?"

"In their minds, you are the princess Odette. Oldest daughter of their queen, and soon to be their ruler." Nicolai finally allowed himself to stride the rest of the way to the bars, his chains rattling. Closing in... "They will do anything you tell them to do."

She released the metal and backed away before he could touch her. As if he were dirty, unworthy. He probably was. "Yes, but why do they believe I'm Odette?"

A muscle ticked below his eye. Her continued questioning irritated him, yes, but her distance irritated him *more*. When close to her, the scent of her was nearly overpowering and so delectable he was probably drooling. "Because."

"Because why?"

Stubborn baggage. "Because my...vampire magic made them," he said flatly. To tell her more was to, perhaps, send her running. Humans were so easily frightened by what they did not understand.

For the moment, he needed this woman on his side, and calm. Although, to be honest, she'd handled things very well so far.

"How?" she insisted.

He shook the bars. "Do as I told you, Jane. We must hurry."

She arched a brow. "You're cute when you're ordering me around, you know that?" The color in her cheeks brightened, and her breath became shallow. "And you... you smell like sandalwood."

She liked his scent as much as he liked hers, he realized. It aroused her. Her nipples were pearling beneath her robe, begging for a touch, a kiss. Did her belly quiver? Was she already moist between her legs?

His hands fisted at his sides. "I don't know why I'm here or how they captured me, but I do know that I don't belong here. I know that if I stay, I will be tortured again and again. Tell me you are not like them, Jane. Tell me you do not like to watch a man be tortured."

Her dark gaze fell to the metal linked around his neck, then dipped lower, perhaps following the beads of dried blood that rode the ropes of his stomach before stopping at his tented loincloth.

Another shiver from her. "I don't," she said on a broken wisp of air. "But what happens if they realize I'm not truly Odette?"

"They won't find out." This lie did not leave him smoothly. "All right? All you need to know to aid the illusion is that you bought me at the Sex Market. You own me. Demand my release, and escort me to your—"

The sound of footsteps echoed, and Nicolai pressed his lips together. Jane tensed. An audience, exactly what they did not need right now. Then Laila rounded the corner, a scowl marring her already ugly face. She was as short and squat as her mother, her cheeks just as padded as Odette's, and her jowls just as noticeable.

Without the hooked nose, however, she was the "beauty" of the family. The length of her dark hair was coiled on top of her head, ringlets hanging at her temples. She wore an opulent gown of bright green velvet to match her eyes, though there was nothing in this kingdom or any other that could make her attractive. The evil of her soul was simply too dark.

A silver timepiece hung from a chain around her

neck. She was never without it, and the sight of it never failed to twist Nicolai's stomach with rage. Why?

She ground to a halt when she spotted Jane, hurriedly smoothing her features into a doting expression. "What are you doing here, sister dear? And in your nightgown, no less." An anxious laugh. "You should be resting. We don't want you getting sick, do we? You've already suffered so much."

Her voice never failed to disgust him, either. He'd heard it over him, under him, behind him, her warm breath trekking over his skin. Now, so close to escape, he had to bite his tongue to hold his curses inside.

Soon, he would destroy her.

Jane gulped, looked at him.

Do what I told you, Jane, he projected at her, a part of him resenting the need to do so. He'd never had to beg for anything in his life. He'd always—a sharp ache erupted in his temples, cutting off his thoughts. A memory, dead and gone before it had a chance to live.

"You are Princess Laila. My sister. Yes." Jane breathed deeply, squared her shoulders, and faced her "sister." "He's—he's mine. I own him." What she lacked in conviction she made up for with determination.

Good girl.

Laila gritted her too-white teeth, and shifted from one sandaled foot to the other. "Yes, but you were gone, darling. I took over his care. He's mine now." She stroked the timepiece. "In situations such as this, Mother always sides with the one in possession."

"I don't care. He's mine."

"Odette, be reasonable." How patient Laila appeared. A falsehood. "He attempted to slay you once, and nearly succeeded. He is too much for you to handle and I have grown used to—"

"I said he's mine."

Good girl, he thought again. So badly Nicolai wished he could unleash the torrent of power inside him, now rather than later. He would crush Laila, smile when she screamed, laugh when she died, then raze this palace brick by brick and dance atop the rubble.

Soon. The word was a constant inside him.

He didn't know what powers he could wield, or if they'd be strong enough to do everything he wanted to this kingdom. Absolute, total destruction. But he wasn't worried. Were his powers not too weak, he would raise his army and they would march—

Another ache tore through his head, another memory destroyed. He hissed from the pain, clearing his mind before he shut down completely.

Both women flicked him a glance before refocusing on each other. But Laila's attention quickly returned to him, to his erection—still pulsing with need of Jane— and her mouth hung open with shock. "You're aroused."

Silent, he reached under his loincloth and stroked his length up and down, taunting her with what he'd never willingly offered her.

Laila gave a strangled choke, her eyes widening as she faced her sister. "How did you arouse him?"

"I—I—" Jane blushed as becomingly as she smiled. So innocent and sweet, sunlight and moonlight twined together. *Taste…*

"Never mind," Laila snapped, all pretense of love and patience vanishing. "It doesn't matter. Mother's on a rampage and demands a word with you. She mourned your death for days, and was ecstatic by your return.

But that happiness will not save you from a whipping if you continue to defy her."

A mother, mourning her child *for days*. How sweet, Nicolai mentally sneered. But then, the Queen of Hearts was known as a brutal tyrant, an unforgiving bitch and a power hungry murderer. Nicolai's own mother had—

He clenched his jaw against the pain.

"I heard you were on your way down here," Laila went on, "and came to get you. You don't want to keep your queen waiting, do you?"

"I—I—"

"No. You don't."

Damn this. Jane was letting Laila direct her, proving she had not the strength of will to lead. His one and only chance for escape was withering with every second that passed.

"Laila, no. I—"

"Your poor, addled mind hasn't yet recovered from your fall, has it, darling? But you like having skin on your back, I know you do. Guards," Laila called.

Jane twisted her fingers together, clearly agitated. "I—I— There's no need. I don't want to be whipped, but I really need to—"

Two armed guards swung around the corner and stopped behind Princess Laila. They kept their gazes straight ahead as they awaited orders.

If they touched Jane, Nicolai would execute them. He would cut their throats, and spit on their remains. The ferocity of the thought should have surprised him. Jane was here for one purpose, and one purpose only, whether she acted like it or not, and remaining untouched by the citizens of Delfina was not it. Surprised, Nicolai wasn't. Nothing would stop him from attacking these men in cold blood. Jane was his. His savior, his to handle. Only his. No one else was allowed.

Until he left her.

He bit his tongue so hard he tasted his own blood.

"Muzzle the prisoner and cart him to my chamber," Laila commanded, and he relaxed somewhat. The men weren't here for Jane, then. "My sister and I will visit with the queen."

"No," Nicolai growled before he could stop himself.

"No?" Astonished, Laila leveled her attention on him. She wrapped her fat little fingers around the time-piece hanging from her neck and squeezed. "You dare issue commands, slave? To *me?*"

"Odette stays." Jane might have fooled the servants and her sister, but she would not find the Queen of Hearts so gullible. She had groomed Odette in her image, and no one knew her better. Jane and her odd speech would be found out. Killed before Nicolai could use her.

Heart...hardening.

Softening...

Laila floundered. "You'll try and kill her again. That's why you want her here. I know it. That's why you're pretending to desire her."

He flicked his tongue over his fangs. "I need inside her. *That's* why I want her here."

Once again, Jane blushed.

"You...you're lying," Laila stammered. "You hate her. You wouldn't want to bed her."

"I crave her."

A pause, heavy with tension. Motions clipped, Laila closed the distance between her and her sister and wrapped an arm around Jane's waist. "Don't listen to him. He'll say anything to gain a second chance to harm you. Come now. I'll protect you."

"No!" Jane jumped from Laila's embrace and glared up at the guards. "Take Nicolai to *my* chamber, but don't muzzle him. And tell M-Mother that I'm in need of rest. I'll speak to her later."

Laila paled as the men leaped into action. Seconds later, hinges were squeaking as the door to Nicolai's cage swung open. There were more footsteps, then a key was inserted into the metal base that pinned him to the wall.

His relief was palpable.

"But...but, Odette. You are placing yourself in danger," Laila said, desperate.

"He. Is. Mine. Nothing more needs to be said."

Wrong words. The claim—*he is mine*—affected him, giving birth to a savage animal inside him. Hers, he was hers, and he would have her before he left her, no matter the consequences. Over and over again. In every way imaginable. He would drink her, and possess her body.

There would be no stopping him, no reasoning with him. Not now.

CHAPTER FOUR

THE GUARDS FORCED NICOLAI onto the bed, the feathered mattress dipping and puffing under his weight. They anchored the metal links curling around his neck to a steel hook in the wall, just above the headboard, then removed the chains from his ankle and wrists—only to cuff him to the bedposts.

Odette had brought slaves here before, Jane realized. The posts were scarred, the deep grooves evidence of their resistance. A *lot* of resistance. How many times had Nicolai suffered this kind of indignity with the princess?

At least he didn't try and bite the guards, and they didn't try to hurt him, and Jane didn't have to side with a "slave," fueling suspicion. Already she felt as if she had a neon sign blinking over her head: Imposter.

Thank God Laila hadn't realized the truth. And wasn't the other princess a shocker? Short, squat and foaming-at-the-mouth-rabies mean. Seriously. If the Wicked Witch of the West had slept with Hannibal Lecter, and the two of them had a baby, that child's name would be Laila.

Pay attention to what's happening around you, Parker!

Right. Jane focused. She watched, flabbergasted, as

one of the guards cleaned Nicolai from head to toe and the other oiled him.

She placed the book on the nightstand, considered protesting what was being done to him, but wasn't sure "Odette" would do such a thing. Therefore, she held her tongue. Through it all, Nicolai remained silent, his expression blank, but his gaze, oh, his gaze was glued to her. His pupils were huge, his irises still sparkling with…desire.

For her, or for her blood? His fangs were sharp and long, revealing the depths of his hunger.

Just then, he was the poster child for bondage, blood and a badass fetish. He was chained, yes, but he would be in control. He was strong, in body and in mind, and he exuded something, pheromones, perhaps, that drew slavelike desires from *her*. Every cell in her body ached, frantic to know his touch. He was the most physically perfect being she'd ever encountered.

Seeing such a proud, strong man bound like that, lying atop a bed of pink lace and ruffles, being readied for her use, should have caused her stomach to churn with sickness. But she only wanted him more.

Her mind had pictured him before she'd ever met him, yes, but her mind had not done him justice. He was tall, at least six foot four, with wide muscled shoulders, a stomach roped and corded, and skin as smooth as cream mixed with coffee. He had shoulder-length hair as dark as midnight, and eyes the color of moonlight glinting off snow, silvery yet threaded with gold.

She didn't see her death in those eyes, as the book had promised. She saw her seduction. How many times had she had to stop herself from reaching out, letting him "mark" her, whatever that meant, just to feel his skin against hers? Too many. That's why she'd jumped away from him when he'd reached for her. She'd feared her reaction, afraid of an increase in the desire she felt. Already being near him was becoming a need as necessary as breathing.

The same force that had brought her here had to be responsible for what she was feeling.

Though he was cut and bruised, with dried blood caked along his arms and legs, he had not a single scar. In fact, he did not have a flaw, period. The closest thing to an imperfection he had was the thin trail of dark hair traveling from his navel to the waist of his loincloth— and that wasn't an imperfection so much as a roadway to heaven.

Speaking of the final destination of that naughty roadway…down in the cell, he'd been aroused by her, and he hadn't tried to hide it. He'd *boasted* about it, drawing attention to his groin. With very good reason. Besides her dreams and single fantasy about him, she had been with only one man. And that man could not compare. She doubted any man could. "Big" was an understatement in Nicolai's case.

When he'd touched himself, running his fingers up and down his length, her body had ached. She'd forgotten her circumstances and imagined dropping to her knees. Tonguing him, drinking him in.

Mind, stop dipping your toes in the gutter pool!

Finally the guards finished and strode toward the door. Her shouted command, "Leave the key," stopped both men.

The shorter of the two faced her and bowed. "You have the key to these restraints, princess."

Oh. Odette would have known that. "Well," she said,

swallowing, "the fall…from the cliffs—you heard about the cliffs, right?—must have caused me to forget. You can, uh, leave us." She waved toward the door, as princessy as possible. God, acting like someone other than who she was—like someone she'd never met—was not fun.

The door shut with a soft *clink*.

She rounded on her "prisoner," closing the distance between them, stopping only when the edge of the bed forced her. Again, she wanted to touch him, but she couldn't allow herself the luxury. Those teeth… He could take her jugular as a souvenir.

"The key is in the drawer of the nightstand," Nicolai said, breaking the silence first. "Use it."

Even his voice was a delight. A sensual feast of tones and nuances. Raspy, husky, a wisp of smoke. She shivered, licked her lips. "You might have summoned me or whatever, but you are not in charge. So listen up. I'll get the key—*after* you tell me more about what's going on."

"You and your 'afters.'" He glared at her, the long length of his lashes fused together and shielding the uniqueness of his dual-colored irises. "This is blackmail." As irritated as he appeared, he also seemed… proud.

Why proud? In and out she breathed, luxuriating in the scent of sandalwood. Far stronger now than when she'd dreamed or read the book. "Yes, it's blackmail, and I won't back down."

Cruel of her, but she suspected the moment she released him, he'd feed first, then race out the door, leaving her behind without giving her a single answer. He had the look of a cornered panther, ready to bite and bolt. Plus, he hadn't wanted to talk to her in the dungeon and wouldn't have, if she hadn't pressed him. Therefore, she would continue to press him.

"Apparently, I'm risking a whipping by being here with you," she added. "You kind of owe me."

"You wouldn't understand," he gritted.

She'd graduated high school at the age of fifteen. Acquired her master's at eighteen. Then, while working toward her doctorate, she'd joined a highly classified branch of the government to research unexplainable abilities and phenomenon, as well as find ways to *accomplish* the unexplainable. The only reason she'd quit and changed the focus of her studies to health sciences was to move back home and help her mother, who had just been diagnosed with breast cancer.

"I think I can keep up," she said dryly. She anchored her hands on her hips, the material pulling tight over her chest.

His gaze lowered to her breasts, and his lips stretched taut over his teeth. "Very well. We'll talk. *After* you straddle me."

She blinked at the sensual request, even as her body responded to him, readying for penetration. "What… why?"

"You get what you want, I get what I want."

"Blackmail?" she parroted, not nearly as controlled as she sounded. Blood rushed through her veins at an alarming rate.

"Yes."

Tempting. So tempting. And probably meant to cow her. "Well, I'm not caving." One of them had to keep things on a business level.

"Are you wet?"

Breath caught in her throat. Clearly that someone was not Nicolai. Really, what kind of question was that? "I—I don't even know you, of course I'm not… I can't be…what you asked."

"Jane. I saw the way you looked at my cock. You can be. So. Are you wet?"

"Yes," she whispered, blushing. She'd done that a lot today. And just as clearly, she wasn't that someone, either.

"I'm hard for you."

I know. I sooo know. "That doesn't matter." Oh, God, that mattered. She wanted to introduce herself to that hardness properly. Meaning, a nice, firm handshake. "I mean, uh, are you planning to hurt me like you hurt the real Odette?"

A beat of silence. "Odette, I hated. Jane, I crave."

Such sweet, intoxicating words, all the more potent because she couldn't accuse him of only lusting for what was available. Laila, too, had wanted him in a bad, bad way, but he hadn't wanted the princess at all. So, logically, Jane had to believe he was as attracted to her as she was to him. Yeah, logically. And not just because she was trembling and desperately wanted it to be true.

He could simply be trying to soften her up.

Oh, great. The upsetting thought poked its way from an ugly place inside her. A place that never wanted her to be happy. A place that felt she didn't *deserve* to be happy. They'd been butting heads for months; more and more, she won the battles. Today, she might not.

"If I hurt you, you would not help me," he said in a silky tone. "I want you to help me, and I am not a foolish man."

No, he was a sexy one. "You're a violent man. I know you are."

"Yes."

His honesty deflated her upcoming argument before she could start.

"Do you fear me, little Jane?"

"Maybe. What if you bite me? Or do that marking thing?"

"You'll like it, the bite and the marking, but I won't do either until you beg. You have my word. Now. Straddle me," he repeated. "I'm also capable of giving pleasure. Giving and taking. That's what we'll do here and now. Give and take pleasure while we talk."

Beg… Sweet heaven, she just might. Because deep inside, at the core of her femininity, she wanted to be with him. As if she'd been born for him, and him alone. Or bespelled. But even the thought of magic couldn't dull her desire for this man. The desire was somehow as familiar as his scent.

"I'm not taking off my robe. Or my panties. We just met. That would be, uh, tacky." *Idiot.* "I'm trusting you to keep your word. And I'm only doing this for answers," she lied.

"Don't care why. Just want to feel you."

Slowly, unsure, she climbed on top of him, placing a knee on each side of his waist. Her robe hiked up, revealing the length of her thighs. Just as slowly, she lowered her body until her female core brushed his erection. She gasped at the contact. He moaned.

This was better than her fantasy. He was hot, so hot. Hard, so hard.

"Talk," she said, flattening her palms on his chest.

Before she did what she'd said she wouldn't and stripped out of her panties.

He arched up, pressing more firmly against her. They moaned in unison, his heart drumming as erratically as hers. She liked that.

A moment passed. "You said you enjoy puzzles," he mentioned huskily. His gaze settled on her neck.

Her pulse fluttered, as though happy to have gained his notice. "Yes."

"We fit together very nicely, don't you think?"

"Yes." God. How moronic she sounded. Yes this, and yes that. It was just, he'd fried her circuits. She was on top of him, poised over his cock. And she ached. Ached like a drug addict in need of a fix. Why else would she have practically thrown herself at a vampire?

He waited. When she said no more, he arched his hips again. "What did you want to know, Jane?"

She rubbed against him. An accident, she told herself, and just once, but enough to leave her sweating. "I want…to know…about you. About why you summoned *me* to free you?" There. She'd found her voice, without panting like she was climbing a mountain. Or a well-endowed man.

"You never said," she continued. "Do I look like Princess Odette or something?" If so, Odette and Laila must have been an odd sight. The blond giant and the brunette toddler. *Jealous?* "I mean, you told me that, in everyone else's mind, I'm their princess." She rubbed again, harder, but slow, so slow, and impossible to label as accidental. Need drove her. "But when I looked at myself in the mirror, I saw, well, myself."

Little beads of perspiration formed on his brow as

he met her, moving with her. "You look nothing like her. Yes, keep doing that."

"Then how does your magic work?" The tip of his erection brushed her most sensitive spot, and she moaned. "Why does everyone assume I'm her?"

"When I summoned you, I also shifted my ability to cast illusions to you, projecting Odette's image." His chains rattled as he attempted to lower his arms. When he realized he couldn't, he scowled. "To everyone around you, with the exception of me, you look and sound like her. But gods, you smell divine."

"So do you." He'd spoken of intrinsic power. So very, very good…uh, *interesting.* Getting answers had never been this wonderfully agonizing in class. "Can you remove the illusion?"

The leather of his loincloth was soft between her legs, a startling contrast to his erection, creating a dizzying friction. Her heart hammered against her ribs with so much force, she feared the bones would crack.

She needed to slow down, or she would explode before the conversation ended.

"No, I cannot. Not while we're together. My power… they did something to me. Bound my abilities in some way, as surely as they bound my body." He licked his lips, revealing and hiding his fangs. So sharp, so deadly. "Do you like this, Jane? Do I please you?"

So much it scared her. "Yes."

"Lean down. Kiss me."

Another urge to obey… She stilled instead. Yes. She wanted to kiss him. Yet she knew that if she leaned down, if she kissed the breath out of his lungs as she wanted him to do to her, they would have sex. They wouldn't be able to help themselves. Look how close she was to begging for it already!

She couldn't have sex with him. They were strangers. Worse, he was a vampire, a drinker of blood, and she'd studied his kind for research. Oh, God. Talk about a mood killer. If he ever found out, the mood wasn't the only thing that would be killed.

He wouldn't find out, she assured herself before she could panic. Wasn't like she'd tell him, and who else knew? No one. Although he might wonder why she knew more about his physiology than she should. Like the fact that he was alive, and not dead, with the same basic organ alignment as a human.

Besides, she would return home at some point. She hoped. More than that, they were in danger and under a time crunch. She needed answers from him, not pleasure. Not kisses.

Reluctantly she crawled off him and stood beside the bed. Her knees almost buckled. Amazing that she was able to maintain her balance, since her muscles had the consistency of Jell-O.

"Jane?"

She couldn't look at him. She would cave. He was just so damn beautiful, those eyes so hungry. For her. Plain Jane, as the kids at school had once called her. Already she was tempted to fling herself back on top of him, rubbing her way to ecstasy. The scent of him clung to her. Sandalwood. Delicious. Every time she inhaled, she smelled him, weakening her resolve.

"Can someone else remove the illusion?" she asked, keeping her profile to him. "While we're together?"

"Why did you leave me?"

"I wasn't concentrating. I was only…"

"Thinking of me. And sex."

Her cheeks heated as she nodded.

He uttered a low growl. "If you will not take pleasure from me, at least sit beside me. I would rather have part of you than none of you."

Said the spider to the fly. A born seducer, this one. Nicolai knew just how to lure, how to tempt. Against her better judgment, she sat. Her fingers brushed his ribs, and the heat of him had her shivering all over again.

"The answer to your question is yes," he said, gruffer still. "If someone's power is greater than mine, my illusion can be broken. But do not go around asking for such a thing. You do not want the witches here knowing what was done to you."

She waited, tense and silent, for him to go on. He didn't. Finally she gasped out, "You can't leave it at that. What happens if they discover the truth?"

Another round of silence.

Her heartbeat increased in speed. "What if your magic fails while I'm here?" Again, she waited. He didn't rush to assure her all would be well. *Still no need to panic. Not yet.*

"Feed me," he said, his fangs extending over his bottom lip, "and I'll strengthen. *No one* will be stronger than me." There, at the end, his words were slurred.

One half of her trembled in pleasure, the other half shuddered in fear. The vampires in the lab had fed from bags of plasma. She'd never been bitten. Had never wanted to be bitten. Until now. If anyone could make her enjoy something like that, it was this man.

"I'll think about it. Now let's backtrack a little. If you can make anyone look like the princess, why did you summon me specifically?" Why place *her* in such danger? Not that he'd truly wanted her, and her alone. She recalled his disdain when he'd learned she was merely a human, recalled his surprise. "I asked before, but you never answered."

He leaned toward her, forcing her fingers to press into his skin. A silent command—and an unrelinquishing demand—for contact. "I did not summon you specifically."

She'd realized that as she'd spoken, but hearing him confirm it depressed her. She had to remain on equal footing with him, and even though he was chained, he kept leaping to the next level without her.

"Who did you mean to summon, then?" she asked, tracing an *X* next to his navel. She blinked. His navel? Damn it! Her willpower sucked. She'd told herself not to touch him so, of course, the first thing she did was claim his belly button as her personal property.

"Jane?"

His deep voice startled her, and she jerked her spine ramrod straight. An instant later, her gaze met Nicolai's. A mistake. Liquid silver eyes, smoldering with passion. Languid expression masking a sea of desires.

"Yes?" *Danger, Jane Parker, danger.*

"I lost you, even though I'm having this conversation only because you wished it. We could be doing—"

"Sorry," she said before he could finish. No reason to discover if what he thought they could be doing meshed with her own desires, and every reason not to. She stuffed her hands under her butt, her weight pinning them in place. Hopefully. "I'll pay attention from now on."

He flicked his tongue over one of his fangs, and she

couldn't help but imagine that tongue flicking between her legs. "I summoned whoever would save me."

Oh, dear God. Her bones melted. Climbing on top of him a second time might actually be a good idea, she mused. She'd be able to hear him better. Yeah, yeah, because she was having trouble hearing him and… *Damn it,* she thought again. *You knew better than to look at him!*

She cleared her throat. "So I release you, and then what happens?" Good. Back on track.

"I am…not sure."

The truth or a lie? That hesitation… "Will I go home?"

"I told you. I do not know. Do you have a man waiting for you?" he asked, the words grated, as if pushed through a grinder.

"No. Otherwise, I wouldn't have straddled you. Fidelity is important." She had nothing and no one except the routine she'd developed. Wake up at six-thirty in the morning and jog five miles. Take a shower, dress, fix breakfast. Read for a few hours, usually something on macroparticles, sometimes a romance, fix lunch. Read for a few hours more, shop online for anything she needed, walk the treadmill to release the knots in her muscles. Bathe, fix dinner. Watch TV, sleep. *Exciting.*

She didn't need to work because one, she'd made so much money through her research, she could never spend it all; and two, she'd made so much money in the car accident settlement, she could never spend it all. Only problem was, she wanted something money couldn't buy. Her family. A second chance.

"But I'm not in danger there," she added softly. "So tell me. What will *you* do when you're free?"

Absolute determination cloaked her features. "Kill my tormentors." Flat, cold. A vow. "After that, I will journey to Elden."

The "kill my tormentors" part shouldn't have cranked her engine, but it did. A lot. All that ferocity... He would protect what was his, and fight for what he wanted. Always. Anyone who tormented him or those he loved would suffer. And with him, a woman would never have to worry about anything. Well, except her panties. Those might be ripped a few times.

"If I summon the healer and she does her thing, and then I let you go, but I don't instantly go home, will you take me with you?"

She was not staying here; she knew that much. Nicolai might plan to kill everyone, but he was only one man. Or vampire, whatever. There would be survivors. Survivors looking to punish the person who had unleashed the big bad vamp.

And the longer she resided in this palace, the more danger she would be in, he'd said. Yet, she couldn't strike out on her own. She knew nothing about this land. This *magical* land, where spells could be cast, memories erased and powerful vampires enslaved.

He opened his mouth, closed it. Then he relaxed, his body sagging against the mattress. His expression softened, heated. "What would you do to stay with me?" he asked, his voice once more like smoke, curling around her, trying to lure her back in.

Her hand itched to reach out, the urge to touch him springing to new life. She wanted to learn the texture of his skin—she hadn't paid enough attention before. She wanted to rediscover the warmth of his body. Was already reaching toward him...

She jumped back to her feet and backed away from him. Sitting next to him had been a mistake. She couldn't concentrate, and she couldn't keep her dumb hands to herself.

"Jane," he said, exasperated.

"What?"

His eyes narrowed, the gold flecks brightening, bursting through the silver. "Forget it. Have I answered your questions?"

"Yes. Wait, no, I—"

"Too late. You said yes. There's no changing your mind. Now summon the healer." He lifted the arm closest to her as best he could, the cuff rubbing against the iron poster. "And remove the chains."

Damn him. He'd never promised to take her with him. "All right. Chains first. Healer second. But you'll owe me. Big time. And don't feed from me. I didn't beg you."

"Noted."

"I'm trusting you. If you go back on your word, I never will again. Once out of my trust circle, always out of my trust circle." She turned and bent over the nightstand, pulling out the top drawer. Sure enough, a long, thin key rested atop a bed of crimson velvet. "Lookie there. So simple."

"Odette!" Hinges squeaked a second before her bedroom door slammed against the wall.

Gasping, Jane spun. A short, obese woman with ruddy cheeks huffed and puffed in the now open entryway. She wore a navy-blue-and-gold robe, the material far too tight for her rotund frame. She had jet-black hair peppered with silver, the strands slicked back and greased.

The city without time had managed to take its toll.

"You dare defy me, girl?"

The queen, she thought with dread and just a little panic. Her "mother." The gal with the whip. *Don't forget you're supposed to be Odette.*

Fear pumped through Jane's veins at an alarming rate, joining the dread and panic. *Danger, danger, danger,* her mind shouted, and it was not the succulent kind Nicolai offered. If this world was anything like her own had once been, this woman, this queen, had absolute power over every one and thing in her kingdom. Including Jane.

"I—I'm sorry." Jane's gaze fell to Nicolai. His expression was now blank, his features smoothed out. Yet, he couldn't hide the coiled tension in his biceps and stomach. He practically vibrated. As stealthily as possible, she tossed the key at him. "I didn't mean to disrespect you, M-Mother. Queen."

"And yet you did. You, my successor, the one my people look to as an example, have made me appear the fool." At least she hadn't noticed the key. "Rather than seek out your doting mother, you sought out a slave." As the queen spoke, two guards filed in beside her.

Jane didn't recognize them; they were taller and meaner-looking than the others.

"Now, you'll be punished."

The men continued to advance.

"But…I… You can't do this! Stop. Don't you dare touch me. Let go!"

A snarl left Nicolai. One that promised pain. Lots and lots of pain. No one but Jane seemed to notice. The guards snagged her by the arms and began dragging her out of the bedroom.

"Mine," Nicolai snapped. "No touching."

Again, he was ignored.

"Stop! Let go!" She struggled, kicking and screaming, but they never loosened their hold.

Behind her, she heard Nicolai jerking against his chains. "Mine!"

"I can do anything I wish," the queen said, so superior Jane wanted to slap her. "Perhaps your little bump on the head made you forget. But no worries, my pet. I will remind you—and ensure you never forget again."

CHAPTER FIVE

SHE NEVER CRIED, NEVER even gasped as the whip flayed her delicate skin.

Nicolai was chained to Odette's bed. He hadn't marked Jane as he'd wanted, but he was somehow attuned to her in a way he doubted he had ever been attuned to another. He should not have been able to focus on her, especially since he'd been fighting sizzling desire for her—her body, her blood—and all other thoughts had become fogged and insignificant in comparison.

Now, he felt fury. So much fury, and every bit of it was leveled on the guards.

They had dragged Jane along the opulent corridor filled with portraits of the queen and her daughters, down the winding stairs with dark velvet carpeting, and to the extravagant banqueting hall. Though she was no longer in the bedroom, Nicolai saw her still. As if their minds were somehow connected. She struggled the entire way. Only when they bent her over the dining table, her face pressed into the polished wood, only when they stripped away the back of her gown, had she settled.

Panting, she twisted her head to gaze over at the queen. The Queen of Hearts, a woman known to dine on the still beating organ during the spells and incantations used in her never-ending quest for youth.

"Don't do this," Jane pleaded. "I meant no offense."

The queen raised one of her many chins, the ones beneath it jiggling. "And yet it was offense that you gave."

"I'm sorry."

"You will be more so."

"Please," Jane said, her skin both pallid with fear and bright with exertion. "Give me another chance."

Perhaps the queen replied. Nicolai would never know. He was too focused on Jane's back. Already she bore scars. More than he could possibly count. They twined from her spine to her rib cage, red and angry, badges of pain. They stretched past the robe's gaping material, perhaps even riding the length of her legs.

What the hell had been done to her?

His guilt sprang back to instant, shattering life, and he was unable to destroy it this time. *He* had placed her in this situation. This delicate, haunted woman with the tantalizing scent, who had offered him the only glimpse of sunlight in a darkened void. She had come to save him, had trusted him enough to straddle him while talking to him. To rub against him, ratcheting his desire to unequaled heights, even without climax. And her resistance…gods, he'd wanted to quash it. Still did. Wanted her to know his bite, his kiss.

His possession.

Perhaps she was merely a challenge he had to triumph above. He didn't care. Quite simply, she was his. That was not in question. *Mine,* his cells continued to scream. *All mine.*

He could not allow her to be whipped.

Nicolai looked at the key resting at his side. Jane

had tossed it at him, and it had landed on the mattress. A brave gesture on her part, but useless. He could not bend enough to reach it with his mouth. He could not angle his hands to grab it. He could not do anything with it. Yet the fact that she'd tried, that she'd thought of him in the face of her own peril…affected him.

He *would* escape. However necessary. He would save her.

Never before had he been left on his own outside of his cell, with no guards within sight or hearing distance. He jerked at his cuffs. The metal links scraped his already cut skin, digging deeper, deeper. He'd pulled at them while straining toward Jane, but at the time he hadn't cared, hadn't felt any sting but that of passion. Now, he felt the pain. That didn't stop him, however.

Just as before, the latches held, both to him and to the bed. He gritted his teeth. His hate for Laila, her mother and even Delfina grew exponentially. *Destroy…*

He closed his eyes, concentrating on the power still swirling inside him. There it was, dark, so dark, churning, an untapped storm just waiting, desperate to be unleashed; and all he had to do was break through the glass cage that had been erected within him.

A glass cage with thin, riverlike cracks running through the center.

Exploit. He banged against the mental glass, over and over again. Nothing. He clawed at it. Still nothing. Damn it!

"Now," he heard the queen say, pulling Nicolai back to the present. To Jane and their connection. Somehow, enough of his magic had escaped to allow him to continue watching her despite the distance between them.

Leather whistled through air. The first blow landed.

Jane squeezed her eyes shut and pressed her lips together. She grimaced, but not a sound did she make.

They had done it. They had whipped her.

Just like that, something inside of Nicolai broke. Not the glass cage, but something far more dangerous, roaring like a wild animal pushed beyond its limits.

From the first moment Nicolai had spotted Jane, his body had reacted to her. He had experienced lust, guilt and possessiveness in varying degrees. Now, the possessiveness simply took over.

Mine, he thought again.

This time, the word sprung from deep inside him, as unstoppable as an avalanche. He did not understand the fierceness accompanying the thought, and refused to ponder it now. Later. He would ponder later. Right now, more than before, he knew only that she was his— his savior, his woman—and nothing else mattered.

The guards had touched her, hurt her. They would die. Painfully. By the time he finished with them they would probably thank him for killing them.

All he had to do was free himself. And he would. Nothing would stop him. Not now, not anymore.

"Soon" had at last arrived.

Being a magical vampire, as Jane had called him, was not going to aid him; he admitted that now. Still his determination intensified, blending with the hate, the burn of that possessiveness. He would reach her by grit alone; he would save her. No matter what he had to do. His gaze strayed to the wrist cuffs and narrowed. Without his thumbs, his hands would slide right through.

He didn't have to think about it. Goodbye, thumbs.

Biting his tongue against the pain he knew was to come, he slammed his hands, thumbs out, into the headboard. *Crunch.* The bones broke with that very first punch. He sucked in a breath, but, like Jane, he did not utter a sound. Punch, punch, punch. Each new blow caused even more damage, ripping tendon, tearing muscle, flattening bone.

By the time he finished, he was sweating, bleeding, his hands limp. But his top half was free. With a growl, he jolted upright. Heard the whistle of leather through air, a soft inhalation of breath. Another lash against Jane's delicate skin.

Skin he wanted to caress.

His hands were too mutilated to grab the key. In fact, his efforts sent the little piece of metal sliding to the floor with a clink. He would need it later, to remove the neck cuff, and so he would pick it up with his mouth— after he'd freed himself.

Through narrowed eyes, he peered down at his feet. At a different angle, those feet would glide straight through the metal rings. And all he had to do to achieve that different angle was break every bone that ran from his ankle to his toes.

Nicolai started kicking the footboard.

JANE CLOSED HER EYES to hide the tears trying so determinedly to form and spill. It wasn't like she'd never experienced pain before. For God's sake, her spine had been broken, her legs unusable for months. Then there'd been the surgeries. Surgery after surgery to pin her bones in their proper places. Then, of course, the rehabilitation.

So, this whipping? Not even a blip on her agony radar. And yet, the humiliation of being bent over a table, her clothing ripped away, her scars revealed to those who sought to harm her, her body bound with ties she couldn't see—magic?—nearly undid her. And for what? For failing to speak with a fat, ugly woman when summoned?

Poor Odette. Was this how she'd lived? Always fearing the next punishment? And poor Nicolai. Jane could not blame him for doing everything within his power to save himself. She would have done the same.

In fact, she could blame only herself for this. Had she listened to Nicolai, had she freed him when he'd wanted, they would have been far, far away from this dreadful place. Well, *he* would have been. He would have left her behind. And he still might, she thought. During their talk, she had not garnered a promise from him. Not to keep her with him, not to protect her. And now, it was too late. There was no way she'd leave him bound after this. Not for any reason. She would free him the moment she was physically able, then take off on her own.

Dumb on her part, maybe. Probably. Okay, definitely. Allowing herself to be separated from the one person who knew who and what she was, the one person who could get her home…so damn foolish. But that still wasn't going to stop her.

And, wow. Jane Parker, considered a dummy. That was a first. She laughed without humor. A novelty in the face of pain. *Nice.*

"This amuses you?" the queen demanded.

Jane refused to acknowledge her.

There was a squeak of outrage. "Clearly you are not hitting her hard enough. You." The queen snapped her fingers. "Take over the whip. Your arms are stronger, as I can well attest."

Oh, gross.

A pause, then the whip continued to descend. Harder, so much harder. Over and over again, minutes ticking by. Still Jane did not utter a sound. She wanted to go home. Back to her boring life, where she was in control.

The whip stopped falling. Finally, a reprieve.

"Have you at last learned your lesson, Odette?" the queen asked, expectant. "Or shall I have him remove the skin on your legs, as well?"

She opened her mouth to tell the bitch to go to hell—no ignoring her this time—but she stopped herself before a single word escaped. Did these people believe in hell, or even know what it was? Would she announce her humanity and lose the protection—what little there was—in being thought of as Princess Odette?

"Silence will not—"

A roar echoed from the walls, harsh, guttural and a promise of pain.

Everyone in the room stilled. Jane forgot to breathe. That sound…she'd never heard its like. There was an animal on the loose, a lion probably, there just had to be. And people were clearly on the menu.

Another roar, followed by the crash of furniture and the shattering of knickknacks. Screams of agony. Gasps, racing footsteps. Had her guards left?

"Don't leave me here," she shouted.

"What's going on?" the queen snapped. Okay. Good. She was still here. Bitch that she was. "You, find out. You, shield me."

"Free me," Jane demanded. "Now."

They paid her no heed.

One of the guards headed toward the entryway, where other guards were pouring inside to *escape* the

beast, but he didn't make it outside the room. Not alive.
There was a blur of movement, then blood was squirt-
ing, a headless body falling.

From the corner of her eye, she spotted Nicolai. He
was a mess, covered in blood, limping, his arms hanging at his sides. His fangs were bared in a fearsome,
crimson scowl, and she knew.

He was the animal.

Thank God. Some of the tension drained from her.
Somehow, some way, he'd managed to escape. His plan
to destroy the people who lived inside this palace was
well under way.

Before, she'd thought there would be survivors. Now,
not so much.

He barreled into another guard, his shoulder slamming into the man's middle and knocking him backward. The guard propelled into another, the one with
the whip. The two fell to the floor. Nicolai slashed into
the whipper's neck and shook, a wolf with his first meal
in months. Screams…silence…death…

Just like that, Jane was freed from whatever had
bound her. She straightened. Sharp lances of pain
shot from her back, spiraling though the rest of her.
She hardly noticed. Her gown sagged from her shoulders, momentarily exposing her breasts. Hurriedly she
righted the material, holding it up.

Nicolai's silver-gold eyes landed on the queen, who
was no longer shielded by a man. Blood—and other
things—dripped from his mouth. His expression was so
dark, so murderous, even Jane backed away from him.
He was a terrifying sight. A warrior lost to bloodlust,
his only goal the destruction of every one and every
thing around him.

He advanced on the queen. "Die. You die."

"How dare you threaten me and my people this way?" the bitch snapped. "I allowed you to live after you tormented my eldest daughter, and now you think to spit on my mercy? Guards!"

No guards came. Perhaps they were too busy being dead.

"She...mine," Nicolai snarled, moving in front of Jane while still advancing on the queen. There was something wrong with his feet, his ankles twisted at an odd angle, yet his steps were measured, clipped with determination.

The queen lifted her mountain of chins. "You think to protect my daughter from me? The daughter you tried to slay?"

"Mine!"

"Come on, then, slave. Come get me."

Jane's heart pounded with renewed force. Her legs shook. This was a showdown the queen couldn't hope to win. Right? *Please be right.*

Nicolai leaped.

Grinning, the queen stretched out one arm and ripples of power pulsated from her. The air around her shimmered, thickened. Nicolai slammed into a wall Jane couldn't see, ricocheting backward.

Another roar ripped from his throat as he jumped to his feet. He pounded his injured fists into that invisible shield, his fangs flashing.

The queen laughed, smug. "Do you see now? Even were you at your strongest, you could not touch me. I am beyond your reach."

Booted footsteps reverberated, and Jane watched, wide-eyed, as the second line of defense marched into the room. So. There were more guards, after all. This new contingent held swords and spears, and when they spotted the bloody Nicolai, they bolted into action.

"No!" Jane threw herself in front of him, the action born of instinct rather than thought. As she well knew, even vampires could be killed, and she didn't want Nicolai to—couldn't watch him—experience that.

Strong arms banded around her waist and jerked her into a hard body. Instinct still drove her and, for a moment, she fought, kicking and elbowing.

"Mine. Be…still."

Nicolai. She relaxed, despite his raging animal nature. He was warm against her. Solid, sturdy despite his wounds. Even decadent. Her inhalations were coming so quickly, she scented the sandalwood she was already coming to love.

Okay, then. They would die together, she thought distantly. She'd survived so much the past year. The car accident, injuries that would have killed most people. Injuries that *should* have killed her. Especially since she'd yearned for death, and hadn't done anything to aid her own cause.

She'd been so lost, wondering. Why her? What was so different, so special, about her that she could endure what others had not? Nothing, that's what.

And now that she wanted to live, she would finally die. Irony at its finest. She would not be allowed to know Nicolai better. She would not get to spend time with him, laugh with him or make love with him.

She should have kissed him earlier.

"Mine," Nicolai repeated against her ear. "Safe." He had stretched out an arm, mimicking the queen, and the air around them had shimmered, forming a…shield? For *them?*

Her jaw dropped as the guards slammed into it and flew backward, just as Nicolai had done.

A gasp escaped her. "How did you—?"

"Walk," Nicolai said in that gravelly voice. His one-word sentences were as frustrating as they were welcome. He nudged her forward.

One step, two, she lumbered over the fallen, savaged bodies sprawled around her. Those who remained standing were pushed out of the way by the shield. Outside the dining room was a foyer. Spacious, with doorways in every direction. Exactly where was she supposed to go?

Laila raced down the staircase, dark hair flying behind her, the silver timepiece banging against her chest. When she spotted Jane and Nicolai, she ground to a halt.

Nicolai snarled at her. He released Jane as if he intended to pound up those steps and attack, but quickly changed his mind. His free arm banded around Jane once more, the other ensuring the shield never wavered. "Mine."

She was really starting to like that nickname.

The younger woman was breathing heavily, her green eyes glittering with jealousy and hate. "Yours? She isn't yours. Odette, he means to kill you. Fight him! Use your magic."

Jane flipped her off.

Shock replaced the anger, but only for a moment. When the princess regained her wits, she shouted, "Someone stop them. Now!" but still the guards could not penetrate the shield. "He's bespelled Odette."

"We need magic, princess," one of them said. "Cast a spell for us. Anything!"

"No magic," Laila gritted without hesitation and with the briefest flare of panic. Then to Nicolai, she said, "You think I'd bind your vampire strength and abilities, and not bespell you to remain here forever? You might be able to leave the palace, but you'll be back. That, I promise you."

Another growl erupted from Nicolai's throat, so fervent even Jane's body vibrated.

"You can kill her if you want," Jane said. "I'll wait."

He tightened his hold. "Mine."

Apparently protecting her was more important than avenging himself. What had changed his mind, she didn't know, but his decision was a gift, better than a diamond and not something she'd ever regift.

Yes, she really should have kissed him when she'd had the chance. Once they were safe, she'd remedy her mistake.

Laila raised her chin(s), reminding Jane of the queen. Smiling, she drew circles around the center of the timepiece with the tip of her index finger. "Go ahead. Try. Fail."

"Walk," Nicolai repeated.

"Where?" Jane asked, tightening her hold on her robe.

He didn't speak again, but guided her toward one of the doorways. He used his big, strong shoulders to nudge it open, careful not to jar her. Endorphins were swimming so potently through her veins, he could have poured salt into her slashed-up back and she wouldn't have felt it. Yet.

Silvery moonlight came into view. As did a large expanse of flatland, with robed men and women moving unhurriedly, happily, children dancing around them. Beyond that, Jane saw trees. Mile after mile of white trees, their leaves swaying, dancing together like drunken ghosts. The landscape was somehow familiar to her, as if she'd been here before. How... Why...?

Jane could only gape, struggling to understand—until Nicolai released her, and her thoughts took a nosedive. He was leaving her already? Disappointment rocked her. She'd liked his touch, had wanted more. Perhaps forever, which made her as dumb now as she'd been earlier. Thankfully, he didn't allow the separation for long. He moved beside her, clasped her hand as strongly as he was able, which wasn't much considering the damage he'd sustained, and jerked her into the throng.

"This way."

A child spotted her, and dropped into a bow. Murmurs arose, and everyone else quickly followed suit. Jane's steps faltered.

"Uh, hi," she said, not knowing what else to say.

"Princess," they muttered. Not happily, but with fear.

"Escape...faster..." Nicolai said with a nudge.

"My pleasure," she muttered, leaping into a sprint.

CHAPTER SIX

THEY TRAVELED FOR HOURS—or so it seemed—though they never managed to exit the forest. Nicolai suspected they were going in circles, his doom in the center. Just when he would think they'd made progress, he would spy the glittering palace rooftop. A rooftop Delfina was famous for, the shingles comprised only of elf tears. No matter what he tried, he could not alter his path.

Fail. The word Laila had used. *Go ahead. Try. Fail.* She had used her magic on him as promised, he realized. But what spell had she used? Unless he figured it out, he could not fight its power. Even as the question and answer formed in his mind, a sharp lance of pain jetted through him. He gnashed his teeth.

At least the guards never caught his trail. Even when the magical shield around him evaporated in a puff of smoke. Magic he wasn't sure how he'd wielded. He knew only that the queen had constructed a shield of her own, and he had instantly known how to do the same.

Now, though, he could not reconstruct it; the ability was gone as if it had never been. And its absence infuriated him. At all costs, he must protect Jane.

Mine. The possessive claim was now so much a part of him, he wasn't sure how he'd survived without her. So, yes, he would protect her. Even from himself. His hunger was completely sated, he'd drained so many guards to reach her, and yet, he could still scent her. His female. So sweet. He still wanted to taste her. So damn badly.

She was injured, though, and needed to rest. Not that she had complained. She had not spoken a word since they'd left the palace courtyard. She had remained behind him the entire time, accepting his every dictate, following his directives. Limping, he thought, and sometimes using his arm as a crutch.

He hadn't allowed himself to look at her, knowing he would have stopped long before now if she appeared fatigued in any way. He wanted her as far from the palace as possible. As far away from Laila and the queen—who should be dead right now, already rotting in a grave.

That they lived…

Worth it. Jane lived, too.

His ankles throbbed as he led her to a cave he'd noticed each time he'd unintentionally backtracked. "Here," he said, voice gruffer than he'd intended. "We'll be safe here." He was sure of it.

"Oh, good. You're back to your normal self."

Normal self? What did that mean? "Rest." Once they were strengthened, he could return to the palace, sneak inside, kill Laila and her mother and find the healer, as planned. Before he left, he would erect defenses so that Jane could stay here, safe.

Once his memories had been returned, his powers restored, he would come back for her. They would travel to Elden together.

His hands tightened into fists. Elden. What awaited him in Elden, besides his desire to kill a king he had never met? At least, not to his knowledge. All he knew was that the man had slaughtered the former sovereigns, claiming the crown by brute force.

Nicolai had heard palace servants gossiping about the royal change. Yesterday, or a hundred years ago, he wasn't sure. Whatever time spell the witches had cast over the palace caused minutes to eke by for everyone inside, the days blending together, a blur you could never count.

Nicolai wondered if he'd ever met the former sovereigns. Perhaps even guarded them. While he could not picture them, he could visualize their palace without problem. A towering monstrosity built more for withstanding attack than aesthetics. A lush green forest surrounded a lake, and that lake surrounded the structure. There was no discernable entryway other than the guard walkway—a walkway he knew better than he knew the angles of his own face.

He *longed* for that palace, that lake, that forest. Knew the land would smell of sea salt and pine. Thought he could hear the echo of his booted footsteps as he ran to…do something, hug someone, perhaps. Thought he could hear a woman's deep-throated chuckle and a man's gruff grunt of approval. A pang of love and homesickness, followed by a wave of hate, swept through him.

Love? Homesickness? Hate? Why? He must learn the answers. He must kill the new king.

A dull ache bloomed in his temples, and he ceased that line of thought. For now.

Jane hobbled in front of him, and placed her hands on his shoulders. At the moment of contact, his fangs lengthened and his gums ached. Just a little taste…

No! Not yet. He soaked in her presence instead, distracting his unnecessary hunger with her electrifying beauty. Electrifying, because she had somehow brought him back to life.

That fall of honey-colored hair, framing a face as pure and unique as a snowflake, begged for a man's fingers. Her ocher eyes were no longer haunted, but determined. Her cheeks were rosy—with desire, despite her weakened, abused condition—a sheen of perspiration from the sultry night air making her glow. She'd tied the fabric of her robe together and the knots on her shoulders teased him. With only a tug, they would unwind and he could—

No, he thought again. He would not entertain such lustful thoughts until she was healed. Then... Oh, yes, then.

Seeing her whipped for his actions had not only broken something inside him, it had awoken something inside him. Not to mention that smile of hers... She shouldn't have smiled at him.

"The key," he said. "Free my neck." He used his tongue to move that key from the side of his mouth to between his teeth.

"My pleasure." She unlocked the ring. The heavy binding tumbled to the ground with a thump. "We should probably get going. The sun will come out soon." Though she'd hobbled, her voice was firm, strong. "If you guys have a sun. And if time has kicked back into gear for us. Someone mentioned Delfina is ageless."

"Not ageless. Those who reside in the palace age much slower. And yes, out here there is a sun, a day and a night."

"We have to hide you, then. We don't want you bursting into flames."

His brow furrowed. "I am not a nightwalker." How had she known about nightwalkers and the way they burst into flames?

"Oh, well..." She paled, swallowed. "Well, in my world, vampires are considered a myth. In books and movies, you guys always burst into flames—or glitter—when you step into sunlight."

Glitter? "I am, perhaps, more sensitive to the sun's rays than others in this realm, but I am nothing like the nightwalkers. At worst, I will burn and blister."

"Oh. Good." Her relief was palpable.

Such a strong reaction, when she'd had no cause to worry. And yet, that worry pleased him. He liked her concern. Liked what it meant. Already she cared.

"I've been thinking," she said, nibbling on her bottom lip.

His stomach clenched at the sight of her teeth, doing what he wanted to do. "Something you enjoy." He placed his throbbing hands over hers, preventing her from drawing away.

"Yes, well." Her tongue emerged, swiping where she'd bitten. "We've been going in circles, which means Laila the harpy told the truth. You are cursed to remain in Delfina."

The sight of her tongue did far more damage to his control than the sight of her teeth. How easy it would be to lean down, lick, sample, savor. *Not until she heals.* Another reminder. *Also, not until she begs. You promised.* "I know," he said more harshly than he'd intended.

"Oh." Her nose scrunched adorably, easing the sting of his self-directed anger. "Well, you could have told me. I've worried, expecting you to argue and trying to formulate my own argument for whichever direction you could have taken. Anyway, you might have been bespelled to think the most dangerous places are the safest, and the safest places the most dangerous. Actually, cancel that 'you might.' You were. You bypassed the water six times!"

River? "You saw a river?" The kingdom of Elden was surrounded by the lake, a lake that connected its northern shore to Delfina. That had always been a point of contention for him while rotting inside his cell. So close to his goal, yet so far away. Now, he was glad.

"No," Jane said. "I didn't see. I *heard* the water."

He hadn't. The only landmark that had stood out to him was a dark, too dark, part of the forest that had made his skin crawl. Had he been alone, he would have braved that forest without hesitation. His mind had been centered upon Jane's protection, however, and he'd opted to brave nothing. A mistake.

His swollen fingers intertwined with hers, squeezing. "Why didn't you say something?"

"You were all scary alpha and in charge, and I didn't want to, you know, poke at the bear. Plus, I was kind of distracted by the scenery and maybe lost in my thoughts. So, here's what we're going to do," she went on. Now who was all alpha and in charge? "You're going to lead us to the most dangerous place in this forest. And when you think you should turn left, you're going to turn right. You're going to do the opposite of everything you feel is correct."

Smart, his Jane. And so damned arousing he doubted he would ever get enough of her.

He wanted to keep her. In his bed, his arms, his fangs buried in her neck, his cock buried between her legs.

Even though he was destined to wed the… Another sharp lance tore through his mind, and he grunted.

"What?" Jane asked, concerned all over again. "Are you okay?"

Her back was a mess of welts, and she asked if *he* was okay. He pressed his tongue to the roof of his mouth and nodded. "You are well enough to travel?"

"Of course," she said, as if there was no doubt in her mind.

"All right, then."

Though his body protested, he trudged forward once again, leaving the cave behind. He followed Jane's advice—orders—and did the opposite of what his "instincts" demanded, even plunging into a patch of thorny clinging vines guarding the darker part of the forest. He expected to be scratched, but the leaves merely caressed him, tickling.

There were no thorns, he realized. Even though he saw them, they were not there. Laila—or her healer—was more powerful than he'd ever suspected.

Male laughter cut through the night, springing from just ahead. Nicolai stopped, stiffened, and Jane bumped into him. Her breasts mashed into his back, and he had to press his lips together to halt his moan.

"Did you hear that?" he whispered.

"Hear what?"

That answered that. Still he did not move forward, but stood there, waiting, listening. Jane's nipples hardened, rasping over his flesh as she breathed. Her scent enveloped him. *Must taste female…soon.*

This physical desire was new to him. Oh, he'd had sex. And recently, too. Many times, but with Laila, or someone of her choosing as the princess watched and directed. Always chained to her bed, muzzled, her mouth and hands forcing him to respond to her, even though he hated her.

Sometimes, when even that failed to arouse him, she had used her witch magic to elicit an erection from him. Unlike her sister, she hadn't needed someone else's pain to spur her into orgasm. She had ridden him with abandon, while he had stared up at the face he despised, scowling, trying with every ounce of his strength to prevent her—and himself—from climaxing.

Sometimes she had, sometimes she hadn't. Sometimes he had, sometimes he hadn't. But each time, no matter the outcome, his hatred for them both had grown.

He did not remember ever being with another woman—besides Odette—though he was sure he'd had many lovers throughout the years. Because, as Laila had writhed atop him, he'd instinctively known what would bring her pleasure. Gliding his thumb along the bundle of nerves between her legs. Laving his tongue there. Kneading her breasts, plucking at her nipples. All the things he had refused to do, and now wanted to do to Jane.

He wanted to watch her expressive face as she reached her peak. Wanted to feel her inner walls clutch at him. Wanted to hear her cry out his name. Sweet heavens, even the thought delighted him.

"Seriously. What are we listening for?" Jane asked. The warmth of her breath trekked down his spine. "I don't hear anything."

Taste…

Distracted again, *Nicki?* The stray thought jolted him back to full awareness. Someone had once said that to him; he knew it. A woman. He wanted to know who, but now was not the time to try and access his memories. He had to remain alert.

"Come," he said, leading Jane deeper into that dark part of the forest. More laughter echoed. Evil, promising retribution. Once again, he stilled. "Did you hear *that?*"

"What?"

More laughter, blending with yet another man's. *"That."*

"No. I hear the rush of water now, but that's all."

Damn it. The laughter must be another trick of Laila's, meant to send him fleeing. Nicolai kicked back into gear. Five minutes passed, an eternity. He remained on guard, without a weapon—he should have grabbed a damned weapon—but willing to shield Jane with his body.

Another five minutes eked by. Then another. He wasn't sure how much longer he could go on, but he felt like he should stop, so he did the opposite. He pushed onward. Another five minutes. Another.

"Wait. Nicolai. You have—"

Jane's words cut off when Nicolai felt the cool rush of water against his feet, droplets splashing up his calf. Brows knitting in confusion, he paused and looked down. He hadn't noticed the water, even though it had been directly in front of him.

The rocks were slippery as he backtracked to the edge. *Dangerous,* he thought. *This place is dangerous. He should—*

Stay. Finally.

"You did it," Jane said. "You found the source." She laughed, soft and carefree.

Without thought, Nicolai found himself whipping

around to catch a glimpse of her. Her expression was lit up, brighter than the sun on its best morning. Her plump pink lips were curved at the corners, inviting him to lick, to finally taste. To devour. The hem of her robe was wet and plastered to her ankles.

She was safe. He could have her. Yes?

His chest constricted, and his stomach quivered. He reached out. A touch, until she healed, he'd allow himself only a touch. Except, his knees gave out just before contact and he fell into the water. His chin resting on his sternum, he breathed quickly and shallowly, trying to fill his lungs but failing.

His energy was draining, absolute fatigue taking its place.

"Oh, no, you don't. Not there. You'll drown." Jane latched onto his arm and managed to drag him to the shore.

Once there, he just kind of fell the rest of the way, crashing into a mossy embankment. He tried to rise, but couldn't find the strength. He needed to forage for food. Jane must be starving. He needed to build a shelter. The bugs would eat his woman alive. He needed to stand guard. She must not be hurt.

"Relax," she said.

"Protect," he murmured.

"Yes, I'll protect you." Gentle hands smoothed over his brow,

"No, I..." Oblivion claimed him before he could utter another word.

NICOLAI...

The deep male voice that called to him was familiar. Always in his dreams, when his defenses were weak-

ened, but it was stronger now than ever before. And...
beloved?

Nicolai...time...save...

In the back of his mind, he heard the *tick, tick, tick*
of a clock.

"Who are you?" he demanded.

An image flashed in his mind. Not of the speaker,
but of huge, grotesque monsters crawling toward him.
Each had eight legs, with sharp, deadly points. They
were black and hairy, their eyes big and beady, their
tails pointed and curling toward him. They were staring him down, as if he were a tasty snack. Bile rose in
his throat, but he pressed on, ignoring them.

"Where are you? What can I do?"

*Nicolai...brother...heal yourself, and come. Time...
save...*

Brother? Nicolai tried to picture a brother. Nothing.
He could not picture his mother, either. Nor his father.
Even in his dreams, pain exploded through his head,
shutting down his memories.

Tick, tick, tick.

Kill! an equally familiar male voice suddenly
boomed. Deeper, harder.

Damn it. He had to find out who was speaking to
him. Had to know. Had to, had to, had to. Life—and
death—rested on his shoulders.

As he considered their identities, he thrashed, his
hand connecting with something solid and warm.

He heard a gasp. For some reason, the female's pain
only increased his agitation. Must protect...

"Everything's fine. You don't have to worry," she
said, soothing him. "I'm here. You're safe now."

Jane, he thought, stilling. His Jane. Such a sweet

voice, such a pretty face. Such a commanding personality, worthy of a queen. She was nearby.

Heal yourself...time...save...

Yes, he thought. With Jane nearby, he could do anything. Heal himself, and even replenish the store of power he'd burned through. He relaxed, willingly sinking back into oblivion. This time, he had a purpose.

CHAPTER SEVEN

JANE SPENT TWO DAYS gathering supplies and making
weapons. She never strayed far from the unconscious
Nicolai, just in case he needed her or they had unexpected visitors, so those supplies were limited. However, she managed to find fruits and nuts to eat, as well
as small, thin twigs and mint leaves. Those, she'd turned
into surprisingly efficient toothbrushes, which she used
liberally on both of them.

Because they were near a stream, bathing her patient was easy. In fact, there'd probably never been two
cleaner people trapped in the wilderness. Nicolai was
no longer oiled, his skin was scrubbed to a healthy pink
shine, and yet, the scent of sandalwood was stronger
than ever. Every time she breathed him in, she tingled,
her blood heating, her mouth watering.

It hadn't helped that in bathing him, she'd had to run
her hands all over him. As dirty as he'd been—cough,
cough—she'd had to bathe him *a lot*. Those muscles…
so hard, thickly roped and laced with sinew. That trail
of hair from his navel to his penis…always tempting
her to wickedness.

And God, she was shame spiraling.

Nicolai might desire her, but he didn't need another
woman lusting after him while he was helpless. What's
more, he didn't need another grabby woman touching

him without permission, and already Jane had pushed the boundaries of his trust by bathing him (so many times).

Hands off from now on, she decided. And one day, she'd apologize for her behavior. Maybe. She wasn't sure she would sound sincere. Despite his past, she'd *liked* touching him. *Bad Jane.* But, well, he'd seemed to like being touched by her. He tossed and turned intermittently, only calming when she was within reach.

Sometimes he questioned a man who needed his help, sometimes he cursed Laila for the vile things she'd done to him, and sometimes he fought ugly monsters, his arms and legs flailing. After the latter two, he always vowed retribution. Painful, slow retribution.

Something he was fully capable of delivering now. The swelling in his wrists and ankles was gone, his thumbs having snapped back into place, his feet having realigned right before her eyes. Even the abrasions on his skin were gone. It was quite an amazing process to witness.

The vampires she had studied had healed quickly, as well, but not *that* quickly. Nor had they slept this long in a single stretch. She worried about him.

Did he need blood? He'd had so much at the palace, and overfeeding could cause as much damage as starvation. Perhaps more so, because overfeeding caused an insatiable need for more, more, more. Nothing else mattered ever again, and dead body after dead body was left in the wake.

She shouldn't know that. She'd almost given herself and her knowledge away with the whole "bursting into flames" thing. And while she hated herself for having experimented on his brethren, she wished she'd done more, knew more. Anything to help Nicolai right now.

Jane sighed. She'd give him another day. And then what? she wondered.

She would have to construct some kind of hamper and drag him through the forest and into a town, find a healer and get him checked out. *If* there was a town other than Delfina nearby.

The problem—besides her lack of strength and direction—was her face. Her magical face. As Odette, she simply couldn't lose herself in a crowd, as proven by the reaction of the people outside the palace. Word of her arrival might travel to Laila. Someone might attempt to capture Nicolai.

That someone would have to die by Jane's hand, and she wasn't quite ready to become a killer.

Another sigh slipped from her, this one weary. As a golden moon settled into a black velvet sky, she placed her handmade weapons—twigs sharpened on rocks until becoming daggers and spears—beside Nicolai. Then she lay next to him.

She'd washed her robe about an hour ago, the still-wet material now draped over a nearby tree limb. Except for her panties, she was naked. By necessity. Of course. So she wasn't going to castigate herself over needing Nicolai's warmth. Well, not too badly. The baths had been frivolous; spooning wasn't.

Lying next to him provided a wealth of wondrous experiences. Peace, after so many months of fear and regret. Soul-deep contentment. Hope for a future she had once dreaded. He shouldn't affect her this quickly and this strongly, even with magic.

After some thought, she'd realized magic could not

change a person's feelings. He had never welcomed his captors; and had they possessed the ability to force the issue, they would have.

Though she was exhausted, falling asleep proved difficult. Her back had scabbed, and those scabs pulled and reopened with her every movement. And her legs… Without her morning jogs and physical therapy, her legs were stiffening up more and more frequently, aching and throbbing. She could practically feel atrophy setting up camp in her muscles.

What she wouldn't give for a handful of painkillers.

At least she didn't have to dread the approach of the sun. Their very first night here, she'd constructed a big, leafy canopy above the small site. Nicolai had claimed he wouldn't burst into flame with ultraviolet contact, but she wasn't willing to risk it. Granted, the sun here was muted, always shaded by clouds, and not nearly as hot as she'd experienced back home. But in her world, she *had* witnessed other vamps burning to ash. Maybe even one of his friends.

Stomach cramp. She wouldn't let herself go there.

Also, the canopy offered them camouflage from the enemy, hiding them from prying eyes. As proud as she was of her efforts, they'd so far been unnecessary. Laila and her men had never even marched past.

Most likely they weren't even looking for the escapee, the princess expecting Nicolai to walk himself straight back to her bed.

Bed. Exactly where *Jane* wanted Nicolai. A soft mattress underneath him, Jane on top of him, her nails digging into his chest as she balanced. A tantalizing rush of desire poured through her, and she moaned.

Nicolai was right beside her. He could wake up at

any moment and realize what she yearned for. But...
maybe another sex fantasy was in order. For his sake.
After all, she had to be disturbing him, rolling around
like this. And last time, she'd fallen asleep the moment
she'd climaxed.

Yes, for Nicolai's sake, she thought dazedly, inhibitions crumbling as she imagined the hard thrust of him
inside her....

A LOW MOAN CAUSED NICOLAI to jolt upright.

Out of habit, he cataloged his surroundings in an
instant. The moon was high, golden, the stars bright,
winking from their scattered perches. Ghost trees
swayed against a cool, sultry breeze. A river rushed
along a pebbled bank.

His brows drew together with confusion. He was enveloped by the sweetest scent of passion...fading...and
the ripe scent of pain...intensifying. Who was in—?

Another low, female moan sounded, broken and
harsh. His attention whipped to the left, down. Jane.
Jane lay beside him. And gods above, she was practically naked. Her only covering was a tiny scrap of white
material between the apex of her thighs.

He should remove it. With his teeth.

Instantly his fangs ached. A familiar sensation in
her presence. For a moment, he could only drink in the
sight of her, his gaze greedy. Her breasts were small,
her nipples pink as berries and beaded deliciously. Her
stomach hollowed, showcasing every single one of her
ribs.

Clearly she had been hungry for a long time. He
would feed her, he thought, delighted by the very idea.
She would never lack for food again. Would eat from

his hand. Only the very best morsels, too. She would close her eyes at the succulent taste, savor every nibble, groan in joy when he sampled the meal with her, and then directly from her.

While blood was the source of his life, he needed food, as well. Perhaps because he was not fully vampire. He had a witch for a mother, and—

A witch for a mother?

Pain sliced through him, and he nearly pounded his fist into the ground. Not again. Frustration ate at him.

Then he spied the scars on Jane's abdomen, and thoughts of offering her the choicest of meats fled, right along with thoughts of his family. Hunger of a different nature asserted itself. He ached to commit murder. Those scars...Dark Abyss... He'd known she had them, but not how many or how deeply they cut her.

From her navel down, she looked as if she'd been sliced up and sewn back together by a blind weaver. Thick, red scars crisscrossed in every direction, badges of pain most in the world would probably never experience.

How had she survived whatever had been done to her?

Whoever had hurt her would die, just as the guards who touched her had.

She deserved pampering. Not just the food from his table, but gowns of rich velvet and a bed of the finest goose feathers. Never would she work. She would relax, enjoy, perhaps spend her days naked, lounging in his bedroom, and her nights sweat soaked from passion.

He would feast from her body, her veins. Sample every part of her, dining between her legs at his leisure. Riding her hard and fast, letting her ride him slow and sweet. Taking her in every position imaginable, then perhaps inventing a few. His cock hardened, already aching.

She needs her rest. Needs to heal. Deep breath in, deep breath out. But gods, much more of her incredible scent and he would fall on her, perhaps drink too much of her blood. She was like the morning dew on the petals of a rose, fragile, and he must always be careful with her.

Trembling, he reached out to smooth that honey hair from her brow…. When he saw his hand, he stilled. Turned his palm up to the moonlight. Wiggled his thumb. Healed. He was completely healed; there was no pain.

How much time had passed?

How long had he left Jane unguarded?

He looked around with fresh eyes, astonished by what he found. Enough time had passed for her to construct a hut, weapons, wash her clothing and his body. He was the man, the warrior, yet *she* had taken care of *him.*

Mine. Worthy of being queen.

She'd told him she did not have a man waiting for her, and he was glad. Had she, he would have killed the man. Not painfully, not unless the man had once hurt her, but he would have died all the same. After Nicolai found a way into her world. And he would have done so. No one but him would lay claim to this woman, not in any time or in any place.

And if you have someone waiting for you? Someone you've forgotten? He frowned, not liking the thought. Fidelity was important. Jane had said as much. He didn't know a lot about himself, but that he, too, believed.

But…he wanted Jane. And right then, he could not even conceive the idea of wanting anyone else, of being with anyone else. Ever. Truly, every cell in his body burned for Jane, only Jane. Somehow, she was already a part of him. Somehow, her essence was rooted so deeply inside him, he suspected they had always been destined to meet, to be together. But…

If someone *was* waiting for him, what would he do? Despite his fearsome temper, he revered the law and never went back on his word. Right?

Perhaps. But… There was that awful, awful word again. The law, his honor, fidelity, none of those applied to this situation. If he didn't want another female, he wouldn't accept another female. He wouldn't cheat *Jane*. It was as simple as that.

While he thought himself somewhat decent in this matter, he did not think he fought honorably. He thought he won his battles through fair means or foul, and punished his enemies without a shred of mercy or remorse. Look at what he'd done to the guards of the Queen of Hearts.

And many years ago, he had led his army through the Wolfyn realm, the moon hidden behind clouds, the citizens of one of the kingdoms sleeping peacefully in their beds. He and his men had razed the entire structure. He'd hated to do it, but that hadn't stopped him. Anything to save his brother….

A sharp pain, his mind shutting down. The memory, lost. For the most part. Once, he'd led an army. He'd thought such a thing before, but now he knew. He had. He'd led them. But…an army of what? Other vampires? Mercenaries? Or had he been royally sanctioned?

The answers were not forthcoming, and he gritted his teeth in renewed frustration.

He focused on the here and now. On Jane. He was willing to fight for her. He wanted her in his life, and she might very well protest. If so, they would verbally brawl and he would do *anything* to keep her.

At last he smoothed the hair from her cheek and…

She had a black eye.

Nicolai stiffened, rage blooming through him, stronger than ever before. Someone had hit her. Who had dared hit her?

The animal instinct roared to the surface, snarling, desperate for blood.

Calm, he had to remain calm. For now. Was she injured further? As tenderly as he was able, he rolled her to her back. There were no other bruises on her face. The long length of her lashes cast spiky shadows over her cheeks, and he traced them just to be sure. They were smooth, soft and warm. Her lips were puffy and red, as if she'd chewed them from worry.

Didn't matter. She was beautiful…a priceless work of art.

There were several cuts on her hands, but those came from the making of the blades. He had borne those same cuts on multiple occasions. Another memory, and it came without pain. He did not pursue it. Jane was more important.

Bruises wrapped around her rib cage, stretching from her back, where she'd been whipped. Thankfully, though, she possessed no other battle marks. So. How had she gotten the black eye?

She shifted in her sleep, and another pained groan left her.

Her back must agonize her in this position. He should have left her on her side. Could he never do the right thing where this woman was concerned? He eased back down and gently worked an arm under her shoulder. Then he lifted her until she was plastered to his side, her injuries free of all contact. She burrowed her head in the hollow of his neck and raised her top leg, fitting herself against him like the puzzle piece she'd once praised.

She flattened her hand over his heart, as if measuring the erratic beat against her own. So trusting she was, so trust*worthy*. She hadn't left him when she'd had the chance. So forgiving, too. He'd allowed her to be whipped, yet still she'd taken care of him. Had even, he mused, cleaned his teeth. His mouth tasted fresh, like mint.

She groaned again, but this time, oh, this time, there was no pain in her voice. Only pleasure. Such a decadent sound. Instantly his cock stood at attention, filling, hardening, readying. He bit his tongue, his fangs sinking deep into the tissue.

"Nicolai?" Jane breathed sleepily.

"All is well, Jane. Go back to sleep."

"No, I—"

"You're right. You may sleep after you tell me who hit you," he interrupted before she could make a demand of her own.

"You did." Warm breath trekked over his chest, tickling his skin.

"What?" he shouted. "Me?"

"Accident. No worries. And I didn't mean to cuddle up to you. I'm sorry."

She was sorry? "Jane. *I* am sorry." Shame beat at him

more stubbornly than any opponent ever had. "Name a punishment and I will render it against myself immediately."

"No punishment necessary, you silly man. I told you, it was an accident."

Even in this, she forgave him so easily. Her worth far surpassed his. "I will never hurt you again, you have my word."

"You were out of it. You couldn't help yourself. I'm just glad you're finally awake. I've been so worried."

She was going to roll away from him, he thought, feeling her muscles bunch, preparing for movement. He tightened his hold on her. "No. I put you here." *And here you will stay.*

"Oh," she said, and he couldn't decide if she was pleased or upset. "Are you, uh, thirsty? For blood, I mean."

Yes. "No." She was in no condition to feed him. But even the idea of tasting her had his fangs extending, moisture filling his mouth.

"Okay. Well, you might be wondering about the number of times I bathed you, but I promise you I never touched you more than necessary. Okay, maybe I did, but not by much. And I cut up the hem of my gown to use as rags, so that you wouldn't have to endure skin-to-skin contact while you were out."

Endure? The thought of her delicate little hands on his body caused his testicles to draw up tight and his erection to throb, close to exploding. "Thank you for taking care of me."

"My pleas— I mean, you're welcome. So how are you feeling?"

"Better." Now that she was relaxing against him. "You?"

"My legs hurt."

Her legs, not her back. It was the first complaint she had ever uttered, yet she'd cast no blame his way. Determination consumed him, suddenly and completely, blending with a sense of urgency. "Hurt, from the walk?"

"From an old injury."

"Tell me."

"Car accident." She paused. "A car is a vehicle used for traveling along roads at high speeds. Anyway, two of them smashed together. I was inside one. My family, too. I survived. They didn't."

He could not imagine what she described, but could identify with her pain. "I will make you better." He eased her to the ground and sat up.

"You can't. Only time can. I only just started walking again a few months ago."

"You could not walk?" When he turned and moved between her legs, a hot blush flooded her cheeks and she quickly covered her breasts and stomach. She also kept her gaze on the large emerald-and-white leaves forming a barrier between them and the sky.

"Not for almost a year. So, hey, did I tell you that I washed my gown and that's why I'm practically naked like this? The material wasn't dry, and I didn't want to wake you up if I accidentally rubbed against you and the gown was cold and wet. But I probably should have risked it," she babbled. "My scars, I know how ugly they are and as perfect as you are, you're probably used to perfect women, too. I mean, not that you had a choice with Laila, and not that she's perfect. But before her you probably—"

"Jane."

She licked her lips. "Yes?"

"Let's tackle this one issue at a time. You think I'm upset by your nakedness?"

"Well, yes. After what Laila did, I—"

"You are not Laila." And every part of him knew it.

"I know that, but you are a victim of sexual abuse and I...I just don't want to push the boundaries and upset you."

Upset him? *Him?* "I've told you how much I crave you, Jane."

"Well, you needed me to save you. You might have been buttering my toast, so to speak." When he looked at her blankly, she added, "You know, softening me up so I'd do what you wanted."

Indeed, that had been the plan. From the first moment he'd spied her, however, everything had changed. He'd operated only on instinct. "You are also too smart for your own good and convince yourself of the silliest notions."

Her eyes narrowed, just not enough to hide the fire inside them. "Anything else you want to complain about, you lazy vampire?"

His lips twitched. Even angry, the woman wasn't concerned with his new position. Her knees were poised at his hips, his erection lifting his loincloth and nearly brushing what was definitely the sweetest spot in this world or the other. Despite her insecurities, she trusted him completely.

She was uncomfortable about her nudity for reasons

that had nothing to do with him, and that he couldn't allow. "You know I've…climaxed recently," he said.

"Well, now I do," she replied cautiously.

"The last time was the morning of your arrival. Mere hours before, in fact. And not once, but twice. Yet, look at my cock, Jane."

A slight gurgle was her only response.

"Look at my cock," he repeated.

This time, she obeyed. Slowly, slowly, her gaze lowered. She gasped when she spotted the angle of his loincloth.

"If I did not want you, I would not be hard."

"I know." A heated sigh.

"Any time you doubt your appeal, just look here." He fisted his length and moved his hand up and down, up and down, hissing in a breath at the painful but very necessary pressure. "You'll remember how exquisite I find you. So much so you are in constant danger of being devoured."

"But my scars…"

"Your scars simply prove how strong and capable you are. They prove you survived a terrible accident. They are lovely."

"Really?" she squeaked, her cheeks brightening another degree.

"Really. And just so you know, there are no boundaries with us."

"There aren't?"

He stopped his assault on himself before he spilled. "No."

"But…but…there are always boundaries."

Oh, really. "Is there something you don't want me to do to you? Some place on your body you don't want me to touch?" He was tense as he awaited her response. He could have misjudged. He could be wrong about her feelings.

She gulped. "No."

He relaxed. "It is the same for me. Therefore, no boundaries."

"Okay, I believe you. But I—I don't think we've explored all the ramifications of this."

"This." A sexual relationship? "I think you think and reason too much. We will mate. One day. Not today, but soon."

Another sigh, her entire body sagging into the ground. "I know that, too. I'm too attracted to you not to give in."

He loved such an open, honest admission. "Good. Now. Have I covered everything that worried you?"

"Well." She chewed at her lip until a tiny bead of blood formed. "I've been thinking."

"I have already mentioned that you do that far too much." Before he realized what he was doing, he reached out, collected the blood with the tip of his finger and licked it away. Her flavor, as sweet as her scent, fizzed and crackled over his taste buds, and he moaned.

Dark Abyss, *nothing* had ever tasted that good. The need for more grew…grew…until he was sweating, panting, fighting for control.

He would not fall on her. He would *not*.

He had known she would delight him in this way, but he had not expected *this*.

"I could return home at any second," she said, unaware of the change in him. "I mean, you're free now and isn't that the reason you summoned me? So it stands to reason that the magic that brought me here will soon begin to fade, whether you want it to or not."

"No," he practically roared, his hunger forgotten in the face of his sudden terror of losing her.

Her eyes widened. "No?"

"I will not allow it." Not now, not ever.

Ever? Yes, he would keep her forever. Would never let her go.

"Just like that?" She snapped her fingers. "You won't allow it, so it won't happen?"

Sweat beaded on his brow as he sat back on his thighs. "I am not safe yet. Therefore, you have not fulfilled all of your duties." He would remain in perpetual danger, if need be. He'd lost so many loved ones already. He could not bear…the pain. The damned pain, wiping his thoughts. "That subject is now closed."

"Fine," she grumbled. "Are you always this grouchy in the semimorning?"

Only when you talk of leaving me. "Would a grouchy vampire tell you that you are the most beautiful female he's ever met?" he asked, determined to soothe them both.

A luscious softening of her eyes, her mouth. "No."

"Then I am not grouchy. Now close your eyes and relax." If that ocher gaze met his, he would forget his purpose, lean down, kiss the breath right out of her, then work his way to her vein. And if his teeth sank inside her, his cock would expect equal measure. "I'm going to ease your hurts."

CHAPTER EIGHT

THE MOST BEAUTIFUL FEMALE he'd ever seen? He must be seeing Odette, then, Jane thought. Thin might be in, at least where she was from, but there was such a thing as too thin and Jane was it. After the accident, she'd been bed bound and tube fed. When she'd finally woken up, able to feed herself, she'd learned of her family's demise and hadn't had an appetite.

Now that her appetite had reasserted itself, she'd been forced to exist on only fruits and nuts.

Fruits…nuts…hmm… In that moment, she realized she was starving. For a juicy steak and a side of fries—on top of another steak. The food could wait, though. She was also starving for a man's touch. A touch Nicolai gave her. Liberally. His strong fingers massaged her calves, deep and hard, hitting her just right. Moaning, she sagged against the moss beneath her.

"Too much?" he asked in a gravelly voice.

"Perfect," she managed to gasp out. She kept her eyes closed, as he'd demanded. Not because of his order, but because his fangs were still out. There was a slight slur to his words.

Those fangs scared her as much as they aroused her. She'd seen the harm they could do, ripping through flesh and bone, but also wondered about the pleasure they could bring. Every time she wondered, she shivered.

Hell, even now she shivered. If he was hungry, she was going to feed him, she decided. After this massage, she would owe him a kidney, anyway. Because, oh, sweet mercy, nothing had ever felt this good. Not even grinding on top of him—in her fantasy and in reality—and that had felt like heaven.

Okay, so, maybe the grinding had felt just as good.

He worked on her calves for over an hour, and by the time he moved up to her thighs, she stopped trying to conceal her breasts and scars. Why should she? He'd already seen them and had claimed to find them exquisite. Her arms slid to the ground, useless. God, the man's hands were magic.

Magic. Yes. Somehow, he was using magic. Warmth flowed from his skin and into hers, an unnatural warmth, a drugging warmth, intoxicating her, stealing into her muscles, her bones, until every part of her was tingling—and his property. Oh, yes. Whatever he touched instantly became his, existing for him and only him.

When his knuckles brushed the edge of her panties, every nerve ending she possessed roared to sudden life, reaching for him. Soon she was panting, groaning, trying to anticipate his next move. At her knee, he rubbed, then stroked up, gliding along her thigh, sweeping over—*yes, there, please there, almost, almost*—only to pause, not quite stroking where she most needed, before reaching for her other thigh. She had to bite her lip to cut off her plaintive cries for more.

If he would prolong the contact, angle it just a little,

she could climax. Oh, God. If she climaxed from this…
it would be embarrassing.

The massage continued. And really, who cared about
being embarrassed? She didn't. When would he brush
across her panties again? She tensed, waiting, hoping,
so damn eager. Her entire body vibrated. Even the air
in her lungs began to heat. But time ticked by, and his
motions became a little jerky as he kneaded the knots,
never offering such wantonness again.

"Distract me," she said. Otherwise, she just might
beg him for a happy ending. Something she couldn't
allow herself to do. He said they would mate soon.
Which meant, now was not the time.

Or *was* she supposed to beg? Before, in the bedroom, he'd said, *Not until you beg me.* Was that what
he wanted now? What he expected? To work her into a
frenzy and hear her plead? Well, she would—

"Distract you how?" he asked, surprising her.

Okay, so begging wasn't on the menu. Astonished
with herself, she fought a wave of disappointment. "Tell
me a story."

He stilled. "A story?"

"Yes." She cracked open her eyelids and added,
"Whatever you do, don't stop massaging!"

His lips twitched despite the tension radiating from
him, something she found endearing. Most likely
amusement had not been a part of his life for a while,
yet he seemed to enjoy her. As she enjoyed him.

"A story about what?" he asked. He remained between her splayed legs, with her knees bent and framing him.

"I don't know. Your family, maybe." The second she
said the words, she wanted to snatch them back. She

remembered the passage from the book. He did not recall his past. His memory—

"I have two brothers and a sister," he said, and stopped breathing.

A moment passed, then another. His fangs slid back inside his mouth, disappearing. Shock and pain replaced the desire and joviality in his expression.

"What's wrong?" she asked, even though she knew the answer. Or thought she did. He needed to speak, to release. Something she had learned—and maybe discarded—in her therapy sessions. But just because *she* hadn't tried it, didn't mean he should not.

"I didn't remember my siblings until just now. I suspected, but…I have two brothers and a sister. Right now I know, *know,* they are real." There was a challenging note in his voice, as if he expected her to argue.

"They're real," she agreed.

He grimaced, nodded. "At last I can see them in my mind. I just can't recall their names. When I try, my head nearly explodes with pain."

"Pain?"

"A *courtesy* of the healer."

"Oh, Nicolai. I am so sorry." To know you had a family and to be unable to recall the past you shared, well, that was a true torture, and far worse than not knowing they existed at all. For months, Jane had survived only on her memories. "Ease away from thinking about their names and describe what you see." Perhaps, when he relaxed, his mind focused on one portion of his past, other memories would follow more easily.

The glaze of pain faded from his eyes, and the corners of his lips quirked up once more. He dug into her muscles with more ferocity. "My youngest brother, just a boy, has green eyes and hair several shades lighter than yours. I see him chasing after me, and that makes me happy."

"I bet he looked up to you," she said to encourage him. "I had an older sister, and I was always chasing after her, desperate to play with her and her friends."

"Yes." Nicolai's eyes widened, but he was looking beyond her, to a place she couldn't fathom. "Yes, he did look up to me. To all of us. And we loved him. He was sweetness and innocence rolled into a mischievous package. I—I see us standing together, smiling, a unicorn prancing in front of us."

A *real* unicorn. Jane wanted details—like, had they saddled the creature and ridden it around?—but didn't want to interrupt the flow of Nicolai's recollection. "What about your other brother?"

"He is younger, as well, though very close to my age." He paused, as if searching his mind for validation. He nodded. "They are all younger than me. Even my darling sister."

"And what are these other siblings like?"

"My sister has her golden head bent over a spell book. I try to convince her to leave with me, as I must visit the market, but she refuses. She wants to stay, has too much to do. She works too hard, wants to please too many people. And he, the brother closest to my age, has black hair, like mine, and he's hunting in the forest, racing alongside the wolves."

The bookworm and the warrior, huh? "You are the dictator, I bet," she said with a smile. "And the youngest is the sweetheart."

"Micah is a sweetheart, yes." His eyes widened, a trace of pain returning. "Micah. Yes, that's his name.

I wonder where he is, where they all are, what they're doing."

"You'll remember, just like you remembered Micah's name. And maybe you don't need a healer to do this. These memories came back without her."

"Maybe they came back because of you." Nicolai's gaze returned to her. He caught sight of her encouraging smile and licked his lips, his expression changing yet again. From wistful to heated, his cheeks flushing, his fangs peeking out. Little beads of sweat popped up on his brow.

"Me?" The rising sun cast muted, golden rays over their camp. Though he remained in the shadows, his bronzed skin seemed to glow. His eyes swirled, liquid silver, hypnotizing her.

"Yes. You are the only change in my life," he said. His attention moved to her breasts, and her nipples pearled for him, as if desperate to please him. "Mine," he added, reminding her of the beast he had become inside the palace.

This time, the beast delighted her.

The tingling reignited, more intense and spreading quickly. She might have moaned. Might have lifted her hips, seeking more of his heat. Hard to tell, because her thoughts were so consumed with what she wanted, *needed,* from him.

"You keep saying that." And she kept hoping it was true. But they'd made no promises to each other, had only stated their desire for each other.

And really, despite his earlier shout that she would stay with him, she had no idea how much longer they would be together. An hour? A week? A year? They were literally from two different worlds, and she could return as suddenly as she'd appeared.

"Mine," he said more forcefully, perhaps sensing her doubts.

"What do you mean by that? Explain."

"Want you. No secret of that. You want me, too."

God, those short, abrupt sentences were sexy as hell. As if his mind was locked on one thought—pleasure—and nothing could penetrate his determination to have it. With her and only her.

But…could she truly satisfy him? More than being from two different worlds, they were completely different people. One, there was his abuse. Would the things she wanted to do to him freak him out? Maybe, maybe not. Nothing had so far. Two, he clearly knew his way around a female body.

Odette and Laila had been willing to enslave him to experience the joy of his body. Jane knew her way around one man's. She knew what he had liked, but had no idea what another male might long for.

Her previous relationship had lasted three years, ending with her accident. Not because of him. Spencer had wanted to stick by her side. She had pushed him away, too grief stricken to deal with him or anyone. And the plain fact was, she had no longer desired him. Not in any way. She had tried, she really had, to make herself want him again. She had planned a date night, with every intention of seducing him. Yet, even the thought of kissing him had made her sick and she had sent him home directly after dinner.

So, the fact was, while she and Spencer had done everything lovers could do, she'd didn't have any other experience. None. In school, she'd been far younger than her classmates, so no one had wanted her. After that, she'd been too busy. Spencer was the first man to distract her enough to start something.

The lack hadn't bothered her before. There'd been no time to consider it, not even when she had been grinding on top of Nicolai. She'd been too busy trying to figure out what had happened to her, trying to survive her sudden appearance here.

Now, however, she wanted to be perfect. The best. She wanted to please Nicolai the way he had pleased her in her fantasy.

She had enjoyed sex. And she had missed it, despite her lack of desire, all these months. Actually, nearly a year now. Mostly, she had loved and missed the afterglow, lying in a man's arms, absorbing his heat, talking, laughing.

"I've lost you to your thoughts." Nicolai cursed under his breath, but there was humor in the undercurrent. "I'm trying to resist you, Jane, and I'm failing. The challenge of engaging your attention isn't helping."

"Why?" A breathy entreaty. "I mean, why are you trying to resist?"

"You need time to recover. And there's something I must tell you first. Something you will not like."

Stomach cramp. "What is it?"

One heartbeat, two. "Without my memories, I can't be sure…a woman could be waiting…"

Another cramp. "Oh, God. You're married?"

"No. No, that much I know. Just before my appearance in the Sex Market, I was with a woman…a servant. Yes. I remember that. I would not have been with a servant if I were married. But I might have *promised* myself to another."

Might have… No. Not possible. "You hadn't." This she said with a sudden surge of confidence. He was too possessive to sleep with a servant if a fiancée waited in the wings.

A glimmer of hope in his expression. "I mention this only as a possibility, not a reality. I could never want anyone as much as I want you right now." He was looming over her a second later, his mouth poised just above hers. He was breathing shallowly, his hands anchored next to her temples, his erection pressed between her legs.

Finally. The contact she'd yearned for. He was hers, hers, only hers. She could believe nothing less. "You may not know yourself, but *I* think I know you," she said. "Trust me, no one is waiting for you."

She wasn't being stubborn or blind about this. Discarding his possessive nature and the fact that any woman he committed to would have his full attention, he was vampire and vampires mated for life. Physically they couldn't stray. Research had proven that. So, memory or not, he would not react to Jane if his heart belonged to another.

"Perhaps I am a horrible person, because I don't care about a faceless stranger," he said. "I can't resist you. I won't resist you. Don't deny me, Jane. Must taste you, all of you. Please." He didn't wait for her reply but leaned the rest of the way down.

"Nicolai—" She meant to tell him that she couldn't resist him, either, and she would never deny him, that he wasn't a horrible person, but the words were lost in a scorching kiss as he meshed their lips together.

His tongue thrust past her teeth and rolled with hers. Hot, so hot.

He tasted of mint and…candy. Mmm. Yes, candy. Sugary sweet, the flavor all his own, consumed her.

Unable to stop herself, she glided her fingers into his hair.

"Yes. Please. Please," she said, finally begging.

Her nails bit into his scalp, holding him to her. She needed more, had to have more, everything else forgotten. Her knees squeezed at his waist, and she rocked herself against him. A gasp of hungry joy escaped her. God! The feel of his erection against her was mind-blowing, shattering, necessary, better than anything she'd ever known. Maybe because she was so damn wet and ready. So she did it again, rocking, rubbing, gasping.

With a growl of approval, he thrust his tongue deeper. Their teeth scraped together. Dizzying friction, welcome but torturous as her need ratcheted up another level. Then he angled his head for even deeper contact, and she felt the graze of his fangs.

No, *this* was need. True, undiluted need. She *wanted* to be bitten, again and again and again. To be everything to him. Lover, sustenance, breath.

Her blood was heating unbearably, her stomach quivering. On and on the kiss continued, until there was no more oxygen left in her lungs. Until Nicolai was her only lifeline.

"Please," she rasped. "Do it."

"Gods, Jane. You're…you're like fire. I want to be burned."

"Yes."

He licked his way to the pulse hammering at the base of her neck. Was he going to bite her at last? But no, he continued laving at her pulse, sucking on it as one of his hands cupped her breast and kneaded. He pinched the throbbing nipple, and a lance of delicious sensation shot through her entire body.

Heaven and hell, so sweetly offered…how close she was to falling over the edge. But when she did, if she did—*please, let her*—where would she land? The clouds, or the fiery pits?

Only one way to find out…

"Nicolai?"

"Yes, sweetheart."

Sweetheart. His sweetheart. "Bite me."

"Jane." A groan. "You tempt me. I shouldn't."

Shouldn't, because he still thought she needed to heal? Or because a part of him still believed another female was out there, waiting for him? If the impossible happened and he *was* committed… Why impossible? she wondered next. Jane was here, wasn't she? *Nothing* was impossible.

The knowledge caused the first tendrils of doubt to surface. Jane despised cheaters, but she also hated stories that forced two people to remain together because of a sense of duty, rather than love. Nicolai wasn't in love. And if he had a woman, why hadn't she searched for him? Saved him? Again, that made Jane think he couldn't possibly be committed. No girlfriend would have let this guy go. Therefore, Jane could still have him.

But, she didn't want him resenting her. Or feeling pressured. Or regretting what they did. "All right. We won't—"

"We will. Just don't want to hurt you."

Relief. So much relief, ecstasy shimmering, within reach. "You could never hurt me. Nicolai, please. Do it."

"Yes, yes, please. *I'll* beg if necessary. I must have more...." His fangs returned to her neck and grazed her sizzling skin. "Must taste, will die if I do not."

"Do it." She hissed out a breath and stiffened as she mentally prepared herself for the onslaught. Of pleasure or pain, she wasn't sure. All she knew was that she needed this, too.

He dragged in a shaky breath. "You are sure? I don't have to. I can stop."

"Don't stop. Please, don't stop. I'm just wary of the unknown."

Liiick. "Do not fear, little Jane. I'll be careful with you. Will control myself." Then, with agonizing slowness, he sank his fangs into her neck, sucked on her, swallowed her blood.

Not once did she experience any pain, but the pleasure, oh, God, the pleasure...exactly as she'd imagined, beautiful in the most erotic way. The missing piece to the puzzle of her life.

The burn of his mouth, the suction of his tongue, both caused riotous reactions in her body. She clutched at his back, pulled at his hair, lost to a bliss that should have been impossible. Soon she was even writhing and thrashing against him, desperate for completion.

He purred against her, his breath warm. Then something hot, so wonderfully hot, entered her system. And okay, she hadn't truly known pleasure before that moment. *This* was pleasure. Pleasure in its purest form. Strength, heat, power. She felt those, too.

Her thrashing became a single-minded pursuit for

the elusive satisfaction that still hovered so close. She ground herself against his erection, over and over again, little shivers of sensation coursing through her every time he swallowed. God. She could climb him like a mountain. Could eat him up, one tasty bite at a time. Could remain in his arms forever.

He wrenched free of her vein. "Have to…stop. Can't take…too much."

There was no such thing as too much. "Take more."

"Promised to be careful." He licked the punctures, shooting more of that liquid heat into her system. He growled, "Now you are marked. Mine."

His, just as he was hers. Hers, and no one else's.

"So good. Never tasted anything…so sweet. Addicted…already…"

Yes. Addicted. He was a drug. Her drug, and she doubted there was a cure.

With her painkillers, she'd had to stop using cold and flat. The withdrawals had been nightmarish. Yet she knew with sudden, shocking clarity that those would not compare to what she'd experience without Nicolai.

He replaced the hand on her breast with his mouth, flicking his white-hot tongue over her nipple, shooting more of those gratifying lances through her. He didn't bite, though, not again.

She wanted him to bite her everywhere. "Please, Nicolai."

"Anything you want, I will give you."

She arched into him, locking her ankles at his lower back. The long, thick length of his erection hit her just right, more liquid dampening her panties. "I want it all."

He still wore the loincloth, but the leather must have bunched up, freeing his cock, because she could feel the heat of his silky skin, soft yet, oh, so hard, pushing at the cotton in a bid to move it out of the way. Just a little more, and they'd be skin-to-skin. Strength-to-wet.

She ached for that. Wanted it with every fiber of her being. But Nicolai had other plans. He continued his downward journey, tracing her scars with his tongue, laving her navel. She would have been humbled by the decadent attention, but she was too aroused. Goose bumps broke out, sensitizing her skin to an almost unbearable degree.

"Mine," he growled.

Yes. *Yes!* His. Always. She frowned. No, not always. The repercussions of his druglike lovemaking hit her like a hammer to the head. She could go home at any moment. This wasn't permanent, and she couldn't forget that fact. Couldn't become attached to him. To this.

You already are.

Yes, she was.

How could she return to her old life now? She'd tasted the forbidden fruit, was addicted just as she'd suspected, and she needed more. More of his hands and his mouth and his teeth and his fingers. More of the heat and the sweetness and the ferocity. But if she didn't finish this, if she attempted to walk away now, she would always wonder about what could have happened.

So, she would worry about the consequences later. Right now, she would simply enjoy.

"Mine," he repeated.

"Yes," she found herself agreeing.

"You want me."

"You, and only you."

"You're so wet for me. I can feel you, feel how ready you are."

"Ready for you, and only you." She was repeating herself, but she didn't care. The words were true.

"You're so hot for me."

"Yes."

"You'll give me everything."

"Yes, I..." Jane's thoughts derailed completely. Finally he was there, between her legs, shoving her panties aside the rest of the way. She anchored her calves over his shoulders as his tongue stroked her.

At first contact, she screamed. So good, so damn good. He licked, sucked and nibbled at her, building her desire to a fever pitch. So close, closer than ever before.

"Like?"

"I like!"

His fingers joined the play. First one, sinking in and out, then another, in and out, in and out, stretching her, preparing her for his possession. "Could stay here forever," he rasped.

She was incapable of responding, what little breath she had left caught in her throat.

"Taste so sweet here, too."

A sound escaped the knot. A whimper.

"Come for me, sweetheart." A command from the animal he'd unleashed at the palace, frothed into a frenzy, desperate, a conqueror. "Let me see that beautiful face light up." With that, he bit her, right there, between her legs.

He sucked the blood that beaded, and then, thank God, then he shot whatever his fangs produced straight inside her core.

Sparks of utter bliss ignited there, then spread, quickly burning her up from top to bottom. Every muscle she possessed clenched, spasmed, shooting her to the stars. Another scream left her, this one tearing through the encroaching daylight.

The climax was intense, soul shattering. Then Nicolai was looming over her, one of his hands ripping at her panties, his cock probing for entrance. His eyes were glitter-bright, his fangs bared in a determined scowl. Not of anger, but of agonizing need.

"More," he said with guttural harshness.

"Let me have you."

"Now," he growled.

Just before he thrust inside, the bushes to their left rattled, the leaves dancing together. His attention whipped there, a growl of pure menace leaving him.

Jane was still too lost in the throes of passion to care. "Nicolai! Please. What are you waiting for?" *Make me your woman in truth.*

"Protect." He jerked upright, severing all contact. She reached for him, but he placed himself in front of her, acting as her shield.

The time for pleasure had ended. The time for fighting had arrived.

CHAPTER NINE

NICOLAI'S MORPH FROM tender lover to savage vampire warrior shocked Jane back to her senses. She was naked—ripped panties didn't count—and her camp had just been invaded. By giants. Four of them.

All four were eyeing her up and down like a barbecued slab of ribs—and they were starving vegetarians.

One by one, they confirmed her thoughts.

"Ugly," the tallest said, the *g* prolonged.

"Hideous."

"Fat."

"Woman," the shortest said. He was probably six-five.

The rest of them shrugged, the universal sign for *I guess she'll do.* Apparently Odette and Laila looked a lot alike, but sex was sex. They might find her repellant, but they'd still do her. Their gazes dipped and glued to her nipples, saliva dripping from the corners of their mouths.

Vegetarians now converted into carnivores.

Jane shuddered. The best thing about her robe, she decided then, was the ease of donning it. She grabbed the material still hanging from the limb where she'd draped it and jerked it over her head. *Boom,* done. She was dressed and ready to face the newest hazard in her life.

She'd expected to battle Laila's guards at some point, but as she snatched up two of her wooden daggers, she realized the giants weren't as humanoid as the guards had been. Their eyes were bright red, like twin crimson suns rising from the pits of hell. Sharp, fanglike teeth, bared now, still dripping, dripping, forked tongues flicking out and swiping over reptile-thin lips. Wide shoulders, with black wings arching above them. Rather than nails, they possessed claws.

Somehow, she recognized them as she'd recognized the forest. They were straight out of her darkest nightmares and deep down she knew these creatures were savage, mindless. And Nicolai was going to fight them? *He drank from you. He's strong enough.*

Please be strong enough.

He snarled a sound of pure menace, his scary animal nature racing back to the forefront. "Mine." He stopped just in front of them, daring them to act.

He was weaponless, his torso bare. His poor back was as scarred as her front. Not from a whip or an accident, she didn't think. There was a wide circular mass of scar tissue, raised and puckered, in the center of his back, as if someone had carved out the patch of skin.

He was a survivor. Like her. He *could* take these men—and win.

"We want woman," the tallest said. He was clearly the leader. Also, he was as dumb as a box of rocks, because he added, "You give. Now," and expected Nicolai to rush to obey.

"No," she and Nicolai said in unison.

"You leave," another said with a frown, just as clearly not understanding why Jane wasn't being given to him.

"She please us. You live."

"No," Jane told them with a shake of her head. "*You* leave." Simple words they might understand. "And *you* will live."

They ignored her.

"Leave," one said to Nicolai. "Last chance."

Another said, "You look like someone. Who?" He shook his head, already losing interest in the question. "No matter. Give woman. We keep."

So. Her will meant nothing. Rape was on their menu du jour. "Rip them to shreds," she told Nicolai.

He didn't reply. He simply leaped forward and raked his claws—claws, longer and sharper than theirs!—along the face of the tallest, the biggest threat, sending the giant stumbling backward.

The grunt of pain that followed was like the starting bell to a UFC match. No rules, just pain.

The five males swarmed together in a tangle of limbs, fangs, blood and adrenaline. The blood, well, that sent Nicolai into an animalistic frenzy. He snarled like a panther, bit like a shark and held on to whatever he clamped his teeth into like a pit bull.

Jane knew better than to interfere. When she'd switched the focus of her work to the human body, hoping to find a cure for her mother, she'd learned quite a bit about physical reactions. A man worked into a rage was completely unaware of his surroundings. The chemicals shooting through his bloodstream would keep Nicolai on a short leash, the end of that leash bound to these giants, where only killing mattered.

So she stood there, and she watched, silently cheering for her man.

Not yours, she forced herself to add. *Not completely, and not yet.* She could share her body with him, her mind, but her heart and soul? No. Not when there was a chance the magic would fade and she would return home. Worse, if he fell in love with her, he would wither and die if she left him.

Oh…damn. She'd forgotten about that. Such a terrible fate had befallen several of the vampires brought to her lab. She couldn't let that happen to Nicolai.

She brushed the depressing, worrisome thoughts aside. No distractions, not now. The fight escalated quickly, the violence seemingly unparalleled. Someone's arm flew past her head—and it wasn't attached to a body.

Just then, Nicolai was walking death. His expression, what few times she glimpsed it, considering how quickly he was moving, was cold. He lacked mercy, never once pulling his punches. He went for the throat, vital organs and groin. Had the giants been human, they would have fallen to his superior power within seconds. But each time he dropped one to the ground, or tore off a limb, the bastard got up for more.

That only revved Nicolai's engine. The lethal grace of him…Jane was riveted, even shocked. Oh, she'd known he was capable of this. There, inside the palace, hatred and determination had radiated from him. And guts had spilled across the floor. Had he not rescued her, he would have stayed until every living being had died by his hand. Or teeth. That, she'd known.

But this man, this warrior, had also given her sizzling pleasure. He'd feasted between her legs, and he'd loved doing it. She thought he might have enjoyed it as much as she had. And, oh, he'd set her blood on fire, thrilled her to her very soul, ensuring both of them existed only for passion. That had happened minutes ago.

Mere minutes ago. Now he was a being capable of rendering pain, only pain.

And all too soon the giants learned to anticipate his moves. They bit at him with their too-sharp saber teeth. They swiped their claws at him, cutting him deep. They spun around him, above him, using their wings to slice at him. Nicolai was forced to jump between them and use his momentum to kick at them. They stumbled, but again, they always rose.

She would have to do something, after all. Nicolai would tire soon, surely. He was losing blood, crimson streaking down his chest where he'd been scratched. How should she—?

In less than a heartbeat of time, strong, trunklike arms banded around her, one just above her breasts, the other around her waist, and jerked her into a thick body. Fear bombarded her, nearly paralyzing her. Then fight-or-flight kicked in—as did a reminder that she held two daggers. Fight won.

She slammed her elbow backward, hitting her attacker in the stomach, meaning to turn and stab. He grunted, but held tight, and she wasn't able to twist around. She opened her mouth to scream. Before even the slightest sound left her, her mind shouted, *You can't distract Nicolai.*

The giant—and she knew a giant held her—dragged her backward, but she didn't allow herself to struggle.

Perhaps they weren't as dumb as she'd first thought. This one had known to hang back, to wait, to watch, and grab her while everyone else was preoccupied. Were any others waiting in the shadows?

How would she fight them all?

A cold rage of her own infused her. Thankfully no

one else appeared, and when Nicolai and company were no longer in sight, leaves and branches shielding them, she erupted. *Fight.* She angled her arms, lifted both of her elbows this time, and then slammed them home. He gave another grunt, finally loosening his hold.

Another angle shift, and she thrust her arms down, using the makeshift daggers. The tips sliced deep into his thighs.

With a howl of pain, he shoved her away from his body. One of the daggers remained lodged, but the other glided free as she stumbled forward. Jane righted herself and whirled around, facing him. This giant was scowling, his fangs dripping with saliva. His red eyes glowed with menace.

"I punish you," he snarled as he ripped the other dagger free. A flick of his wrist. The sharpened wood clanked on the ground, now useless.

Fight. "Wrong. *I'll* punish *you.*"

That confused him for a moment. He blinked, brows knitting together. Then he shook his head. "No. I punish you."

Okay. Back to her original assessment. Calling these things dumb as rocks was an insult to the rocks. "Bring it, big boy." Six months of self-defense lessons were about to pay off.

Or not. She'd never had to use her "skills" in a genuine life-and-death situation.

He stomped toward her, booted feet kicking up dirt with every step, the ground shaking. Blood poured down his pant-covered legs, yet he didn't limp or even seem to notice his injuries.

When he was within reach, he tried to grab her. She ducked, and when his claws encountered only air, she twisted and stabbed. This time, her dagger sank into his middle. Another howl rent the air. Before she could dart out of the way this time, his fingers were fisting her hair and pushing her face-first into the dirt.

Seriously? Over that quickly? Oh, hell, no! She rolled into a ball before he could pin her with his massive weight, maneuvered to her back and worked her legs between their bodies. She pushed. He didn't budge an inch. Damn it!

Think, Parker. She still had one of the daggers. She stabbed again, going for his neck. He reared back. Too late. Contact, just not where she'd hoped. His cheek split open, and blood poured.

He flashed his saber-fangs as he snarled.

"Punish." Then he was leaning down, those fangs sinking into her neck. This bite lacked the pleasure and heat of Nicolai's. This one provided only pain. So much pain.

He thought to drain and weaken her. A mistake on his part, she thought darkly, steeling herself against every ache and throb. He'd left himself wide-open. Before her mind could fog from blood loss, she wilted into the ground. Either he assumed that she had been properly subdued or that she'd passed out. His fingers left her hair to move to her breasts and squeeze.

She struck, finally slamming the dagger into his jugular, all the way to the other end. His entire body spasmed, his fangs locking down tight.

Okay, reassessment time. *This* was pain. She nearly screamed from the intensity of it.

There was no dislodging him, even when he sagged against her. His weight shoved the air from her lungs.

She lay there, trying to catch her breath, his blood pouring over her.

For a moment, she was transported back to her car. Her mother dying, her blood dripping onto Jane. Both of them crying, because they knew the others were already gone. Unsavable.

I love you, Janie.

I love you, Mom.

Something sharp dug into her scalp, ripping strands of her hair. Her body was pulled out from under the giant. His teeth had still been buried deep, and the movement caused his fangs to tear through skin and vein, leaving teeth tracks down her neck, chest and stomach.

Another scream fought its way from her throat. *Still can't risk distracting Nicolai.* His battle royale hadn't ended. Otherwise, he would have been here. And she knew it wasn't Nicolai who had grabbed her, even before bright, crimson eyes were glowing down at her. Nicolai would have been gentle, would have tried to soothe her.

"Woman. Ugly. I will bed, anyway."

Peachy. Her eyesight fogged. Had this guy escaped Nicolai, or was he new? Even if she'd had twenty-twenty vision just then, she doubted she would have been able to tell. One hideous monster was the same as any other, she supposed.

"I'm a...princess," she said, trying anything to scare him. "Princess...Odette. Of Delfina. You have to...let me go."

Like the caveman he was, he continued to drag her through the dirt. Twigs and rocks scratched at her scabbed back, and she winced. Soon her robe was in tatters and tears burned her eyes.

She tried again, even as the fog migrated to her mind. "My mother…queen…will kill—"

"Witch queen not my queen. No queen. Only king." He rounded a corner and the new angle hurt worse. "He have you."

Extra peachy. "You're taking me…to your king?"

"After."

After. The same word she'd once thrown at Nicolai, while he'd been chained and helpless. Never again. *After* was now stricken from her vernacular. "You keep this up…and I'll be dead…before we get there."

A confused silence. Then a triumphant, "You not dead. You alive."

Box. Of. Rocks. "Pick me up…stupid shit. Carry me."

The simple order worked. He stopped, swooped down and hefted her up—over his shoulder, fireman style, squashing her stomach into her kidneys, but hey, anything was better than leaving a trail of scabs and blood on the ground. A trail Nicolai didn't need. Wherever this brute took her, Nicolai would find her. He'd marked her, he'd said. And thank God he had.

She and her abductor ran into another giant along the way, and stopped. An angry conversation ensued. She caught words like *king* and *now,* and curses so dark her ears were probably bleeding. Just like the rest of her.

Didn't take a genius to figure out the problem. Word of a female's capture had already spread to the king. Ugh-O here was not to sample her goods. He was to bring her in and allow the king to decide her fate, as well as become the first to rape her.

Come on, Nicolai. Where are you?

Ugh-O leaped back into motion, the messenger remaining close to his side, not trusting him to obey. Or maybe not. Maybe she was the glue that held them together. A few times, the bastard reached out and patted her ass. This always angered the hell out of Ugh-O, and he would swat at the offending appendage, jarring her.

In fact, his footfalls were so heavy, she slammed up and down, losing her breath over and over again. By the time they reached a twisted maze of caverns, she was convinced her lungs were flat as pancakes, and her intestines were wrapped around her spine.

Even with her still-dimming eyesight, she watched for Nicolai, hoping to catch a glimpse of him shadowing the beast, ready to strike. While she did spy other beings following her captor—little things with wings, darting through the air, and wolflike creatures skulking around the trees—none of them were the vampire.

And when she heard a roar, pain-filled and broken, echoing in every direction, she wanted to vomit. That had been Nicolai's voice. What the hell were the giants doing to him?

Then the sound cut off abruptly, and she found the silence was even more disturbing than the roar. Had the giants just…killed— *No!* No, no, no. But what if…?

Oh, God. A sob caught in her throat. If he lived, he would have come for her.

She was his, he'd said so. Many times. And somehow, he was hers. She barely knew the man but she felt something deep and inexorable for him.

Only minutes before, she'd thought her heart and soul safe from his appeal, her mind too concerned with the danger to him. Now, as she was dragged to the unknown, death a possibility, when she thought *him* dead, the truth hit her.

Her heart and soul had never been safe.

Nicolai fascinated her. He was bossy and arrogant, yet protective when it mattered. He was a killer with a lover's hands. In his arms, she'd come alive, had been utterly undone. He was already a part of her. In her blood, her head, her everything. So, no. No, no, no. He couldn't be dead. He just couldn't be.

Whatever had been done to him, he would heal. He had to heal. His roar had probably cut off because he'd passed out or something. Yes, that was it. And since he healed when he slept, that was a good thing.

Right?

The beast had to duck to enter one of the caverns, and she forced herself to concentrate. The hallways were narrow, suffocating. Footsteps echoed as he marched, creating a symphony of terror in her mind. She attempted to memorize the path he took, but it was difficult. So many turns, so dizzying. Alice's rabbit hole, she thought with a humorless laugh.

Finally they reached a spacious chamber bursting with more of those winged giants. Murmurs of approval abounded the moment she was spotted, and those approvals swiftly mutated into lusty catcalls. Growling, stiff with anger, Ugh-O tossed her atop a pallet in the center.

Jane scrambled to her feet. More waves of dizziness accompanied the action, and she swayed. When her vision cleared, she spun in a circle, studying her new surroundings. A throne of glittering crystal grew directly from the wall. That throne would have made a majestic sight, if not for the bare-chested maniac seated on top of it.

His nose was so far out of place, the left side rested against his cheek. One of his eyes was missing, and there was a hole in his bottom lip, as if one of his saber teeth had punched right through. His chest was a mass of scars, like slices of roast beef that had been glued together—but the glue hadn't held.

At least twenty others stood beside him, guarding him. All eyes were on her, bright red lasers she couldn't escape. Sweat dripped between her breasts, even as her blood chilled. Not one of these creatures would aid her. They all wanted, and expected, a turn.

In fact, only two people in the room were uninterested in her presence. The only other females. Both were naked, old and wrinkled, unwashed, with straggly hair and dead eyes. They'd been well used, multiple times, and were covered in bite marks and bruises. No wonder these guys were so hot for the repulsive "Odette."

Footsteps behind her caused her to spin. More dizziness, intent on lingering. Only when it passed did she realize these were the men who had attacked Nicolai. They were bloody, limping, missing a few body parts and barely breathing, but they were here.

"Where's my vampire?" she screeched.

Ignoring her, they fell before their king. "Vampire disappear."

He'd disappeared. That meant he was alive. Thank God. Oh, thank God.

"No fresh meat?" the king asked, speaking up for the first time.

"No fresh meat."

A rumble of angry muttering sprung from the sovereign, and he waved his fingers toward the men. Four other giants stepped forward, palming swords and swinging before Jane could compute what was going on. Heads rolled, stopping at her feet.

She hunched over and finally vomited. No, not vomited. She dry heaved. There was nothing in her stomach. Laughter and applause abounded as the bodies were gathered up.

"Fresh meat now. Cook," the king said with a nod of approval. "We dine."

They were going to eat their own kind. Oh, God, oh, God, oh, God. She straightened, preparing to run.

Ugh-O settled a hard hand on her shoulder, ending her escape attempt before she'd taken a single step. "I found. I get."

The king lost his good humor and frowned. "I give you my hag." He motioned toward one of the old women. The hag in question stepped forward automatically and bowed. "Now give me yours."

"No. I want the fat one."

Hisses abounded.

Telling the king no was a crime, she supposed. "Fight," she suggested, her voice trembling as much as her body. "Fight over me. Winner gets me." Fingers crossed they killed each other.

That dark frown leveled on her. "Fight, yes. After." He crooked his finger at her, expecting her to close the distance between them.

After. There was that word again. Gulping, she shook her head. Ugh-O squeezed her shoulder harder, harder still, and she winced.

"Come," the king demanded, speaking more sharply

now. He waved her over, and if she wasn't mistaken, next waved to his crotch. As if he expected her to jump on board right here, right now.

He probably did. She'd heard the unspoken *Or else,* and rallied her wits. *Come on. I can do this.* "Take me to your bedchamber." Never in her life had Jane attempted to seduce someone who repulsed her, and she mentally cringed at the huskiness of her tone. Better she fight this man alone than with all his people watching—and able to join in. "I'll do things you've only dreamed about." *If your dreams involve strangling on your own intestines.*

"Just want your mouth on cock."

I would rather die. "And I want to put my mouth on your cock." *Lightning, strike me down. Please.* "So let's go to your bedchamber. Because, and here's the kicker, I do my best work in private."

He was on his feet in an instant, stalking toward her.

CHAPTER TEN

NICOLAI'S HEAD WAS a seething cauldron of thoughts, his body a tuning fork of emotion. One moment he'd been fighting the giants, protecting Jane, the next he was shouting in pain, unable to control the turmoil in his mind. Faces, so many faces. Voices, so many voices.

Clutching at his ears, he fell to his knees. The jarring helped. The faces faded and the voices quieted, allowing rational thought to form. Had to…protect… Jane…again… But when he pried his eyelids apart, he saw that the giants were gone.

So was Jane.

He was no longer near the river, no longer in the forest. A barren wasteland surrounded him. What trees he saw were gnarled, their leaves withered. Ash floated in an acidic wind, black snow scented with death and destruction. And he smelled something…rotting.

He recognized nothing.

He turned, saw a snakelike vine slither from one of the trees, then another, both headed in his direction. They dove for him, bit at him and, when they tasted his blood, seemed to cackle with glee. When they dove a second time, he jumped out of the way—and onto a pile of bones.

A need to slay the Blood Sorcerer, the new king of

Elden, filled him, consumed him entirely. Was the bastard nearby? If so, this wasteland was Elden. Had to be.

Elden. *Elden*. The word reverberated in his head. And just like that, the faces returned to his mind, forcing their way to the surface of a man somehow unprepared for them. Faces, blurring together, becoming one. A scene built.

A blonde woman crouched in front of him, studying his skinned knee with soft concern in her green eyes. He was a boy, just a boy, and as she chanted a spell and blew warm breath on his wound, peace and love infused him. The torn flesh knitted back together, blood no longer dripping from it.

When the healing process completed, she grinned over at him. "See? All better, yes?" Such a sweet voice, tender and carefree. She brushed his frustrated, angry tears away with her knuckles. The tears had not formed because of any pain he felt, but because he'd wanted, *needed,* to inflict more damage on his opponents. "You have to stop fighting, darling. Especially boys who are twice your age, and far bigger."

"Why? I beat them." And he could have hurt them a lot worse!

"I know, but the more you damage their pride, the more they will hate you."

"They cannot hate if they do not survive."

"Besides that," his mother continued sternly, "you are in a position of power, and they are not. You must be a voice of reason, not a blast of violence."

He crossed his arms. "They deserved what I did to them."

"And what, exactly, did they do to deserve your claws in their necks?"

"They hurt a girl. Pushed her around in a circle and tried to look up her skirt. They scared her so badly she cried. And then they touched her. In one of her private places. Here." He flattened a palm on his chest. "And she screamed."

The woman sighed. "All right. They deserved your wrath. But, Nicolai, my love, there are other ways to punish those who do wrong. Permissible ways."

"Such as?" He could think of no way other than what he'd done. Like for like, hurt for hurt.

"Tell your father what they've done, and he'll lock them away or banish them from the kingdom."

"So that they can do more harm elsewhere? Or one day seek revenge?" he scoffed. "No."

"And what if you are hurt while you are hurting them?" she demanded.

"I'll come to you. You are the most powerful witch in all the world."

Another sigh, some of her upset fading. "You're incorrigible. And your faith in me is very sweet, if somewhat misguided. Yes, I am powerful, but not as powerful as you will be one day. That's why I want you to be careful. One day, your temper might cause you to accidentally destroy more than a few lives."

"All right, Mother. I will try and be careful, but I can't promise."

"Oh, your honesty…" She flashed a soft smile. "Off you go. After you pay my spell casting fee."

He scrunched up his face, leaned forward and kissed the softness of her cheek. "I'm a prince. I shouldn't have to pay."

"Well, I'm a queen, so you'll *always* have to pay. Go on, now. Find your brother and *study* with him, my darling. No more running away from your tutors to avenge the world."

With a wave, he was darting off, away from her—but not for the classroom. He had too much energy and needed to swim. Swimming always calmed him.

In the here and now, darkness swooped in, blanking Nicolai's mind. Another reprieve. He fell the rest of the way to the ground. One of the vines sliced his cheek, but he hardly noticed. He was remembering his past.

Why was he remembering? Why were the memories flooding him like this?

The healer who had bound his powers had not unbound them. Perhaps more of Nicolai's abilities had found their way free. That would also explain the split-second location switch. Perhaps those abilities had demolished the glass cage.

Except, a quick mental check proved the cage was still there, his abilities and memories still swirling inside it, faster and faster. However, now streaks of crimson were dripping from the top, eroding the glass.

Crimson…blood?

The guards from Delfina? No. Days had passed, and he'd had no reaction to what he'd consumed at the palace. And while he had bitten the ogres, he hadn't swallowed their blood, unconsciously knowing it was poison to him.

The last person he'd drunk from was Jane. He'd gulped from her neck, her taste so decadent he'd wanted to stay there forever. And maybe he would have. Maybe he would have drained her if the thought of losing her had not slammed through him. That, followed by the thought of sampling the heaven between her legs, had driven him to leave her neck and descend. And he'd never been so glad to end a meal. Between her legs, she was sweeter than the nectar of honeysuckle.

He wanted to taste her there again. Wanted to at last sink inside her, possess her fully, become a part of her. Wanted her passion cries in his ears, her limbs all around him, clinging to him. Wanted her nails in his flesh, leaving her own mark.

Where was she? Had she—?

Another memory grabbed hold of his attention, using so much force he could only grunt with the pain. Images, voices, blurring together, painting another scene.

"Tighten your hold, boy. You'll lose your sword in seconds with that puny of a grip."

He was still a boy, a little older now, standing in front of a tall, muscled man. Black-as-night hair, eyes of polished silver. He wore a fine silk shirt and leather trousers, his boots unscuffed and tied just under his knees. A man of wealth, no question. A man of authority and knowledge.

A warrior.

They stood in the center of a courtyard, lovely plants and flowers thriving all around them. The air was sweet, the ground beneath their feet a lush, springy emerald. Smooth marble walls enclosed the entire area, yet there was no ceiling, allowing morning sunlight to pour inside and reflect off the veins of gold. And just above them, balconies opened up from each of the royal bedrooms, welcoming spectators.

A young dark-haired boy was perched on the ledge of the balcony to Nicolai's right, watching while twirling a dagger. He wanted to puff up his chest and pound. He was about to be all kinds of impressive for his younger brother. He could toss with deadly accuracy, stab with lethal force and, when he concentrated, wield two swords at once.

"Nicolai," the man in front of him said, impatient. "Are you paying attention to me?"

"Of course not. Otherwise, I would have heard what you said, and you wouldn't be about to repeat yourself."

Dayn chuckled.

Father was not amused, and did not reward Nicolai for his honesty. "I have meetings to attend, son. Meetings in another kingdom, which means *you* will be in charge while I'm gone. I need to know you can defend yourself and those you love. Pay attention. Now."

"Yes, sir." He focused on the happenings before him, weighing the metal in his hands. "Why must we practice over and over again? I'm good."

"You're good, but you need to be great. Last time I managed to stab you in the back so badly you scarred!" There was hard admonishment in his father's voice. "You must learn to work with all weapons, at all times of the day and night. You must work with one hand, both hands, standing, sitting and injured. *Without* becoming distracted."

Nicolai raised his chin. "Why can't I just kill my opponents with my fangs and be done with it?" He'd done so before. Many times. Until his mother's prediction had come true, and he'd destroyed an entire village simply to punish a man for beating his wife.

He'd at last taken control of his emotions and hadn't lost his temper since. That didn't mean his fangs were useless, though.

"And if your fangs have been pried out of your mouth?" his father demanded.

"No one would ever be foolish enough to remove my

fangs. Mother says I'm the most powerful vampire in the world. I can walk in the light, and I can steal power from anyone I choose."

"No, she says you *will be*." His father's expression hardened. "You are a prince, Nicolai. The *crown prince*. Many in this world and the other will covet your direct line to my throne. Many will try and hurt you simply to hurt me. You must know how to defend yourself, always, for every situation."

Nicolai gave the sword another once-over. Long, thin and polished to a vibrant shine. He was not used to its heaviness, or the thickness of the hilt. "Very well. I will train some more, but why are you not teaching Dayn?"

"So many questions." His father sighed.

"Why must he watch? He's a prince, too, you know." And so very eager to learn. Each day, after Nicolai's lessons, Dayn begged to be taught. Nicolai could never resist him.

He loved his brother, and would die for him. A boy most in the palace feared. Dayn had an affinity with the animals that roamed the grounds, preferring to run with them rather than to walk alongside his own people.

Nicolai understood his brother's need. Sometimes he, too, felt animalistic in nature, most especially when his temper used to overtake him, shattering his control and leaving only a need to destroy, to hurt others.

"His time will come," the king said. "Soon."

"But not the new princess, right? She'll always be too delicate." He sneered the last.

"Breena is newly born, and she is not a blood drinker like you and Dayn. She is a witch like her mother. You and Dayn must always protect her. In turn, she will heal your people after battle as your mother used to do."

Shame had Nicolai looking down at his dirty boots. He was the reason his mother could no longer heal the wounds of others. He hadn't meant to, but he had stolen her ability. She hadn't blamed him, hadn't even yelled at him.

He would do anything to return the ability to her. Yet, he could not. Once taken, he could not give back. Ever. He'd tried, over and over again. The only thing he could do, his mother had said, was learn how to control his newly discovered talent for absorbing the magic of others. And he had, remaining in his bedroom for weeks, reading, studying and practicing.

"Do you think I'll be a great leader, like you?" he asked.

"I think you and your questions will be the death of me, boy." The king held out his own sword, touching the metal against Nicolai's. "Let us begin."

Darkness.

Nicolai was panting now, sweating uncontrollably. Trembling. His hands ached. He looked at them. He must have clawed at his temples, trying to stop the pain from exploding through him, because his nail beds were bloody, his claws mere stumps.

His father had warned him.

His father. The king.

His name truly was Nicolai. Odette had not lied about that. She'd known who and what he was. They all had. *So highborn,* Laila had liked to say, and now he knew why. He was a prince. A crown prince, and one day, a king.

A brother to Breena. His sister. His beautiful baby sister with her golden curls. She'd grown into a lovely woman with a heart of fire, despite the fact that she was always protected, always guarded. Nicolai had snuck her out a few times, wanting her to have a taste of the freedom he took for granted. Where was she now?

Dayn, the brother closest to him, as dark and dangerous as the night, and just as beloved. Where was he?

His father, proud and strong. Honorable, determined. Unwilling to back away from any challenge. Where was he?

His mother, soft and gentle, so nurturing, even in the face of his most violent tempers. Where was she?

Micah, the youngest son, so full of life. Where was he?

Nicolai pulled himself into a crouch. Somehow, he had moved out of the forest. He was now in front of a lake. Not the lake he'd shared with Jane. This water was thick and red. Every few seconds, a hissing, snapping, flesh-colored fish would fly from the surface, arch in the air, then dive back in.

The rocks around him were dagger sharp. A hundred yards away, in the center of all that crimson, was a castle. Dark mold clung to the walls, more of those slithering plants crawling in every direction. There was a walkway, a line of monsters patrolling it.

They hadn't noticed him, but they would. He was out in the open and needed to find shelter. Perhaps feed to strengthen himself. Then he needed to find Jane. She was out there, somewhere. If she was hurt…

She had better not be hurt. He must protect her at all cost. Yet, even as determined as he was, he only managed to crawl a few feet before the next memory hit him, welding him in place.

In this newest scene, he was a grown man, his dark hair shagging around his shoulders. He was bare chested and seated on a bank of rocks, much like the one he'd just seen. Only, the rocks were smooth, the water clear. He'd removed his boots before sitting down, and those were dry, waiting for him on the beach, but his pants were soaked through and caked in salt.

The moon was high, golden, the sky bright with scattered stars. They winked down at him, mocking him with their tranquility. His mind offered more chaos than he thought he could bear.

His father, King Aelfric, was sick.

The healers did not know if he would recover. Nicolai's mother, Queen Alvina, was frantic with worry. She'd tried countless spells and incantations, yet nothing she'd done had worked. *Nicolai* had tried countless spells, using the healing magic he'd stolen from her. Not even that elicited favorable results. Alvina suspected foul play, but until she figured out what kind of magic had been used, her hands were as good as tied.

Nicolai loved his father, gruff though the king was. Besides that, he wasn't ready to take the throne. He wasn't sure if he would ever be ready. Becoming king would mean his father was dead, and he wanted his father to live forever.

And, to be honest, despite Nicolai's best efforts, despite a few years without a single episode, his temper sometimes got the better of him. When that happened, entire villages suffered. He was simply too volatile to rule an entire kingdom.

His father might be gruff, but he was fair. Fair, except when it came to Nicolai's marriage. Though his father had demanded, ranted, raved, Nicolai had refused to settle down. He wasn't ready to take a queen.

Being saddled with the same woman forever? That

could become a hell as dark as the Abyss. He spent every night with a new female. Sometimes two new females. And once, three.

And all right, fine. Perhaps that lifestyle had grown tiresome. Perhaps the prize was never worthy of the chase. But some of his friends had married, and though a few were happy, the rest were miserable—and there was nothing they could do to change their fate. Marriage was forever.

His father wanted him to wed a princess from a neighboring kingdom, but he had not found one that appealed to him. Giving such creatures his name, sharing his kingdom, would grate every hour of every day.

"Nicki," a young voice called. "Nicki!"

Nicolai was on his feet a second later, hopping along the rocks and racing toward his youngest brother. The youngest prince was on the beach, beside Nicolai's boots, and unharmed. Relief speared him.

"Micah, damn it. What are you doing out here? Until you're older, you're not supposed to be near the water on your own."

The little boy screwed up his lips, all determination and courage. "I'm not on my own! You're here." A mischievous glint in his eyes.

"Damn it." Just like that, Nicolai's anger deflated. As always, he could not stay angry with the scamp. Micah looked up to him, wanted to spend time with him, and Nicolai loved that. Loved *him*. Even though the boy had butchered his name while learning to speak, and his family sometimes still teased him with the nickname. "O-lie."

At least he had later moved on to "Nicki."

The females who made their way to Nicolai's bed

often called him by the shortened Nicki, as well, but that invited a familiarity he never seemed to feel toward them, and after a quick admonishment, they never did it again.

He was almost afraid something was wrong with him. He loved his family with his whole heart, but no one else could penetrate the barrier he'd unwittingly constructed.

"Did you come to swim?" Micah asked when Nicolai reached him.

"No, to think."

"Can I help?" the boy asked eagerly. Golden hair gleamed in the moonlight. He smiled, two of his teeth missing. He was not a vampire, like Nicolai and Dayn, but he was powerful all the same. Though he had a warrior's heart, he took after their mother and sister in so many ways.

"Of course you can." Nicolai sat and patted the sand.

Micah plopped down beside him. For several seconds, they breathed in the moist, salt-laden air, silent. Of course, Micah did not do this calmly. He shifted and he kicked out his legs, trying to get comfortable but never quite succeeding.

"Thinking makes me tired," Micah finally said. "Not like playing."

Nicolai bit back a smile. "What do you want to play?"

The image changed in a heartbeat, not giving way to a single moment of darkness. Nicolai was suddenly lying in the bed beside his father. Somehow, he knew a few days had passed since his night on the beach.

The king was recovering. Healers had drained him and Nicolai had fed him blood straight from his own vein. Every drop that he could spare, Nicolai had given—and even some that he couldn't. Finally, success. The poison had been vanquished, and now, the two men were recovering together.

"Pick a female and marry her," his father said. "If not one of the princesses, someone. Anyone. Please, Nicolai. I nearly died. Might still, though I feel stronger every hour. Please. You need an anchor, like your mother is to me. Someone to pull you back from the madness. *Please*."

His father had never begged for anything. That he was now, over this...Nicolai did not have the heart to fight him any longer. He'd been pushing himself to this conclusion, anyway.

"As you wish, Father. It will be done. A princess from a neighboring kingdom, as you've already approved."

Tides of relief permeated the room. "Thank you. Thank you, my son."

Darkness, there again. Indomitable.

Nicolai heard a female scream, jolting him.

This time, when he came back to himself, he was crouched on a flat rock in the middle of the crimson lake. Closer to the moss-covered castle. The monsters had scented him, and were peering over at him through beady eyes. Their tails swayed, ready to strike at him if he dared move any closer.

The moon was still high, the hooked edges bleeding into a sky covered in a thick film of ash, hiding all the stars.

Those fiendish fish darted around him, teeth chomping at him, closer, closer. He was soaked with sweat, his heart a sledgehammer against his ribs, his muscles trembling. His mind, still lost. Aelfric. Alvina. Names. Every member of his family now had a name.

Damn it, where were they? Did they still live? How long had he been away from them?

Quite a while, if this landscape was any indication.

He needed to search for them, but that scream... female... His female, he realized. Jane was screaming. *Jane!*

His blood burned in his veins, singeing, leaving blisters. Those blisters caught fire, tiny infernos that swiftly spread. With a growl, he pushed to his feet. His boots slipped on the slimy rock, but he managed to maintain his balance.

The monsters tensed. He should challenge them. Wipe the castle stones with their entrails. Yes... His heartbeat slowed, becoming a sporadic fist in his chest. No, he decided next. He would have revenge, would find his family—after. Jane needed him now.

His gaze skated over the violated water, the crumbling cliffs farther ashore, the hideous castle straight from a nightmare. He'd traveled here through his memories. Therefore, it stood to reason he could reach Jane through his memories, as well.

He closed his eyes, pictured her as he'd last seen her. Underneath him. Her naked body splayed for his pleasure.

Her expression was soft and heated, her teeth nibbling on her lush bottom lip. Her eyes were at half-mast, the long length of her lashes casting shadows over her flushing cheeks. That long, glorious mane of honey-colored hair was spread around her, the ends curling.

Her breasts were small but firm, her nipples pink and beaded. He'd kissed them, sucked them. Her stomach was flat, her navel a work of art. He'd licked, down... down. Between her legs was the sweetest patch of honey-colored curls, shielding his new favorite place in this world or any other.

Her legs were long and lean, and they wrapped around him just right.

Nicolai, he thought he heard her whisper.

He would have liked *her* to call him Nicki. Anything that promoted familiarity between them. He wanted her tied to him, in every possible way, forever. A forever that Jane might refuse to give him. If he had proposed to a neighboring princess—and he did not delude himself into thinking that princess was Odette, making his life simple—someone *was* waiting for him.

They had not wed, though. Marriage was forever to his people, and his body would react to no one save his wife. But. Yes, but. He would have pledged his name, his life. Easy to dismiss when he'd had no memory of agreeing to do so. Not so easy now, but that wouldn't stop him.

Nicolai did not want to be without Jane. He *wouldn't* be without her. He would find her and return to Elden. *She* would be his queen.

Elden. This decimated land truly was Elden.

The bloody lake was as much a part of his kingdom as the wasteland he'd first appeared in. His kingdom. *Not* the Blood Sorcerer's. A man Nicolai had dreamed of destroying. Would destroy.

Sickness churned in his stomach, because he knew what that meant. The Blood Sorcerer had slain his parents. Aelfric and Alvina would never have allowed their lands to wither like this.

Nicolai ached with the need to return the favor.

Don't think about that now. Find Jane.

He opened his eyes, realized he had transported himself back to the wasteland. Those slithering vines were closing in... He squeezed his lids shut, imagined Jane, felt his body disintegrate, the ground disappearing from beneath his feet. When next he looked, the lush forest of Delfina surrounded him. However, he did not see the camp or Jane.

He breathed deeply, catching her scent. He kicked into motion, running faster and faster, cutting the distance between them as rapidly as possible. All the while, he continued to picture her, the trees around them, until he blinked and at last found himself in the camp she had constructed.

Unable to slow his momentum, he smacked into a thick trunk and stumbled backward, into the water.

Another scream reverberated in his head, this one louder and far more desperate. His fangs lengthened, slicing into his bottom lip. His hands curled into fists, but his claws, not yet healed, merely tickled his skin. The daggers Jane had made lay at his feet. He strapped as many as he could to his arms and legs.

He started forward, his stride determined. Her scent was stronger now...tinged with fear... Every step closer to her heated his blood with fury. She was marked, his, the path she'd taken suddenly a beacon in the night.

Anyone who had touched her would suffer. It was time the entire kingdom of Delfina—and all the kingdoms in this realm—realized that truth. Even if that meant unleashing the deadliest force of his temper.

I'm coming, little Jane.

CHAPTER ELEVEN

MOVING THE FESTIVITIES to the king's bedroom, Jane thought, had been smart. In theory. But she hadn't known all the variables, or "monkey wrenches" as she'd called them, while working in her lab, which very often proved to be fatal while experimenting. The biggest monkey wrench this time around? In the throne room, she would have performed on the king of the monsters, and the king alone, while everyone else watched and probably cheered. In the "privacy" of his bedroom, he expected her to service him and friends. At the same time.

This was explained to her on the march down the hallway.

So, even though they'd switched locations, and even though his personal guards had remained behind with the hags to keep them company, there were now four men waiting for Jane to kick things off.

Not that she planned to put on a performance. She would rather die. And she just might.

The moment the newest giants spotted her, their eyes began to glow that dark, eerie red. Their bodies tensed, getting ready for the pleasure they expected to receive. Like Nicolai, they wore loincloths. Those loincloths were now tented.

The king pushed her forward, and she spun to keep

her eyes on him. Already he was stripping. Leather crisscrossed over his chest, creating *X*'s—*so* not a treasure map—but a second later off came the crisscrosses, then the cloth. Daggers were strapped to his waist. Those he kept on. Dread and horror blended, rushing through her.

Okay, think, Parker. Think.

He pointed to the spot at his feet. "On knees. Use mouth on me. Hands on men. Orloft fuck you."

The guards licked their lips, every one of them. Okay. Okay. Options appeared and disappeared in an instant—and all of them were disappointing. She could do as ordered, and bite the king so hard he wouldn't be using his penis on anyone for a long time. If ever. He'd hit her and dislodge her teeth. A blow that would break her jaw, surely. After that, he'd be able to shove whatever he wanted into her mouth and she wouldn't be able to stop him.

She could run. There was no door to stop her. In fact, the entryways and exits were open and airy. But as good as that was for her, that was also good for the men. Four here, plus twenty or so in the throne area. They would give chase. Nothing would block them, and she would be caught. They knew this cavern better than she did, after all. She'd probably be gangbanged.

She could fight the king and his personal guards, here and now. They would win, no question, but she would have tried. And she might die *before* actual penetration, so that was a plus. If Nicolai was out there, this might give him time to find her.

He was out there.

All right, then. She had a plan of action. Next up, finding a weapon.

The cavern boasted no luxuries. There was a pallet in the far corner. In the other corner was a pile of bones. Bones. Okay. Not the greatest weapons of all time, but beggars couldn't be choosers. She could use one as a club.

"Woman. Knees. Mouth. Pleasure. Now."

Jane tried the easiest approach: walking to the pile. Midway, the king jumped in her path. Very well. Easy way, out. She pretended to lunge left. He followed. She quickly switched and ran to his right. The four giants who'd been watching and waiting moved directly in front of the pile and crossed their arms over their chests. Okay, so. Hard way, out, too.

There was only one thing left to do. She widened her stance and prepared for an attack. "My answer is no."

The king frowned, glanced at his men with splayed arms, all *Women, so stupid, but what can we do?* before again pointing at his feet. "You. Knees. Now."

"I understand what you're saying." Moron. Some people drank at the fountain of knowledge. He must have gargled and spit. Then again, he might not have done even that. "That's why I'm telling you no."

He flashed his saber teeth at her. "But you said—"

"I lied. You're ugly and mean and I wouldn't give myself to you even if a flesh-eating bacteria was ravaging this world, and your cock held the only immunization."

Confusion followed by relief bathed his monstrous features. "Cock. You. Yes."

Of course that's the only word he cared about. *"No."*

His eyes narrowed to tiny slits, and she would not have been surprised to find a red bull's-eye in the center of her forehead. "I make you."

"That's what I thought you'd say." She lifted her chin and waved her fingers. "You're very predictable, after all. So, let's cut the chitchat and do this."

Growling low in his throat, he advanced. He stretched out a hand to grab her, and she ducked, swung around and elbowed him in the stomach. He grunted, hunching over to gasp for air. The others laughed and snickered. Their merriment surprised her. She'd expected fury.

The king straightened before she could render another blow, found her with his gaze and advanced. Again, she ducked and swung; again, she elbowed him. Again, he hunched over, breathless.

This time, the guards clapped. They must think this was foreplay.

She raced behind the king before he could gain his bearings and kicked. He stumbled forward. She jumped up and, as she came down, elbowed the top of his head. He went down, face-first. The success of her moves thrilled and strengthened her, pumping adrenaline through her system. One more blow to the king for good measure, and she'd turn her attention to the guards.

Except, as she thrust out her leg to kick him in the stomach, he rolled and latched onto her ankle. With only a tug, he sent her crashing to her ass. Oxygen exploded from her lungs. Black and white winked before her eyes, little spiderwebs and starbursts.

Before she had time to act, the king swung out his meaty fist. *Contact.* Her poor cheekbone cracked. Skin split. Her brain rattled against her skull, and the black in her vision completely overpowered the white.

Just like that, her advantage was lost. Not that she'd ever really had one.

Crawl away. Curl into a protective ball. Something!

Too late. Another punch landed, this one on her jaw. For an endless span, pain and dizziness and nausea became her only companions. Then the spiderweb of black expanded, closing in. *Don't you dare pass out!*

Another punch.

So. Much. Pain. *Okay, you can pass out now.*

Of course, that's when the darkness thinned against another blast of adrenaline, sharpening her wits. Jane wanted to scream for help, but knew no one here would do anything to help her. Only hurt her further. Plus, physically, she *couldn't* scream. As she'd feared, her jaw was broken.

Another punch.

More pain. No, *pain* wasn't an adequate word for what she experienced. *Agony,* perhaps, but even that seemed too tame a descriptor.

Hard fingers wrapped around her biceps and shook her, causing the agony to radiate through the rest of her. "Look at me."

She blinked opened her eyes. Or eye. One of them was already sealed shut, the upper and lower lid glued together, concealing what felt like a golf ball. She lay on her back, and the king loomed over her. The moment he realized she was awake, he began ripping at her robe.

He liked to fight his conquests, then. Well, she would give him one to remember. She gritted her teeth against a new onslaught of suffering and kicked him in the face. The action was unexpected, and he stumbled backward before at last hitting the floor. Somehow, she managed to pull herself into a sitting position. The starbursts returned, pushing a moan out of her.

"Hold her," the king said with an evil grin. He rubbed

at his erection. His bare erection. He'd already removed his loincloth.

Eager to please—as well as get their hands on her, she was sure—the men jumped to obey. In a blink, she was flat on her back, her hands anchored over her head and her legs pinned and spread.

Just. Like. That.

In another blink, her breasts were being squeezed and her nipples pinched. And all four giants were staring between her thighs, waiting for her femininity to be revealed.

"No," she snapped, but the word was intelligible. "No!" Was this what Nicolai had endured?

They laughed. The king fisted the tattered hem of her robe. The rest of the fabric ripped.

Beyond the cavern, a scream echoed. Her attackers paused, frowned, looked at one another. Another scream echoed, followed by another. And another. Each was pain-filled and panicked. Were the beasts fighting among themselves, perhaps over the hags, or had Nicolai arrived?

Hope bloomed within her.

The king shrugged, his attention returning to her body. She wore only her panties now, and they already were ripped in the crotch and therefore useless as far as barriers went. He licked his lips as he stroked his cock once, twice, preparing to penetrate her.

"Big," he said, practically patting himself on the back. In this, he was right. His penis was thick, too thick, and as long as a battering ram. She would be torn apart.

Her hope withered, died. Tears blurred her good eye,

and she whimpered, the sound as broken as her jaw. Any second now, and...

A snarl reverberated, deep and ominous. Closer now, so close.

Neither the guards nor the king looked away from her to check who had uttered the enraged warning. But suddenly Jane knew, sensed. Nicolai *was* here.

"You're gonna die real bad," she said flatly. Again, her injuries made the words incomprehensible, but she didn't care. Saying them offered a small measure of satisfaction.

"Never die." Still grinning, the king fell to his knees. The guards leaned closer, their hands inching up her arms and legs. Then, as the king guided his cock toward her, something swiped out faster than her eye could track. Blood sprayed. The king roared in pain and shock.

That same something—a real dagger Nicolai must have stolen from the ogres—swiped at the guards, hitting two at a time. More blood, more roars. The men fell away from her, and finally she was free. She lay there, panting, shaking. Then gentle arms were slipping under her and lifting her. She was carted to the pallet and laid down. Fingertips tenderly brushed her swollen cheek. Nicolai's face came into view. He was covered in blood, every part of him soaked with crimson.

Flames leaped and cracked within his eyes. "Rape?"

She gave a slight shake of her head.

Those flames died, leaving something far worse: cold, merciless rage. Then he was gone.

He attacked the guards first, those who had maneuvered back to their feet, ripping their tracheas out with his teeth and spitting them to the floor. But that wasn't enough for him, and he used the dagger to remove their heads from their bodies. Bodies he piled in the entry, effectively locking the king inside the room with him.

The two men circled each other.

"Suffer," Nicolai said, the length and sharpness of his fangs causing him to slur the words.

"Yes. You suffer."

"She's mine. Mine! You will die for touching what's mine."

The king blinked, his head tilting to the side. "You familiar. You vampire. You…prince?" A gasp of horror accompanied the realization. "Yes. You prince. Dark prince. Majesty, I beg sorry. I thought you dead. We all thought you dead."

Nicolai, the slave, was a prince?

The king dropped to one knee, a show of submission. "I give my sorries. So many sorries. Majesty. No offense. Take woman. She is yours."

Nothing Jane had done had humbled the king. Nothing had evoked fear in him. Now, at the thought of battling royalty, he was on his knees, pleading.

"You die," Nicolai said simply. The king never stood a chance. Her man removed his limbs, one by one. And though the king screamed and screamed and screamed, he didn't once struggle. As if he knew struggling would earn him an even worse fate.

Next to go, his eyes. After that, his groin. At that point, his screams became pleas for mercy. Mercy Nicolai did not have. Oops, there went the king's tongue. No more begging or screaming. Just whimpering.

"Nicolai," Jane finally managed, her voice so weak even she had trouble hearing what she'd said. Fatigue was riding her hard, and she knew she wouldn't be awake much longer.

Nicolai glanced at her, barely able to catch his breath. The need to hurt clung to him like a second skin, visible to all. Never had she seen a more primitive male, wild and uncontrollable, a Pict warrior straight from battle. A sight most people would only ever see in their nightmares.

"Need you," she said.

"Yes." He swung back to the dying king. With a quick flick of his wrist, he removed the man's head, just as he'd done to the others. Then he was poised over Jane, stroking her gently. "I'm so sorry, sweetheart. So sorry."

"Will be…fine. Been…worse. Just need…you."

The words were meant to comfort him. They failed. Absolute anguish cloaked his features. He wiped his arm on a nearby cloth, bit into his own wrist and held the bleeding wound to her mouth. "Drink."

While Nicolai chanted words she did not understand, the warm liquid cascaded down her throat. At first, she experienced the most delicious tingling, starting in her stomach and moving through her veins. To her jaw, her arms, her legs. The tingling soon sharpened, heated, and she felt as if little molten daggers were slicing through her.

What the hell was his blood doing to her?

"Nicolai," she screeched. "Hurts."

"You're healing, sweetheart. I'm sorry. I'm sorry. The hurt is good."

Even as he spoke, her jaw snapped back into place. She screamed, the shrill sound echoing off the cave walls. The lid of her swollen eye split apart, and she groaned. At first, her vision was hazy, as if her corneas had been smeared with Vaseline, but as the heat and the daggers continued to work through her, Windex was sprayed and she could see again. Perfectly.

When the healing process was complete, she lay there, still panting, sweating and trembling, but a woman reborn. She stretched her jaw, and while there was a lingering ache, she could move it unfettered.

"Thank you," she said, tears of relief filling her eyes.

Nicolai sprawled beside her and gathered her in his arms. He held her for a long while before the dam inside her broke and she sobbed against his chest, clutching him tightly to her. All of her book smarts, and she'd been helpless.

"I killed them, sweetheart. I killed them all. They'll never hurt you again. This I swear to you."

The evil of the king stunned her. The complete disregard for her will, the violence he had unleashed... Oh, she'd known there were people capable of such dark deeds, but never before had those deeds been brought to her door. It was frightening and heartbreaking to have seen the evidence firsthand.

"That's the way. Let it out. I've got you," he said soothingly.

"I was so scared."

"Never again. *Never again*," he vowed. "Unless... were you afraid of me?"

She shook her head.

"Good, that's good. I would never hurt you. Even lost in a temper, I couldn't hurt you."

Soon her tears dried. The physical damage, as well as the pain of the healing, had taken their toll, and she sagged against him, sighing and shuddering. "What were you chanting when you gave me your blood?"

"More of my vampire magic. I cast a healing spell to aid the powers of my blood."

She sniffled, her nose stuffy. "It was better than Vicodin."

"Vicodin?"

"A painkiller from my world."

"A killer of pain. Did you love him?" The words were growled.

A burst of unexpected humor gave her strength. "No. In fact, he was hard to shake. He, uh, stalked me, that kind of thing. I had to pretend he didn't exist."

Nicolai kissed her temple and relaxed against her. "Shall I hunt and destroy him for you, sweetheart? It would be my pleasure, believe me."

"You have enough enemies. Besides, I destroyed him a while back."

Another kiss. "Because you are strong."

Lovely praise, but she was completely undeserving of it and couldn't pretend otherwise. "I wasn't strong enough to save myself today." The tears returned. She brushed them away with a shaky hand. "I took self-defense lessons for a while, but they didn't help. Not really. He would have…he was going to…"

"Never again," Nicolai repeated, tightening his hold. "I will train you further. And when I'm done with you, not even *I* will be able to defeat you."

"Really?"

"Oh, yes. Your safety is a personal mission of mine. A mission I will not fail."

Maybe the turmoil of the day had made her emotional, but she got teary eyed all over again. That was the sweetest thing a guy had ever said to her. Even better than what he'd said to Laila. "Enough about me. I was afraid the giants had killed *you*."

"I doubt even death would have kept me away from you."

Okay. She was wrong. *That* was the sweetest. She kissed the pulse at the base of his neck. "What—what were those things?"

"Ogres."

A yawn snuck up on her, her eyelids dipping heavily. "The king seemed to know you."

He stiffened. "Yes."

And he didn't want to discuss it. She changed the subject, suddenly too tired to reason out why or press for answers. "You found me because you'd marked me, right?"

"Yes," he said again. He traced his fingertips along her spine. "And I have never been gladder for something."

"Have you marked other women?" Oh, God. She shouldn't have asked. She wasn't ready for the answer. Not here, not like this. Not after what had happened. He clearly did not have to be wed or engaged to mark a woman, so there could be a *thousand* out there. She should have….

"Not to my knowledge," he said cautiously.

She sighed with relief. She would be willing to bet "marking" was more than a memory, that marking was an instinct, biology at its finest, a knowledge that went bone-deep. After all, dogs did it. Of course, they peed on what they wanted, leaving their scent behind. And they didn't need to remember doing it; they simply needed to smell and catch a hint of the desired aroma.

Nicolai had not honed in on any other woman. As easily as he'd found Jane, he would have found any others, without difficulty. *If* they were out there. So, logically, she had to believe she was the only one.

Yes, logically. He was free.

Maybe you're the one who's as dumb as a box of rocks. A good scientist studies both sides of the coin. Fine. She'd argue in favor of the other side. Nicolai could very well be engaged, as he'd feared, as she'd tried to deny. And maybe he hadn't marked the woman yet, wanting to wait for the actual ceremony to complete the connection.

Or, like the ogres, he could have had a harem of women. Perhaps one woman had not satisfied him for long, so he'd plowed through them like he had a cold and they were tissues. Perhaps there'd been too many to mark. Or perhaps he'd simply never cared enough to do it.

That certainly fit the image of a pampered prince. *Was* he a prince, though? *Had* he been pampered? A man given everything he wanted, never really satisfied?

Sometimes she hated her brain. And coin flipping.

The man she knew was volatile and possessive. He didn't play nice with others, and he didn't know how to share. Yet he was as far from pampered as a man could be. *And he's mine,* she thought, burrowing her head deeper into the hard line of his body. His strong, warm body.

He knew her, and wasn't bothered by her verbal and mental tangents. He'd cared enough about her to come back for her—twice—saving her life. That had to count for something.

"Stop thinking and sleep, Jane," he said.

"All right." Nothing would happen to her while they were together. She knew it. He would guard her with his life. "Hold me and don't let go."

"Always," he vowed.

Oh, yes. He cared. She drifted off to sleep with a smile.

CHAPTER TWELVE

When Jane awoke, she was still in the cave. She wasn't sure how much time had passed. All she knew was that she'd never felt so rested. She stretched like a contented kitten, warm despite her nakedness, her muscles liquid, and gazed around.

Startled by what she saw, she sat up. Enough time had passed for Nicolai to clean every speck of blood from the floor and walls. He'd also removed the bodies and subsequent body parts. If not for the lingering taint of evil, this could have been some kind of underground resort.

There was no reason for Nicolai to have done such a thing. They weren't going to live here. Weren't even going to spend the day. Unless he'd hoped to spare her any upset. Her eyes widened. That was exactly why he'd done it, she realized. The sweet, darling man.

Hello again, emotional roller coaster. She sniffled, her chin trembling.

"Don't cry, sweetheart. Please don't cry." He was perched beside her, looking away from her, and holding out a bundle of wrinkled material. And God, his profile was gorgeous. Still streaked with blood, though some had been washed away, his cheeks were sharp, his lips lush and his expression relaxed. No ill effects from the fighting. "It kills me inside."

After everything he'd done for her, she would do anything he asked. Besides, despite his relaxed expression, lines of tension branched from his eyes, as if permanently etched there. Something more *was* bothering him, and she wouldn't add to his troubles.

"I won't." She used the hem of the offered fabric to clean her face.

The corners of his mouth twitched, his inner worries momentarily forgotten. What did he find so humorous? "Did you sleep well?" he asked.

"Yes, thank you."

"Good. Now. Will you dress for me?" A question layered with apprehension.

She thought she knew why. Her nakedness aroused him—or at least, she hoped it did—but he didn't want to do anything about it. Not after what had happened here. She was grateful.

She knew the old adage "replace the bad with the good." She also knew there was nothing better than Nicolai's touch. He could play her like a piano, stroking all the right keys and creating a symphony. But she didn't want their first time to spring from any need but the one to be together.

"Jane?" he prompted.

Dress. Right. "With what?" Her robe was ruined beyond repair.

"Your tissue."

"Oh." She chewed on her bottom lip as she studied the "tissue." A faded yellow cotton robe, clean, and free of rips. Perfect. "Where did you get this?"

He motioned behind him with a tilt of his head. "The only other females here were so grateful to be free of their ogre masters, they stayed long enough to help me clean this room and offered you all of their possessions."

"That was thoughtful of them."

"They also offered me the use of their bodies."

"I will wipe the floor with their blood!" She jerked the robe over her head.

When Nicolai came back into view, she saw that he was grinning. That grin...decadent and shameless. Her blood heated. Blood that belonged to him, had once been a part of him.

"I sent them on their way," he said. "*Without* accepting."

"Like I care what you do," she groused. This conversation, on the heels of her harem worries, brought out the fires of *her* temper.

That wiped away his amusement completely. "You had better care."

She sighed. Honesty was needed if they were going to have any kind of relationship. And she wanted a relationship with him, however long they had left together. A day, a week, a month? Or would she remain here forever?

She wouldn't worry about that now.

"Fine," she said on a sigh. "I care." Her stomach growled from hunger, and in the quiet of the cave, the sound echoed loudly. She blushed. "Do you?"

"More than I can say."

"I just...don't want you to be hurt if I leave."

"You won't leave. Now, come." He stood and waved his fingers. "I'll feed you."

He cared! And how could he be so certain she would remain? "What time is it?" she asked, accepting his aid with a tender smile. A smile that quickly fled. Her bones creaked and ached as she straightened.

"Close to midnight."

Back home, she would have been in her bed right now, tossing and turning and dreading the coming morning.

They made their way back to the river. Limping at first, but muscles relaxing with the exercise, she gathered mint leaves and twigs, and they brushed their teeth as they walked. Afterward, Nicolai foraged for fruits and nuts to tide her over. As she nibbled, she kind of expected creatures from childhood storybooks to jump out and grab her, or Laila to scream a curse and appear, but no. The thirty-minute journey was incident free.

Nicolai stepped into the water, dipped all the way in, came up wet and sputtering and motioned for her to do the same. "Bathe, and I'll gather the fish you scare away."

"Ha, ha. Shows what you know. Fish adore me. Don't be surprised if they dance at my feet."

"Are you trying to make me kill the fish in a jealous rage so you can have more to eat?" he teased.

"Maybe." More than gorgeous, he was sexy. Amused, playful, all that wet dark hair plastered to his scalp and dripping down his face, crystalline droplets scorching a path down his mouthwatering pectorals, the ropes of his stomach—and, sweet heaven, there were a lot of ropes—and finally catching in the waist of his loincloth.

Without the taint of the cave, there was nothing to dilute her need. Jane hungered for her man more than anything else.

You've gotta clean up if you want to get dirty with him.

"Prepare to be awed," he said, giving her his back.

I already am. She removed her new robe and jumped into the water—such cool, refreshing water—before he could turn and see her beaded nipples. She scrubbed up until her skin tingled. Well, tingled from more than desire.

All the while, she snuck secret glances at Nicolai. He caught several fish and tossed them ashore. As time ticked by, he became more and more apprehensive, his motions clipped. And he was utterly oblivious to her stare. Not once did he glance back at her.

Moonlight spotlighted him, golden and magical. He was so strong, so capable. She chewed her bottom lip as she treaded water. The water might be cool, but the liquid between her legs was warm.

Perhaps she should have been scared or experienced post-traumatic stress symptoms. Flashbacks at the very least. After all, she'd nearly been raped and *had* been beaten. But this was Nicolai. Her protector. Not even bad memories would dare attack her while he was nearby.

"Nicolai," she said, a husky note in her voice. She hadn't meant to call him, but his name had emerged unbidden, unstoppable.

Finally he turned to her. Her breath caught. His eyes were brighter than she'd ever seen them, the gold flecks out to play, mingling seductively with the silver. His cheeks were flushed, his fangs long and sharp.

"Awed yet?" he demanded.

"Yes." Oh, yes. Was that why he was so distressed and distant? She hadn't properly praised his skills? "You're the best fisherman I've ever met. Granted, you're the only one I've ever met, but…"

No hint of a smile. "I'll feed you," he said, adding darkly, "After."

"After?"

"I smell your desire for me, little Jane, and I gave you time to grow used to the idea of being with me. Time is up. Come here." He crooked his finger. "I want you."

After wasn't such a bad word anymore. "About time." She didn't hesitate. She swam the distance, the water caressing her skin. When she was only a whisper away, she let her feet drop to the bottom and stood. The waterline reached just under her breasts.

"I'm going to have you," he said fiercely.

"Yes."

"All of you."

"Yes." Please.

He stepped closer. Every time they inhaled, their chests rubbed together, creating the most dizzying friction.

"Nothing will stop me," he said.

"Not even thoughts of another woman waiting for you?" She hated herself the moment the words left her, but she was still glad they had. Another woman was the reason he had resisted her before.

Shadows couched his features, turning him into the warrior of the night before. "There...is. A woman. Most likely."

Oh, God. "Who?" A plug was lifted, and the desire drained from her, leaving her cold, hollow. "Do you... did you love her?"

"No. My father arranged the marriage. I do not remember my intended's face or her name, or even my proposal. I know only that I promised my father I would wed her."

Don't cry. Don't you dare cry. At least his heart did not belong to someone else. That should help.

That didn't help. She wanted all of him. For herself.

"You're remembering?" she croaked.

"Not everything, only bits and pieces at a time. I tell you this, not to upset you, Jane, but to warn you. No matter what happens, I'm keeping you. You are mine. That will not change."

No matter what happens—as in, if he had to marry another woman. "No."

The possibility of his involvement with another had been so easy to dismiss before. And she could very easily dismiss it now, when it was a reality. *If* he had decided to end the engagement.

She wouldn't be the other woman. She wouldn't! She had too much pride. Didn't she? Oh, God. The fact that she'd even asked meant she already wanted to consider the option.

No. No, no, no. Her parents had loved each other, respected each other, and that's what she wanted for herself. A deep, abiding love that placed her first. She didn't want to spend her nights wondering if her man was in bed with his wife, giving her pleasure and babies. She didn't want to find herself regulated to the fringes of his life. She didn't want to be the one everyone blamed for their troubles.

She deserved better.

When she returned home and thought back on her time here—she knew she couldn't stay now, because somehow, some way, she would find a path home—this was the night that would haunt her. Not those pain-filled hours with the ogres. Not even the humiliation of her whipping. *This* hurt the most.

She backed away from him. Not allowing the retreat, he reached out and gripped her shoulders, tugging her back to him. Closer this time, until not even a whisper separated them. They were flush against each other, his erection smashed against her belly.

"I know what you're thinking, Jane."

"What, you're a mind reader as well as an engaged man?" She threw the words like weapons, needing to lash out even in the smallest way.

"No, but I know you. You are not leaving me." The command didn't come from the tender savior who had held her while she'd slept, but from the dangerous predator who had removed a man's limbs just to hear him scream. "I told you these things, not to worry you, but to reassure you. Betrothals can be broken. And mine will be. I will have you, and no other."

"I—I—" Was that a declaration? A proposal? Her emotions ran the gamut, and her mind didn't know whether to release the despair and accept the sudden tide of joy, or wallow in both. "I know you said I wouldn't, but what if I do, in fact, leave your world? You would…" Die. She shouldn't know that, couldn't yet admit that she did, but then, he hadn't asked her to forever mate with him, had he?

If he did, mating could very well tie her to this world forever. Her eyes widened. Was *that* how he knew she would stay?

"You will not leave," he said. "I will make sure of it, whatever I have to do. Now, we finish this, Jane. Here. Now." He didn't wait for her reply, but swooped down, thrusting his tongue deep inside her mouth.

Joy won.

She couldn't help herself. She welcomed him. He

still tasted of mint, warm, wet mint, and she couldn't get enough. And when he tilted her head, taking more, sampling deeper, her nerve endings erupted with sensation. This was what a kiss was meant to be, a possession, a claiming. An awakening of every sense.

Her hands wound around his neck, her fingers sinking into his hair. Later. She'd ask him what he'd meant by "whatever I have to do" later. Right now, she had the most important fact. He wasn't pledging himself to someone else. Here, now, she would enjoy him.

They stood like that, kissing and rubbing against each other forever. And every second of that forever ramped up her desire, until she was trembling, needy, aching with a fever only he could assuage.

"Wrap your legs around me," he commanded harshly.

"Yes." Even the thought left her reeling. She jumped up and did as commanded, expecting him to possess her in the next instant. He didn't enter her, though. No, he carried her to the shore, his hard length sliding against her. She moaned as he laid her down and stretched out on top of her. Still he didn't enter her.

"Don't stop," she breathed.

"I won't." He placed his hands beside her temples, removed his loincloth and anchored his weight.

"So lovely, my female."

"Prove it. Prove that I'm yours."

His lips peeled back from his fangs. "When I'm done, you might regret such a request."

"Promises, promises."

Once again, he defied her expectations. He didn't go in for the kill, didn't deliver instant relief to her raging desires. Instead, he spent the next few minutes kneading her breasts and laving her nipples, his fingers tracing erotic patterns on her stomach, but he never quite reached where she needed him most.

When he began kissing the same white-hot path his fingers had taken, her legs fell open, a silent plea for contact.

He didn't give it to her.

He licked her inner thighs, between her damp lips, even speared her core with his tongue, sinking inside for the briefest of seconds, teasing her with what could be, but he was always careful to bypass her clit.

She needed to come, damn it.

"Nicolai. Stop teasing."

Warm breath trekked over her. "Who do you belong to, Jane?"

Well, well. Now she knew his game. Work her over, tease her with what he could give her, until she gave him what he wanted—what she'd demanded of him. Ownership.

"Look at me," she said.

He rested his chin on her pubic bone. His lashes lifted, and his gaze met hers. Tension strained his features. He wanted to come as badly as she did. "Yes?" he said.

Who would break first? "My turn."

She flattened her feet on his shoulders and pushed. A second later, he was the one flat on his back and she was looming over him.

"What are you doing, Jane?"

"Having my turn." She laved her tongue over his nipples, loving how they speared her tongue. "If I do anything you don't like, just say stop."

"I'll like." His hands tangled in her hair. His claws must have regrown, because she could feel them biting into her scalp, and she loved it. "Anything you do, I'll like."

"Well, then, let's see what you like most." She licked her way to his navel and dipped inside. His muscles quivered with anticipation. Her breasts cradled his erection, and she rubbed up and down, up and down, fueling his passion. Soon the tip of him grew moist, allowing a smoother glide.

She wanted him out of control. Mindless. Desperate. Exactly as she was when she was with him. She may not have very much experience, but she wouldn't let that stop or intimidate her, she decided. She would learn his body, his every secret desire.

"Jane," he rasped.

"Yes, Nicolai."

"I need… I want…"

"Me to taste you?"

"Oh, gods, Jane." His voice was a croak. "Yes. Please."

She crouched between his legs and peered down at his cock. He was so long, so thick and hard. Down, down she leaned…but she didn't gobble up that delicious length. Not yet. She lavished attention on his testicles, teasing him as he had teased her, until his hips were lifting in supplication.

"Please," he said again.

"Who do you belong to?" she asked as he'd asked her.

He didn't even try to hold out. "You. Jane."

The admission affected her as strongly as a caress, and she shivered. "I'm going to make you so happy you said that." She fit her lips around the head of his penis. His flavor hit her taste buds, and she groaned in eagerness. More, she wanted more. She slid her mouth all the way down, until he reached the back of her throat.

A hoarse cry left him. Up she glided, lightly scraping him with her teeth. Another cry. She hovered there, unmoving, tormenting. Waiting.

"Jane, I like this most."

Down she slid; up she glided, repeating the process over and over, slowly at first, then increasing her speed. Soon he could no longer speak, could only moan and groan as she had. Having him like this, at her mercy, his desire for her consuming him, directing all of his thoughts and actions, was a powerful aphrodisiac to her.

Just as his testicles tightened, signaling the start of his climax, she stilled, clamping her lips on the base of his cock, preventing him from going further. A little trick she'd read about but never tried. His roar of need blasted through the forest.

"Jane," he panted. "Jane, please."

He was trembling, moist with perspiration, but he didn't come. And when the danger passed, she crawled up his body, trembling just as violently. His fangs were so long they'd cut into his lip, leaving trails of blood down his chin.

"Why didn't you..."

"I want you inside me." Her blood was molten in her veins, causing sweat to bead on her brow.

"*Need* to be inside you, but not yet, not yet." His hands returned to her hair, his fingers pulling at the strands. "Must control urge to bite you first."

"Don't control the urge." She leaned down and flicked her tongue against one of his fangs, quickly cutting the soft tissue. "Give in to it. I'm fine."

He groaned as if in pain. "Delicious."

"More?"

The world suddenly spun. He'd tossed her on her back, and was looming over her. "More," he slurred, his gaze locked on her hammering pulse. "No, can't. Not yet, not yet," he repeated. "Baby."

"Yes?" Why *not yet?* Maybe she was greedy. Maybe she was selfish. She wanted now, now, *now*.

He chuckled, a broken sound. "No. Baby. I could give you a baby. Do you want a baby?"

Understanding dawned. Sadness and fear suddenly swamped her, dulling some of her desire. "I can't have children." Would he think less of her? No longer want her?

The woman his father had picked could probably have children.

Oh, ouch.

Jane had thought she'd come to terms with her lack. But now…the thought of starting a family with Nicolai… She wanted that, she realized. Not now, but later. When they were safe. To be with him, to have his child growing inside her… She would never know that joy.

The lack was another reason she'd dumped Spencer when she had. Once, they'd talked about getting married and starting a family, and she'd known how badly he had wanted that. With her, he would never have it. So she'd let him go, knowing he would thank her one day, when he was wed to another woman, his kids running around and laughing in their home.

"After the accident, my body is ruined," she said, pushing the words past the lump in her throat. "So, you don't have to worry about getting me pregnant. Ever.

And if you want to stop and never take this thing between us any further, I'll understand."

He peered down at her, a dark warrior whose ire had been pricked. "Jane?"

"Yes?"

"I want you no matter what. *Need* you. Never think otherwise." With that, he gripped her thighs, spread them and surged up, hitting her deep inside with that one powerful thrust.

She forgot her sadness as instant, necessary, all-consuming desire flooded her. He was so big he stretched her; she was so wet, her once-neglected body gave him only minimal resistance.

"Nicolai!" His name, oh, how she loved his name.

"I like this, too," he said. In and out he moved. "Changed my mind. Like this most."

Her mind clouded, her nerve endings razed to the point of pleasure-pain, and she screamed. She'd been so turned on, the slightest stroke would have sent her shooting off to the stars. But this…sweet heaven, this.

Oh, God, it was so good, and she was so lost, she never wanted to be found, wanted this forever… Nicolai, Nicolai, hers, always hers. She was babbling to herself, and she knew it, couldn't control it. Didn't want to control it. Just wanted more. Of him, of this.

"Shouldn't bite, must bite."

"Bite. *Please.* I'm yours, Nicolai. I'm yours."

He growled, and then his fangs were in her neck and she was climaxing, squeezing at him, clutching at him. Taking everything he had to give and demanding more. And he gave it to her.

He rode the waves of her satisfaction, thrusting inside her with a fervor that left her breathless. He was all around her, a part of her, the sole light in her world. Drinking, drinking, oh, yes, drinking. Soon she became dizzy, and little doubts peeked from the shadows of her mind, as if they'd been hiding all along, waiting for her defenses to crumble.

Maybe his words—*want you no matter what, need you*—were preorgasm talk, meant to lure her into bed and keep her from running. Maybe the cloud of desire had been leading him all along. Maybe he would later change his mind about wanting her.

Maybe, when this was over, he would let her go.

No. She fought back. *No.* This wasn't temporary. He wouldn't discard her. Even if he learned the truth about some of the things she'd done to his kind?

Cold, hard reality. Again, she fought back. Nothing would destroy this moment, not even that. Here, pleasure mattered. Only pleasure.

He hooked one of his arms under her knee and lifted, opening her wider, increasing the depths he reached. Instantly her body prepared for yet another climax, needing it just as desperately as the others, as if sex with him was a prerequisite for her survival. She should fear *that*. She needed him too intently, was no longer complete without him.

Hell, if she left, would she be the one to wither? Had *she* mated him and just didn't know it? What did she know about the road to mating? Nothing really.

Nicolai took hold of her other leg and lifted, surging impossibly deeper, and she forgot even that. There was no part of her left untouched. She was Nicolai's woman, plain and simple, branded by him, a part of *him*. After this, she would never be the same, didn't want to be the same.

She sank her nails into his scalp and forced his head up. His teeth slid from her vein. "Nicolai…"

"I'm sorry." He eyed her, blood dripping from the corner of his mouth. "I didn't mean… Did I take too much?" Agony wafted.

"No." He could have it all, every last drop. "Kiss me," she demanded.

"Yes." He met her halfway. Their lips pressed together, their tongues dueled. His flavor filled her, and this time it was mixed with hers. Together, every part of them together…intoxicating.

"Mine," she said.

"Yours."

Forever, she didn't let herself add, but, oh, did she want to. Later, they would talk. Yes, the dreaded conversation about feeling and intentions. About the future.

The kiss continued, spinning out of control, their teeth scraping together, as he slipped and slid within her. He released one of her legs to move his hand between their bodies, and pressed his thumb against her clitoris. Just like that, she exploded again, spasming around him.

He hissed out a breath, pushed deep once more, and came, every muscle he possessed clenching and unclenching. She'd never made love without a condom, and loved the feel of him jetting inside her.

When he stilled, she wrapped herself around him, holding him as close as possible. He collapsed on top of her, but quickly rolled to relieve the pressure of his muscled weight. They were both sweat soaked and feverish, trembling.

"My Jane," he said, so much satisfaction in his voice she couldn't fear the upcoming discussion.

She kissed his shoulder. "My Nicolai."

Forever.

She hoped.

"Don't leave...need to talk," she breathed, just before drifting off to sleep.

CHAPTER THIRTEEN

PANTING, SWEATING, SATED in the most perfect way, Nicolai snuggled Jane in to his side. Her blood flowed through his veins like champagne, bubbling and fizzing, claiming every thought and beating back a painful realization he wasn't quite ready to face. He wanted to close his eyes and savor, but he had a few things to work out in his mind first.

She'd wanted to talk. About what? If she thought to push him away after what they'd shared… Well, that wasn't going to happen.

What they'd just done could not be called "sex."

Sex was an urge. Sex was something you could do with anyone. Sex could be consensual or forced, as he well knew. What they'd done was a mating. Primal, wild, necessary, and as essential as a beating heart.

He would have died if he'd been denied access to her body. He'd simply *had* to be inside her. Nothing could have stopped him. Not attack, not death, hell, not even her disappearance. If she had returned to her world, he would have found a way to follow her.

There was no resisting this woman, not for him, and he wasn't going to try anymore. Not in any way. His betrothed might be waiting for him, but so what. Like he'd told Jane, he would have her and no other.

She'd changed him.

When he'd first seen her, scented her, his hunger for her had bloomed. Perhaps he'd become obsessed. Because when he'd watched her being whipped, he'd forgotten his plan to save himself and had gone after her. Then, when he'd heard her scream, had realized the ogres were hurting her, his rage had been unequaled. Seeing her beaten face and body had made a mockery of the rage, however, and he'd become fully beast, his darker nature taking over.

All the times before, he'd only thought he had a temper.

The fighting had ended too early. He'd wanted to torture the king, wanted to keep him at the brink of death and agony for centuries. For Jane's sake, he'd finished the bastard off and gathered his woman close, just like this.

She had slept then, too, but he hadn't calmed. The need to brand her, to let the world know exactly who she belonged to, had been driving him as forcefully as the rage had. But he hadn't wanted to hurt her when he took her—and he'd known he would take her.

So he'd brought her here, intending to swim and pacify himself. He'd meant to feed her the fish, as well, but she'd watched him while he'd captured them, and he'd felt the rise of her desire.

He'd forgotten his good intentions. His hope to be careful.

Now he'd had her, had branded her, just as he'd wanted, needed, but he realized even that wasn't enough. Nothing would ever be enough with her. He would always want her. Always want more.

Were his parents alive, they would understand. He knew this to be true.

He'd loved them, and they had loved him. They would want him to be happy, and he could not be happy without Jane. His father had settled on a neighboring princess only because Nicolai had shown no preference.

Now, he had.

Jane could not have children, and that bothered her, but it did not bother him. He hadn't lied to her. He liked her just as she was. When Nicolai became king in his father's stead—the need lit, caught fire—he would be expected to have an heir. But he had three siblings well capable of seeing to that.

So. His new plan of action: secure Jane to his side, return to Elden, kill the Blood Sorcerer who had slain his parents and claim the throne. He didn't want to wait to discuss this. Urgency rode him. Instinct that drove him to settle things now.

"Jane…"

A moment passed.

"Jane. Sweetheart." Gently he shook her.

"Yes," she muttered groggily.

"We will talk now."

Her slight catch of breath was encouraging. "Really?"

"Yes, really. When you first came to me, you mentioned a book. Where is the book now?"

"Oh. *That's* what you want to talk about." She sounded disappointed. "I left it at the palace in Delfina. I don't think that matters, though. It was the right book, just newer. And blank."

He frowned. "When you read it, the story was about me?"

"Yes. About your enslavement. There was a pink bookmark in the middle, and that's the page that told about your imprisonment. Then, written by the same hand, was a note from you, commanding me to help you, to come to you. The rest of the pages were blank, though."

He'd wondered before if he'd written the thing and forgotten. For all he knew, the witches had cursed him to forget everything but what they did to him. Why had the ink disappeared when Jane had shown up in Delfina, though? Because she'd arrived before he'd actually written the book? But, if he'd commanded her to come here—commanded *her* specifically—he would have met her already. And she would have left him.

He tensed. He did *not* like that notion and he quickly discarded it. He hadn't said "come back to me." He'd said "come to me." So…magic might have shown her to him, and like the book, he'd forgotten.

Still, the fear that he could lose her took root and refused to leave him. "Do you want to stay here with me, Jane?" He geared for battle. A battle he would fight viciously to win. She had a life he knew nothing about, and were the situation reversed, were he stuck in her world, he would have to find a way to leave to avenge his family and home. And he would have stolen away with her, he thought.

Now she was the one to tense. "Okay, I could answer your question with a question of my own. Do you want me to stay? But I won't. Because I shouldn't have to qualify my opinion. I'm not a coward." She licked her lips, as she did each time she felt desire for him, and he felt the hot slide of her tongue on his chest. "So. Here it is. Yes. I want to stay with you. That's what I wanted to talk to you about."

Thank the gods. He had worried for nothing. "I am

glad." Inadequate words. "I want you to stay with me, too."

"Really? You're not just saying that?"

"Jane, when have I ever just said anything?"

"Well, men say stuff they don't mean to get women into bed. All the time."

Some did, yes, but he never had. He'd always been up front, offering a single night of his attention, his body, but nothing else, and no longer. That was it, the end. Although, to get Jane into his bed again, he'd do and say just about anything.

"I will always be honest with you. Always. As long as you desire me. Stop, and I will change my dealings with you."

She laughed, the sexiest purr he'd ever heard. "Thank you for the warning."

Having her near him was arousing. Feeling her lick him, more so. But that laugh…he was hard as a rock in seconds. "I want you with me, Jane. In bed and out."

A tremor drove through her, vibrating into him, relief replacing her humor. "I don't know what I would have done if you'd tried to take away my magic green card. And before you ask, that means get rid of me."

"Get rid of you? Sweetheart, I'm doing everything in my power to keep you."

"Really?" Another soft entreaty.

He would have rolled his eyes if he weren't so happy with her. "Really."

"Thank you. I mean it. Thank you."

"And now you thank me. I should be thanking you. And I do. Humbly. You have become the reason I live, Jane."

He thought he heard her sniffle. She buried her head

in the hollow of his neck, rubbing her cheek against him. "So what's next?"

"I need to return to the kingdom of Elden. I think my siblings are there. Trapped, perhaps. I don't know. All I know is that, deep down, I am so hungry to slay the new king, I tremble. Like eating, this is a need. I *must* do it."

She didn't hesitate. "I'll help you."

He did not want her involved in such a violent, dangerous plan, but he did not want her out of his sight, either. "I need to find a way to keep you bound to me and to this land first. Should I write another book for you?" His magic was stronger now.

"If you do, we will be operating under the assumption that I'll return, no matter what we do or try."

"And perhaps such an assumption is what would send you back." Damn this! There had to be a way. "I wonder what spell I used to bring you here. If I knew, I would know if you would leave after a certain time, or after I am truly free. Or if I bound you to the land forever. I remember so many things, but not that, not yet, and I cannot risk another spell. It might interfere with the first."

She eased up, her hair tumbling over her bare shoulder, golden moonlight illuminating her. "When I first read the book and realized it wasn't a joke, I wondered how you could have known me when we'd never met."

"And you figured out the answer." His words were a statement, not a question. He'd known his woman was smart. She was the perfect combination of beauty and intelligence.

"Yes. I dreamed of you before I ever read the book.

Saw you chained, but never spoke to you. Now I think they were visions rather than dreams."

"But why have visions of me *before* I used my magic?"

"Maybe part of me crossed into this world long ago. Some things are familiar to me, like the ghost trees and ogres. Maybe you saw me, too, and that's how your magic knew to focus on me."

"That makes sense, but I wonder how you crossed over."

She gulped. "I…I…"

He reached up to cup her cheek. "Don't fear, Jane. We will figure this out. You won't leave. I won't let you."

"There's something I should tell you. About me. My job. You might change your mind about me." She traced the tip of her finger along his sternum. "I said I wasn't a coward and that means full disclosure, even about this. The things I did, horrible things, to learn about your—"

"I told you before, Jane, that your job—" A pang exploded through his head, silencing him, reminding him of what had happened after he'd fought the ogres here in this very spot. The same spot he'd first drunk from Jane. Pain, then opening his eyes in a new location.

He grunted. What was…? Another pang, this one rattling his brain against his skull.

The cage holding his memories and abilities was crumbling, bit by bit.

"What's wrong?" Jane eased to her elbow and smoothed his hair from his brow, her expression soft and luminous with concern. "Are you sick?"

Her emotions were in turmoil, yet she cast aside her own concerns to nurture him. No wonder he'd fallen for her so quickly and so easily. "Drinking your blood empowers me as never before," he confessed, "but as more of my memories and abilities escape, I experience a...wee little pinch of sensation."

Even as he spoke, one of those "wee little pinches" migrated from his head to his chest, and he hissed a breath. That one had been stronger than any of the others.

"Oh, Nicolai. Now I know why you were reluctant to drink from me. I'm so sorry I made you."

"I'm not. And you didn't make me, Jane. I wanted to. Badly. Besides, that isn't why. Want you healthy."

A sound of frustration. "Now you're doing what you said you wouldn't, and weaving pretty words to make me happy."

Another pang, another grunt.

"What can I do? Besides never feed you again?"

"Stay with me. And you *will* feed me again." Every day for eternity. "This will pass."

"I'll stay," she whispered. "Don't worry. And, Nicolai, we've never talked about my job before."

"We haven't? You researched...experimented..." What kind and on who were answered inside his mind, but he was having trouble reaching the information.

The color drained from her face. "That's right. And you still like me?"

"Jane..."

"Yes, of course. We'll discuss it when you're better." A pause. Then a whispered, "Could we have talked in my visions? Could *I* have forgotten conversations? Could whatever magic was used on you bleed into me?" She was talking to herself, trying to reason things out.

"Yes," he replied, anyway. "There's a chance."

"Sorry, sorry. I'll be quiet. You rest."

Trusting her, he closed his eyes, breathed slowly, deeply, and simply let the memories come. The first to hit him was of a pretty maid quietly entering his bedroom. Hinges squeaked as his gaze sought her. He didn't know her name, only that he'd smiled at her earlier that day, and she'd taken that smile for the invitation it was. He was lying on his mattress of plush goose feathers, naked, waiting. She stripped as she approached him.

Just before she reached him, the door opened and closed again. He looked. Another maid. The three of them were going to play. Good. He hadn't looked forward to a night with only one, a single conquest too easy. Too…boring. He needed to try something new.

His mind shied away from that particular memory.

Once, he might have been looking for more than one partner at a time. Once, he might have wanted to try anything and everything. And that one, he still wanted. With Jane. He wanted to do everything with her, but only with her. Everything they did was a new experience. Exciting, and most of all, soul shattering.

That wasn't going to change. She affected him too deeply, too intensely. And she hadn't had much pleasure in her life, he didn't think. Every new touch from him had left her gasping, writhing, her expression one of wonder and need.

He wanted her to wear that expression forever. Would see to it, make it a personal mission of his.

And what she could do with her mouth…*that* was magic.

Darkness suddenly fell over his mind, reality becoming clear. He felt Jane's soft fingers, still smoothing over his brow. Her warm, sweet breath trekked over his cheeks. She had kept her promise. She was staying put.

He couldn't lose her, he thought. There had to be a way to keep her. Forever.

The book, Jane, her dreams of this world. His spell to bring her here. He focused on those things, hoping to spur the memories in that direction. Shifted glamor, the illusion of someone else's face masking her own, he knew that much. Also an incantation in the words he'd written? Yes...yes... He'd murmured a spell as he'd written in the book. He'd wanted Jane to be standing beside him—and then she was.

A memory played.

Don't do this to me. He heard her voice so clearly. *I will find a way to help you.*

She *had* spoken to him before their first meeting. Their first remembered meeting.

I must. I need you. Until your body joins your mind, you are useless to me. His reply. Cold, harsh.

But to take my memory, she'd said.

He had taken her recollection of their conversations?

Their voices faded, and his father's image filled his head. An important memory, but he needed to know about Jane right now. She was the most pressing. The book. Jane. The spell—spells—he'd used.

His father was speaking to him, but Nicolai couldn't hear the words. The book. Jane. The spells he'd used. *Come on. The book. Jane. The spells he'd used.* Gradually, the image shifted. The towering form of his father shrunk. Black hair grew, curling, lightening. Harsh features became soft, delicate. Jane's.

This was his past with Jane, the memory resurfacing.

More than a whisper of conversation this time, more than a glimpse.

And there she was, his beautiful Jane, pacing in front of him. They were in his cell. He wore his loincloth and bruises. He lay on his pallet, watching her. From the moment she'd first appeared, untouchable, like a phantom, yet smelling of something wild and primal, he had wanted her.

Honey-colored hair streamed down her back, bouncing with every agitated step she took. She wore a long shirt that bagged on her, and he wished he could present her with silks and velvets.

"How are you tugging me here?" she asked. "Why can't you tug all of me?"

"I told you. Magic. And don't forget, *you* first came to *me* like this."

"As if I could forget. I closed my eyes and just…appeared. As if I'd been teleported, even though I never completed my teleportation research, never tested humans. And the plastic I sent over and back was solid and remained solid. I am not solid!"

"But you wake up at home, and you are always returned to your body."

"Yes." He didn't like that he couldn't touch her or drink from her, but no matter how many times she appeared—and she had, countless—her condition remained the same. Insubstantial. So, they would talk and she would entertain him.

She'd become something to look forward to, his only enjoyment. And he knew she enjoyed their time together, as well. Knew she liked him. She'd confided in him about her work; he'd told her about his frustration and anger that his memories had been destroyed.

But they couldn't go on like this. He couldn't stay here. He couldn't remain a prisoner forever. There had to be a way to bring her here—all of her. Had to be a way she could aid his escape. A way they could be together physically.

"Tell me the last thing you remember before coming here that first time," he demanded.

"Nothing. I was sleeping! I just woke up, and poof, I was in the Delfina palace and headed straight for you."

"Before that, then. Think. Maybe something was done or said about my world. Years could have passed since it happened, but you would remember."

A heavy pause. "There is something." Though she was spectral, her footsteps seemed to pound into the floor. "Once, I interviewed a vampire at my lab. I asked him question after question, but he refused to answer. I stood to leave. Suddenly he spoke up. He told me to let him go, to let him find his female before it was too late. I couldn't. I didn't have the authority. The next day, I returned."

Urgency filled him. "And?"

"And my boss told me the vampire had screamed all night. I entered his room—he was quiet by then, but this time he spoke up instantly. He said one day I would meet a man, fall in love with him and lose him. Just as my lack of action had caused him to lose his female. Then he broke free of his restraints. I thought he would fly at me, but he merely lifted his hand and used his claw to slash his own throat. He died right in front of me."

Nicolai's stomach dropped. "He cursed you, then. A blood curse." Unbreakable—for the most part.

"That was two years ago, and I thought he was just

spouting off. Trying to make me feel guilty for his incarceration!"

"No. He gave his life force to the words, breathing them into existence, lending them his heartbeat. The curse waited for the perfect time to strike."

"So I'm destined to only ever see you while in spirit form? No matter what we do?" She laughed bitterly. "If that's the case, no wonder you end up leaving me. I mean, we can't even touch each other!"

He scrubbed a hand down his face, his chains rattling. He couldn't answer her. Not without condemning them both. "What do you take pleasure in doing at home, Jane?"

"You want to discuss that now? Seriously?"

"Tell me."

She stopped, tossed up her arms. "I exercise and I read. That's all."

"Then I'll write you a book. I'll bespell the words. You will come to me in body, as well as spirit."

"Only to lose you later?"

He pursed his lips.

"I'll take that as a yes. Which means my answer is no. I don't want to come here, be with you, only to lose you forever."

"You can save me."

"And I want to save you, but what I won't do is watch you die." Her gaze narrowed on him. "I know how these things work, Nicolai. You've told me you care about me. And yeah, that could be your incarceration talking, but maybe not. If we take things to the next level and you lose me, you will wither."

He would rather wither than remain enslaved. "That's a chance I'm willing to take."

"I'm not."

"Then I will take your memory, Jane."

Her mouth fell open. "You can do that? You *would* do that?"

"Yes, and yes. I would do that and a whole lot more."

"You know the pain of having memories taken. How could you even think of doing that to me?"

Sound reasoning, which he ignored. "I will only take the memories of me."

"So I'll see you but won't recognize you?" Suddenly she couldn't quite catch her breath. Tears ran down her cheeks, leaving little wet tracks. "Will you recognize me?"

"I don't know. Perhaps."

"Don't do this, Nicolai."

"I must. I need you. Until your body joins your mind, you are useless to me." Useless, but so necessary.

"But to take my memories…"

"You've forced my hand." Flat, no room for compromise.

"And if we hate each other in this new beginning, as we did before?"

At first, she had watched him with those haunted amber eyes, her scent so sweet he could practically taste it. He'd wanted her, craved her, but she had kept her distance.

When at last she deigned to speak to him, he'd been worked into such a frenzy for her that he had lashed out and tried to bite her, only to waft right through her—as well as scare the Abyss out of her. She had vanished. Hadn't returned for days. Frustration and anger had eaten him.

The next time, he forced himself to speak softly to

her, to maintain his own distance, gentling her, even though such things went against the very fiber of his nature. After that, she'd come back again, and again, and camaraderie soon morphed into caring.

What he planned to do to her was a betrayal. He knew that.

He did it, anyway. He used his magic to create the book, the pen. Used his magic to write to Jane. Used his magic to send her away, back to her world, to her body. Used his magic to wipe her memories. Used his magic to bring her back to him.

And in the process, his own memories of her *were* taken. Not because of the witches, but because of him. He'd taken them on purpose. He'd known knowledge of his past with her would influence his future. Might even prevent him from using her.

Something was shaking him, dislodging the recollection. He tried to hold on, had to know what happened next, but the shaking continued, and he growled.

"Nicolai. Nicolai, you have to snap out of it." Jane's voice, closer, in the present, frantic and fearful. "Someone's coming. Nicolai, please. Wake up."

Please.

He released the past completely, allowing his mind to snap back into focus. He'd hurt her enough already. And, as she had feared, he would lose her again. The spell he'd used had not disrupted the very first spell cast on her. The one that would force her to lose her lover. Nothing could disrupt that spell, and none Nicolai had tried had brought her back to him. Until he'd worked *with* the first.

He'd brought Jane here, bound her body to his, on

the condition that she leave him when—if—she fell in love with him.

So, he could keep her, as long as he prevented her from loving him.

"Nicolai."

The present. Yes. He heard footsteps. A lot of them. Booted. Spears scraping against the ground. Power saturated the air. Laila, definitely. With her army? Probably.

Different emotions warred for dominance. Fury, elation, anticipation, hatred, anxiety. Nicolai wanted to attack, to kill, but that would place Jane in jeopardy, and that he wouldn't do. Ever.

He jolted upright, a blur of motion. Jane had already pulled on her robe, was ready to go.

"Come." He grabbed her arm, and jerked her away from their camp.

CHAPTER FOURTEEN

NICOLAI DRAGGED JANE through the forest, branches slapping at him. She was limping again, and he wanted to carry her, but Laila's guards must have caught his scent, because the echo of their footsteps increased, and the sense of magic intensified in the night air.

They were closing in.

He could have moved from one location to another with only a thought. From here, back to the withered, perverted kingdom of Elden. His heart clenched in his chest, and he gritted his teeth. Now was not the time to think of his home. Or the condition of his home. Or his parents, and the sorcerer he would soon destroy.

What if he disappeared, but Jane did not go with him? She would be left on her own in an inhospitable environment, the enemy all around.

Damn this. He had to try something. He'd managed to beat the flood of memories back, but they were knocking at his mind, demanding release. If they overtook him again…

He focused on what was most important. He and Jane shared a past he'd barely touched on. One she still couldn't recall. What he knew was that he wouldn't repeat his previous mistakes.

He needed that book, the one in Delfina. Had to write something more inside of it. For when she left him. Oh, gods. Yes, that meant he would be operating under the assumption she would love and leave him, but he *had* to plan for the worst. Maybe, just maybe, a new spell would bring her back.

Elden had not planned for defeat, and look what had happened.

"Nicolai," Jane panted. "I'm used to jogging, but this is like Extreme Jogging, Jungle Edition, and I don't know how much longer I can keep up. Can we rest?"

He heard her. Distantly. Tried to concentrate on her, but the darkness was closing in on him, another memory fighting its way free.

All his life, he had absorbed the powers and magic of others. What they could do, he could then do. That was how he'd formed the air shield inside the palace. The Queen of Hearts had done so; therefore, he had done so, too. And that was why Laila had forbidden anyone from practicing their craft around him.

Some abilities lasted days, weeks. Others lasted a lifetime.

He'd remembered most of this already, so of course his mind tried to shove it aside to make room for something else, something new.

"Nicolai. Please."

He couldn't lock on her. More details unfolded. His ability to cast illusions, as well as move from one location to another with only a thought, had come from a witch. A lover who had tried to kill him as he lay sleeping. She had wanted to become his bride, but he had wanted only the sex. She'd tried several different identities with him, amusing him.

He'd never told her that he knew who she was, each and every time she approached, because he recognized her scent. He'd let her continue to come to him, and every time he'd made his intentions clear. Still she'd tried, hoping to change his mind. When she realized she could not, in any incarnation, she finally attacked.

One moment Nicolai was leading Jane through the forest, the next he was inside a bedroom. His bedroom, he thought. The one in his memory, with the homicidal witch. He did not realize the switch soon enough and slammed into the wall, propelling backward. He hit the floor with a black curse.

Jane was nowhere to be seen.

Nicolai popped to his feet, his blood flashing hot. He would return to the forest, now, now, damn it, now, and if anyone had touched Jane…

He remained in the bedroom.

Fangs bared, he spun, looking for the way out. Blood stained the walls, crimson splattered in every direction. The floor possessed deep grooves, each in patterns of four, as if multiple swords had been dragged over it and had cut into the wood.

The giant, hairy creatures, their legs—four on each side—sharp and deadly. They had been here. They had come for him.

Nicolai had been pumping into a woman, a servant. His door had flown open, and he'd heard the screams echoing from below, in the great hall. He should have heard them sooner, but his partner had been screaming, too, distracting him.

Nicolai had reached for his blood daggers, the ones he kept on his nightstand, intending to fight the monsters, wondering about his family, but he'd…disappeared, falling straight into a winding black hole.

Had his siblings died alongside his parents? Or fallen

into the same hole? He remembered curses around him, echoing.

Now he stopped breathing. He hadn't wanted to remember this, not yet, but… Was he certain his parents were dead? Was there no longer any question in his mind?

He didn't need to think about it. Yes. He was certain. They were dead. The knowledge practically seeped from the mold-covered walls around him. He hadn't seen them die, but he'd felt the drain of their life forces. They were gone.

Oh, gods. And his siblings?

No, not dead. Now that he knew what to check for, he could feel their energy swirling inside him still; only, the energy was…different than before. Were they trapped somewhere? Unable to free themselves? Probably. Otherwise, Dayn would have destroyed the Blood Sorcerer and reclaimed the palace.

Dayn and his ability to hunt anyone or thing. Micah, sweet baby-faced Micah, would have been running down the halls and laughing. Breena would have been trying her hand at magic, messing up her spells.

With these thoughts, he wanted to drop to his knees, roar to the heavens, curse, rant and rail, fight everything and everyone. How to find them? How to free them?

Now he also realized he'd heard Dayn's voice in his dreams. Calling to him, telling him to heal himself. They shared a blood connection, something that could never be destroyed. They could speak again.

Where are you, brother?

A moment passed. There was no reply. Very well. He would try again later.

A sense of urgency reignited, and Nicolai checked

for his daggers. They were gone, as were his clothing and all his other weapons. The room had been totally cleaned out.

He ground his molars and pictured the rest of the castle, which was surprisingly easy. Towering, more rooms than he could count. Winding hallways and secret passages. He whisked to every bedroom, every cell in the dungeon. He saw people he did not recognize, more bloodstains, more monsters patrolling the gates. Rage consumed him. The need to kill the new king, the sorcerer, intensified. But his family was not here, nor was the sorcerer.

He would have to return. Soon. Always soon. Right now, he had to protect Jane. A full-time job, he was coming to realize. One he cherished and wouldn't trade.

After a last glance at the castle he'd once loved, he closed his eyes and pictured the forest and the last spot he'd seen Jane. He was there a second later—easier every time—but found no sign of his woman. No sign of Laila and her army, either.

He sniffed…sniffed… There. He locked on to Jane's sweet scent, mixed with the disgusting aroma of Laila and her men. They were following her.

He gave chase.

JANE HEARD THE VOICES before she spotted the town, and nearly toppled over with relief. She increased her speed, and finally, blessedly, reached civilization. The sun was steadily rising in the sky, casting a violet haze on the people just now starting their day. Warming Jane, and even burning her. Her skin itched, prickling as if little bugs were crawling through her veins.

She did not want to contemplate the possible reasons for such an occurrence.

People—humans?—strode along cobbled streets, some carrying wicker baskets piled high with clothing, some carrying bags of—she sniffed, moaned—bread and meat. Her stomach grumbled as her mouth watered. She was light-headed, her blood supply a little low. She *needed* to replenish.

Jane paused beside a tree, watching, thinking. She had two choices. Keep moving, remaining on her own, and risk being found by Laila. Or enter the town, eat and risk being found by Laila. At least the second option provided a meal plan. So, okay. No contest.

Except, she was still Odette. If these people recognized her, word would spread, and she would be found far more quickly. On the plus side, Laila wouldn't hurt her and Nicolai was no longer with her. He was no longer in danger—she didn't think—and that was a good thing.

He'd disappeared in a heartbeat of time, shocking her. She'd waited in the area for what seemed an eternity, but he'd never reappeared and she'd had to move on. He would find her, wherever she was. She couldn't believe otherwise.

Laila's army had nearly discovered her, marching right over her hiding place. But they'd lost Nicolai's trail and backtracked in an attempt to find it again. That's when Jane bolted, forcing her protesting body to act before it shut down completely and Laila returned.

If—when—Jane was discovered, she wanted to be well-fed, stronger. So again, no contest. She limped forward, entering the town. The moment the people caught sight of her, they stopped what they were doing, horror consuming their features, and knelt.

Yep. She'd been recognized. What the hell had Odette done to them?

She closed the distance between her and one of the groups with food. "Please. I'm so hungry. May I—"

"Take whatever you wish, princess," the man closest to her said, thrusting the basket in her direction.

"I don't have any money, but I'll find a way to pay you back. I swear." The scent of roasted chicken hit her, transporting her straight to heaven. She stretched out a shaky hand, reached inside the confines of the wicker and claimed a bowl of something creamy. Was she drooling? *You can't dive in like an animal.* "What's your name?"

"Hammond, princess." There was a trace of anger in that husky voice.

"Thank you for the food, Hammond."

"Anything for you, princess." The anger morphed into hatred.

Jane sighed, looked around. "Please stand. All of you. There's no reason to bow."

Several seconds ticked by before they obeyed, as if they feared she would attack them for rising, even though she'd told them to. Other than that, they didn't move. Though she wanted to limp away, find a deserted, shadowed corner and shove her face right into the food, she couldn't. They might suspect she was not who they thought she was.

"I need a room," she announced. "And water. And clean clothing. Please. If one of you could point me in the right direction, I would be grateful."

At first, no one stepped forward. Then, reluctantly,

a middle-aged female curtsied and said, "If you'll follow me, princess, I will see to your needs."

"Thank you."

Ten minutes later, an eternity, Jane was inside a bedroom, alone. She devoured the contents of the bowl—some kind of chicken salad—before bathing in the steaming tub the woman had filled with a muttered spell. Not human, after all, but a witch. The water soothed Jane's sensitive skin, relieving the itching. Afterward, she donned a clean, blue robe the witch had laid out for her.

All she lacked was Nicolai, and this day would be perfect.

Where was he?

With a weary sigh, she sprawled out on the bed. Firm, lumpy, but heaven for her still aching muscles and bones. What to do, what to do. Nicolai was, at heart, a protector. Fierce, unwavering. Which meant he hadn't left her voluntarily.

So. Either his abilities—whatever they were—were responsible, or someone had used magic to draw him away from her. The first was more likely. As strong as Nicolai was becoming, she doubted anyone would be able to simply spell him someplace anymore. Because, if that were the case, Laila would have done it days ago.

Laila. The bitch was a problem. A big one. As long as she was out there, Nicolai would be hunted, in danger. Jane could turn herself in, she supposed, and try to convince the princess to leave "the slave" alone. Would that help, though? Having tasted the man herself, she knew how impossible it would be to forget him.

Laila probably craved him more than the air she breathed. The thought alone caused jealousy to rise up, sharp and biting. Jane ignored the unproductive response. A few problems with turning herself in. One, Laila could wield magic. Jane could not. Two, Jane's secret could be found out. And if the queen whipped her own daughter, what would she do to an enemy impersonating one of her children? Three, what if Nicolai followed her to Delfina? He could be captured again, his memories wiped. His body used.

His body belonged to Jane. No one else.

She rolled to her side, clutching the pillow to her middle, suddenly reminded of the day she had received Nicolai's book. She'd read a few passages and had thought of him for hours afterward. She had been obsessed with him, really. After reading a few more passages, she had fantasized about him, practically making love to her pillow. Then, she had gone to him.

Maybe she could reach him again.

She closed her eyes and imagined him inside her cabin, puttering around, fixing things, then seducing her into bed. There, he touched her, stripped her. Kissed her, tasted her. Consumed her. Goose bumps spread. She could almost feel the warmth of his breath, the slick glide of his skin.

"Nicolai," she breathed.

Jane.

His voice, so deep, so familiar. For a moment, she experienced a wave of dizziness, felt as if she were floating. Then the mattress was beneath her again, and… cold. Cold? In less than a second, the mattress had gone from warmed to chilled. Impossible. Unless— Her eyelids popped open, hope unfurling.

Hope dying. She hadn't whisked to Nicolai. She was inside her cabin. On her own bed.

Jane jolted upright, trying to suck air into her lungs. A knot formed in her throat, and nothing could penetrate it. No. She couldn't be here. No, no, no. She popped to her feet, nearly toppling as her knees shook. She rushed around, stumbling a few times, grabbing her knickknacks to see if they were real or imagined.

Please be imagined.

They were solid, dusty, as if they hadn't been cleaned in weeks. They were real. She choked back a sob.

No! Tears blurred her vision. She swiped her arms over her dresser, knocking everything to the floor. A glass vase shattered. A hairbrush clattered. How the hell had she gotten here? She'd wanted to be with Nicolai. She needed to be with him and had to get back. She *would* get back.

She just had to figure out how.

CHAPTER FIFTEEN

JANE RAGED FOR HALF AN HOUR. Panicked for an hour after that. Then she did what she did best—reasoned. There was a logical explanation for what had happened. There always was. So, she brushed her teeth, showered and redressed in her robe. No way she'd dress in jeans and a T-shirt. She didn't belong here anymore, and wouldn't dress as if she did.

She belonged there. With Nicolai.

She stretched out on her bed, and her comforter plumped around her. Okay. She could do this. What had she been doing before she'd ended up here? Lying in bed, just like this, thinking about Nicolai. Imagining the two of them making love, actually. Good, that was good. She would just do that again.

She cleared her mind with a little shake of her head, drew in a deep breath, released the air…slowly…and forced her muscles to relax. A picture of Nicolai rose front and center. Dark hair shagging around his head, silver eyes liquid with desire. For her. Lips parted as he breathed shallowly, his own desire raging. His fangs peeked out.

Her stomach quivered, but other than that, nothing happened. No dizziness, no movement whatsoever. *Keep going.* In her mind, she saw him remove his shirt, slowly pulling the material over his head. His skin, his beautifully bronzed skin, glistened exquisitely. His nipples were small and brown, utterly lickable. That scrumptious trail of hair lead from his navel to a cock she'd once loved with her mouth.

Warm moisture pooled between her legs. But again, no floating, no changing locations.

Damn it. She hadn't been this unsuccessful since the age of eight, when she'd read about making synthetic diamonds in the microwave. Diamonds she'd hoped to present to her mother on her birthday. The charcoal bricks and peanut butter necessary for the conversion had survived the lengthy cook time. The dish she'd put them in had not. Neither had the microwave.

A chuckle escaped her as she suddenly recalled her mother's reaction. They'd been standing in the kitchen, her darling mother looking through the thick, dark smoke to Jane, who was holding the book that explained exactly how to do it. Her disbelieving expression was comical.

"Diamonds?" her mother asked.

"I followed every step, didn't miss a single one."

Her mother coughed as she claimed the book. Several minutes passed before she turned her attention to the blackened mess inside the microwave. "You followed every step, did you?"

"Yes!"

"And you used a Pyrex dish?"

Jane blinked. "P-Pyrex?"

Dizziness caused the image to waver, fade, and that dizziness caused a bubble of excitement to burst through her chest. This was it. She was returning....

The moment the dizziness passed, she popped open her eyelids and sat up. For a moment, her unfamiliar surroundings simply couldn't register. She was perched on a linoleum floor in the center of a kitchen. There was a stainless-steel stove, a sink, scuffed cabinets. The layout was familiar—she'd just seen it in her mind—but the colors were not.

Once, the walls had been painted yellow. Now they were painted blue. Once, the refrigerator had been silver. Now it was black. Still she knew. This had been her kitchen. She'd grown up here. Her mother had stood just in front of that sink, coughing from the smoke wafting from the microwave. A high-pitched scream suddenly echoed, a jumble of words following. "Intruder! Thief! Murderer! What the hell are you doing here?" a woman gasped from behind her. "Who are you? Get out! Get out right now! Billy, call 9-1-1."

Jane whipped around, instinctively holding up her hands in a you-can-trust-me gesture. "I'm not going to hurt you."

Absolute fear coated the woman's features. She grabbed a knife from the counter, waving the sharp tip in Jane's direction. "That's what all the psychos say."

Jane backed away.

"Billy!"

"What?" a sleepy male voice growled from around the corner.

Oh, crap. Reinforcements. Remembering the house's layout, Jane bolted, heading straight for the front door. She raced into the morning sunlight, the length of her robe tangling around her feet. And sure enough, she was in her old neighborhood. Not much had changed. The houses were small, a little run-down and crowded too close together.

Fearing the woman and her Billy would give chase—

and grab a shotgun—she sprinted about half a mile along the gravel road, turned sharply and ducked behind Mrs. Rucker's giant oak. She'd hidden here a lot as a kid.

She was panting and sweating as she slid to her ass. And damn. Her feet throbbed. The little rocks had sliced them to ribbons.

Well, that was fun. Not. What the hell had just happened?

She ran the variables through her mind, weighed each of the possible outcomes, compared them and discarded all but one. His blood. She'd had Nicolai's blood; he'd fed it to her to heal her. His abilities must have transferred to her. Like him, she could move from one place to the other, disappearing and reappearing. In essence, teleporting.

She just had to picture where she wanted to go, and boom. She was there in a snap. Amazement filled her. She'd studied the manipulation of macroparticles for years before she'd succeeded in teleporting plastic, basically faxing a small portion from one station to another. Now, to move a living being between planes with only a thought…it was everything she'd worked for, gift-wrapped and handed to her.

So, when she'd imagined her old kitchen, she had traveled to her old kitchen. Before, in that town, she had imagined Nicolai in her bed, and had therefore traveled back to her bed. So simple, so easy, an answer that made sense. Finally.

She could return to her man.

She was grinning as she closed her eyes and pictured the quaint little bedroom she'd previously occupied. The wooden tub, the feathered bed. Yes, the bed. Where she'd sprawled, hoping Nicolai would find her.

Dizziness rolled through her, and she couldn't contain her gasp of excitement. Next time she opened her eyes, she would be there. Back in Delfina. And if she retained this ability, she would never have to worry about losing Nicolai to magic again. She could stay with him always. If she didn't retain it automatically, she could drink from him every day to ensure that she did.

"Well, well," a female voice said. "There you are, using your magic to become invisible again. Who were you spying on this time, sister dear?"

Dread replaced Jane's excitement as she opened her eyes. She was in the little room, all right, but that room was now overflowing with Laila and her soldiers. Two of them held a teary-eyed woman. The very woman who had brought Jane here, who had fed her, clothed her.

Laila stood at the edge of the bed, peering down at her. There was no sign of Nicolai.

Slowly Jane sat up. *Careful.* "Yes, I was using my invisibility again." As far as lies went, that was a good one. Irrefutable. "How did you find me?"

"Is that any way to greet your loving sister? A sister who has searched and searched for you, desperate to save you from a madman's clutches."

A thought hit her: despite traveling between worlds, the Odette mask was still in place. Sweet! But really, Jane knew if Laila had "searched and searched" for her, it had been to slay her and claim Nicolai for her own. Two could play the deceit game, however.

"Thank you for saving me, darling. All I've done these past few days is miss you."

Emerald eyes narrowed to tiny slits.

"Now," Jane added before Laila could reply. "What are you doing to the woman?"

"Oh." Laila waved a dismissive hand. "I knew you were here, I could sense your magic, but I couldn't find you and feared she had killed you." Was that relish in her tone?

"As you can see, she didn't." As she spoke, she said a prayer that Nicolai did not come for her, yet. She didn't want him walking in on this. Didn't want Laila to see him.

"True." Laila twisted and eyed the guards holding her. "She's no longer of any use to us. Dispose of her."

"Dispose of her" had better not mean… A third guard stepped up behind the woman, who had begun to flail and panic, grabbed her by the jaw and jerked, breaking her neck in seconds. Her body sagged forward, going limp. Lifeless.

Jane could only gape in shock, in horror. "Wh-why did you do that?"

The guards dragged the body away, and Laila shrugged. "She irritated me."

"You…" *Bitch.* The urge to murder the princess flashed white-hot through her veins. And she'd once thought herself unready for such an act.

That she remained in place, seemingly unaffected, saved her. There was a little voice of reason in the back of her head, reminding her that she was outnumbered and outgunned.

Jane had never been a violent person. Perhaps Nicolai's dark side was rubbing off on her, too, because she *liked* the thought of hurting Laila. Welcomed it. *One day, I will destroy you.*

Laila eased onto the mattress, pressing close. Jane

barely stopped herself from scooting away in disgust. "Now, sister dear, we have much to discuss."

NICOLAI REMAINED IN the shadows, bypassing huts and outdoor vendors pedaling their wares. Jane's scent, so sweet…stronger now…so close…mixed with a hundred others. Some rotten, pungent. Some sweat soaked, some magic ripe.

Laila and her army were here.

The moment realization struck, he stopped caring about stealth. He leaped into action, feet hammering at the ground. The citizens paused when they spotted him, some doing a double take. Murmurs soon arose.

Did they know him?

He caught words like *prince* and *dead,* each a question. They did know him, then. Knew he was a prince of Elden. They'd thought him dead. Did they think the same about his family?

He almost stopped to question them. Almost. Jane was in danger. That preceded *everything.* He quickened his pace. His intense sense of smell took him to a little hut at the edge of the town. Guards spilled from it, filing into the streets. There were even guards posted at the neighboring homes, all watching and waiting for their princess.

Nicolai returned to the shadows. Thankfully no one in this area had noticed him. People were perched in front of their windows, nervously eyeing the guards. Potential allies?

Some were witches, but most were humans. Humans who had crossed into this realm throughout the centuries, for whatever reason. They had congregated here, settled and sprouted roots. That had been a mistake, for this town was part of Delfina and under the rule of the Queen of Hearts. They couldn't help him.

He drew in a heated breath, released it. Well, he didn't need help. He was a prince. A vampire. Powerful beyond imagining. He had led an army of his own, had conquered kingdoms and female hearts. He could absorb the abilities of others, and it was time he used that to his advantage—and not accidentally.

Eyes narrowing, he homed in on the house. Jane was inside. He felt her energy, as sweet as her scent and… now blended with his own. He gave a primitive grunt of approval. *Mine.* He had done more than mark her; he had branded her. *I'm coming for you, sweetheart.*

He switched his focus to Laila. She was rotten to her core, with a scent to match. Magic swirled inside her, dark and potent. Ability after ability, honed over centuries of living with such a slowly ticking clock. He rifled through them.

She could hypnotize others; that could aid him, yes, but she could only entrance one person at a time. She could heal her own wounds. He could already do that. She could *cause* wounds. Another maybe. She could spark false desire. No. A muscle ticked in his jaw, though. How many times had she used that ability on him?

Doesn't matter. He continued his search, discarding…discarding… There! Remote viewing, like what he'd done inside the palace with Jane. Perfect, and now his earlier ability made sense. He wondered how many times Laila had used the ability on him. Watched him without his knowledge.

No matter the answer, she would never be able to do so again.

He grabbed on to the ability and gave a soft mental tug, drawing it closer and closer to him. A little more… just a little more… His chest puffed as his every cell suddenly absorbed the magic necessary to see places he could not physically reach. Still he kept tugging, and tugging, and tugging. Drawing the magic away from her and into him.

Laila wouldn't know what he was doing. His victims never did, until it was too late. Right now, she would be experiencing only mild fatigue. If he attempted to draw *all* of her abilities, all of her power, however, she would know and could try to stop him, erecting mental blocks.

Suddenly his mind opened up. In a blink, he was looking at Jane, as if he were sitting beside her. Only, he saw her through Laila's eyes. And Laila saw the mask. Saw Odette. Odette's dark hair, Odette's green eyes. Her too-long nose and thick jowls.

Knowing Jane rested under that mask was enough to light his body on fire and soothe the sharpest edges of his fear for her safety. She was alive, unharmed. He would have her again.

"What did the slave do to you? Tell me before I perish from worry." Laila ruined the effect of the demand with a yawn.

Jane fluffed her hair, every inch the princess. "Like you said before, he desired me. I desired him, one thing led to another, and we were steaming up the forest, if you know what I mean."

"Did you bespell him to desire you?" Each word was tauter than the last. "You must have. Otherwise, he would be with you now. Yet, I have caught no sign of him. So where is he?"

"No, I didn't bespell him." Jane offered no more.

"Then how did you elicit his desire? He hated you, tried to kill you. You did something, I know you did. Just admit it."

Jane smirked over at her, and it was a glorious sight. "Hold on to your panties, Laila dear, because this might shock you. I—wait for it—treated him with respect. You should try it sometime. You might be delighted with the results."

Hate burned through Laila so relentlessly, Nicolai felt the heat of it inside his own body. "You lie. You've never treated anyone with respect. I doubt you even know what the word means."

"Are we showing our claws now, *darling?* Because I promise you, mine are sharper."

Pride filled him. No one would doubt she was Odette now. Not even the queen herself. She wore confidence as snugly as a cloak.

"I will ask you one more time," Laila gritted out.

"Or what?"

"Where. Is. He?"

"Dead." A casual shrug. "He's dead."

Laila's mouth dropped open, a strangling sound emerging. "You killed him?"

"Yes. Yes, I did." Jane threw her legs over the mattress, and winced. They must be paining her, he thought, wishing he were there to ease her hurts. She straightened. "Now, let's go home. I'm eager to sleep in my own bed."

Laila remained in place and crossed her arms over her middle. "Where's his body?"

"I fed it to the ogres, of course," she replied blithely.

"What's with all the questions, anyway? Nicolai did not belong to you."

She was giving him what he'd told her he wanted, he thought. A chance to destroy Laila, undetected. Time to reach Elden, to kill the new king. And yes, the urgency was still there, simmering inside him, stronger with every minute that passed, but he still couldn't, wouldn't, leave her.

Relief bathed Laila, bleeding into him, but the emotion was as quickly schooled as the hatred. "I found the ogre cave. Nicolai's body was not there. Others' were, which has to mean he killed them and escaped."

Jane didn't miss a beat. "Wrong. *I* massacred the ogres. After they finished with him."

The shock returned. "How?"

A buff of her nails. "A girl never reveals her fighting secrets. She might need them later on."

A heartbeat of silence. A low growl.

"How dare you!" Laila shouted, no longer able to contain her emotions. She jumped to her feet, stomped her foot. "He was mine."

Jane got in her face, putting them nose to nose. "Actually, you spoiled brat, he's mine. Was mine."

Tension thickened the air, practically vibrating between them. Long moments passed, the only sound that of their breathing. Finally Laila backed down. She stepped away, widening the distance.

"Of course. You're right." Grudgingly offered. "So tell me. *Why* did you kill him?"

"I no longer desired him."

Even though Nicolai knew why she said what she said, his inner beast did not like hearing those words. Later, he would have to be soothed. Later, he would have to explain his past with her and apologize for what he'd done.

Would her claim then become true?

"Now, then. Let's return to the palace," Jane said. "Guards. Move out."

They hesitated.

"Now!" she screamed, her patience clearly gone.

This time, they scrambled to obey. Jane followed them, forcing Laila to trail after her. Nicolai could feel the princess's desire to stab her sister in the back. But she didn't, and as they marched out of the town, he skulked after them.

Soon…

CHAPTER SIXTEEN

EVEN THOUGH, AS A PRINCESS of Delfina, she was carried on a plush velvet lounge, the sun blocked by a canopy of dark netting, Jane much preferred traveling with Nicolai. Where was he? Close, she thought. She could almost scent him, a hint of magic, a pinch of seductive spice. She prayed he'd opted not to follow her.

Laila thought he was dead. So, in a way, he was finally free of the bitch. He could travel to Elden, and do what needed doing. And Jane could deliver his vengeance—a special care package of lethal—for him.

The princess had killed an innocent woman for no damn reason. No wonder the people in town had been afraid of Odette. The royal family abused their power, and Jane wasn't going to let them do so anymore.

Then she and Nicolai could be together again.

When Laila finally decided to stop for the evening, Jane's legs were stiff from disuse. Not as stiff as they could have been, at least. In fact, not even close to what she was used to dealing with. No throbbing pain, no bone-crushing aches. However, a walk would have been nice.

Sadly, a walk wasn't in the forecast for some time to come. She had to continue to lounge as the guards erected her tent. And decorated the inside. And carted in her trunks. Trunks Laila had brought with her, perhaps hoping to bribe her for a night with Nicolai.

When they finished, bowing before her and awaiting dismissal, Laila climbed down from her own raised lounge, stepping on their backs to reach the ground.

"There will be a celebration of your return," the princess announced with a clap of her hands. "We will dine in my tent. My slaves will dance for us, and you may choose whichever you desire to warm your furs."

Gee. Thanks. "Sorry, but I'm tired." Jane climbed down, too, feeling guilty the entire time. Although the guards blinked with surprise at her slighter weight and that sparked a kernel of fear. "I wish only to bathe and sleep. And eat. I haven't been fed properly in days."

"Bathe, yes. Then join me. I will feed you. Since your return from the grave, there has been too much friction between us. I do not like it, and long for the ease of our former relationship."

A lie, Jane knew. Laila hated Odette with the same passion she had craved Nicolai in her bed, but to protest was to, perhaps, act against the real Odette's character. "Very well," she said on a sigh. "I'll join you in an hour." A small reprieve, but a reprieve all the same. She made her way to her own tent.

A long soak in the portable tub did much to appease her aches and pains. A tub Rhoslyn had filled. The girl was a surprisingly welcome sight.

Jane scrubbed from head to toe, using the floral-scented soap that had rested on the rim. "Did Laila demand that you come on this journey or did you volunteer?"

Frizzy red hair bobbed. "I volunteered, princess."

She unfolded a vivid green robe from a trunk. "Just in case we found you, and you had need of me."

I should have been nicer to this girl. "I didn't see you until you entered my tent. Where were you in the procession?"

"Behind the third line of defense, with the rest of the servants and slaves."

"I wished I'd known. You could have ridden in the carriage with me." Jane emerged from the water and grabbed the towel resting on a nearby bench.

"I will help you," Rhoslyn said, rushing over. The robe dangled from her arms.

"No, thanks." There were some things she was now capable of doing herself—things she hadn't been able to do while practically chained to a hospital bed—and she would never again allow anyone to do them for her.

Dried, she pinched one corner of the robe and lifted. Her lips curved down in distaste. Though finely made, the material was too wide for her, and far too thick. She'd melt from the heat. And, where the robe gaped, she'd fry like battered shrimp when in the sun.

"I am sorry if the cloth is not to your liking." Free of her burden, Rhoslyn bowed her head. "You may beat me if you wish."

Jane caught the layer of fear in her voice. "Beat you? Rhoslyn, I'm not going to beat you. Ever."

The girl continued as if she hadn't heard a word Jane had said. "I thought you would prefer something durable, rather than enticing. And your sister was quite eager to reach you, so I did not have much time to pack your things. I am not complaining," she rushed to add. "I simply wished to explain why there are not many robes to choose from, and why I did not bring your very best."

"You did great, I swear. I love the gown. Love it. See?" She dressed and twirled. "I've never felt lovelier."

Rhoslyn offered her a genuine smile. "I am glad, princess. Oh. And I am happy to tell you that I brought your book."

Jane paused, her heart suddenly thumping. "Really? Where is it?"

The girl crossed to the other side of the tent. Slowly, Jane realized, and with care. "Hey. Are you okay? Did you hurt yourself carrying those buckets?" Great. Something else to feel guilty about.

Rhoslyn stiffened, stumbling over her own feet, before continuing on. "I am fine, princess." She hunched over another trunk, dug inside and lifted the leather-bound tome.

Jane gasped with horror. As the girl had bent over, her hair had fallen forward and Jane had caught sight of bruising on her neck. Black and blue and clearly spreading farther down. "What happened to your back?" This time, her tone was firm, unyielding, demanding an answer.

Rhoslyn's thin arm shook as she held out the book. "I allowed you to be abducted by the slave. I was punished. As I deserved."

Whipped, then. Laila hadn't given the girl time to pack properly, but she'd damn sure made time to use the cat-o'-nine-tails. Jane claimed the offered item, hating Laila a little more. "That wasn't your fault. You couldn't have stopped him. Hell, you weren't even there."

No reply was forthcoming.

She sighed. "I'm headed to my sister's tent. While

I'm gone, I want you to soak in the tub. If you want. If you don't, don't. Then, I want you to rest. Do not wait up for me. And that's an order."

Eyes wide with surprise, Rhoslyn gave another nod.

Jane stepped outside. Overhead, the sun was setting, muted and a deep purple. And yet, it still managed to burn her newly sensitive skin, making her itch all over again. Now wasn't the time to consider what that meant, either.

Laila's tent was a mere ten steps away. At the entrance, Jane stopped and squared her shoulders. *You can do this.* The sound of laughter and music wafted toward her as she brushed past the flap. She scouted her new surroundings, trying to take everything in at once. To the right, Laila was perched on a hastily constructed dais. Lounging, of course, and eating pastries. There was an empty seat beside her.

Six naked men slow danced in the center. They were tall, leanly muscled and oiled to a glossy shine. Two blonds, two redheads and two with dark hair. Math at its finest. Hands roamed, and bodies bumped and grinded. Each man had an erection, but Jane doubted they liked what they were doing. Their eyes were glazed and lifeless. Were they bespelled?

To the left was a band. Well, the Delfina version of a band. A naked harpist, a naked violinist and a naked vocalist. Jane was sensing a theme. And, well, shit. This had the makings of an orgy. Participation had better not be mandatory. Her body belonged to Nicolai, and no one else.

"Odette," Laila called, catching sight of her. "Thank you for coming."

What ulterior motive do you have? Jane wondered

as she closed the distance between them. No way the princess had thrown this little shindig together out of the goodness of her heart. Fact: she didn't have a heart.

Jane eased into her chair and stretched out. "My... pleasure." Something about the princess was off, she immediately realized. No, not off. Different. Yes, that was a better word. She pulsed with power, stronger than before. Had she cast some sort of spell on herself? Could witches even do that?

Wasn't like Jane could ask. She was supposed to be a witch herself.

Laila waved her hand over the tray of pastries. "Have anything you like."

Hmm, sugar. Her stomach twisted with hunger. How many hours had passed since she'd had that delicious chicken salad? The same number of hours that had passed since the princess had killed that innocent woman. Goodbye, appetite. "I'm fine."

"You must drink." Laila clapped. "Fix my sister a goblet of wine."

The servant behind their chairs jumped to obey, and seconds later, Jane was holding a bejeweled, golden goblet. Rather than refuse it, she held on. Drinking the wine was out of the question, though. She needed her wits. All of her wits.

If an opportunity presented itself, she was going to deliver her care package tonight. Poison? A stabbing? Whatever method she picked, she would have to be careful. She couldn't win against the princess's magical abilities. Especially since she had no idea what the girl could do.

"Now," Laila purred. "Enjoy."

For over an hour, the men danced and Laila watched,

eating and drinking. Jane watched *her,* studying her like a lab rat. Soon the princess was giggling and throwing grapes at the men. When the giggles subsided, she became aroused. Unabashedly, she moved her hand underneath her robe and rubbed herself between her legs.

"Touch his chest," the princess called huskily. "Yes, like that. Now lick his nipples. Oh, good boy. That's the way." With her free hands, she cupped one of her breasts.

Jane blushed. She'd nailed the happenings of the night like most of these slaves were probably going to nail Laila. Any minute now, and every single one of them would be orgying.

Oh, gross. She'd just turned the word *orgy* into a verb.

She was just about to excuse herself when the tent flap lifted. A new man, a slave, entered, and he was as naked as the others. He, too, was tall and oiled, though he was lean and lanky. Jane didn't recognize him, and yet, her eyes ate him up. Her heart sped up, her blood heated. Her skin tingled deliciously.

He had hair so pale it was like falling snow. His eyes. were as black as a stormy night, and thickly lined with kohl. He was probably five-ten, his shoulders a little narrow, and his belly flat, almost concave. His skin was bronzed to a mochalike shimmer.

There was an almost feminine sense of gentleness about him. A gentleness that didn't seem to fit the hard gleam of his eyes, as if it were a winter coat that belonged to someone else.

Like Jane had done, he paused in the doorway to take everything in. Anger flared his nostrils. Hate wafted from him, then desire. True desire, overshadowing everything else. He sniffed, gaze panning, then locking on her. He was striding forward a second later. Then he stilled, catching himself.

Breath caught in Jane's throat. She might not recognize that face and body, but she recognized that purposeful, powerful stride. Nicolai. He was projecting someone else's image, she knew it.

He was here. He was alive, healthy and whole, she thought, giddy with the knowledge. She should have been upset. He was ruining her plan, putting himself in danger. And yet, she reacted to his nearness…needed him. His body, his blood.

Her eyes widened as she realized what she'd just contemplated. She wanted to drink…his blood?

Oh, yes, she thought, her gaze zeroing in on his vein. She could see the slight fluttering there and wanted to sink her teeth in. Teeth. Was she…? She ran her tongue along the edge of her teeth. They felt the same, no fangs having sprouted unexpectedly. A wave of disappointment hit her.

She hadn't allowed herself to contemplate such an idea because she hadn't wanted to face that very sense of disappointment.

Vampires were not able to turn humans into blood drinkers. She knew because testing their blood, mixing it with human blood, had been one of her experiments. Nothing had happened, nothing had changed.

Hope did not abandon her completely. Nicolai was a little more…*everything* than any other vampire she'd known, so if anyone could change her, it was him. And she wanted to change. Wanted to live as long as he would.

"Oh, there he is," Laila said. "My special slave. Come here, darling boy. Let me show you off to my sister."

At first, Nicolai did not obey. Jane was glad. She didn't want him anywhere near the princess and her slutty hands. And if the princess *dared* to put those hands on him, Jane couldn't be held responsible for her actions. Actions that would involve the removal of the offending appendages.

Nicolai kicked into gear, and all too soon he stood between the lounges. He bowed his head, subservient.

"So pretty," Laila cooed. "Isn't he pretty, Odette?"

"Yes," she managed to choke out.

Laila sat up and petted his chest.

You are going to die, bitch. Jane fisted her hands on her thighs, her nails cutting, drawing blood.

"I found him days ago, as I was scouring Delfina to save you. He did not wish to travel with me. At first. He had another love, you know, and wished to remain with him. But I quickly changed your mind, didn't I, precious?"

His eyes narrowed, but he offered no reply. Not so subservient, after all.

Petting, petting, the bitch was still petting him. Jane was reaching out before she could stop herself, wrapping her fingers around Laila's wrist and squeezing. "I want him."

Triumph filled those green eyes. "Well, you can't have him. He's mine."

"Laila—"

"No. Do you recall when I wanted *your* slave, and you would not share?"

So. That's what this night was about. Tempting Jane, then denying her. "Let me explain something to you,

Laila. I am older than you. Which means I am the future queen. *Your* future queen. What I want, I get. Even if that 'what' belongs to you." She might not know Delfina law, but she knew the construction of a matriarchal culture, as well as social hierarchy.

In the end, top dog always won. Right now, Jane was top dog.

"You—you—"

"Can do anything I want, yes." Jane tossed the girl's hand into her lap. "So don't you dare touch him. I've claimed rights. Do you understand?"

Bright red spots of color bloomed on Laila's cheeks. "Mother will have something to say about this."

"Yes, and I'm sure it will be 'job well done.'" Jane pushed to her feet, standing beside Nicolai. She curbed the urge to link their hands, to bury her head in the hollow of his neck, and simply breathe him in. "Bottom line. She's not here. Is she?"

"No." The color spread to Laila's nape.

"And that means…"

"Your word is law," Laila gritted out. "Very well. I will let you have him without a fight. *If* he wishes to belong to you. Darling," she said, standing and peering deep into his eyes.

Magic crackled between them.

Jane experienced a momentary wave of nervousness. Could Nicolai be entranced, or whatever Laila was doing to him? "That's enough," she barked.

Laila ignored her. "Tell my sister how much you desire me, precious. Tell her whose body you crave."

His lips compressed into a thin line.

"Tell her! Now."

Even the harp and violin drowned out, overshadowed

by the thud of Jane's heartbeat. Then Nicolai shook his head and said, "I desire the princess Odette," and the world outside their circle reentered her awareness.

A shocked gasp. An angry growl. "No. No, you lie."

"Why would he lie?" Jane demanded.

Laila's narrowed gaze swung to her. "What did you do to him? How did you steal his affections from me? *What did you do?*" she screeched.

"She did nothing. I simply want her." There was enough truth in Nicolai's voice to prove his claim.

"I will—" Laila raised her hand, either to hit Nicolai or cast a spell.

Either way, Jane didn't care. She grabbed on to the bitch's wrist a second time. "You haven't yet learned the concept of the phrase *my property*. Touch him, and you'll regret it."

Several seconds passed before Laila schooled her features and dropped her arm to her side. She released a shuddering breath. "You're different, Odette. You never treated me this shabbily before."

Jane shrugged, as if unconcerned, but deep inside she trembled. "Near-death experiences have a way of leaving their mark. Good night, sister dear." Finally she claimed Nicolai's hand and ushered him out of the tent, hurrying to hers.

Rhoslyn had taken her at her word, and had not remained to see to her needs. Jane and Nicolai were alone.

She whirled to face him. He'd dropped the mask, and she could see his dark, shaggy hair, his bright silver eyes. His towering height, wide shoulders and rock-solid strength. Her desire intensified, burning through her.

"We have much to discuss," he said. He cupped her

cheeks, his grip strong and sure. "But first, I need you. I missed you more than I can say." And then he wasn't saying anything at all. He was kissing her hungrily, and she was kissing him back.

CHAPTER SEVENTEEN

NICOLAI WRAPPED JANE in his arms, taking her passion and returning it with equal measure. He'd nearly dropped to his knees the moment he'd spotted her, perched beside his enemy, in danger but alive. Relief, yes, he'd experienced that emotion. Fury, that, too. Laila had been within his reach, his to kill.

Fear had accompanied the fury, however. He'd felt the magical spell protecting the bitch from physical injury, and returning whatever violence was dished to the one doing the attacking.

If he'd gone for her throat…if Jane *had*…

They would have died.

Didn't happen. Jane's safe now.

Laila must know Nicolai was coming for her, or she would not have cast the spell. A spell most witches avoided. No one could hurt her, it was true, but no one could help her, either. If she injured herself accidentally, the spell would turn on *her,* seeing her as the threat. She would not only suffer with her injury, she would suffer a hundredfold with the magic.

"Nicolai," Jane rasped.

He'd feared she would not recognize him, that he would have to steal Laila's ability to hypnotize to force her to leave with him. Something he hadn't known he could succeed in doing, not with Laila's spell waiting to strike. He should have had more faith in his woman. Jane was as aware of him as he was of her. The face he wore didn't matter.

"Yes, sweetheart." The sweetness of her scent infused with his cells. Her decadent taste filled his mouth. His blood heated, and every muscle in his body hardened, anticipating her touch.

"What did you…do with the…real slave?" Her tongue licked at his each time she paused to breathe.

"Set him free." In more ways than one. Laila had scrambled the poor man's brain, until he hadn't known up from down, left from right, making herself the only tangible thing in his world, forcing him to cling to her.

Nicolai could have simply chained the poor man for the night and hidden him, but he'd thought, *That could have been me.* He'd used his own abilities to break through and remind the man of who he was and who he loved, removing Laila from the equation.

"Nice." Jane's hold tightened on him, nearly breaking his ribs. Worth it, he thought. "Shouldn't we…escape, while we…have the chance?"

"No. When the princess sleeps, I can invade her dreams, force her to hurt herself." Another ability he possessed. "Then we'll leave. Return to Elden." Each sentence was punctuated with a deep, wet kiss that rocked him to his soul.

"So we need to do something to pass the time, huh?" Jane returned her full attention to his tongue, sucking and rolling it with her own. Her hands slid through his hair, her nails scraping his scalp and leaving their mark.

He loved that she accepted his need for vengeance so easily. He loved that she clung to him, as desperate for closer contact as he was. But nothing would ever be close enough, not for either of them. He loved that she was smarter than he, and sometimes got lost in her own thoughts.

He just loved…her. Yes, he realized. He did. He loved her. He'd fallen in love with her soon after she first appeared in his world. They'd been strangers, but they'd soon bonded. From the bond, caring had sprung. From the caring, love. But the desire…oh, the desire had always been there.

A glimmer of resentment in his chest. Not directed at her, but to the vampire who had cursed her. Nicolai could never tell her how he felt. She might return the sentiment and vanish.

"I missed you. So much," he said, willing to confess that much but no more. "The separation was like being stabbed." Over and over again, the wound and pain never ending.

"I missed you, too." She kissed and nipped a path along his jaw, his neck, licking and laving. "Where'd you go?"

"Elden."

"Home?"

"Yes."

"Me, too."

"What?" He disengaged from the erotic contact, and peered down at her. "Home *home?*"

She refused to stop. With a little leap, she was back in his arms and sucking on his pulse. "Yes, home home. My world."

Nicolai cupped her chin, forcing her to still, to look at him. Her eyes were glazed with passion, her lids at half-mast. His heart constricted at such a lovely sight. A shake of his head was required to put him back on track. "Let me be clear on this. You left my world and returned to yours."

"Yes."

He'd almost lost her again. And he'd had no idea! "How did you get back?" he croaked.

A secret smile played at the edges of her lips. One that burned through him, deepening his arousal. "Apparently, when you gave me your blood, you gave me your ability to teleport, too."

Dark Abyss. He had never considered that possibility. Maybe because he'd only ever shared his blood with his father, and his father had already possessed some of Nicolai's abilities.

"And you came back to me." He'd never been one to see fate's hand in his life, but now...if Jane hadn't been injured by the ogres, he wouldn't have given her his blood. If he hadn't given her his blood, he wouldn't have found a way to tie her to his side for the rest of their lives.

"I'll always come back to you."

A heavy weight lifted from his shoulders. The curse had somehow lost its power over her. Otherwise, she would have remained in her world.

He traced his thumbs over her cheekbones. "I've told you this before, but I want you to listen closely. I don't care if I have a thousand betrothed females waiting on me. You are all that matters." He would have only one woman. This woman. Forever.

He swooped back down, plunging his tongue past her teeth and into the sweet recesses of her mouth. She welcomed him with a moan.

He'd been cold and detached with females most of his life. Oh, he'd treated his mother and sister as the treasures they were, but everyone else he had never even given a second thought. He'd been a prince, and they his due. Or so he'd convinced himself.

Fate, he mused again. Had he not been a slave, desperate to escape, he might have treated Jane the same way. And that would have been a shame, to never have known her and the nuances of her personality. Unselfish, brave, stronger than anyone he knew, capable and honorable.

Honorable. Yes. He would never have to wonder where he stood with her. She would always tell him, whether he was a prince or a pauper. She would never be intimidated by him, would always challenge him.

"I want you naked." He tugged at the shoulder straps of her robe, shoving the material to the floor. In seconds, emerald material pooled at her feet. He lifted her out of it, and settled her more firmly against his body. Skin-to-skin. Finally.

Every time she exhaled, their chests rubbed together, and he thrilled at the contact. She was hot and silky against him. Her nipples were beaded, rasping against the fine mat of hair he possessed. His shaft pressed to both their bellies, moisture seeping from the tip. He arched his hips, creating a delicious glide.

She arched to meet him, the friction sparking exquisitely. "I can't ever get enough of you."

"Good." He traced his hands down the ridges of her spine, loving the goose bumps that jumped up to meet him. He cupped her ass. "No panties?"

"None were given to me."

"I'm glad." If he had his way, she'd never wear them again.

"I—I want you. Now."

"You've got me. Nothing will separate us, Jane. Do you understand?"

Her breath hitched. She toyed with the ends of his hair. "I think so, yes."

"Know so. I don't want to lose you. I *can't* lose you. I want to wed you. To be with you always. I choose you, Jane. Over my crown, my people and my vengeance."

Tears welled in her eyes, creating amber pools. Nicolai tensed, waiting, unsure in a way he'd never been before.

"Just as I choose you," she said brokenly.

Thank the gods. He would have dropped to his knees and begged if necessary. "I want to be your family."

"You are."

A soft touch along his check. Jane's expression was so tender, tears filled *his* eyes.

"Jane. I love you." No reason to deny it now. "I want to show you. Let me show you."

Her mouth fell open on a gasp. "You…you love me? I mean, I know you mentioned marriage, but this is the first you've said of love and I…I…"

"I love you. With all my heart."

"Oh, Nicolai." She threw herself at him, laughing and crying at the same time. "I love you, too. So much."

Hearing her declaration was like stepping into a warm ray of the sun after an eternity spent in the cold darkness of winter. Something he hadn't known he needed, but now that he had it, he knew he couldn't live without it.

He drew her down to the floor. Her nipples were flushed and rosy, and he couldn't resist. He circled one with his tongue, flicked it until she moaned, then moved to the other. His fangs extended and ached. Now wasn't the time to indulge in the delight that was her blood, however. He'd fed before coming to her, hoping to dull his hunger for her.

No other blood had ever affected him the way Jane's did. So powerful, so consuming. And while he wanted his memory back in full *now,* he would rather not disappear without warning again and have to track his woman's location, leaving her in danger.

Danger she could handle, as she'd proven over and over again.

He eased up to study her. That honey-colored hair was spread around her shoulders, her eyes glazed and ravenous. She chewed on her bottom lip as she glided her hands along the roped planes of his stomach. She was a wanton sight, a goddess come from the heavens.

He rose to his knees and guided her legs apart. So wet, so pink. He wanted to dive in, both with his mouth and with his cock. Sweat was already sheening his brow, his cells like little knives in his veins, demanding he take her, claim her. His woman. Now, always.

Not yet, not yet.

He had to prepare her. The first time they had sex, he'd hurt her. Not that she'd protested. She'd been too tight, and he'd been too eager. Not this time. This time she would enjoy every second.

He traced a finger up her hot center and she jerked as if struck by lightning.

"Yes!" She fisted her hands on the rug beneath her, and lifted her hips.

With the movement, his finger slid inside her of its own accord. Those inner walls closed around him, squeezing. He could have spilled then and there. *Breathe, damn it.* He worked that finger in and out, in and out, until she was writhing, mindless, gasping his name. Then he worked in a second finger. In and out, in and out.

Soon she was moaning every few seconds, rolling her hips in circles, seeking his thumb on her center. He gave it to her. For a moment. She cried out in relief—and then groaned in distress when he took the pressure away.

A third finger joined the other two, in and out, in and out. Stretching her, spreading that sweet, sweet dew. When her muscles tensed, ready to lock down in climax, he severed all contact.

"Please!" she shouted.

Such a succulent entreaty. He used the hand wet with her juices on his cock, slicking himself up. He closed his eyes in ecstasy, loving the pressure as much as Jane had. Needing it. He stroked up…down.…

"Oh, no, you don't." Her legs wound around his back, her ankles locking just above his ass; she tugged him down. Without anything to balance him, he fell on top of her. She gasped when his weight hit. "Please, Nicolai. Do it."

"Yes," he rasped. He couldn't wait a second more, either.

He guided his tip to her entrance and thrust, deep and sure. They cried out in unison. Then she was coming, clenching around him, driving his need higher… higher. More, he had to have more. Wanted to bite her, wouldn't let himself bite her.

Instead, he sank his fangs into his own wrist. Blood laced his tongue. Blood still flavored with Jane. He wanted to suck, but he forced himself to release his vein and hold the wound over Jane's mouth.

"Drink," he commanded. They would do this every day. Would never risk her losing the ability to move between worlds.

Obeying, she closed her eyes. She looked as if she were…savoring? Oh, gods above, she was. The very idea sent his need soaring. His testicles drew up tight. Any moment now, he would explode. He wanted her with him, though, all the way.

"Harder, Jane," he said, even as he increased the speed of his thrusts. He hit her so damned deep, making her gasp, but she never stopped drinking, and soon her hips were once again rising up to meet him. She was gulping greedily, moaning with every swallow.

My woman. Mine.

Maybe he'd shouted the words. "Yes," Jane responded, inner walls closing tighter and tighter around him as her second orgasm rocked her. "Yours."

This time, there was no holding back. She milked him, and he gave her every drop, shooting it inside her.

They clung together for several minutes, hours, years, shivering and shuddering until finally sagging to the floor. He couldn't quite catch his breath, couldn't quite form a rational thought, but even then he knew he didn't want to hurt her and rolled to his side.

"I thought I was turning into a vampire, then convinced myself I wasn't," she said sleepily. "But I must be. Your blood…it tastes so damn good. I've been craving it, like a drug. And now that I've had more of it—" she shivered "—I feel so *good.*"

He frowned. He hadn't known such a thing was possible. Unlike the nightwalkers, he was a living being, born rather than created. Making others simply wasn't—hadn't been—possible.

Besides, even if he'd wanted to share his blood with others, which he hadn't, his human lovers had not wanted to drink from him. In fact, they had found the very idea disgusting. Same with the witches, and same with the shifters, though their objections had stemmed more from contamination of the species.

"You crave all blood or just mine?" he asked.

"Just yours. Though the thought of drinking from others isn't as abhorrent as it should be."

"Any other symptoms?" He liked the thought of sharing this with her, but the complications scared him to his soul.

"My skin is a little more sensitive than normal. More sensitive than yours, I think. But, if I'm becoming a vampire, a heightened sensitivity would make sense because I haven't yet had time to adjust."

How many other humans would tell him that becoming a vampire "makes sense"? He almost smiled. Almost.

He would have to teach her how to feed, just in case they were parted for any amount of time. He tensed at the thought of her mouth on someone else. *It's the only way.* Cutting through a vein was not a skill you developed naturally, but one you had to learn.

"How do you feel about changing?" he asked.

"A little afraid. A little excited."

"Tell me if you experience any other signs."

"I will."

He kissed her temple. "Rest now, sweetheart. I'll wake you in a few hours."

"And we'll kill Laila?"

See? Jane knew him better than anyone else he'd ever known. "Yes. We'll kill Laila." He wondered if he could draw Jane into the dream, guarding her, preventing Laila from lashing at her while she was defenseless.

"Good." Her warm sigh caressed his skin as she snuggled more firmly against him. "I love you."

"I love you, too."

She fell asleep, and he began to plan their future together, ignoring a sudden and intense sense of foreboding.

CHAPTER EIGHTEEN

THEY DRESSED QUICKLY, quietly, and Jane packed a little bag of necessities. Such as the book—Nicolai had been overjoyed to see it—a few robes, snacks and a canteen of water. Laila had not brought any weapons for Odette to use, a fact that disappointed Jane but didn't surprise her.

"How are you going to invade her dreams?" she asked Nicolai.

"I'll tell you all about it." He moved in front of her and gripped her shoulders. Once again he wore the slave's mask. "When I'm done."

She knew what that meant—he would be in danger—and her answer was hell, no. "I'm going with you."

He sighed as if he'd expected such a response and had already resigned himself to it. "I do want to take you into the dream with me, and I will try to do so. Having never done something like that before, I don't know if it will work. Meanwhile, I want you to stay here."

"Why?"

He flicked his tongue over an incisor. "If I can't force her to harm herself, I'll have to absorb her powers. All of her powers and all the spells she has cast upon herself."

Jane's eyes widened. "You can do that?"

A stiff nod. "Most likely I will have to go that route.

I tried to invade her dreams while you were sleeping and encountered an unexpected resistance. If the resistance is still there, while I'm in close proximity to her, I'll have to do something to lower her guard to steal her magic. Something…nonviolent."

She began to understand, and wanted to throw up. Or maybe throw a punch. "Like…kissing her?" Or more?

Another nod, this one barely discernable.

"You can't just stab her?" she asked hopefully.

"Not without dying myself. She's cast a spell that causes any injury I attempt to inflict on her to be directed at myself."

"Okay, so that's out." Jane nibbled on her bottom lip, felt the cuts already there and realized she had been doing a lot of nervous chewing lately. "That explains the power I felt wafting from her, I guess."

"You felt that?"

"Yep." She squared her shoulders. "And okay, fine. If you have to kiss her, you have to kiss her. And believe me, I do not envy you. That's taking one for the team a little far. I mean, I think I'd rather endure the stabbing myself instead of having to kiss her."

He nearly choked on a laugh. "This is not funny, Jane."

"I know." But she'd much rather he laugh than worry over her reaction. "As long as you survive, I'm good with the plan. Please tell me you'll be able to hurt her once you absorb her powers."

"Yes." Absolute determination radiated from him. "I will."

"Then I guess sticking your tongue down the devil's throat has a nice enough payoff." She punched him in the arm. "Good luck, tiger."

He laughed again, this time far less strained. "Thank you. Now. Will you please stay here?"

"Nope, sorry. I may not possess any magic of my own, but Laila still assumes I'm Odette. You might need me. Therefore, I'm sticking to your side as if I've been glued there."

A moment passed in silence, then another. Finally he pinched the bridge of his nose. "All right. You may come with me. If things do not progress as I hope, you are to run to Elden, and search out the prince Dayn. Trust no one else. Tell him you belong to me. Tell him you are my betrothed."

How sad he suddenly sounded. At the thought of losing her? "And he'll believe me?" Not that she would leave. She wouldn't, not for any reason. They *would* be together.

"I've marked you, so yes. Yes, he will. He is a blood drinker, like me."

When he turned away, she grabbed his arm. A puny move but one that worked all the same. "You found your brother?"

"Not yet. I have a feeling you will succeed where I have failed."

Again, he went to leave. Again, she held on to him. "So you *are* a prince?"

"Yes," he repeated. "The crown prince, destined to rule all of Elden."

This time, he remained in place, awaiting her response. She released him and shrugged. "That explains *a lot.*"

He blinked down at her. "That's all you have to say on the subject?"

"Yeah." He was royalty. So what? Everyone had a flaw.

She bent down, grabbed the strap of her pack and hefted the heavy thing onto her shoulder. The cord dug into her muscle, but she didn't allow herself to wince. Nicolai would take the burden upon himself, and he needed his hands free.

"Just don't expect me to be all humble and obey your every whim. That's not going to happen. So are we doing this or what?"

His lashes fused, hiding his irises, as he leaned down, wrapped her in his arms and kissed her, softly, sweetly, a tender lover expressing his gratitude. For what? she wondered, then she forgot the question. Her lips tingled. Their tongues met briefly, and she tasted him. Wanted more. Always, she wanted more.

He straightened and sighed. "I do not want her magic affecting you, Jane. If I fail and she turns on you—"

"Sticks and stones may break my bones, but I might be a vampire so I don't give a shit. I'll heal."

His brow knitted with confusion and anger. "No one will be breaking your bones."

She patted his cheek. "I believe I've already told you that I'm going with you and that's final. Stop trying to talk me out of it."

Maybe he could feel her determination. Maybe he hated the thought of being apart as much as she did. Either way, his hands left her and he nodded. "Stubborn baggage."

"I'll take that to mean *delightful female*."

"You'd be right." He twined their fingers and ushered her outside, into the night. The moon was hidden behind thick, dark clouds, the air cool and moist. A storm must be brewing.

There was a campfire crackling a few feet away, casting golden rays and heat, but no guards around it. Actually, there was no sign of life anywhere. Not even in front of Laila's tent. Jane knew men patrolled the perimeter, however. She could hear their hearts beating. *Thump-thump. Thump-thump.*

"Something's off," Jane said.

"I know," Nicolai replied, his voice flat.

"She should have guards in front of her tent. Why did she send them away?"

"She must be expecting me."

Could they never catch a break? "We should leave. Come back another day. If she knows who you are, she'll attack."

"Oh, yes, she will." His voice was still flat, but resolve gave it a dangerous edge. "We may be giving her too much credit. She may not know, may only suspect. Either way, she dies tonight."

He spoke like a man who knew he didn't have a lot of time. Jane recalled his need to return to Elden. A physical need that was slowly killing him, he'd said. Perhaps that was the case here.

So, when he strode the short distance and swept inside the tent without pause, Jane made no protests. Lanterns were still lit, and her eyes adjusted instantly. Unlike earlier, no slaves danced in the center.

To her consternation, Laila was not asleep on her bed. She still lounged on her chaise, sipping from a goblet. Waiting.

"Finally," she said casually. She stroked the timepiece hanging around her neck. A timepiece that had not been there earlier. "And now I have my answers."

"About?" Nicolai shoved Jane behind him.

She placed her hands on his back, felt the muscles knot.

Fury colored Laila's expression for a split second before she smoothed her features. "You'll stay where you are, slave. And believe me, you won't be able to move from one location to another with only a thought, so don't even try."

Had she used her magic to root him in place? Jane moved beside him—and yes, that was exactly what Laila'd done, she realized as her own feet became as heavy as boulders. Laila hadn't moved, hadn't even blinked, yet somehow she'd used her magic.

Dread blasted through her, little bombs that spread their poison quickly. "Mother will be very disappointed in you," she said.

"Will she?" Laila smiled, shifting her attention to Jane. "Or will she be proud of me for destroying an imposter?"

Breathe, just breathe.

"Earlier, when I had that human female killed, I felt your upset and disgust. I wondered why. That is not something my sister ever felt. Then, I felt someone digging through my powers. I wondered who, but I didn't cast a spell to stop—or hurt—the person, because I also wondered what they wanted. Imagine my surprise when they—he—chose my magic mirror."

She wouldn't ask. Couldn't. Not yet.

"Then, imagine my further surprise when my very loyal slave ceased to desire me. The same way another slave of mine ceased to desire me."

"Nicolai never desired you," Jane spat.

Laila shrugged, unconcerned. "He never desired you, either. In fact, I think he was relieved when I took over his care. Then, suddenly, you return from the grave, and he can't tear his eyes away from you. He yearns for you, abducts you. Not to use you as a shield, but because he can't bear to be away from you. Something was wrong, and I knew it. Now, I know what that something is."

"And just what do you know?" Nicolai asked as calmly as if they were having Sunday brunch and discussing the next day's forecast.

Jane looked up at him. He'd dropped the mask. There was his dark hair, his silver eyes. His wide shoulders, his muscles stretching the fabric of his dark blue robe. A beautiful man she would protect with her own life.

"The woman beside you is not my sister," Laila said. "Her name is Jane, correct?"

Breathe. "I am Odette. You can't prove otherwise."

"Really? Well, perhaps you are right." Anger laced the princess's tone, the words as sharp as daggers. "Once, I could look through the eyes of others. Now that ability has been taken from me. No matter, though. I remembered how Nicolai used to talk to someone inside his cell. A woman. Jane. No one else could see her. We assumed him insane." She laughed smugly, and even her humor sliced. "But your name is Jane, I would bet, and you are human."

Jane could feel the fury pulsing off of Nicolai. "Perhaps you're the insane one."

Laila unfolded from the chair and stood. Her gaze swung to Nicolai. "Oh, no, you don't, slave. As you can tell, I've cast a spell to prevent you from stealing any more of my powers. While the two of you…frolicked, I fortified my magic." Had he tried?

"Except," he said with a smile of his own, all white and lethal, "any powers you use are mine to use, as well. That, you cannot prevent from happening."

"No, you can't…" Laila screeched. She'd tried to step toward them, but her foot had stopped midair.

"Yes, I can. Holding you in place doesn't harm you physically, and, in fact, saves you from my claws. So you should be happy. Your protective spell is working."

"Release me, or I will scream for the guards."

He arched a brow, taunting her. "And you think they'll believe you concerning Odette? They won't, and we both know it. Your only chance is to release her. Do it, and we'll talk. You and I. Alone."

"Right. Because I'm a fool."

"Well…" Jane said.

Laila scowled at her, but continued. "Vow that you won't try to kill me or use the powers that I use, and I'll consider it."

Nicolai opened his mouth to reply, probably to agree, but Jane stopped him. "I'm not going anywhere. I don't care what the two of you decide." And as soon as she was able, she was taking a crash course in Magic 101. She wanted to know the rules. What a witch could and couldn't do. She wanted to know how to stop them. How to defeat them.

"How about this, Nicolai," Laila said, smiling again. "We'll find out what kind of damage I can do to your Jane without ever taking a step."

A moment later, Jane felt as if her head was about to explode. She cried out, clutched her ears, felt warm drops of blood spill onto her palms. Her entire world focused on her throbbing brain, and she lost sight of everything around her.

Her knees buckled, but her feet were still locked into the rug-covered floor. She could only crouch, screaming and crying and praying for death. An eternity seemed to pass. But then, the pain stopped just as suddenly as it had hit her.

Gradually she became aware of her surroundings and realized *Laila* was now screaming.

Nicolai, Jane thought distantly. Nicolai must have stolen her ability to squeeze minds—or whatever she'd done—and was using it against the princess. But he was grunting, too, as if the pain was exploding through him.

Laila's screams ceased abruptly. Nicolai quieted a second later.

The only sound to be heard were panting, labored breaths. Jane tried to stand, but didn't have the strength. She saw that her bag had fallen and rested a few inches away. She was soaked with sweat, her robe seemingly a hundred pounds heavier.

She managed to turn her head and glance up at Nicolai. He wasn't looking at her, but at Laila, his eyes narrowed, hatred radiating from him.

"You saw what I saw," Laila gritted out. "Your precious human studied your kind. Cut them up, hurt them. Tell me, were they your friends?"

Oh, no, Jane thought. No, no, no. Somehow he'd known she had researched and done experiments on his kind, but he hadn't known the identities of her victims. *Had* she hurt one of his friends?

"Do you still wish to protect her?" Laila demanded. "Do you still wish to be her lover?"

Silence.

Such heavy silence.

Please don't tell me you knew any of them. If he had, he would hate her.

"What do you want, princess?" Nicolai said, his voice devoid of all emotion.

A knot grew in Jane's throat, practically cutting off her air. He did. He hated her. She needed to apologize, to explain, but couldn't do so here, now.

He can't hate you. He loves you. He'll forgive you. Eventually. She hoped.

Laila's chin lifted, triumph flashing through her eyes. Such cruel green eyes. "I want you to bind yourself to me. Forever."

He snorted. "No. What do I gain in return? Nothing."

"I'll allow you to kill the girl." She motioned to Jane with a wave of her hand.

Acid burned a hole in her stomach.

"I'll kill her," he said, matter-of-fact, "but I don't need to enslave myself to do it."

Oh, God. Jane had become one of his enemies, his hated, must-be-destroyed-at-any-cost enemies. "Nicolai. Please. I'm so, so sorry."

He didn't deign to look at her. Just held up his hand to silence her. "I took your memories. *Me.* I wanted you to save me. So, as you can see, I never truly wanted you. Only what you could do for me. Save your apologies."

He'd…what? Why would he…?

Everything rushed back, as if a glass cage had been shattered inside her mind. They had talked, they had shared. Discovered that she was cursed. He'd known that forcing her to cross over, to save him, would endanger him. For that very reason, she had refused. He'd taken her memory and forced her to do it.

At the time, she'd thought she would resent him. Instead, she was glad he'd done it. Glad she'd helped him, freed him, made love with him. She even understood his reasoning. When she had been bed bound, she had tried to bargain with God for freedom. In that state of mind, you did things. Things you weren't always proud of.

Why hadn't she returned home permanently, though, as the curse dictated? She loved him. She should have lost him already.

Or was his hatred the thing that would keep them apart, not her absence? Her stomach somersaulted.

"*I'll* kill her, then," Laila said.

"With magic?" Nicolai laughed. "Please do. Then I'll have the power to kill *you*."

"Not if I kill you, *then* the girl."

"You don't want me dead, princess. You want me pliant." His head tilted to the side. "Why did you bury *my* memories? Not of the girl, but of everything else. I know why you blocked my powers, but the memories…"

A smug gleam entered her eyes. "You want to know, fine. I'll tell you. I'm not the beast you think me, you know."

He crossed his arms over his chest.

"You appeared at the slave market in Delfina, and everyone assumed you were a Prince Nicolai look-alike. Everyone wanted to buy you. Me, Odette. The wealthy, the poor. Only Odette and I knew you truly were Prince Nicolai of Elden, crown prince, vampire, powerful beyond imagining." Again, she stroked the timepiece. "You fought wildly and managed to slay several people who simply approached you to study you closer. Then, you escaped."

His eyes widened ever so slightly, an involuntary reaction Jane was sure. She figured he hadn't recalled that part of his life yet. She wanted to reach out to him, but feared he would reject her.

"Odette had set you free, after blocking your powers. She wanted you away from the market, away from the prying eyes of others. News had just come from Elden that the king and queen had been slain."

A sharp intake of breath was Nicolai's only response. How Jane ached for him.

"As you can guess, Odette wouldn't have freed you if she had no way of capturing you. Yet still you proved elusive. She nearly succeeded a dozen times, because you kept trying to return to Elden, yet you always found a way to abandon her. When she at last caught you, she scoured the depths of your mind. You might not have witnessed the event, but you knew. You had heard the news, as we had, and magic had filled in the rest."

"Tell me," he rasped.

"In a bid to gain control of the lands, the Blood Sorcerer attacked. Your mother and father lay dying, and each cast a spell. Your mother, to send you away to safety. Your father, to fill you with a need for vengeance."

Jane could feel Nicolai's fury growing…sharpening.…

"Odette couldn't allow you to keep trying to return," Laila went on. "Nor could she allow you to search for your brothers and sister. Had they known you still lived, they would have come for you. So, they had to think you were dead, slain with your parents. That way, no one would ever come to your rescue."

His hands fisted.

"And now," Laila went on, "now it's too late."

"What do you mean?" he gritted out.

"Twenty years have passed since the Blood Sorcerer attacked the palace."

"No." He shook his head, once, twice. "No."

"Oh, yes." A fleeting smile. "You were as unaware of the passage of time as you were of your past. Odette made sure of it." Laila lifted her chin. "So. How about this for a bargain? I will help you defeat the Blood Sorcerer, *if* you kill the human. Right here, right now."

"And forget the crimes *you* have committed against me?" he seethed.

At least he hadn't accepted right away, Jane thought darkly, dryly. That he would turn on her so savagely… she could not forgive. Unless this was a trick. Unless he meant to gain Laila's trust.

Hope eternal.

"It's either that, or I let the healer wipe your memory once again. We've had to do so several times, you know."

Tighter and tighter those hands curled. "You would trust me not to hurt you?"

"No. You will take a blood oath not to. *Before* I release you, and after you kill the girl."

Jane gulped, her mouth going dry.

This time, Nicolai didn't hesitate. "Very well. Release us from your magical hold, and I vow never to kill or hurt you. Help me slay my enemy, and I…I will kill the girl."

CHAPTER NINETEEN

SUDDENLY JANE'S FEET were freed. Nicolai snaked out an arm, catching her before she could bolt. Not that she would have. Or, yeah. She would have. Actually, even with his grip, she still could. All she had to do was disappear. To disappear, all she had to do was think of her home.

As the man she loved tugged her closer…closer… panic took over, her thoughts too chaotic to tame. Then, an unexpected calm took hold of her. This *was* the man she loved. The man who claimed to love her. The man who *did* love her. He might be angry with her—furious, even—but he wouldn't kill her.

This *was* a trick to trap Laila.

He wouldn't ever hurt her. She knew that on a bone-deep level. He was beautiful and wanton, wicked and yet principled. She'd given herself to him body and soul. Now and forever, just as he'd given himself to her. Nothing would change that, not even her past. She trusted him.

Blind trust had never come easily to her. She'd always believed in proof. Testing theories, changing variables and watching reactions, but blind trust was what she was giving her man. He'd come through for her time after time, and he would again.

Yes, she knew there was a dark side to his nature.

Hell, she'd seen him in action on multiple occasions. No matter what, however, he would never turn that dark side on her. So, he had a plan. Pretending to want to kill her was part of it.

"Release me, too, princess," Nicolai said.

"No. Just the girl."

He growled, but that was the only indication he gave that he'd heard her.

Jane couldn't let another moment go by without telling him how she felt. "I'm so sorry, Nicolai. I didn't mean to—"

"Silence." A lash, and yet he gave her the subtlest of nods, as if he wanted her to continue.

Still he dragged her closer, until her body was flush with his. His heat enveloped her, so familiar she relaxed.

"I worked for the government, and yes, I studied your kind, but I never tortured and I never killed. I didn't know you at the time, and I didn't know what I did would hurt you or someone you loved. I just tried to help my people understand what—"

"Be. Quiet." His fangs flashed down at her, but again, he gave her the barest hint of a nod.

"I love you. No matter what happens or what you have to do, I will always love you."

"What are you waiting for?" Laila snapped. "Do it."

Jane could hear the rush of Nicolai's blood. While his expression was calm, stern, his heart beat erratically. He was not as unaffected as he seemed.

He didn't look away from her when he said, "I'm going to drink from her neck, princess. I'm also going to cover her mouth to prevent her from screaming."

"Let her scream," Laila said, anger soothed. "I'll like it."

"I will not have anyone rushing into this tent and watching. Nor do I want you nearing us until she's… dead."

Pretend. This is pretend, she reminded herself. Otherwise, he would have simply swooped down, savagely bit and sucked the life right out of her. Yet, here he stood, arguing with his tormentor, demanding certain concessions.

"Do not tell me what to do, slave. I—"

"Will accept my terms or we are back to where we started."

A pause. Jane drew in a deep breath and tilted her head to the side as she exhaled, giving him easier access to her vein. His eyes widened, his pupils flaring. His fangs lengthened and sharpened a little more.

"I want her on the floor," he croaked. "Release my feet, Laila. You can stop me again if I lunge for you."

Another pause.

"Very well," Laila said on a sigh.

A second later, Nicolai was urging Jane the rest of the way to the ground.

He loomed over her as he had countless other times. Her hair splayed around her shoulders, and her robe sagged.

"Nicolai," she breathed.

"Not another word, Jane." The gold flecks in his eyes seemed to swirl. Down, down he leaned. Breath emerged from her lungs and mouth shallowly. Just as his teeth sank home, he flattened his hand over her mouth.

Her eyes flared. Her body bowed. Warm, electric pleasure entered with his teeth, shooting through every inch of her. He was sucking slowly, so slowly, taking little sips. And his hand…his hand was cut, his blood dripping into her mouth, down her throat and swirling in her belly.

He was feeding her even as he drank from her. His fingers tapped at her cheek, a bid for…something.

She had only to reason this out.

He'd told Laila he would kill her. Therefore, he was pretending to kill her. And any time Jane had spoken up to soften him, he'd told her to shut the hell up but had really wanted her to keep talking. So…he must want her acting panicked and disbelieving while acting un-caring himself.

She tested her theory, struggling against him, giving Laila a show. When Nicolai grunted his approval, she knew beyond any doubt. She pounded her fists into his shoulders, as if trying to shove him away. She bucked, as if trying to dislodge him.

When the wound in his hand closed up, he ground his palm against her teeth to reopen the flesh. Once again, his blood trickled down her throat.

Then, he groaned, sucking a little harder at her vein, drawing a little more blood.

Enough, she thought she heard him say, but that was impossible. His lips were still on her vein. *Enough. You have to stop.* He lifted his head, panting, licked his lips, then dove back down, biting her in a new place. This, too, pumped pleasure straight into her veins.

Careful, careful, careful. Don't take too much. Slow down.

Jane frowned. Nicolai was speaking, but he was doing so straight into her head.

Have to time this just right. Again, his voice drifted through her head. The pressure against her vein eased.

Nicolai?

His body jerked against hers. *Jane?*

Yes. I can hear you, and now I'm guessing you can hear me. How is that possible?

He licked her neck, careful not to let Laila see. *Some blood drinkers share a mental connection.*

"Hurry," the princess snapped.

I need you to kill the princess for me.

Though he wanted the pleasure of doing so, he couldn't. He'd vowed not to. Which meant, someone had to do it for him. So, that was his plan. To have Jane strike the lethal blow.

Consider it done.

Thank you. A pause. *I'm sorry for what I did to you. Before. And now.*

I'm sorry, too. Her heart skipped a beat.

The princess has lowered her defenses, just as we hoped, and I've absorbed some of her power. The spell that stopped anyone from hurting her is now mine. She'll still be strong, however, just not as *strong.*

Nicolai didn't drink much more. He even dribbled several mouthfuls of blood down Jane's neck and onto the ground. He was creating a mess, she knew. The illusion of death. She forced her struggles to slow... slow...until sagging limply, arms falling uselessly to her sides. She lay there, breathing as shallowly as possible. So much so she knew not even Nicolai could see the rise and fall of her chest.

Through tiny slits in her eyelids she watched him lift his head. Blood continued to drip from his chin, splashing on her collar and absorbing into her robe. He pressed two fingers into her nape, searching for a pulse. She knew what he felt: a wild, strong beat.

"It's done." Nicolai severed all contact as he stood. "I've done my part. Now you do yours."

"Step away from her," Laila said. "I will check for myself."

He didn't hesitate. He moved to the other side of the tent, away from Jane, away from the princess.

But...just how was she supposed to kill the woman? She had no weapons, and Laila wasn't devoid of all her powers. She could cast a spell in the blink of an eye.

Come on, Parker. Think. Footsteps pattered. Body heat wafted. *Think faster.* Then the creak of bones echoed as Laila crouched. The body heat drew closer... closer...as the princess reached out.

The flicker of an idea presented itself. Dangerous, untested, but the only way. *Nicolai, can she travel with only a thought, like you?* Jane rushed out.

No.

Perfect. Laila's fingers pressed into Jane's neck. Jane opened her eyes, reached up and latched onto her wrist. A gasp of shock sounded. At the same time, Nicolai swooped in and grabbed the timepiece from around Laila's neck.

"Mine," he snapped. "Jane. Now."

"What are you—?" Laila began.

Before the princess could begin casting, Jane closed her eyes and pictured her home—with Laila in it. Now that her mind was calm, her focus cold, it wasn't difficult. She saw her kitchen, experienced a wave of dizziness. Laila struggled against her, but as the dizziness intensified, the struggles slowed. For a moment, Jane felt as if she were floating, and tightened her grip on the princess.

"What are you…what…?" Laila's voice was weak, and Jane could hear an underlay of pain.

"Jane," Nicolai shouted. "Jane! What are you doing?"

When the dizziness left her, when she felt something hard and chilled pressing into her back, she looked around. She and Laila were inside her kitchen. Sunlight streamed in through the window, burning her so badly she actually sizzled. She rolled away with a hiss of pain, seeking the shade.

Nicolai hadn't teleported with Jane that night in the forest, but then, he hadn't been operating at full tilt. Most of his abilities had still been locked away. Tonight, he'd been like a powder keg—and so was Jane.

She stopped, flat on her back, Laila still in a crouch. The princess was pallid, sweating and…falling. She hit the floor, face-first.

Jane meant to leap away, grab a knife. That's the reason she'd brought the witch here. Suddenly she could scent Laila's blood. It wasn't an altogether pleasant smell, and yet hunger twisted her stomach. Such raw, consuming hunger.

Before she realized she'd even moved, she was angled toward the princess, her teeth sinking into her vein. Only a trickle of blood met her tongue. Frustration clawed at her. She angled her head, bit again. Again, only a trickle. She lifted, found the princess's pulse with her gaze, then swooped back down. This time, the blood flowed like a newly awakened river.

She should have had to chew to get what she wanted, a thought that grossed her out, but her gums were aching terribly, and her teeth—fangs?—had slid right in.

Warm, rushing life continued to fill her mouth. She

moaned, dug her teeth in deeper, sucked harder, replenishing what she'd lost.

She must have hit a nerve because Laila came out of her faint with a jolt, and tried to push Jane away. She tightened her hold, gulping and gulping and gulping. Soon, Laila ceased struggling. Went as limp as a rag. Jane continued to drink, physically unable to pull herself from the drug that was this woman's blood. Drug, yes. Because, with the blood, something else, something warmer, almost…fizzy, rushed through her.

Her cells practically exploded with energy.

Stop, you have to stop. If she took any more, she would kill the princess. She could hear the distant *thump-thump* of a heartbeat, and knew it was slowing, almost beyond repair. The flow of blood was trickling off, thinning.

I don't want to stop. I brought her here to kill her. Stopping defeats the purpose.

But in the back of her mind, she knew—somehow, as if the memory were not her own—that to kill this way was to live this way. One death would not be enough. She would drain everyone she drank from. Always. No one would be safe from her. Not even Nicolai.

Nicolai.

Panting, she jerked her teeth out of Laila. She flicked her tongue and, sure enough, she had fangs.

Nicolai had made her a vampire.

With a shaky hand, she brushed the hair from her face. When she caught sight of that hand in the light, she gasped.

She…glowed. Bright, golden, white lightning exploded from her skin. And the crackling in her veins… she felt like she could do *anything*. Until she moved her hand into a ray of that sunlight and started sizzling. She groaned with pain, her arm falling to her side.

Note to self: avoid the sun.

Another thing of note: *You're here for a reason. Don't forget.*

As if she could.

She leaped up and, knowing exactly where her knives were, grabbed one, careful to remain in the shadows. As she peered down at the woman who had enslaved Nicolai, taken away his rights, abused him physically and sexually—for over twenty years!—she found that she couldn't stab her. Couldn't kill the bitch that way, either.

Death would be too easy for Laila. *You have to do* something. *When she wakes up, she'll use her magic against you.*

Could she, though? This world was different from Laila's, with different metaphysical laws, different atmospheres. Would her magic work here? Nicolai's ability to cross from one world to the other worked in both places, but while Nicolai could withstand his own sun, he would not be able to withstand Jane's. Proof: she could tolerate his, but not hers. And she'd dealt with this sun all her life.

She wished she had interviewed or dissected a witch—and she didn't care what kind of monster people would think her for such a desire. But one had never been brought to her lab. Could that be because no one had known they were here? Could they not use any of their powers in this world, and were rendered human?

There was one way to find out.

Jane dragged the princess to her bedroom, which was hard to do with her windows and drapes all open, found rope and tied the bitch to the bedposts. Not once did Laila awaken. Jane showered quickly, cleaning off the blood, then dressed in familiar jeans and a T-shirt. Felt odd, wearing her "normal" clothes. Felt…wrong.

Trembling, she threw the robe in the washer. *Nicolai?* she cast out mentally, hoping for a reply. *Are you out there? Are you okay?* Soon as she took care of Laila, she would go back to him.

They hadn't yet bonded fully. Otherwise, neither of them would have been able to drink from others. She wanted to bond fully.

Jane returned to her bedroom, pushed a chair in front of the princess and waited. She wouldn't let herself think about Nicolai yet.

Hours passed, ticking by slowly. Finally, though, Laila cracked open her eyes. She moaned, tugged at her bonds, frowned. Realization jolted her upright—or rather, as much as possible.

"Relax," Jane told her. "I haven't done anything to you that you haven't done to someone else."

"You'll pay for this," Laila snarled.

"And you're stuck here."

A moment passed, then another. Then, suddenly, Jane could hear the woman's voice in her head, as clearly as she'd heard Nicolai's. *What did she do to me? Why can't I use my magic?*

Jane smiled. Well, well. One blessing at least. "You can't use your magic because you're in my world now."

Laila gasped. "How did you know that?" *Oh, great goddess. She has my powers. She has my powers!*

"No, I don't. I am a vampire, though."

"Stop that!" *She's reading my mind, the bitch. I hate*

*her! Now clear your mind. How did she become like
Nicolai?*

"I drank his blood."

"Stop doing that, I said."

Jane chewed on her bottom lip. If she could read
minds, she could go deeper than surface thoughts.
Right?

She focused more intently on Laila's thoughts....
*Have to escape... How do I escape without my powers?
I have to steal my powers back.*

She probed a little deeper. Suddenly she was reliv-
ing the episode on her kitchen floor. Except, she saw
and felt and heard through Laila's senses. Waking up to
untutored fangs in her neck, weakened, unable to use
her powers. Powers she'd relied on her entire life.

She *had* taken the princess's powers, Jane realized.
That was what fizzed inside her veins.

Nicolai could absorb other people's powers, and
when Jane had consumed his blood, she must have developed that ability just like the teleportation.

She probed even deeper. There seemed to be a thousand different voices, a thousand flashes from the girl's
life. She listened and watched for the things concerning
Nicolai... There!

She watched, listened. Hated the princess all over
again.

"*You* wiped Nicolai's mind," she growled as she came
back to the present. She was shaking. "You told him—
and he thought—a healer had done it."

Laila paled. "I'm not saying anything to you."

"You don't have to." Laila had wiped his mind and
bound his powers, then planted a new memory, one of
the healer doing so. She hadn't wanted him to blame

her. She'd also tried to plant suggestions of love and adoration, but while she had manipulated his thoughts, she hadn't been able to manipulate his emotions.

And now I can do so, Jane thought. She wasn't exactly sure how to use the ability, so she latched onto every memory she could, pictured a black box and stuffed them inside, hiding them away.

"What are you doing?" Laila demanded. "Stop... What...why...?"

Jane remained silent. She worked for hours, grabbing and stuffing, grabbing and stuffing. When she finished, the cabin was dark and musty, and her body so weak she had already slid out of her chair.

She met Laila's gaze. A blank gaze. "Who—who are you?" Panic sprouted. "Who am I?"

"Tit for tat," Jane said with a forced smile. When the sun set, she loaded Laila into her car, drove her into the nearest town and dropped her off. She was without powers, memory and money. She would have to place herself at someone else's mercy.

Mercy she might not find.

Jane returned home, pulled on her robe and threw herself on her bed. She pictured the tent where she'd last seen Nicolai, but...nothing happened. She tried again... with the same result.

She tried for hours, the entire night. By morning she was a sobbing mess, weak, sick to her stomach. She couldn't do it. She couldn't return.

The curse had finally kicked in.

CHAPTER TWENTY

THREE DAYS. WITHIN THREE DAYS, Nicolai's full memory was returned.

And now, holding his timepiece, he knew exactly what had happened to his parents. The Blood Sorcerer had launched a sneak attack, going for the king and queen first, allowing his monsters to ravage them. The hideous monsters from Nicolai's nightmares, the ones he'd seen on the castle walkway and inside his bedroom.

Laila had it right. As the pair lay dying, they had cast separate spells. The queen, to send her children away. The king, to spark a need for vengeance. Both spells had bonded with him—and his timepiece. A gift from his parents. All their children had one. Even Micah, the youngest.

Micah, just a baby.

Now, twenty years had passed. Micah was a man. Unless he'd been trapped in a time standstill like Nicolai. And if he still lived.

Nicolai knew Dayn lived. Now that his memory and abilities were restored, so was his mind connection to the other blood drinker in the family. He could hear the turmoil of his brother's thoughts. Could feel the man's desperation.

Breena was out there, too. Rumor was, she was living with Berserkers. An impossibility. Berserkers had been wiped out long ago. So…where was she really?

And Jane…his Jane. Sometimes he could hear her as he heard Dayn. Distantly, the words and emotions muted. *Don't think about her right now. You'll collapse.*

He'd never gotten to tell his beloved siblings good-bye. Nor had he gotten to tell his parents. His father had wanted so badly to see him wed. Betrothed at the very least, and Nicolai had agreed to bind himself to someone. Only, he never had. Not really. He'd finally settled on the princess of Brokk, but he had never made a formal offer. And, oh, how his father had despaired.

While he could not give his father a bride—if he couldn't have Jane, he would have no one—he could at last give his father the vengeance he'd used his last breath ensuring.

Nicolai knew he was not too late, for the timepiece continued to tick. When the hands stopped, then and only then would it be too late. But the hands were moving more quickly than they should have, meaning time was running out.

He would return to Elden, kill the sorcerer and claim his rightful place on the throne. Nothing would stop him. Tomorrow, he added. Nothing would stop him *tomorrow*. He could not bring himself to leave Laila's tent. Not yet. This was the last place he'd seen and held Jane.

Jane.

You aren't supposed to think about her.

Beyond the tent, he could hear the rest of the camp rousing. Footsteps pounded closer and closer and he knew it was only a matter of minutes before someone ventured inside again. He pictured the Princess Laila, as he had done before, cloaking himself in her image.

Sure enough, the tent flap rose and two guards stepped inside, awaiting orders.

"Leave this place," he found himself saying. "Gather everything and everyone else and return home."

"What of you, princess?"

"I'm staying. Now go."

They bowed and exited, used to her abruptness. He'd been casting illusions for years, and had once teased his brothers and sisters, pretending to be them—in front of them. They had laughed, and begged for more.

The memory had his chest constricting. He would have liked to tease Jane that way.

Jane, he thought again. Her blood flowed through his veins, heating him up, making him ache and tingle. How was he supposed to live without her?

He didn't care what she'd done in the past. How could he? She had already confessed her past to him, when he'd been imprisoned, and she'd appeared to him in phantom form.

He knew she thought he blamed her and perhaps even hated her. Was that why she stayed away? Had he failed to convince her otherwise when they'd spoken in their minds?

There'd been no other way. He'd had to convince Laila he would kill her. So even though he'd wanted to hug and kiss her and tell her how much he loved her, how there was nothing she could ever do to earn his hatred, he had glared at her, snapped at her.

She'd returned to her own time. To save him. And now, enough time had passed that he feared she no longer possessed the ability to travel here. Or was the curse keeping her there? The curse he'd thought he'd overcome. Oh, yes, he realized. There was his answer.

He stalked to Jane's bag and dug inside, withdrawing the book. He'd flipped through the blank pages a thousand times already. Each of those thousand times he'd imagined casting another spell, one to bring her back to him.

Yet, how could he make such a spell work? How could he circumvent the curse that separated them? So far he had not…thought of…

A way.

Heart galloping, Nicolai found a pen, sat on Laila's lounge and started writing.…

TWO WEEKS LATER, JANE returned from her midnight jog and found a box on her porch. The same box she'd found before. She knew what rested inside it and gulped.

Not a day had passed that she hadn't thought about Nicolai, cried for him, prayed to see him again. She found herself racing up the porch steps, grabbing the box and shoving her way inside the cabin.

Every day she'd changed a little more. She still ate food, still needed it, but she also needed blood. Her midnight jogs, which she no longer needed to work the stiffness out of her muscles because her muscles didn't get stiff anymore, had become snack time. The deer ran from her, but like a lion with a gazelle, she always caught one.

The biggest change of all? She was pregnant. She'd realized the truth only a few hours ago, and had been in a shocked daze ever since. She should have figured it out before now, having spent the past several mornings vomiting. More than that, Nicolai's blood had healed her spine and legs, so why not her reproductive system, too?

She wanted to see Nicolai, needed to tell him. Had to make love with him, laugh with him, hold on to him and never let go.

The bookbinding creaked as she opened the front flap. There was a tattered pink ribbon—from one of her robes, she realized, her eyes filling with tears. Heart pounding against her ribs, she mentally read, her voice too wobbly to speak.

"My name is Nicolai, and I am the crown prince of Elden. I will become king the day I kill the Blood Sorcerer. And I will kill him. After I tell my female that I love her."

She swiped at her burning eyes.

"I will always love my Jane, and I am miserable without her. She thinks I despise her, but for the first time in her life, my too-intelligent woman is wrong. I did and said what I had to only to save her life."

"I know," she managed to work past the knot.

"Her life is far more important to me than my own."

The words swam. Again, she swiped at her eyes.

"But she is cursed. Cursed to lose the man she loves. And she has. She's lost him. Absolutely. But now…now she can find him again. If not through magic or abilities, than with her mind."

Jane wiped her eyes with the back of her wrist, trembling, hopeful, joyous, excited and scared. Scared, because Nicolai was offering her the world, but she had no way to tell him.

"Come back to me, Jane. Please. Come back to me. I await you. I will await you forever."

The rest of the pages were blank.

Oh, Nicolai. I want to. I want to so badly. She stood on her shaky legs and walked, trancelike, into her shower. She sat and let the water pour over her, clothes and all. Nicolai wanted to see her, but she couldn't return. Every time she tried, she destroyed a little piece of her soul.

And yet, she gave it another try.

She closed her eyes and pictured the tent. Just like before, nothing happened. Just as she'd feared. She tried again. And again. And again. Only when the water was cold as ice did she emerge from the stall. *Don't give up hope. There's another way.*

Yes. *Yes.* With her mind, he'd said.

Her mind.

The next evening, she gathered all the necessary tools for transfer. Crudely, quickly constructed, but hopefully adequate. She donned her robe and placed the sensors of the machine along her bedposts. Trembling, she stretched out on her mattress, flipped the switch and closed her eyes. If she died because of this, okay. If she hurt herself, whatever. She refused to allow fear or anything else to stop her from doing whatever was necessary to reach her man. Refused to deny her baby the chance to know a father's love.

A slight buzzing in her ears. Sickness in her stomach. Her machine could work, she reminded herself, and *had* worked with plastic.

I'm not plastic. Oh, God. Jane pictured her destination, trying to use Nicolai's ability alongside the man-made appliance. Several seconds ticked by. Seconds that felt like separate eternities. Finally she felt her body begin to heat…heard the buzzing increase in volume… felt the bed disappear from beneath her… Heat…more heat…

Buzzing, gone. Nothing. She was nothing.

"Jane. Sweetheart."

Nicolai. There was his voice, so close. Panting, she pried her eyelids open, and she saw that she was lying on the floor of the tent, Nicolai looming over her, his hands wrapped around her arms as he shook her.

She'd done it. She'd crossed over. Traveled to him, her mind the guide.

"Jane," he said on a sigh of relief. There was no need for more words. Not yet.

An instant later they were kissing and pulling at each other's clothes. In seconds, they were naked and falling to the floor. No preliminaries. Nicolai shoved open her legs and thrust deep. Thrust home.

Jane cried out, already wet for him, needing him like she needed air to breathe. He pounded in and out, pushing her to heights she'd only dreamed about these past two weeks.

Her nipples rasped his chest, sparking a fire. An inferno. Spreading through her, consuming her, and she erupted, screaming, screaming, clutching at him, scratching his back. And then his fangs were in her neck, and he was drinking, and she was climaxing again, angling her head and biting into *his* neck.

He roared as she drank him down, bucking against her, going even deeper, and soon shooting inside her. Glorious, necessary, life affirming.

When he collapsed against her, she held on tight. She didn't think she'd ever been happier. She was with her man, her love, the future bright.

"You got the book," he said, planting little kisses along her jaw.

"Oh, yes. Thank you for sending it. I couldn't get here. I wanted so badly to come back to you, but I couldn't move from one location to another in a blink anymore."

He propped his weight on his elbows and peered down at her. "Thank you. Thank you for coming back."

"My pleasure." She cupped his cheeks. "You'll be happy to know Laila is now in the same position she placed you in." She'd watched the news. Laila had been found, her image flashed, calling for anyone who might know her. And until someone claimed her, she'd been locked in a mental institution for the violently insane.

"I don't care about her. How are *you?*"

"Good." Now. "I have something to tell you."

He lost a little of his good humor. "You look worried. Jane, you can tell me anything. I will never hate you. Never turn away from you."

"I… Do you remember when I told you I couldn't have children?"

He nodded, his brow furrowed.

"Well, I can." A smile grew. "And I'm going to. I found out a few days ago. We're going to be parents."

His mouth fell open, snapped closed. Fell open again. "Jane…I… Jane!" With a whoop, he leaned down and kissed her again. "You are sure?"

"Yes."

Another kiss. "Are you happy?"

"Yes."

"Me, too." His smile was radiant. "Oh, Jane." He kissed her again and again, his hand constantly rubbing over her still-flat belly. "I love you, and want you with me. Tell me you'll stay. Tell me you'll live with me. Marry me."

"Yes, yes, yes!" She laughed, hugging him tight. "In case you don't understand, yes means yes."

He chuckled against her lips. "I must still return to Elden."

"And so you will. With me. I adore you, Prince or King or whatever you are!"

"As I adore you, Jane. My heart and my queen."

"Good." She cupped his cheeks, loving him more with every minute that passed. "Now let's go to Elden and kick some ass."

* * * * *

THE DARKEST ANGEL

CHAPTER ONE

FROM HIGH IN THE HEAVENS, Lysander spotted his prey. *At last. Finally, I will end this.* His jaw clenched and his skin pulled tight. With tension. With relief. Determined, he jumped from the cloud he stood upon, falling quickly…wind whipping through his hair…

When he neared ground, he allowed his wings, long and feathered and golden, to unfold from his back and catch in the current, slowing his progress.

He was a soldier for the One True Deity. One of the Elite Seven, created before time itself. With as many millennia as he'd lived, he'd come to learn that each of the Elite Seven had one temptation. One potential downfall. Like Eve with her apple. When they found this…thing, this abomination, they happily destroyed it before it could destroy them.

Lysander had finally found his.

Bianka Skyhawk.

She was the daughter of a Harpy and a phoenix shape-shifter. She was a thief, a liar and a killer who found joy in the vilest of tasks. Worse, the blood of Lucifer—his greatest enemy and the sire of most demon hordes—flowed through her veins. Which meant *Bianka* was his enemy.

He lived to destroy his enemies.

However, he could only act against them when they

broke a heavenly law. For demons, that involved escaping their fiery prison to walk the earth. For Bianka, who had never been condemned to hell, that would have to involve something else. What, he didn't know. All he knew was that he'd never experienced what mortals referred to as "desire."

Until Bianka.

And he didn't like it.

He'd seen her for the first time several weeks ago, long black hair flowing down her back, amber eyes bright and lips bloodred. Watching her, unable to turn away, a single question had drifted through his mind: Was her pearl-like skin as soft as it appeared?

Forget desire. He'd never wondered such a thing about *anyone* before. He'd never cared. But the question was becoming an obsession, discovering the truth a need. And it had to end. Now. This day.

He landed just in front of her, but she couldn't see him. No one could. He existed on another plane, invisible to mortal and immortal alike. He could scream, and she would not hear him. He could walk through her, and she would not feel him. For that matter, she would not smell or sense him in any way.

Until it was too late.

He could have formed a fiery sword from air and cleaved her head from her body, but didn't. As he'd already realized and accepted, he could not kill her. Yet. But he could not allow her to roam unfettered, tempting him, a plague to his good sense, either. Which meant he would have to settle for imprisoning her in his home in the sky.

That didn't have to be a terrible ordeal for him, however. He could use their time together to show her the right way to live. And the right way was, of course, his way. What's more, if she did not conform, if she *did* finally commit that unpardonable sin, he would be there, at last able to rid himself of her influence.

Do it. Take her.

He reached out. But just before he could wrap his arms around her and fly her away, he realized she was no longer alone. He scowled, his arms falling to his sides. He did not want a witness to his deeds.

"Best day ever," Bianka shouted skyward, splaying her arms and twirling. Two champagne bottles were clutched in her hands and those bottles flew from her grip, slamming into the ice-mountains of Alaska surrounding her. She stopped, swayed, laughed. "Oopsie."

His scowl deepened. A perfect opportunity lost, he realized. Clearly, she was intoxicated. She wouldn't have fought him. Would have assumed he was a hallucination or that they were playing a game. Having watched her these past few weeks, he knew how much she liked to play games.

"Waster," her sister, the intruder, grumbled. Though they were twins, Bianka and Kaia looked nothing alike. Kaia had red hair and gray eyes flecked with gold. She was shorter than Bianka, her beauty more delicate. "I had to stalk a collector for days—days!—to steal that. Seriously. You just busted Dom Pérignon White Gold Jeroboam."

"I'll make it up to you." Mist wafted from Bianka's mouth. "They sell Boone's Farm in town."

There was a pause, a sigh. "That's only acceptable if you also steal me some cheese tots. I used to highjack them from Sabin every day, and now that we've left Budapest, I'm in withdrawal."

Lysander tried to pay attention to the conversation, he really did. But being this close to Bianka was, as always, ruining his concentration. Only her skin was similar to her sister's, reflecting all the colors of a newly sprung rainbow. So why didn't he wonder if *Kaia's* skin was as soft as it appeared?

Because she is not your temptation. You know this.

There, atop a peak of Devil's Thumb, he watched as Bianka plopped to her bottom. Frigid mist continued to waft around her, making her look as if she were part of a dream. Or an angel's nightmare.

"But you know," Kaia added, "stealing Boone's Farm in town doesn't help me now. I'm only partially buzzed and was hoping to be totally and completely smashed by the time the sun set."

"You should be thanking me, then. You got smashed last night. And the night before. And the night before that."

Kaia shrugged. "So?"

"So, your life is in a rut. You steal liquor, climb a mountain while drinking and dive off when drunk."

"Well, then yours is in a rut, too, since you've been with me each of those nights." The redhead frowned. "Still. Maybe you're right. Maybe we need a change." She gazed around the majestic summit. "So what new and exciting thing do you want to do now?"

"Complain. Can you believe Gwennie is getting married?" Bianka asked. "And to Sabin, keeper of the demon of Doubt, of all people. Or demons. Whatever."

Gwennie. Gwendolyn. Their youngest sister.

"I know. It's weird." A still-frowning Kaia eased down beside her. "Would you rather be a bridesmaid or be hit by a bus?"

"The bus. No question. That, I'd recover from."

"Agreed."

Bianka did not like weddings? Odd. Most females *craved* them. Still. *No need for the bus,* Lysander wanted to tell her. *You will not be attending your sister's wedding.*

"So which of us will be her maid of honor, do you think?" Kaia asked.

"Not it," Bianka said, just as Kaia opened her mouth to say the same.

"Damn it!"

Bianka laughed with genuine amusement. "Your duties shouldn't be too bad. Gwennie's the nicest of the Skyhawks, after all."

"Nice when she's not protecting Sabin, that is." Kaia shuddered. "I swear, threaten the man with a little bodily harm, and she's ready to claw your eyes out."

"Think we'll ever fall in love like that?" As curious as Bianka sounded, there was also a hint of sadness in her voice.

Why sadness? Did she want to fall in love? Or was she thinking of a particular man she yearned for? Lysander had not yet seen her interact with a male she desired.

Kaia waved a deceptively delicate hand through the air. "We've been alive for centuries without falling. Clearly, it's just not meant to be. But I, for one, am glad about that. Men become a liability when you try and make them permanent."

"Yeah," was the reply. "But a fun liability."

"True. And I haven't had fun in a long time," Kaia said with a pout.

"Me, either. Except with myself, but I don't suppose that counts."

"It does the way I do it."

They shared another laugh.

Fun. Sex, Lysander realized, now having no trouble keeping up with their conversation. They were discussing sex. Something he'd never tried. Not even with himself. He'd never wanted to try, either. Still didn't. Not even with Bianka and her amazing (soft?) skin.

As long as he'd been alive—a span of time far greater than their few hundred years—he'd seen many humans caught up in the act. It looked…messy. As un-fun as something could be. Yet humans betrayed their friends and family to do it. They even willingly, happily gave up hard-earned money in exchange for it. When not taking part themselves, they became obsessed with it, watching others do it on a television or computer screen.

"We should have nailed one of the Lords when we were in Buda," Kaia said thoughtfully. "Paris is hawt."

She could only be referring to the Lords of the Underworld. Immortal warriors possessed by the demons once locked inside Pandora's box. As Lysander had observed them throughout the centuries, ensuring they obeyed heavenly laws—since their demons had escaped hell before those laws were enacted, no one having thought escape possible, they had not been killed but thrust into that box first, and the Lords second—he knew that Paris was host to Promiscuity, forced to bed a new person every day or weaken and die.

"Paris is hot, yes, but I liked Amun." Bianka stretched to her back, mist again whipping around her. "He doesn't speak, which makes him the perfect man, in my opinion."

Amun, the host of the demon of Secrets. So. Bianka liked him, did she? Lysander pictured the warrior. Tall, though Lysander was taller. Muscled, though Lysander was more so. Dark where Lysander was light. He was actually relieved to know the Harpy preferred a different type of male than himself.

That wouldn't change her fate, but it did lessen Lysander's burden. He hadn't been sure what he would have done if she'd *asked* him to touch her. That she wouldn't was most definitely a relief.

"What about Aeron?" Kaia asked. "All those tattoos…" A moan slipped from her as she shivered. "I could trace every single one of them with my tongue."

Aeron, host of Wrath. One of only two Lords with wings, Aeron's were black and gossamer. He had tattoos all over his body, and looked every inch the demon he was. What's more, he had recently broken a spiritual covenant. Therefore, Aeron would be dead before the upcoming nuptials.

Lysander's charge, Olivia, had been ordered to slay the warrior. So far she had resisted the decree. The girl was too softhearted for her own good. Eventually, though, she would do her duty. Otherwise, she would be kicked to earth, immortal no longer, and that was not a fate Lysander would allow.

Of all the angels he'd trained, she was by far his favorite. As gentle as she was, a man couldn't help but want to make her happy. She was trustworthy, loyal and all that was pure; she was the type of female who should have tempted him. A female he might have been able to accept in a romantic way. Wild Bianka…no. Never.

"However will I choose between my two favorite

Lords, B?" Another sigh returned Lysander's focus to the Harpies.

Bianka rolled her eyes. "Just sample them both. Not like you haven't enjoyed a twofer before."

Kaia laughed, though the amusement didn't quite reach her voice. Like Bianka, there was a twinge of sadness to the sound. "True."

Lysander's mouth curled in mild distaste. Two different partners in one day. Or at the same time. Had Bianka done that, too? Probably.

"What about you?" Kaia asked. "You gonna hook up with Amun at the wedding?"

There was a long, heavy pause. Then Bianka shrugged. "Maybe. Probably."

He should leave and return when she was alone. The more he learned about her, the more he disliked her. Soon he would simply snatch her up, no matter who watched, revealing his presence, his intentions, just to save this world from her dark influence.

He flapped his wings once, twice, lifting into the air.

"You know what I want more than anything else in the world?" she asked, rolling to her side and facing her sister. Facing Lysander directly, as well. Her eyes were wide, amber irises luminous. Beams of sunlight seemed to soak into that glorious skin, and he found himself pausing.

Kaia stretched out beside her. "To co-host *Good Morning America?*"

"Well, yeah, but that's not what I meant."

"Then I'm stumped."

"Well…" Bianka nibbled on her bottom lip. Opened her mouth. Closed her mouth. Scowled. "I'll tell you, but you can't tell anyone."

The redhead pretended to twist a lock over her lips.

"I'm serious, K. Tell anyone, and I'll deny it then hunt you down and chop off your head."

Would she truly? Lysander wondered. Again, probably. He could not imagine hurting his Olivia, whom he loved like a sister. Maybe because she was not one of the Elite Seven, but was a joy-bringer, the weakest of the angels.

There were three angelic factions. The Elite Seven, the warriors and the joy-bringers. Their status was reflected in both their different duties and the color of their wings. Each of the Seven possessed golden wings, like his own. Warriors possessed white wings merely threaded with gold, and the joy-bringers' white wings bore no gold at all.

Olivia had been a joy-bringer all the centuries of her existence. Something she was quite happy with. That was why everyone, including Olivia, had experienced such shock when golden down had begun to grow in her feathers.

Not Lysander, however. He'd petitioned the Angelic Council, and they'd agreed. It had needed to be done. She was too fascinated by the demon-possessed warrior Aeron. Too…infatuated. Ridding her of such an attraction was imperative. As he well knew.

His hand clenched into a fist. He blamed himself for Olivia's circumstances. He had sent her to watch the Lords. To study them. He should have gone himself, but he'd hoped to avoid Bianka.

"Well, don't just lie there. Tell me what you want to do more than anything else in the world," Kaia exclaimed, once again drawing his attention.

Bianka uttered another sigh. "I want to sleep with a man."

Kaia's brow scrunched in confusion. "Uh, hello. Wasn't that what we were just discussing?"

"No, dummy. I mean, I want to sleep. As in, conk out. As in, snore my ass off."

A moment passed in silence as Kaia absorbed the announcement. "What! That's forbidden. Stupid. Dangerous."

Harpies lived by two rules, he knew. They could only eat what they stole or earned, and they could not sleep in the presence of another. The first was because of a curse on all Harpy-kind, and the second because Harpies were suspicious and untrusting by nature.

Lysander's head tilted to the side as he found himself imagining holding Bianka in his arms as she drifted into slumber. That fall of dark curls would tumble over his arm and chest. Her warmth would seep into his body. Her leg would rub over his.

He could never allow it, of course, but that didn't diminish the power of the vision. To hold her, protect her, comfort her would be…nice.

Would her skin be as soft as it appeared?

His teeth ground together. There was that ridiculous question again. *I do not care. It does not matter.*

"Forget I said anything," Bianka grumbled, once more flopping to her back and staring up at the bright sky.

"I can't. Your words are singed into my ears. Do you know what happened to our ancestors when they were stupid enough to fall asl—"

"Yes, okay. Yes." She pushed to her feet. The faux fur coat she wore was bloodred, same as her lips, and a vivid contrast to the white ice around her. Her boots were black and climbed to her knees. She wore skintight pants, also black. She looked wicked and beautiful.

Would her skin be as soft as it appeared?

Before he realized what he was doing, he was standing in front of her, reaching out, fingers tingling. *What are you doing? Stop!* He froze. Backed several steps away.

Sweet heaven. How close he'd come to giving in to the temptation of her.

He could not wait any longer. Could not wait until she was alone. He had to act now. His reaction to her was growing stronger. Any more, and he *would* touch her. And if he liked touching her, he might want to do more. That was how temptation worked. You gave in to one thing, then yearned for another. And another. Soon, you were lost.

"Enough heavy talk. Let's get back to our boring routine and jump," Bianka said, stalking to the edge of the peak. "You know the rules. Girl who breaks the least amount of bones wins. If you die, you lose. For, like, ever." She gazed down.

So did Lysander. There were crests and dips along the way, ice bounders with sharp, deadly ridges and thousands of feet of air. Such a jump would have killed a mortal, no question. The Harpy merely joked about the possibility, as if it were of no consequence. Did she think herself invulnerable?

Kaia lumbered to her feet and swayed from the liquor still pouring through her. "Fine, but don't think this is the last of our conversation about sleeping habits and stupid girls who—"

Bianka dove.

Lysander expected the action, but was still surprised by it. He followed her down. She spread her arms, closed her eyes, grinning foolishly. That grin…affected him. Clearly she reveled in the freedom of soaring. Something he often did, as well. But she would not have the end she desired.

Seconds before she slammed into a boulder, Lysander allowed himself to materialize in her plane. He grabbed her, arms catching under hers, wings unfolding, slowing them. Her legs slapped against him, jarring him, but he didn't release his hold.

A gasp escaped her, and her eyelids popped open. When she spotted him, amber eyes clashing with the dark of his, that gasp became a growl.

Most would have asked who he was or demanded he go away. Not Bianka.

"Big mistake, Stranger Danger," she snapped. "One you'll pay for."

As many battles as he'd fought over the years and as many opponents as he'd slain, he didn't have to see to know she had just unsheathed a blade from a hidden slit in her coat. And he didn't have to be a psychic to know she meant to stab him.

"It is you who made the mistake, Harpy. But do not worry. I have every intention of rectifying that." Before she could ensure that her weapon met its intended target, he whisked her into another plane, into his home—where she would stay. Forever.

CHAPTER TWO

BIANKA SKYHAWK GAPED at her new surroundings. One moment she'd been tumbling toward an icy valley, intent on escaping her sister's line of questioning, as well as winning their break-the-least-amount-of-bones game, and the next she'd been in the arms of a gorgeous blond. Which wasn't necessarily a good thing. She'd tried to stab him, and he'd blocked her. Freaking blocked her. No one should be able to block a Harpy's deathblow.

Now she was standing inside a cloud-slash-palace. A palace that was bigger than any home she'd ever seen. A palace that was warm and sweetly scented, with an almost tangible sense of peace wafting through the air.

The walls were wisps of white and smoke, and as she watched, murals formed, seemingly alive, winged creatures, both angelic and demonic, soaring through a morning sky. They reminded her of Danika's paintings. Danika—the All-Seeing Eye who watched both heaven and hell. The floors, though comprised of that same ethereal substance, allowing a view of the land and people below, were somehow solid.

Angelic. Cloud. Heaven? Dread flooded her as she spun to face the male who had grabbed her. "Angelic" described him perfectly. From the top of his pale head to the strength in that leanly muscled, sun-kissed body, to the golden wings stretching from his back. Even the white robe that fell to his ankles and the sandals wrapped around his feet gave him a saintly aura.

Was he an angel, then? Her heart skipped a beat. He wasn't human, that was for sure. No human male could ever hope to compare to such blinding perfection. But damn, those eyes…they were dark and hard and almost, well, empty.

His eyes don't matter. Angels were demon assassins, and she was as close to a demon as a girl could get. After all, her great-grandfather was Lucifer himself. Lucifer, who had spent a year on earth unfettered, pillaging and raping. Only a few females had conceived, but those that had soon gave birth to the first of the Harpies.

Unsure of what to do, Bianka strode around her blond; he remained in place, even when she was at his back, as if he had nothing to fear from her. Maybe he didn't. Obviously he had powers. One, he'd blocked her—she just couldn't get over that fact—and two, he'd somehow removed her coat and all her weapons without touching her.

"Are you an angel?" she asked when she was once again in front of him.

"Yes." No hesitation. As if his heritage wasn't something to be ashamed of.

Poor guy, she thought with a shudder. Clearly he had no idea the crappy hand he'd been dealt. If she had to choose between being an angel and a dog, she'd choose the dog. They, at least, were respectable.

She'd never been this close to an angel before. Seen one, yes. Or rather, seen what she'd thought was an angel but had later learned was a demon in disguise. Either way, she hadn't liked the guy, her youngest sister's father. He considered himself a god and everyone else beneath him.

"Did you bring me here to kill me?" she asked. Not that he'd have any luck. He would find that she was not an easy target. Many immortals had tried to finish her off over the years, but none had succeeded. Obviously.

He sighed, warm breath trekking over her cheeks. She had accidentally-on-purpose closed some of the distance between them; he smelled of the icecaps she so loved. Fresh and crisp with just a hint of earthy spice.

When he realized that only a whisper separated them, his lips, too full for a man but somehow perfect for him, pressed into a mulish line. Though she didn't see him move, he was suddenly a few more inches away from her. Huh. Interesting. Had he increased the distance on purpose?

Curious, she stepped toward him.

He backed away.

He had. Why? Was he scared of her?

Just to be contrary, as she often was, she stepped toward him again. Again, he stepped away. So. The big, bad angel didn't want to be within striking distance. She almost grinned.

"Well," she prompted. "Did you?"

"No. I did not bring you here to kill you." His voice was rich, sultry, a sin all its own. And yet, there was a layer of absolute truth to it, and she suspected she would have believed anything he said. As if whatever he said was simply fated, meant to be. Unchangeable. "I want you to emulate my life. I want you to learn from me."

"Why?" What would he do if she touched him? The tiny gossamer wings on her own back fluttered at the thought. Her T-shirt was designed especially for her kind, the material loose to keep from pinning those wings as she jolted into super-speed. "Wait. Don't answer. Let's make out first." A lie, but he didn't need to know that.

"Bianka," he said, his patience clearly waning. "This is not a game. Do not make me bind you to my bed."

"Ohh, now that I like. Sounds kinky." She darted around him, running her fingertips over his cheek, his neck. "You're as soft as a baby."

He sucked in a breath, stiffened. "Bianka."

"But better equipped."

"Bianka!"

She patted his butt. "Yes?"

"You will cease that immediately!"

"Make me." She laughed, the amused, carefree sound echoing between them.

Scowling, he reached out and latched onto her upper arm. There wasn't time to evade him; shockingly, he was faster than she was. He jerked her in front of him, and dark, narrowed eyes stared down at her.

"There will be no touching. Do you understand?"

"Do you?" Her gaze flicked to his hand, still clutching her arm. "At the moment, you're the one touching me."

Like hers, his gaze fell to where they were connected. He licked his lips, and his grip tightened just the way she liked. Then he released her as if she were on fire and once again increased the distance between them.

"Do you understand?" His tone was hard and flat.

What was the problem? He should be begging to touch her. She was a desirable Harpy, damn it. Her body was a work of art and her face total perfection. But for his benefit, she said, "Yeah, I understand. That doesn't mean I'll obey." Her skin tingled, craving the return of his. *Bad girl. Bad, bad girl. He's a stupid angel and therefore not an appropriate plaything.*

A moment passed as he absorbed her words. "Are you not frightened of me?" His wings folded into his back, arcing over his shoulders.

"No," she said, raising a brow and doing her best to appear unaffected. "Should I be?"

"Yes."

Well, then, he'd have to somehow grow the fiery claws of her father's people. That was the only thing that scared her. Having been scratched as a child, having felt the acid-burn of fire spread through her entire body, having spent days writhing in agonizing, seemingly endless pain, she would do anything to avoid such an experience again.

"Well, I'm still not. And now you're starting to bore me." She anchored her hands on her hips, glaring up at him. "I asked you a question but you never answered it. Why do you want me to be like you? So much so, that you brought me into heaven, of all places?"

A muscle ticked below one of his eyes. "Because I am good and you are evil."

Another laugh escaped her. He frowned, and her laughter increased until tears were running from her eyes. When she quieted, she said, "Good job. You staved off the boredom."

His frown deepened. "I was not teasing you. I mean to keep you here forever and train you to be sinless."

"Gods, how— Oops, sorry. I mean, golly, how adorable are you? 'I mean to keep you here forever and train you,'" she said in her best impersonation of him. There was no reason to fight about her eventual escape. She'd prove him wrong just as soon as she decided to leave. Right now, she was too intrigued. With her surroundings, she assured herself, and not the angel. Heaven was not a place she'd ever thought to visit.

His chin lifted a notch, but his eyes remained expressionless. "I am serious."

"I'm sure you are. But you'll find that you can't keep me anywhere I don't want to be. And me? Without sin? Funny!"

"We shall see."

His confidence might have unnerved her had she been less confident in her own abilities. As a Harpy, she could lift a semi as if it were no more significant than a pebble, could move faster than the human eye could see and had no problem slaying an unwelcome host.

"Be honest," she said. "You saw me and wanted a piece, right?"

For the briefest of moments, horror blanketed his face. "No," he croaked out, then cleared his throat and said more smoothly, "No."

Insulting bastard. Why such horror at the thought of being with her? *She* was the one who should be horrified. He was clearly a do-gooder, more so than she'd realized. *I am good and you are evil,* he'd said. Ugh.

"So tell me again why you want to change me. Didn't anyone ever tell you that you shouldn't mess with perfection?"

That muscle started ticking below his eye again. "You are a menace."

"Whatever, dude." She liked to steal—so what. She could kill without blinking—again, so what. It wasn't like she worked for the IRS or anything. "Where's my sister, Kaia? She's as much a menace as I am, I'm sure. So why don't you want to change her?"

"She is still in Alaska, wondering if you are buried inside an ice cave. And you are my only project at the moment."

Project? Bastard. But she did like the thought of Kaia searching high and low but finding no sign of her, almost like they were playing a game of Hide and Seek. Bianka would totally, finally win.

"You appear...excited," he said, head tilting to the side. "Why? Does her concern not disturb you?"

Yep. A certified do-gooder. "It's not like I'll be here long." She peeked over his shoulder; more of that wisping white greeted her. "Got anything to drink here?"

"No."

"Eat?"

"No."

"Wear?"

"No."

Slowly the corners of her lips lifted. "I guess that means you like to go naked. Awesome."

His cheeks reddened. "Enough. You are trying to bait me and I do not like it."

"Then you shouldn't have brought me here." Hey, wait a minute. He'd never really told her why he'd chosen her as his *project,* she realized. "Be honest. Do you need my help with something?" After all, she, like many of her fellow Harpies, was a mercenary, paid to find and retrieve. Her motto: if it's unethical and illegal and you've got the cash, I'm your girl! "I mean, I know you didn't just bring me here to save the world from my naughty influence. Otherwise, millions of other people would be here with me."

He crossed his arms over his massive chest.

She sighed. Knowing men as she did, she knew he was done answering that type of question. Oh, well. She could have convinced him otherwise by annoying him until he caved, but she didn't want to put the work in.

"So what do you do for fun around here?" she asked.

"I destroy demons."

Like you, she finished for him. But he'd already said he had no intention of killing her, and she believed him—how could she not? That voice… "So you don't want to hurt me, you don't want to touch me, but you do want me to live here forever."

"Yes."

"I'd be an idiot to refuse such an offer." That she sounded sincere was a miracle. "We'll pretend to be married and spend the nights locked in each other's arms, kissing and touching, our bodies—"

"Stop. Just stop." And, drumroll please, that muscle began ticking under his eye again.

This time, there was no fighting her grin. It spread wide and proud. That tic was a sign of anger, surely. But what would it take to make that anger actually seep into his irises? What would it take to break even a fraction of his iron control?

"Show me around," she said. "If I'm going to live here, I need to know where my walk-in closet is." During the tour, she could accidentally-on-purpose brush against him. Over and over again. "Do we have cable?"

"No. And I cannot give you a tour. I have duties. Important duties."

"Yeah, you do. My pleasure. That should be priority one."

Teeth grinding together, he turned on his heel and strode away. "You will find it difficult to get into trouble here, so I suggest you do not even try." His voice echoed behind him.

Please. She could get into trouble with nothing but a toothpick and a spoon. "If you leave, I'll rearrange everything." Not that there was any furniture to be seen.

Silence.

"I'll get bored and take off."

"Try."

It was a response, at least. "So you're seriously going to leave me? Just like that?" She snapped her fingers.

"Yes." Another response, though he didn't stop walking.

"What about that bed you were going to chain me to? Where is it?"

Uh-oh, back to silence.

"You didn't even tell me your name," she called, irritated despite herself. How could he abandon her like that? He should hunger for more of her. "Well? I deserve to know the name of the man I'll be cursing."

Finally, he stopped. Still, a long while passed in silence and she thought he meant to ignore her. Again. Then he said, "My name is Lysander," and stepped from the cloud, disappearing from view.

CHAPTER THREE

LYSANDER WATCHED AS TWO newly recruited warrior angels—angels under his training and command—finally subdued a demonic minion that had dug its way free from hell. The creature was scaled from head to hoof and little horns protruded from its shoulders and back. Its eyes were bright red, like crystallized blood.

The fight had lasted half an hour, and both angels were now bleeding, panting. Demons were notorious for their biting and scratching.

Lysander should have been able to critique the men and tell them what they had done wrong. That way, they would do a better job next time. But as they'd struggled with the fiend, his mind had drifted to Bianka. What was she doing? Was she resigned to her fate yet? He'd given her several days alone to calm and accept.

"What now?" one of his trainees asked. Beacon was his name.

"You letsss me go, you letsss me go," the demon said pleadingly, its forked tongue giving it a lisp. "I behave. I return. Ssswear."

Lies. As a minion, it was a servant to a demon High Lord—just as there were three factions of angels, there were three factions of demons. High Lords held the most power, followed by Lords, who were followed by the lowest of them all, minions. Despite this one's lack of status, it could cause untold damage among humans. Not only because it was evil, but also because it was a minion of Strife and took its nourishment from the trouble it caused others.

By the time Lysander had sensed its presence on earth, it had already broken up two marriages and convinced one teenager to start smoking and another to kill himself.

"Execute it," Lysander commanded. "It knew the consequences of breaking a heavenly law, yet it chose to escape from hell anyway."

The minion began to struggle again. "You going to lisssten to him when you obviousssly ssstronger and better than him? He make you do all hard work. He do nothing hissself. Lazy, if you asssk me. Kill *him*."

"We do not ask you," Lysander said.

Both angels raised their hands and fiery swords appeared.

"Pleassse," the demon screeched. "No. Don't do thisss."

They didn't hesitate. They struck.

The scaled head rolled, yet the angels did not dematerialize their swords. They kept the tips poised on the motionless body until it caught flame. When nothing but ash remained, they looked to Lysander for instruction.

"Excellent job." He nodded in satisfaction. "You have improved since your last killing, and I am proud of you. But you will train with Raphael until further notice," he said. Raphael was strong, intelligent and one of the best trackers in the heavens.

Raphael would not be distracted by a Harpy he had no hopes of possessing.

Possessing? Lysander's jaw clenched tightly. He was not some vile demon. He possessed nothing. Ever. And when he finished with Bianka, she would be glad of that. There would be no more games, no more racing around him, caressing him and laughing. The clenching in his jaw stopped, but his shoulders sagged. In disappointment? Couldn't be.

Perhaps *he* needed a few days to calm and accept.

HE'D LEFT HER ALONE for a week, the sun rising and setting beyond the clouds. And each day, Bianka grew madder—and madder. And madder. Worse, she grew weaker. Harpies could only eat what they stole (or earned, but there was no way to earn a single morsel here). And no, that wasn't a rule she could overlook. It was a curse. A godly curse her people had endured for centuries. Reviled as Harpies were, the gods had banded together and decreed that no Harpy could enjoy a meal freely given or one they had prepared themselves. If they did, they sickened terribly. The gods' hope? Destruction.

Instead, they'd merely ensured Harpies learned how to steal from birth. To survive, even an angel would sin.

Lysander would learn that firsthand. She would make sure of it. Bastard.

Had he planned this to torture her?

In this palace, Bianka had only to speak of something and it would materialize before her. An apple—bright and red and juicy. Baked turkey—succulent and plump. But she couldn't eat them, and it was killing her. Liter-*fucking*-ally.

At first, Bianka had tried to escape. Several times. Unlike Lysander the Cruel, she couldn't jump from the clouds. The floor expanded wherever she stepped and remained as hard as marble. All she could do was move from ethereal room to ethereal room, watching the murals play out battle scenes. Once she'd thought she'd even spied Lysander.

Of course, she'd said, "Rock," and a nice-sized stone had appeared in her hand. She'd chucked it at him, but the stupid thing had fallen to earth rather than hit him.

Where was he? What was he doing? Did he mean to kill her like this, despite his earlier denial? Slowly and painfully? At least the hunger pains had finally left her. Now she was merely consumed by a sensation of trembling emptiness.

She wanted to stab him the moment she saw him. Then set him on fire. Then scatter his ashes in a pasture where lots of animals roamed. He deserved to be smothered by several nice steaming piles. Of course, if he waited much longer, *she* would be the one burned and scattered. She couldn't even drink a glass of water.

Besides, fighting him wasn't the way to punish him. That, she'd realized the first day here. He didn't like to be touched. Therefore, touching him was the way to punish him. And touch him she would. Anywhere, everywhere. Until he begged her to stop. No. Until he begged her to continue.

She would make him *like* it, and then take it away. *If* she lasted.

Right now, she could barely hold herself up. In fact, why was she even trying?

"Bed," she muttered weakly, and a large four-poster appeared just in front of her. She hadn't slept since she'd gotten here. Usually she crashed in trees, but she wouldn't have had the strength to climb one even if the cloud had been filled with them. She collapsed on the plush mattress, velvet coverlet soft against her skin. Sleep. She'd sleep for a little while.

FINALLY LYSANDER COULD STAND it no more. Nine days. He'd lasted nine days. Nine days of thinking about the female constantly, wondering what she was doing, what she was thinking. If her skin was as soft as it looked.

He could tolerate it no longer. He would check on her, that was all, and see for himself how—and what— she was doing. Then he would leave her again. Until he got himself under control. Until he stopped thinking about her. Stopped wanting to be near her. Her training had to begin sometime.

His wings glided up and down as he soared to his cloud. His heartbeat was a bit…odd. Faster than normal, even bumping against his ribs. Also, his blood was like fire in his veins. He didn't know what was wrong. Angels only sickened when they were infected with demon poison, and as Lysander had not been bitten by a demon—had not even fought one in weeks—he knew that was not the problem.

Blame could probably be laid at Bianka's door, he thought with a scowl.

First thing he noticed upon entering was the food littering the floor. From fruits to meats to bags of chips. All were uneaten, even unopened.

Scowl melting into a frown, he folded his wings into his back and stalked forward. He found Bianka inside one of the rooms, lying atop a bed. She wore the same clothing she'd been clad in when he'd first taken her— red shirt, tights that molded to her perfect curves—but had discarded her boots. Her hair was tangled around her, and her skin worryingly pale. There was no sparkle to it, no pearl-like gleam. Bruises now formed half-moons under her eyes.

Part of him had expected to find her fuming—and out for his head. The other part of him had hoped to find her compliant. Not once had he thought to find her like *this*.

She thrashed, the covers bunched around her. His frown deepened.

"Hamburger," she croaked.

A juicy burger appeared on the floor a few inches from the bed, all the extras—lettuce, tomato slices, pickles and cheese—decorating the edges of the plate. The manifestation didn't surprise him. That was the beauty of these angelic homes. Whatever was desired—within reason, of course—was provided.

All this food, and she hadn't taken a single bite. Why would she request— It wasn't stolen, he realized, and for the first time in his endless existence, he was angry with himself. And scared. For her. He hated the emotion, but there it was. She hadn't eaten in these last nine days because she couldn't. She was truly starving to death.

Though he wanted her out of his head, out of his life, he hadn't wanted her to suffer. Yet suffer she had. Unbearably. Now she was too weak to steal anything. And if he force-fed her, she would vomit, hurting more than she already was. Suddenly he wanted to roar.

"Blade," he said, and within a single blink, a sharp-tipped blade rested in his hand. He stalked to the side of the bed. He was trembling.

"Fries. Chocolate shake." Her voice was soft, barely audible.

Lysander slashed one of his wrists. Blood instantly

spilled from the wound, and he stretched out his arm, forcing each drop to fall into her mouth. Blood was not food for Harpies; it was medicine. Therefore her body could accept it. He'd never freely given his blood to another living being and wasn't sure he liked the thought of something of his flowing inside this woman's veins. In fact, the thought actually caused his heartbeat to start slamming against his ribs again. But there was no other way.

At first, she didn't act as if she noticed. Then her tongue emerged, licking at the liquid before it could reach her lips. Then her eyes opened, amber irises bright, and she grabbed on to his arm, jerking it to her mouth. Her sharp teeth sank into his skin as she sucked.

Another odd sensation, he thought. Having a woman drink from him. There was heat and wetness and a sting, yet it was not unpleasant. It actually lanced a pang of…something unnameable straight to his stomach and between his legs.

"Drink all you need," he told her. His body would not run out. Every drop was replaced the moment it left him.

Her gaze narrowed on him. The more she swallowed, the more fury he saw banked there. Soon her fingers were tightening around his wrist, her nails cutting deep. If she expected some sort of reaction from him, she would not get it. He'd been alive too long and endured far too many injuries to be affected by something so minor. Except for that pang between his legs… *What* was that?

Finally, though, she released him. He wasn't sure if that gladdened him or filled him with disappointment.

Gladdened, of course, he told himself.

A trickle of red flowed from the corner of her mouth, and she licked it away. The sight of that pink tongue caused another lance to shoot through him.

Definitely disap—uh, gladdened.

"You bastard," she growled through her panting. "You sick, torturing bastard."

He moved out of striking distance. Not to protect himself, but to protect her. If she were to attack him, he would have to subdue her. And if he subdued her, he might hurt her. And accidentally brush against her. *Blood...heating...*

"It was never my intent to harm you," he said. And now, even his voice was trembling. Odd.

"And that makes what you did okay?" She jerked to a sitting position, all that dark hair spilling around her shoulders. The pearl-like sheen was slowly returning to her skin. "You left me here, unable to eat. Dying!"

"I know." Was that skin as soft as it looked? He gulped. "And I am sorry." Her anger should have overjoyed him. As he'd hoped, she would no longer laugh up at him, her face lit with the force of her amusement. She would no longer race around him, petting him. Yes, he should have been overjoyed. Instead, the disappointment he'd just denied experiencing raced through him. Disappointment mixed with shame.

She was more a temptation than he had realized.

"You know?" she gasped out. "You know that I can only consume what I steal or earn and yet you failed to make arrangements for me?"

"Yes," he admitted, hating himself for the first time in his existence.

"What's more, you left me here. With no way home."

His nod was stiff. "I have since made restitution by saving your life. But as I said, I am sorry."

"Oh, well, you're sorry," she said, throwing up her arms. "That makes everything better. That makes almost dying acceptable." She didn't wait for his reply. She kicked her legs over the bed and stood. Her skin was at full glow now. "Now you listen up. First, you're going to find a way to feed me. Then, you're going to tell me how to get off this stupid cloud. Otherwise I will make your life a hell you've never experienced before. Actually, I will anyway. That way, you'll never forget what happens when you mess with a Harpy."

He believed her. Already she affected him more than anyone else ever had. That was hell enough. Proof: his mouth was actually watering to taste her, his hands itching to touch her. Rather than reveal these new developments, however, he said, "You are powerless here. How would you hurt me?"

"Powerless?" She laughed. "I don't think so." One step, two, she approached him.

He held his ground. He would not retreat. Not this time. *Assert your authority.* "You cannot leave unless I allow it. The cloud belongs to me and places my will above yours. Therefore, there is no exit for you. You would be wise to curry my favor."

She sucked in a breath, paused. "So you still mean to keep me here forever? Even though I have a wedding to attend?" She sounded surprised.

"When did I ever give you the impression that I meant otherwise? Besides, I heard you tell your sister you didn't want to go to that wedding."

"No, I said I didn't want to be a bridesmaid. But I love my baby sis, so I'll do it. With a smile." Bianka ran her tongue over her straight, white teeth. "But let's talk about you. You like to eavesdrop, huh? That sounds a little demonic for a goody-goody angel."

Over the years he'd been called far worse than demonic. The goody-goody, though… Was that how she saw him? Rather than as the righteous soldier he was? "In war, I do what I must to win."

"Let me get this straight." Her eyes narrowed as she crossed her arms over her middle. Stubbornness radiated from her. "We were at war before I even met you?"

"Correct." A war he would win. But what would he do if he failed to set her on the right path? He would have to destroy her, of course, but for him to legally be allowed to destroy her, he reminded himself, she would first have to commit an unpardonable sin. Though she'd lived a long time, she had never crossed that line. Which meant she would have to be encouraged to do so. But how? Here, away from civilization—both mortal and immortal—she couldn't free a demon from hell. She couldn't slay an angel. Besides him, but that would never happen. He was stronger than she was.

She could blaspheme, he supposed, but he would never—never!—encourage someone to do that, no matter the reason. Not even to save himself.

The only other possibility was for her to convince an angel to fall. As she was *his* temptation, and as he was the only angel of her acquaintance, he was the only one she could convince. And he wouldn't. Again, not for any reason. He loved his life, his Deity, and was proud of his work and all he had accomplished.

Perhaps he would simply leave Bianka here, alone for the rest of eternity. That way, she could live but would be unable to cause trouble. He would visit her every few weeks—perhaps months—but never remain long enough for her to corrupt him.

A sudden blow to the cheek sent his head whipping to the side. He frowned, straightened and rubbed the now-stinging spot. Bianka was exactly as she'd been before, standing in front of him. Only now she was smiling.

"You hit me," he said, his astonishment clear.

"How sweet of you to notice."

"Why did you do that?" To be honest, he should not have been surprised. Harpies were as violent by nature as their inhuman counterparts, the demons. Why couldn't she have looked like a demon, though? Why did she have to be so lovely? "I saved you, gave you my blood. I even explained why you could not leave, just as you asked. I did not have to do any of those things."

"Do I really need to repeat your crimes?"

"No." They were not crimes! But perhaps it was best to change the subject. "Allow me to feed you," he said. He walked to the plate holding the hamburger and picked it up. The scent of spiced meat wafted to his nose, and his mouth curled in distaste.

Though he didn't want to, though his stomach rolled, he took a bite. He wanted to gag, but managed to swallow. Normally he only ate fruits, nuts and vegetables. "This," he said with much disgust, "is mine." Careful not to touch her, he placed the food in her hands. "You are not to eat it."

By staking the verbal claim, the meal did indeed become his. He watched understanding light her eyes.

"Oh, cool." She didn't hesitate to rip into the burger, every crumb gone in seconds. Next he sipped the chocolate shake. The sugar was almost obscene in his mouth, and he did gag. "Mine," he repeated faintly, giving it to her, as well. "But next time, please request a healthier meal."

She flipped him off as she gulped back the ice cream. "More."

He bypassed the French fries. No way was he going to defile his body with one of those greasy abominations. He found an apple, a pear, but had to request a stalk of broccoli himself. After claiming them, he took a bite of each and handed them over. Much better.

Bianka devoured them. Well, except for the broccoli. That, she threw at him. "I'm a carnivore, moron."

She hardly had to remind him when the unpleasant taste of the burger lingered on his tongue. Still, he chose to overlook her mockery. "All of the food produced in this home is mine. Mine and mine alone. You are to leave it alone."

"That'd be great if I were actually staying," she muttered while stuffing the fries in her mouth.

He sighed. She would accept her fate soon enough. She would have to.

The more she ate, the more radiant her skin became. Magnificent, he thought, reaching out before he could stop himself.

She grabbed his fingers and twisted just before contact. "Nope. I don't like you, so you don't get to handle the goods."

He experienced a sharp pain, but merely blinked over at her. "My apologies," he said stiffly. Thank the One True Deity she'd stopped him. No telling what he would have done to her had he actually touched her. Behaved like a slobbering human? He shuddered.

She shrugged and released him. "Now for my second order. Let me go home." As she spoke, she assumed a battle stance. Legs braced apart, hands fisted at her sides.

He mirrored her movements, refusing to admit, even to himself, that her bravery heated his traitorous blood another degree. "You cannot hurt me, Harpy. Fighting me would be pointless."

Slowly her lips curled into a devilish grin. "Who said I was going to try and hurt you?"

Before Lysander could blink, she closed the distance between them and pressed against him, arms winding around his neck and tugging his head down. Their lips met and her tongue thrust into his mouth. Automatically, he stiffened. He had seen humans kiss more times than he could count, but he'd never longed to try the act for himself.

Like sex, it seemed messy—in every way imaginable—and unnecessary. But as her tongue rolled against his, as her hands caressed a path down his spine, his body warmed—far more than it had when he'd simply thought of being here with her—and the tingle he'd noticed earlier bloomed once more. Only this time, that tingle grew and spread. Like the shaft between his legs. Rising…thickening…

He'd wanted to taste her and now he was. She was delicious, like the apple she'd just eaten, only sweeter, headier, like his favorite wine. He should make her stop. This was too much. But the wetness of her mouth wasn't messy in the least. It was electrifying.

More, a little voice said in his head.

"Yes," she rasped, as if he'd spoken aloud.

When she rubbed her lower body against his, every sensation intensified. His hands fisted at his sides. He couldn't touch her. Shouldn't touch her. Should stop this as she'd stopped him, as he'd already tried to convince himself.

A moan escaped her. Her fingers tangled in his hair. His scalp, an area he'd never considered sensitive before, ached, soaking up every bit of attention. And when she rubbed against him again, *he* almost moaned.

Her hands fell to his chest and a fingertip brushed one of his nipples. He did moan; he did grab her. His fingers gripped her hips, holding her still even though he wanted to force her to rub against him some more. The lack of motion didn't slow her kiss. She continued to dance their tongues together, leisurely, as if she could drink from him forever. And wanted to.

He should stop this, he told himself yet again.

Yes. Yes, he would. He tried to push her tongue out of his mouth. The pressure created another sensation, this one new and stronger than any other. His entire body felt aflame. He started pushing at her tongue for an entirely different reason, twining them together, tasting her again, licking her, sucking her.

"Mmm, yeah. That's the way," she praised.

Her voice was a drug, luring him in deeper, making him crave more. More, more, more. The temptation was too much, and he had to—

Temptation.

The word echoed through his mind, a sword sharp enough to cut bone. She was a temptation. She was *his* temptation. And he was allowing her to lead him astray.

He wrenched away from her, and his arms fell to his sides, heavy as boulders. He was panting, sweating, things he had not done even in the midst of battle. Angry as he was—at her, at himself—his gaze drank in the sight of her. Her skin was flushed, glowing more than ever. Her lips were red and swollen. And he had caused that reaction. Sparks of pride took him by surprise.

"You should not have done that," he growled.

Slowly, she grinned. "Well, you should have stopped me."

"I wanted to stop you."

"But you didn't," she said, that grin growing.

His teeth ground together. "Do not do it again."

One of her brows arched in smug challenge. "Keep me here against my will, and I'll do that and more. Much, much more. In fact…" She ripped her shirt over her head and tossed it aside, revealing breasts covered by pink lace.

Breathing became impossible.

"Want to touch them?" she asked huskily, cupping them with her hands. "I'll let you. I won't even make you beg."

Holy…Lord. They were lovely. Plump and mouthwatering. Lickable. And if he did lick them, would they taste as her mouth had? Like that heady wine? *Blood… heating…again…*

He didn't care what kind of coward his next action made him. It was either jump from the cloud or replace her hands with his own.

He jumped.

CHAPTER FOUR

LYSANDER LEFT BIANKA alone for another week—bastard!—but she didn't mind. Not this time. She had plenty to keep her occupied. Like her plan to drive him utterly insane with lust. So insane he'd regret bringing her here. Regret keeping her here. Regret even being alive.

That, or fall so in love with her that he yearned to grant her every desire. If that was the case—and it was a total possibility since she was *insanely* hot—she would convince him to take her home, and then she would finally get to stab him in the heart.

Perfect. Easy. With her breasts, it was almost too easy, really.

To set the stage for his downfall, she decorated his home like a bordello. Red velvet lounges now waited next to every door—just in case he was too overcome with desire for her to make it to one of the beds now perched in every corner. Naked portraits—of her—hung on the misty walls. A decorating style she'd picked up from her friend Anya, who just happened to be the goddess of Anarchy.

As Lysander had promised, Bianka had only to speak what she wanted—within reason—to receive it. Apparently furniture and pretty pictures were within reason.

She chuckled. She could hardly wait to see him again. To finally begin.

He wouldn't stand a chance. Not just because of her (magnificent) breasts and hotness—hey, no reason to act as if she didn't know—but because he had no experience. She had been his first kiss; she knew it beyond any doubt. He'd been stiff at first, unsure. Hesitant. At no point had he known what to do with his hands.

That hadn't stopped her from enjoying herself, however. His taste…decadent. Sinful. Like crisp, clean skies mixed with turbulent night storms. And his body, oh, his body. Utter perfection with hard muscles she'd wanted to squeeze. And lick. She wasn't picky.

His hair was so silky she could have run her fingers through it forever. His cock had been so long and thick she could have rubbed herself to orgasm. His skin was so warm and smooth she could have pressed against him and slept, just as she'd dreamed about doing before she'd met him. Even though sleeping with a man was a dangerous crime her race never committed.

Stupid girl! The angel wasn't to be trusted, especially since he clearly had nefarious plans for her—though he still refused to tell her exactly what those plans were. Teaching her to act like him had to be a misdirection of the truth. It was just too silly to contemplate. But his plans didn't matter, she supposed, since he would soon be at her mercy. Not that she had any.

Bianka strode to the closet she'd created and flipped through the lingerie hanging there. Blue, red, black. Lace, leather, satin. Several costumes: naughty nurse, corrupt policewoman, devil, angel. Which should she choose today?

He already thought her evil. Perhaps she should wear

the see-through white lace. Like a horny virgin bride. Oh, yes. That was the one. She laughed as she dressed.

"Mirror, please," she said, and a full-length mirror appeared in front of her. The gown fell to her ankles, but there was a slit between her legs. A slit that stopped at the apex of her thighs. Too bad she wasn't wearing any panties.

Spaghetti straps held the material in place on her shoulders and dipped into a deep vee between her breasts. Her nipples, pink and hard, played peekaboo with the swooping make-me-a-woman pattern.

She left her hair loose, flowing like black velvet down her back. Her gold eyes sparkled, flecks of gray finally evident, like in Kaia's. Her cheeks were flushed like a rose, her skin devoid of the makeup she usually wore to dull its shimmer.

Bianka traced her fingertips along her collarbone and chuckled again. She'd summoned a shower and washed off every trace of that makeup. If Lysander had found himself attracted to her before—and he had, the size of his hard-on was proof of that—he would be unable to resist her now. She was nothing short of radiant.

A Harpy's skin was like a weapon. A sensual weapon. Its jewel-like sheen drew men in, made them slobbering, drooling fools. Touching it became all they could think about, all they lived for.

That got old after a while, though, which was why she'd begun wearing full body makeup. For Lysander, though, she would make an exception. He deserved what he got. After all, he wasn't just making Bianka suffer. He was making her sisters suffer. Maybe.

Was Kaia still looking for her? Still worried or per-haps thinking this was a game as Bianka had first supposed? Had Kaia called their other sisters and were the girls now searching the world over for a sign of her, as they'd done when Gwennie went missing? Probably not, she thought with a sigh. They knew her, knew her strength and her determination. If they suspected she'd been taken, they would have confidence in her ability to free herself. Still.

Lysander was an ass.

And most likely a virgin. Eager, excited, she rubbed her hands together. Most men kissed the women they bedded. And if she had been his first kiss, well, it stood to reason he'd never bedded anyone. Her eagerness faded a bit. But that begged the question, why hadn't he bedded anyone?

Was he a young immortal? Had he not found anyone he desired? Did angels not often experience sexual need? She didn't know much about them. Fine, she didn't know anything about them. Did they consider sex wrong? Maybe. That would explain why he hadn't wanted to touch her, too.

Okay, so it made more sense that he simply hadn't experienced sexual need before.

He'd definitely experienced it during their kiss, though. She went back to rubbing her hands together.

"*What* are you wearing? Or better yet, not wearing?"

Heart skidding to a stop, Bianka whipped around. As if her thoughts had summoned him, Lysander stood in the room's doorway. Mist enveloped him and for a moment she feared he was nothing more than a fantasy.

"Well?" he demanded.

In her fantasies, he would not be angry. He would be overcome with desire. So…he was here, and he was real. And he was peering at her breasts in openmouthed astonishment.

Astonishment was better than anger. She almost grinned.

"Don't you like it?" she asked, smoothing her palms over her hips. *Let the games begin.*

"I—I—"

Like it, she finished for him. With the amount of truth that always layered his voice, he probably couldn't utter a single lie.

"Your skin…it's different. I mean, I saw the pearlesque tones before, but now…it's…"

"Amazing." She twirled, her gown dancing at her ankles. "I know."

"You know?" His tongue traced his teeth as the anger she'd first suspected glazed his features. "Cover her," he barked.

A moment later, a white robe draped her from shoulders to feet.

She scowled. "Return my teddy." The robe disappeared, leaving her in the white lace. "Try that again," she told him, "and I'll just walk around naked. You know, like I am in the portraits."

"Portraits?" Brow furrowing, he gazed about the room. When he spotted one of the pictures of her, sans clothing, reclining against a giant silver boulder, he hissed in a breath.

Exactly the reaction she'd been hoping for. "I hope you don't mind, but I turned this quaint little cloud into a love nest so I'd feel more at home. And again, if you remove anything, my redesign will be a thousand times worse."

"What are you trying to do to me?" he growled, facing her. His eyes were narrowed, his lips thinned, his teeth bared.

She fluttered her lashes at him, all innocence. "I'm afraid I don't know what you mean."

"Bianka."

It was a warning, she knew, but she didn't heed it. "I think it's my turn to ask the questions. So where do you go when you leave me?"

"That is not your concern."

Was he panting a little? "Let's see if I can make it my concern, shall we?" She sauntered to the bed and eased onto the edge. Naughty, shameless girl that she was, she spread her legs, giving him the peek of a lifetime. "For every question you answer, I'll put something on," she said in a sing-song voice. "Deal?"

He spun, but not before she saw the shock and desire that played over his harshly gorgeous face. "I do my duty. Watch the gates to hell. Hunt and kill demons that have escaped. Deliver punishment to those in need. Guard humans. Now cover yourself."

"I didn't say what item of clothing I'd don, now did I?" She gave herself a once-over. "One shoe, please. White leather, high heel, open toe. Ties up the calf." The shoe materialized on her foot, and she laughed. "Perfect."

"A trickster," Lysander muttered. "I should have known."

"How did I trick you? Did you ask for specifics? No, because you were secretly hoping I wouldn't cover myself at all."

"That is not true," he said, but for once, she did not hear that layer of honesty in his voice. Interesting. When he lied, or perhaps when he was unsure about what he was saying, his tone was as normal as hers.

That meant she would always know when he lied. Did things get any better than that?

This was going to be even easier than she'd anticipated. "Next question. Do you think about me while you're gone?"

Silence. Thick, heavy.

Wait. She could hear him breathing. In, out, harsh, shallow. He *was* panting.

"I'll take that as a yes," she said, grinning. "But since you really didn't answer, I don't have to add the other shoe."

Again, he didn't reply. Thankfully, he didn't leave, either.

"Onward and upward. Are angels allowed to dally?"

"Yes, but they rarely want to," he rasped.

So she'd been right. He didn't have firsthand knowledge of desire. What he was now feeling had to be confusing him, then. Was that why he'd brought her here? Because he'd seen her and wanted her, but hadn't known how to handle what he was feeling? The thought was almost…flattering. In a stalkerish kind of way, of course. That didn't change her plans, however. She would seduce him—and then she would slice his heart in two. A symbolic gesture, really. An inside joke between them. Well, for herself. He might not get it.

Still, she couldn't deny that she liked the idea of being his first. None of the women after her would compare, of course, and that— Hey, wait. Once he tasted the bliss of the flesh, he would want more. Bianka would have escaped him and stabbed him—and he would have recovered because he was an immortal—by then. He could go to any other female he desired.

He would kiss and touch that female.

"I'm waiting," he snapped.

"For?" she snapped back. Her hands were clenched, her nails cutting her palms. He could be with anyone; it wouldn't bother her. They were enemies. Someone else could deal with his Neanderthal tendencies. But gods, she might just kill the next woman who warmed his bed out of spite. Not jealousy.

"I answered one of your questions. You must add a garment to your body. Panties would be nice."

She sighed. "I'd like the other shoe to appear, please." A moment later, her other foot was covered. "Back to business. Did you return so that I'd kiss you again?"

"No!"

"Too bad. I wanted to taste you again. I wanted to touch you again. Maybe let you touch me this time. I've been aching since you left me. Had to bring myself to climax twice just to cool the fever. But don't worry, I imagined it was you. I imagined stripping you, licking you, sucking you into my mouth. Mmm, I'm so—"

"Stop!" he croaked out, spinning to face her. "Stop."

His eyes, which she'd once thought were black and emotionless, were now bright as a morning sky, his pupils blown with the intensity of his desire. But rather than stalk to her, grab her and smash his body into hers, he held out his hand, fingers splayed. A fiery sword formed from the air, yellow-gold flames flickering all around it.

"Stop," he commanded again. "I do not want to hurt you, but I will if you persist with this foolishness."

That layer of truth had returned to his voice.

Far from intimidating her, his forcefulness excited her. *I thought you didn't like his Neanderthal tendencies.*

Oh, shut up.

Bianka leaned back, resting her weight against her elbows. "Does Lysandy like to play rough? Should I be wearing black leather? Or is this a game of bad cop, naughty criminal? Should I strip for my body-cavity search?"

He stalked to the edge of the bed, his thick legs encasing her smaller ones, pressing her knees together. He was hard as a rock, his robe jutting forward. Those golden flames still flickering around the sword both highlighted his face and cast shadows, giving him a menacing aura.

Just then, he was both angel and demon. A mix of good and evil. Savior and executioner.

Her wings fluttered frantically, readying for battle— even as her skin tingled for pleasure. She could be across the room before he moved even a fraction of an inch. Still. She had trouble catching her breath; it was like ice in her lungs. And yet her blood was hot as his sword. This mix of emotions was odd.

"You are worse than I anticipated," he snarled.

If this progressed the way she hoped, he would be very happy about that one day. But she said, "Then let me go. You'll never have to see me again."

"And that will purge you from my mind? That will stop the wondering and the craving? No, it will only make them worse. You will give yourself to others, kiss them the way you kissed me, rub against them the way you rubbed against me, and I will want to kill them when they will have done nothing wrong."

What a confession! And she'd thought her blood hot before… "Then take me," she suggested huskily. She traced her tongue over her lips, slow and measured. His gaze followed. "It'll feel sooo good, I promise."

"And discover if you are as soft and wet as you appear? Spend the rest of eternity in bed with you, a slave to my body? No, that, too, will only make my cravings worse."

Oh, angel. You shouldn't have admitted that. A slave to his body? If that was his fear, he more than craved her. He was falling. Hard. And now that she knew how much he wanted her…he was as good as hers. "If you're going to kill me," she said, swirling a fingertip around her navel, "kill me with pleasure."

He stopped breathing.

She sat up, closing the rest of the distance between them. Still he didn't strike. She flattened her palms on his chest. His nipples were as beaded as hers. He closed his eyes, as if the sight of her, looking up at him through the thick shield of her lashes, was too much to bear.

"I'll let you in on a little secret," she whispered. "I'm softer and wetter than I appear."

Was that a moan?

And if so, had it come from him? Or her? Touching him like this was affecting her, too. All this strength at her fingertips was heady. Knowing this gorgeous warrior wanted her—her, and no other—was even headier. But knowing she was the very first to tempt him, and so strongly, was the ultimate aphrodisiac.

"Bianka." Oh, yes. A moan.

"But if you'd like, we can just lie next to each other." Said the spider to the fly. "We don't have to touch. We don't have to kiss. We'll lie there and think about all the things we dislike about each other and maybe build up an immunity. Maybe we'll stop *wanting* to touch and to kiss."

Never had she told such a blatant lie, and she'd told some big ones over the centuries. Part of her expected him to call her on it. The other part of her expected him to grasp on to the silly suggestion like a lifeline. Use it as an excuse to finally take what he wanted. Because if he did this, simply lay next to her, one temptation would lead to another. He wouldn't be thinking about the things he disliked about her—he would be thinking about the things he could be doing to her body. He would feel her heat, smell her arousal. He'd want—need—more from her. And she'd be right there, ready and willing to give it to him.

She fisted his robe and gently tugged him toward her. "It's worth a try, don't you think? *Anything*'s worth a try to make this madness stop."

When they were nose to nose, his breath trickling over her face, his gaze fastened on her lips, she began to ease backward. He followed, offering no resistance.

"Want to know one of the things I dislike about you?" she asked softly. "You know, to help get us started."

He nodded, as if he were too entranced to speak.

She decided to push a little faster than anticipated. He already seemed ready for more. "That you're not on top of me." Just a little more persuasion, and that would be remedied. Just a little… "How amazing would it feel to be that close?"

"Lysander," an unfamiliar female voice suddenly called. "Are you here?"

Who the hell? Bianka scowled.

Lysander straightened, jerking away from her as if

she had just sprouted horns. He stepped back, disengaging from her completely. But he was trembling, and not from anger.

"Ignore her," she said. "We have important business to attend to."

"Lysander?" the woman called again.

Damn her, whoever she was!

His expression cleared, melted to steel. "Not another word from you," he barked, backing away. "You tried to lure me into bed with you. I don't think you meant to make me dislike you at all. I think you meant to—" A low snarl erupted from his throat. "You are not to try such a thing with me again. If you do, I will finally cleave your head from your body."

Well, this battle was clearly over. Not one to give up, however, she tried a different strategy. "So you're going to leave again? Coward! Well, go ahead. Leave me helpless and bored. But you know what? When I'm bored, bad things happen. And next time you come back here, I just might throw myself at you. My hands will be all over you. You won't be able to pry me off!"

"Lysander," the girl called again.

He ground his teeth. "Return to your *cloud*," he threw over his shoulder. "I will meet you there."

He was going to meet another girl? At her cloud? Alone, private? Oh, hell, no. Bianka hadn't worked him into a frenzy so that someone else could reap the reward.

Before she could inform him of that, however, he said, "Give Bianka whatever she wants." Talking to his own cloud, apparently. "Anything but escape and more of those...outfits." His gaze intensified on her. "That should stave off the boredom. But I only agree to this on the condition that you vow to keep your hands to yourself."

Anything she wanted? She didn't allow herself to grin, the girl forgotten in the face of this victory. "Done."

"And so it is," he said, then spun and stalked from the room. His wings expanded in a rush, and he disappeared before she could follow. But then, there was no need to follow him. Not now.

He had no idea that he'd just ensured his own downfall. *Whatever she wants,* he'd said. She laughed. She didn't need to touch him or wear lingerie to win their next battle. She just needed his return.

Because then, *he* would become *her* prisoner.

CHAPTER FIVE

HE'D ALMOST GIVEN IN.

Lysander could not believe how quickly he'd almost given in to Bianka. One sultry glance from her, one invitation, and he'd forgotten his purpose. It was shameful. And yet, it was not shame that he felt. It was more of that strange disappointment—disappointment that he'd been interrupted!

Standing before Bianka, breathing in her wicked scent, feeling the heat of her body, all he'd been able to recall was the decadent taste of her. He'd wanted more. Wanted to finally touch her skin. Skin that had glowed with health, reflecting all those rainbow shards. She'd wanted that, too, he was sure of it. The more aroused she'd become, the brighter those colors had glowed.

Unless that was a trick? What did he truly know of women and desire?

She was worse than a demon, he thought. She'd known exactly how to entrance him. Those naked photos had nearly dropped him to his knees. Never had he seen anything so lovely. Her breasts, high and plump. Her stomach, flat. Her navel, perfectly dipped. Her thighs, firm and smooth. Then, being asked to lie beside her and think of what he disliked about her...both had been temptations, and both had been irresistible.

He'd known his resolve was crumbling and had

wanted to rebuild it. And how better to rebuild than to ponder all the things he disliked about the woman? But if he had lain next to her, he would not have thought of what he disliked—things he couldn't seem to recall then or now. He might have even thought about what he *liked* about her.

She was brilliant. She'd had him.

He'd never desired a demon. Had never secretly liked bad behavior. Yet Bianka excited him in a way he could not have predicted. So, what did he like most about her at the moment? That she was willing to do anything, say anything, to tempt him. He liked that she had no inhibitions. He liked that she gazed up at him with longing in those beautiful eyes.

How would she look at him if he actually kissed her again? Kissed more than her mouth? How would she look at him if he actually touched her? Caressed that skin? He suddenly found himself wanting to watch mortals and immortals alike more intently, gauging their reactions to each other. Man and woman, desire to desire.

Just the thought of doing so caused his body to react the way it had done with Bianka. Hardening, tightening. Burning, craving. His eyes widened. That, too, had never happened before. He was letting her win, he realized, even though there was distance between them. He was letting his one temptation destroy him, bit by bit.

Something had to be done about Bianka, since his current plan was clearly failing.

"Lysander?"

His charge's voice drew him from his dark musings. "Yes, sweet?"

Olivia's head tilted to the side, her burnished curls bouncing. They stood inside her cloud, flowers of every kind scattered across the floor, on the walls, even dripping from the ceiling.

Her eyes, as blue as the sky, regarded him intently. "You haven't been listening to me, have you?"

"No," he admitted. Truth had always been his most cherished companion. That would not change now. "My apologies."

"You are forgiven," she said with a grin as sweet as her flowers.

With her, it was that easy. Always. No matter how big or small the crime, Olivia couldn't hold a grudge. Perhaps that was why she was so treasured among their people. Everyone loved her.

What would other angels think of Bianka?

No doubt they would be horrified by her. *He* was horrified.

I thought you were not going to lie? Even to yourself. He scowled. Unlike the forgiving Olivia, he suspected Bianka would hold a grudge for a lifetime—and somehow take that grudge beyond the grave.

For some reason, his scowl faded and his lips twitched at the thought. *Why* would that amuse him? Grudges were born of anger, and anger was an ugly thing. Except, perhaps, on Bianka. Would she erupt with the same amount of unrelenting passion she brought to the bedroom? Probably. Would she want to be kissed from her anger, as well?

The thought of kissing her until she was happy again did *not* delight him.

Usually he dealt with other people's anger the way he dealt with everything else. With total unconcern. It was not his job to make people feel a certain way. They were responsible for their own emotions, just as he was responsible for his. Not that he experienced many. Over the years, he'd simply seen too much to be bothered. Until Bianka.

"Lysander?"

Olivia's voice once more jerked him from his mind. His hands fisted. He'd locked Bianka away, yet she was still managing to change him. Oh, yes. His current plan was failing.

Why couldn't he have desired someone like sweet Olivia? It would have made his endless life much easier. As he'd told Bianka, desire wasn't forbidden, but not many of their kind ever experienced it. Those that did only wanted other angels and often wed their chosen partner. Except in storybooks, he had never heard of an angel pairing with a different race—much less a demon.

"—you go again," Olivia said.

He blinked, hands fisting all the tighter. "Again, I apologize. I will be more diligent the rest of our conversation." He would make sure of it.

She offered him another grin, though this one lacked her usual ease. "I only asked what was bothering you." She folded her wings around herself and plucked at the feathers, carefully avoiding the strands of gold. "You're so unlike yourself."

That made two of them. Something was troubling her; sadness had never layered her voice before, yet now it did. Determined to help her, he summoned two chairs, one for him and one for her, and they sat across from each other. Her robe plumed around her as she released her wings and twined her fingers together in her lap. Leaning forward, he rested his weight on his elbows.

"Let us talk about you first. How goes your mission?" he asked. Only that could be the cause. Olivia found joy in all things. That's why she was so good at her job. Or rather, her former job. Because of him, she was now something she didn't want to be. A warrior angel. But it was for the best, and he did not regret the decision to change her station. Like him, she'd become too fascinated with someone she shouldn't.

Better to end that now, before the fascination ruined her.

She licked her lips and looked away from him. "That's actually what I wanted to speak with you about." A tremor shook her. "I don't think I can do it, Lysander." The words emerged as a tortured whisper. "I don't think I can kill Aeron."

"Why?" he asked, though he knew what she would say. But unlike Bianka, Aeron had broken a heavenly law, so there could be no locking him away and leading him to a righteous path.

If Olivia failed to destroy the demon-possessed male, another angel would be tasked with doing so—and Olivia would be punished for her refusal. She would be cast out of the heavens, her immortality stripped, her wings ripped from her back.

"He hasn't hurt anyone since his blood-curse was removed," she said, and he heard the underlying beseeching.

"He helped one of Lucifer's minions escape hell."

"Her name is Legion. And yes, Aeron did that. But he ensures the little demon stays away from most humans.

Those she does interact with, she treats with kindness. Well, her version of kindness."

"That doesn't change the fact that Aeron helped the creature escape."

Olivia's shoulders sagged, though she in no way appeared defeated. Determination gleamed in her eyes. "I know. But he's so...nice."

Lysander barked out a laugh. He just couldn't help himself. "We are speaking of a Lord of the Underworld, yes? The one whose entire body is tattooed with violent, bloody images no less? That is the male you call *nice?*"

"Not all of the etchings are violent," she mumbled, offended for some reason. "Two are butterflies."

For her to have found the butterflies amid the skeletal faces decorating the man's body meant she'd studied him intently. Lysander sighed. "Have you...felt anything for him?" Physically?

"What do you mean?" she asked, but rosy color bloomed on her cheeks.

She had, then. "Never mind." He scrubbed a hand down his suddenly tired face. "Do you like your home, Olivia?"

She blanched at that, as if she knew the direction he was headed. "Of course."

"Do you like your wings? Do you like your lack of pain, no matter the injury sustained? Do you like the robe you wear? A robe that cleans itself and you?"

"Yes," she replied softly. She gazed down at her hands. "You know I do."

"And you know that you will lose all of that and more if you fail to do your duty." The words were harsh, meant for himself as much as for her.

Tears sprang into her eyes. "I just hoped you could convince the council to rescind their order to execute him."

"I will not even try." Honest, he reminded himself. He had to be honest. Which he preferred. Or had. "Rules are put into place for a reason, whether we agree with those reasons or not. I have been around a long time, have seen the world—ours, theirs—plunged into darkness and chaos. And do you know what? That darkness and chaos always sprang from one broken rule. Just one. Because when one is broken, another soon follows. Then another. It becomes a vicious cycle."

A moment passed as she absorbed his words. Then she sighed, nodded. "Very well." Words of acceptance uttered in a tone that was anything but.

"You will do your duty?" What he was really asking: Will you slay Aeron, keeper of Wrath, whether you want to or not? Lysander wasn't asking more of her than he had done himself. He wasn't asking what he *wouldn't* do himself.

Another nod. One of those tears slid down her cheek.

He reached out and captured the glistening drop with the tip of his finger. "Your compassion is admirable, but it will destroy you if you allow it so much power over you."

She waved the prediction away. Perhaps because she did not believe it, or perhaps because she believed it but had no plans to change and therefore didn't want to discuss it anymore. "So who was the woman in your home? The one in the portraits?"

He…blushed? Yes, that was the heat spreading over his cheeks. "My…" How should he explain Bianka? How could he, without lying?

"Lover?" she finished for him.

His cheeks flushed with more of that heat. "No." Maybe. No! "She is my captive." There. Truthful without giving away any details. "And now," he said, standing. If she could end a subject, so could he. "I must return to her before she causes any more trouble." He must deal with her. Once and for all.

OLIVIA REMAINED IN PLACE long after Lysander left. Had that blushing, uncertain, distracted man truly been her mentor? She'd known him for centuries, and he'd always been unflappable. Even in the heat of battle.

The woman was responsible, she was sure. Lysander had never kept one in his cloud before. Did he feel for her what Olivia felt for Aeron?

Aeron.

Just thinking his name sent a shiver down her spine, filling her with a need to see him. And just like that, she was on her feet, her wings outstretched.

"I wish to leave," she said, and the floor softened, turning to mist. Down she fell, wings flapping gracefully. She was careful to avoid eye contact with the other angels flying through the sky as she headed into Budapest. They knew her destination; they even knew what she did there.

Some watched her with pity, some with concern— as Lysander had. Some watched her with antipathy. By avoiding their gazes, she ensured no one would stop her and try and talk sense into her. She ensured she wouldn't have to lie. Something she hated to do. Lies tasted disgustingly bitter.

Long ago, during her training, Lysander had commanded her to tell a lie. She would never forget the vile flood of acid in her mouth the moment she'd obeyed. Never again did she wish to experience such a thing. But to be with Aeron...maybe.

His dark, menacing fortress was perched high on a mountain and finally came into view. Her heart rate increased exponentially. Because she existed on another plane, she was able to drift through the stone walls as if they were not even there. Soon she was standing inside Aeron's bedroom.

He was polishing a gun. His little demon friend, Legion, the one he'd helped escape from hell, was darting and writhing around him, a pink boa twirling with her.

"Dance with me," the creature beseeched.

That was dancing? That kind of heaving was what humans did as they were dying.

"I can't. I've got to patrol the town tonight, searching for Hunters."

Hunters, sworn enemy of the Lords. They hoped to find Pandora's box and draw the demons out of the immortal warriors, killing each man. The Lords, in turn, hoped to find Pandora's box and destroy it—the same way they hoped to destroy the Hunters.

"Me hate Huntersss," Legion said, "but we needsss practice for Doubtie'sss wedding."

"I won't be dancing at Sabin's wedding, therefore practice isn't necessary."

Legion stilled, frowned. "But we dance at the wedding. Like a couple." Her thin lips curved downward. Was she...pouting? "Pleassse. We ssstill got time to practice. Dark not come for hoursss."

"As soon as I finish cleaning my weapons, I have to run an errand for Paris." Paris, Olivia knew, was keeper of Promiscuity and had to bed a new woman every day or he would weaken and die. But Paris was depressed and not taking proper care of himself, so Aeron, who felt responsible for the warrior, procured females for him. "We'll dance another time, I promise." Aeron didn't glance up from his task. "But we'll do it here, in the privacy of my room."

I want to dance with him, too, Olivia thought. What was it like, pressing your body against someone else's? Someone strong and hot and sinfully beautiful?

"But, Aeron…"

"I'm sorry, sweetheart. I do these things because they're necessary to keep you safe."

Olivia tucked her wings into her back. Aeron needed to take time for himself. He was always on the go, fighting Hunters, traveling the world in search of Pandora's box and aiding his friends. As much as she watched him, she knew he rarely rested and never did anything simply for the joy of it.

She reached out, meaning to ghost a hand through Aeron's hair. But suddenly the scaled, fanged creature screeched, "No, no, no," clearly sensing Olivia's presence. In a blink, Legion was gone.

Stiffening, Aeron growled low in his throat. "I told you not to return."

Though he couldn't see Olivia, he, too, always seemed to know when she arrived. And he hated her for scaring his friend away. But she couldn't help it. Angels were demon assassins and the minion must sense the menace in her.

"Leave," he commanded.

"No," she replied, but he couldn't hear her.

He returned the clip to his weapon and set it beside his bed. Scowling, he stood. His violet eyes narrowed as he searched the bedroom for any hint of her. Sadly, it was a hint he would never find.

Olivia studied him. His hair was cropped to his scalp, dark little spikes barely visible. He was so tall he dwarfed her, his shoulders so wide they could have enveloped her. With the tattoos decorating his skin, he was the fiercest creature she'd ever beheld. Maybe that was why he drew her so intensely. He was passion and danger, willing to do anything to save the ones he loved.

Most immortals put their own needs above everyone else's. Aeron put everyone else's above his own. That he did so never failed to shock her. And she was supposed to destroy him? She was supposed to end his life?

"I'm told you're an angel," he said.

How had he known what—the demon, she realized. Legion might not be able to see her, either, but as she'd already realized, the little demon knew danger when she encountered it. Plus, whenever Legion left him, she returned to hell. Fiery walls that could no longer confine her but could welcome her anytime she wished. Olivia's lack of success had to be a great source of amusement to that region's inhabitants.

"If you are an angel, you should know that won't stop me from cutting you down if you dare try and harm Legion."

Once again, he was thinking of another's welfare rather than his own. He didn't know that Olivia didn't need to bother with Legion. That once Aeron was dead, Legion's bond to him would wither and she would again be chained to hell.

Olivia closed the distance between them, her steps tentative. She stopped only when she was a whisper away. His nostrils flared as if he knew what she'd done, but he didn't move. Wishful thinking on her part, she knew. Unless she fell, he would never see her, never smell her, never hear her.

She reached up and cupped his jaw with her hands. How she wished she could feel him. Unlike Lysander, who was of the Elite, she could not materialize into this plane. Only her weapon would. A weapon she would forge from air, its heavenly flames far hotter than those in hell. A weapon that would remove Aeron's head from his body in a mere blink of time.

"I'm told you're female," he added, his tone hard, harsh. As always. "But that won't stop me from cutting you down, either. Because, and here's something you need to know, when I want something, I don't let anything stand in the way of my getting it."

Olivia shivered, but not for the reasons Aeron probably hoped. Such determination...

I should leave before I aggravate him even more. With a sigh, she spread her wings and leapt, out of the fortress and into the sky.

CHAPTER SIX

"YOU, CLOUD, BELONG TO ME," Bianka said. That was not an attempt to escape, nor another sexy outfit, therefore it was acceptable. "Lysander gave you to me, so as long as I don't touch him, I get what I want. And I want you. I want you to obey me, not him. Therefore, you have to heed my commands rather than his. If I tell you to do something and he tells you not to, you still have to do it. *That's* what I want."

And oh, baby, this was going to be fun.

The more she thought about it, the happier she was that she couldn't touch Lysander again. Really. Seducing—or rather, trying to seduce—him had been a mistake. She'd basically ended up seducing herself. His heat…his scent…his strength… *Give. Me. More.*

Now, all she could think about was getting his weight back on top of her. About how she wanted to teach him where she liked to be touched. Once he'd gotten the hang of kissing, he'd teased and tantalized her mouth with the skill of a master. It would be the same with lovemaking.

She would lick each and every one of his muscles. She would hear him moan over and over again as *he* licked *her.*

How could she want those things from her enemy? How could she forget, even for a moment, how he'd

locked her away? Maybe because he was a challenge.
A sexy, tempting, frustrating challenge.

Didn't matter, though. She was done playing the role
of sweet, horny prisoner. She still couldn't kill him;
she'd be stuck here for eternity. Which meant she'd have
to make him want to get rid of her. And now, as master
of this cloud, she would have no problem doing so.

She could hardly wait to begin. If he stuck to past
behavior, he'd be gone for a week. He'd return to "check
on" her. Operation Cry Like A Baby could begin. Tomorrow she'd plan the specifics and set the stage. A
few ideas were already percolating. Like tying him to
a chair in front of a stripper pole. Like enforcing Naked
Tuesdays.

Chuckling, she propped herself against the bed's
headboard, yawned and closed her eyes.

"I'd like to hold a bowl of Lysander's grapes," she
said, and felt a cool porcelain bowl instantly press atop
her stomach. Without opening her eyes, she popped one
of the fruits into her mouth, chewed. Gods, she was tired.
She hadn't rested properly since she'd gotten here—or
even before.

She couldn't. There were no trees to climb, no leaves
to hide in. And even if she summoned one, Lysander
could easily find her if he returned early—

Wait. No. No, he wouldn't. Not if she summoned
hundreds of them. And if he dismissed all the trees,
she would fall, which would awaken her. He would not
be able to take her unaware.

Chuckling again, Bianka pried her eyelids apart.
She polished off the grapes, scooted from the bed and
stood. "Replace the furniture with trees. Hundreds of
big, thick, green trees."

In the snap of her fingers, the cloud resembled a forest. Ivy twined around stumps and dew dripped from leaves. Flowers of every color bloomed, petals floating from them and dancing to the ground. She gaped at the beauty. Nothing on earth compared.

If only her sisters could see this.

Her sisters. Winning a game or not, she missed them more with every second that passed. Lysander would pay for that, too.

She yawned again. When she attempted to climb the nearest oak, her lingerie snagged on the bark. She straightened, scowled—reminded once again of the way her dark angel had stalked to her, leaned into her, hot breath trekking over her skin.

"I want to wear a camo tank and army fatigues." The moment she was dressed, she scaled to the highest bough, fluttering wings giving her speed and agility, and reclined on a fat branch, peering up into a lovely star-sprinkled sky. "I'd like a bottle of Lysander's wine, please."

Her fingers were clutching a flagon of dry red a second later. She would have preferred a cheap white, but whatever. Hard times called for sacrifices, and she drained the bottle in record time.

Just as she summoned a second, she heard Lysander shout, "Bianka!"

She blinked in confusion. Either she'd been up here longer than she'd thought or she was hallucinating.

Why couldn't she have imagined a Lord of the Underworld? she wondered disgustedly. Oh, oh. How cool would it be if Lysander oil-wrestled a Lord? They'd be wearing loincloths, of course, and smiles. But nothing else.

And she could totally have that! This was her cloud, after all. She and Lysander were now playing by her rules. And, because she was in charge, he couldn't rescind his command that she be obeyed without her permission.

At least, she prayed that was the way this would work.

"Remove the trees," she heard him snap.

She waited, unable to breathe, but the trees remained. He couldn't! Grinning, she jolted upright and clapped. She'd been right, then. This cloud belonged to her.

"Remove. The. Trees."

Again, they remained.

"Bianka!" he snarled. "Show yourself."

Anticipation flooded her as she jumped down. A quick scan of her surroundings revealed that he wasn't nearby. "Take me to him."

She blinked and found herself standing in front of him. He'd been shoving his way through the foliage and when he spotted her, he stopped. He clutched that sword of fire.

She backed away, remaining out of reach. No touching. She wouldn't forget. "That for me?" she asked, motioning to the weapon with a tilt of her chin. She'd never been so excited in her life and even the sight of that weapon didn't dampen the emotion.

A vein bulged in his temples.

She'd take that for a yes. "Naughty boy." He'd come to kill her, she thought, swaying a little. That was something else to punish him for. "You're back early."

His gaze raked her newest outfit, his pupils dilated and his nostrils flared. His mouth, however, curled in distaste. "And you are drunk."

"How dare you accuse me of such a thing!" She tried for a harsh expression, but ruined it when she laughed. "I'm just tipsy."

"What did you do to my cloud?" He crossed his arms over his chest, the picture of stubborn male. "Why won't the trees disappear?"

"First, you're wrong. This is no longer your cloud. Second, the trees will only leave if I tell them to leave. Which I am. Leave, pretty trees, leave." Another laugh. "Oh, my gods. I said leave to a tree. I'm a poet and I didn't know it." Instantly, there was nothing surrounding her and Lysander but glorious white mist. "Third, you're not going anywhere without my permission. Did you hear that, cloud? He stays. Fourth, you're wearing too many clothes. I want you in a loincloth, minus the weapon."

His sword was suddenly gone. His eyes widened as his robe disappeared and a flesh-colored loincloth appeared. Bianka tried not to gape. And she'd thought the forest gorgeous. Wow. Just…wow. His body was a work of art. He possessed more muscles than she'd realized. His biceps were perfectly proportioned. Rope after rope lined his stomach. And his thighs were ridged, his skin sun-kissed.

"This cloud is mine, and I demand the return of my robe." His voice was so low, so harsh, it scraped against her eardrums.

The sweet sound of victory, she thought. He remained exactly as she'd requested. Laughing, she twirled, arms splayed wide. "Isn't this fabulous?"

He stalked toward her, menace in every step.

"No, no, no." She danced out of reach. "We can't have that. I want you in a large tub of oil."

And just like that, he was trapped inside a tub. Clear oil rose to his calves, and he stared down in horror.

"How do you like having your will overlooked?" she taunted.

His gaze lifted, met hers, narrowed. "I will not fight you in this."

"Silly man. Of course you won't. You'll fight…" She tapped her chin with a fingernail. "Let's see, let's see. Amun? No. He won't speak and I'd like to hear some cursing. Strider? As keeper of Defeat, he'd ensure you lost to prevent himself from feeling pain, but that would be an intense battle and I'm just wanting something to amuse me. You know, something light and sexy. I mean, since I can't touch you, I want a Lord to do it for me."

Lysander popped his jaw. "Do not do this, Bianka. You will not like the consequences."

"Now that's just sad," she said. "I've been here two weeks, but you don't know me at all. Of course I'll like the consequences." Torin, keeper of Disease? Watching him fight Torin would be fun, 'cause then he'd catch that black plague. Or would he? Could angels get sick? She sighed. "Paris will have to do, I guess. He's handsy, so that works in my favor."

"Don't you dare—"

"Cloud, place Paris, keeper of Promiscuity, into the tub with Lysander."

When Paris appeared a moment later, she clapped. Paris was tall and just as muscled as Lysander. Only he had black hair streaked with brown and gold, his eyes were electric blue and his face perfect enough to make her weep from its beauty. Too bad he didn't stir her body the way Lysander did. Making out with him in front of the angel would have been fun.

"Bianka?" Paris looked from her to the angel, the angel to her. "Where am I? Is this some ambrosia-induced hallucination? What the hell is going on?"

"For one thing, you're overdressed. You should only be wearing a loincloth like Lysander."

His T-shirt and jeans were instantly replaced with said loincloth.

Best. Day. Ever. "Paris, I'd like you to meet Lysander, the angel who abducted me and has been holding me prisoner up here in heaven."

Instantly Paris morphed from confusion to fury. "Return my weapons and I'll kill him for you."

"You are such a sweetie," she said, flattening a hand over her heart. "Why is it we haven't slept together yet?"

Lysander snarled low in his throat.

"What?" she asked him, all innocence. "He wants to save me. You want to subjugate me for the rest of my long life. But anyway, let me finish the introductions. Lysander, I'd like you to meet—"

"I know who he is. Promiscuity." Disgust layered Lysander's voice. "He must bed a new woman every day or he weakens."

Another grin lifted the corners of her lips, this one smug. "Actually, he can bed men, too. His demon's not picky. I do hope you'll keep that in mind while you guys are rubbing up against each other."

Lysander took a menacing step toward her.

"What's going on?" Paris demanded again, glowering now. Bianka knew he was picky even if his demon wasn't.

"Oh, didn't I tell you? Lysander gave me control of his home, so now I get whatever I want and I want you guys to wrestle. And when you're done, you'll find Kaia and tell her what's happened, that I'm trapped with a stubborn angel and can't leave. Well, I can't leave until he gets so sick of me he allows the cloud to release me."

"Or until I kill you," he snapped.

She laughed. "Or until Paris kills *you*. But I hope you guys will play nice for a little while, at least. Do you have any idea how sexy you both are right now? And if you want to kiss or something while rolling around, don't let me stop you."

"Uh, Bianka," Paris began, beginning to look uncomfortable. "Kaia's in Budapest. She's helping Gwen with the wedding, and thinks you're hiding to get out of your maid of honor duties."

"I am not maid of honor, damn it!" But at least Kaia wasn't worried. *The bitch,* she thought with affection.

"That's not what she says. Anyway, I don't mind fighting another dude to amuse you, but seriously, he's an angel. I need to return to—"

"No need to thank me." She held out her hands. "A bowl of Lysander's popcorn, please." The bowl appeared, the scent of butter wafting to her nose. "Now then. Let's get this party started. *Ding, ding,*" she said, and settled down to watch the battle.

CHAPTER SEVEN

LYSANDER COULD NOT BELIEVE what he was being forced to do. He was angry, horrified and, yes, contrite. Hadn't he done something similar to Bianka? Granted, he hadn't stripped her down. Hadn't pitted her against another female.

There was the tightening in his groin again.

What was wrong with him?

"I will set you free," he told Bianka. And sweet Holy Deity, she looked beautiful. More tempting than when she'd worn that little bit of nothing. Now she wore a green and black tank that bared her golden arms. Were those arms as soft as they appeared? *Don't think like that.* Her shirt stopped just above her navel, making his mouth water, his tongue yearn to dip inside. *What did I just say? Don't think like that.* Her pants were the same dark shades and hung low on her hips.

He'd come here to fight her, to finally force her hand, and judging by that outfit, she'd been ready for combat. That…excited him. Not because their bodies would have been in close proximity—really—and not because he could have finally gotten his hands on her—again, really—but because, if she injured him, he would have the right to end her life. Finally.

But he'd come here and she'd taught him a quick yet unforgettable lesson instead. He'd been wrong to whisk her to his home and hold her captive. Temptation or not. She might be his enemy in ways she didn't understand, but he never should have put his will above hers. He should have allowed her to live her life as she saw fit.

That's why he existed in the first place. To protect free will.

When this wrestling match ended, he would free her as he'd promised. He would watch her, though. Closely. And when she made a mistake, he would strike her down. And she would. Make a mistake, that is. As a Harpy, she wouldn't be able to help herself. He wished it hadn't come to that. He wished she could have been happy here with him, learning his ways.

The thought of losing her did not sadden him. He would not miss her. She'd placed him in a vat of oil to wrestle with another man, for Lord's sake.

There was suddenly a bitter taste in his mouth.

"Bianka," he prompted. "Have you no response?"

"Yes, you will set me free," she finally said with a radiant grin. She twirled a strand of that dark-as-night hair around her finger. "After. Now, I do believe I rang the starting bell."

Her words were slightly slurred from the wine she'd consumed. A drunken menace, that's what she was. And he would not miss her, he told himself again.

The bitterness intensified.

A hard weight slammed into him and sent him propelling to his back. His wings caught on the sides of the pool as oil washed over him from head to toe, weighing him down. He grunted, and some of the stuff—cherry-flavored—seeped into his mouth.

"Don't forget to use tongue if you kiss," Bianka called helpfully.

"You don't lock women away," Paris growled down at him, a flash of scales suddenly visible under his skin. Eyes red and bright. Demon eyes. "No matter how ir-ritating they are."

"Your friends did something similar to their women, did they not? Besides, the girl isn't your concern." Ly-sander shoved, sending the warrior hurtling to *his* back. He attempted to use his wings to lift himself, but their movements were slow and sluggish so all he could do was stand.

Oil dripped down his face, momentarily shielding his vision. Paris shot to his feet, as well, hands fisted, body glistening.

"So. Much. Fun," Bianka sang happily.

"Enough," Lysander told her. "This is unnecessary. You have made your point. I'm willing to set you free."

"You're right," she said. "It's unnecessary to fight without music!" Once again she tapped her chin with a nail, expression thoughtful. "I know! We need some Lady Gaga in this crib."

A song Lysander had never heard before was playing through the cloud a second later. Like a siren rising from the sea, Bianka began swaying her hips seductively.

Lysander's jaw clenched so painfully the bones would probably snap out of place at any moment. Clearly there would be no reasoning with Bianka. That meant he had to reason with Paris. But who would ever have thought he'd have to bargain with a demon?

"Paris," he began—just as a fist connected with his face.

His head whipped back. His feet slipped on the slick floor and he tumbled to his side. More of the cherry fla-vor filled his mouth.

Paris straddled his shoulders, punched him again. Lysander's lip split. Before a single drop of blood could form, however, the wound healed.

He frowned. He now had the right to slay the man, but he couldn't bring himself to do it. He did not blame Paris for this battle; he blamed Bianka. She had forced them into this situation.

Another punch. "Are you the one who's been watching Aeron?" Paris demanded.

"Hey, now," Bianka called. No longer did she sound so carefree. "Paris, you are not to use your fists. That's boxing, not wrestling."

Lysander remained silent, not understanding the difference. A fight was a fight.

Another punch. "Are you?" Paris growled.

"Paris! Did you hear me?" Now she sounded angry. "Use your fists like that again and I'll cut off your head."

She'd do it, too, Lysander thought, and wondered why she was so upset. Could she, perhaps, care for his health? His eyes widened. Was *that* why she preferred the less intensive wrestling to the more violent boxing? Would she want to do the same to him if he were to punch the Lord? And what would it mean if she did?

How would he feel about that?

"Are you?" Paris repeated.

"No," he finally said. "I'm not." He worked his legs up, planted his feet on Paris's chest and pressed. But rather than send the warrior flying, his foot slipped and connected with Paris's jaw, then ear, knocking the man's head back.

"Use your hands, angel," Bianka suggested. "Choke him! He deserves it for breaking my rules."

"Bianka," Paris snapped. He lost his footing and tumbled to his butt. "I thought you wanted me to destroy him, not the other way around."

She blinked over at them, brow furrowed. "I do. I just don't want you to hurt him. That's my job."

Paris tangled a hand through his soaked hair. "Sorry, darling, but if this continues, I'm going to unleash a world of hurt on your frenemy. Nothing you say will be able to stop me. Clearly, he doesn't have your best interests at heart."

Darling? Had the demon-possessed immortal just called Bianka *darling*? Something dark and dangerous flooded Lysander—*mine* echoed through his head—and before he realized what he was doing, he was on top of the warrior, a sword of fire in his hand, raised, descending…about to meet flesh.

A firm hand around his wrist stopped him. Warm, smooth skin. His wild gaze whipped to the side. There was Bianka, inside the tub, oil glistening off her. How fast she'd moved.

"You can't kill him," she said determinedly.

"Because you want him, too," he snarled. A statement, not a question. Rage, so much rage. He didn't know where it was coming from or how to stop the flow.

She blinked again, as if the thought had never entered her mind, and that, miraculously, cooled his temper. "No. Because then you would be like me and therefore perfect," she said. "That wouldn't be fair to the world."

"Stop talking and fight, damn you," Paris commanded. A fist connected with Lysander's jaw, tossing him to the side and out of Bianka's reach. He maintained his grip on the sword and even when it dipped into the oil, it didn't lose a single flame. In fact, the oil heated.

Great. Now he was hot-tubbing, as the humans would say.

"What'd you do that for, you big dummy?" Bianka didn't wait for Paris's reply but launched herself at him. Rather than scratch him or pull his hair, she punched him. Over and over again. "He wasn't going to hurt you."

Paris took the beating without retaliating.

That saved his life.

Lysander grabbed the Harpy around the waist and hefted her into the hard line of his body. Soaked as they both were, he had a difficult time maintaining his grip. She was panting, arms flailing for the demon-possessed warrior, but she didn't try to pull away.

"I'll teach you to defy me, you rotten piece of shit," she growled.

Paris rolled his eyes.

"Send him away," Lysander commanded.

"Not until after I—"

He splayed his fingers, spanning much of her waist. He both rejoiced and cursed that he couldn't feel the texture of Bianka's skin through the oil. "I want to be alone with you."

"You—what?"

"Alone. With you."

With no hesitation, she said, "Go home, Paris. Your work here is done. Thanks for trying to rescue me. That's the only reason you're still alive. Oh, and don't forget to tell my sisters I'm fine."

The sputtering Lord disappeared.

Lysander released her, and she spun around to face him. She was now grinning.

"So you want to be alone with me, do you?"

He ran his tongue over his teeth. "Was that fun for you?"

"Yes."

And she wasn't ashamed to admit it, he realized. Captivating baggage. "Return the cloud to me and I will take you home."

"Wait. What?" Her grin slowly faded. "I thought you wanted to be alone with me."

"I do. So that we can conclude our business."

Disappointment, regret, anger and relief played over her features. One step, two, she closed the distance between them. "Well, I'm not giving you the cloud. That would be stupid."

"You have my word that once you return it to me, I will take you home. I know you hear the truth in my claim."

"Oh." Her shoulders sagged a little. "So we really would be rid of each other. That's great, then."

Did she still not believe him? Or... No, surely not. "Do you want to stay here?"

"Of course not!" She sucked her bottom lip into her mouth, and her eyes closed for a moment, an expression of pleasure consuming her features. "Mmm, cherries."

Blood...heating...

Her lashes lifted and her gaze locked on him. Determination replaced all the other emotions, yet her voice dipped sexily. "But I know something that tastes even better."

So did he. Her. A tremor slid the length of his spine. "Do not do this, Bianka. You will fail." He hoped.

"One kiss," she beseeched, "and the cloud is yours."

His eyes narrowed. Hot, so hot. "You cannot be trusted to keep your word."

"That's true. But I want out of this hellhole, so I'll keep it this time. Promise."

Hold your ground. But that was hard to do while his heart was pounding like a hammer against a nail. "If you wanted out, you would not insist on being kissed."

Her gaze narrowed, as well. "It's not like I'm asking for something you haven't already given me."

"Why do you want it?" He regretted the question immediately. He was prolonging the conversation rather than putting an end to it.

Her chin lifted. "It's a goodbye kiss, moron, but never mind. The cloud is yours. I'll go home and kiss Paris hello. That'll be more fun, anyway."

There would be no kissing Paris! Lysander had his tongue sliding into her mouth before he could convince himself otherwise. His arms even wound around her waist, pulling her closer to him—so close their chests rubbed each time they breathed. Her nipples were hard, deliciously abrading.

"Out of the oil," she murmured. "Clean."

He was still in the loincloth, but his skin was suddenly free of the oil, his feet on soft yet firm mist. The cloud might belong to him once more, but she could still make reasonable demands.

Bianka tilted her head and took his possession deeper. Their tongues dueled and rolled and their teeth scraped. Her hands were all over him, no part of him forbidden to her.

Goodbye, she had said.

This was it, then. His last chance to touch her skin. To finally know. Yes, he planned to see her again, to watch her from afar, to wait for his chance to rid himself of her permanently, but never again would he allow himself to get this close to her. And he had to know.

So he did it.

He glided his hands forward, tracing from her lower back to her stomach. There, he flattened his palms, and her muscles quivered. Dear Deity of Light and Love. She was softer than he'd realized. Softer than anything else he'd ever touched.

He moaned. *Have to touch more.* Up he lifted, remaining under her shirt. Warm, smooth, as he'd already known. Still soft, so sweetly soft. Her breasts overflowed, and his mouth watered for a taste of them. Soon, he told himself. Then shook his head. This was it; the last time they would be together. Goodbye, pretty breasts. He kneaded them.

More soft perfection.

Trembling now, he reached her collarbone. Her shoulders. She shivered. Still so wonderfully soft. More, more, more, he had to have more. Had to touch all of her.

"Lysander," she gasped out. She dropped to her knees, working at the loincloth before he realized what she was doing.

His shaft sprang free, and his hands settled atop her shoulders to push her away. But once he touched that soft skin, he was once again lost to the sensation. Perfection, this was perfection.

"Going to kiss you now. A different kind of kiss." Warm, wet heat settled over the hard length of him. Another moan escaped him. Up, down that wicked mouth rode him. The pleasure…it was too much, not enough, everything and nothing. In that moment, it was necessary to his survival. His every breath hinged on what she would do next. There would be no pushing her away.

She twirled her tongue over the plump head; her fingers played with his testicles. Soon he was arching his hips, thrusting deep into her mouth. He couldn't stop moaning, groaning, the gasping breaths leaving him in a constant stream.

"Bianka," he growled. "Bianka."

"That's the way, baby. Give Bianka everything."

"Yes, yes." Everything. He would give her everything.

The sensation was building, his skin tightening, his muscles locking down on his bones. And then something exploded inside him. Something hot and wanton. His entire body jerked. Seed jetted from him, and she swallowed every drop.

Finally she pulled away from him, but his body wouldn't stop shaking. His knees were weak, his limbs nearly uncontrollable. That was pleasure, he realized, dazed. That was passion. That was what human men were willing to die to possess. That was what turned normally sane men into slaves. *Like I am now.* He was Bianka's slave.

Fool! *You knew this would happen.* Fight. It was only as she stood and smiled at him tenderly—and he wanted to tug her into his arms and hold on forever—that a measure of sanity stole back into his mind. Yes. Fight. How could he have allowed her to do that?

How could he still want her?

How could he want to do that to her in return?

How could he ever let her go?

"Bianka," he said. He needed a moment to catch his breath. No. He needed to think about what had happened and how they should proceed. No. He tangled a hand in his hair. What should he do?

"Don't say anything." Her smile disappeared as if it had never been. "The cloud is yours." Her voice trembled with…fear? Couldn't be. She hadn't showed a moment of fear since he'd first abducted her. But she even backed away from him. "Now take me home. Please."

He opened his mouth to reply. What he would say, he didn't know. He only knew he did not like seeing her like that.

"Take me home," she croaked.

He'd never gone back on his word, and he wouldn't start now. He nodded stiffly, grabbed her hand, and flew her back to the ice mountain in Alaska, exactly as he'd found her. Red coat, tall boots. Sensual in a way he hadn't understood then.

He maintained his grip on her until the last possible second—until she slipped away from him, taking her warmth and the sweet softness of her skin with her.

"I don't want to see you again." Mist wafted around her as she turned her back on him. "Okay?"

She…what? After what had happened between them, *she* was dismissing *him?* No, a voice roared inside his head. "Behave, and you will not," he gritted out. A lie? The bitter taste in his mouth had returned.

"Good." Without meeting his gaze, she twisted and blew him a kiss as if she hadn't a care in the world. "I'd say you were an excellent host, but then, you don't want me to lie, do you?" With that, she strolled away from him, dark hair blowing in the wind.

CHAPTER EIGHT

FIRST THING BIANKA DID after bathing, dressing, eating a bag of stolen chips she had hidden in her kitchen, painting her nails, listening to her iPod for half an hour and taking a nap in her secret basement was call Kaia. Not that she had dreaded the call and wanted to put it off or anything. All of those other activities had been necessary. Really.

Plus, it wasn't like her sister was worried about her anymore. Paris would already have told her what was going on. But Bianka didn't want to discuss Lysander. Didn't even want to think about him and the havoc he was causing her emotions—and her body and her thoughts and her common sense.

After making out with him a little, she'd wanted to freaking stay with him, curl up in his arms, make love and sleep. And that was unacceptable.

The moment her sister answered, she said, "No need to throw me a Welcome Home party. I'm not sticking around for long." *Do not ask me about the angel. Do not ask me about the angel.*

"Bianka?" her twin asked groggily.

"You were expecting someone else to call in the middle of the night?" It was 6:00 a.m. here in Alaska. Having traveled between the two places multiple times since

Gwen had gotten involved with Sabin, she knew that meant it was 3:00 a.m. there in Budapest.

"Yeah," Kaia said. "I was."

Seriously? "Who?"

"Lots of people. Gwennie, who has become the ultimate bridezilla. Sabin, who is doing his best to soothe the beast but whines to me like I care." She rambled on as if Bianka had never been abducted and she'd never been worried. Sure, she'd thought Bianka was merely shirking her duties, but was a little worry too much to ask for? "Anya, who has decided she deserves a wedding, too. Only bigger and better than Gwen's. William, who wants to sleep with me and doesn't know how to take no for an answer. He's not possessed by a demon so he's not my type. Shall I go on?"

"Yes."

"Shut up."

She imagined Kaia high in a treetop, clutching her cell to her ear, grinning and trying not to fall. "So really, you were *sleeping?* While I was missing, my life in terrible danger? Some loving sister you are."

"Please. You were on vacay, and we both know it. So don't give me a hard time. I had an...exciting day."

"Doing who?" she asked dryly. Only two weeks had passed since she'd last seen Kaia, but suddenly a wave of homesickness—or rather, sistersickness—flooded her. She loved this woman more than she loved herself. And that was a lot!

Kaia chuckled. "I wish it was because of a *who.* I'm waiting for two of the Lords to fight over me. Then I'll comfort them both. So far, no luck."

"Idiots."

"I know! But I mentioned Gwen has become the

bride from hell, right? They're afraid I'll act just like her, so no one's willing to take a real chance on me."

"Bride from hell, how?"

"Her dress didn't fit right. Her napkins weren't the right color. No one has the flowers she wants. Whaa, whaa, whaa."

That didn't sound like the usually calm Gwen. "Distract her. Tell her the Hunters captured me and performed a handbotomy on me like they did on Gideon." Gideon, keeper of Lies. A sexy warrior who dyed his hair as blue as his eyes and had a wicked sense of humor.

The thought of seducing him didn't delight her as it once might have. Stupid angel. *Do not think about him.*

"She wouldn't care if you were chopped up into little pieces. You're too much like me and apparently we take nothing seriously so we deserve what we get," Kaia said. "She's driving me freaking insane! And to top off my mountain-o-crap, I was totally losing our game of Hide and Seek. So anyway, why'd you decide to rescue yourself? I'm telling you, you have a better chance of survival in the clouds than here with Gwen."

"Survival schmival. It wasn't fun anymore." A lie. Things had just started to heat up the way she'd wanted. But how could she have known that would scare her so badly?

"Good going, by the way. Allowing yourself to be taken into the clouds where I couldn't get to you. Brilliant."

"I know, *right?*"

"So was it terrible? Being spirited away by a sexy angel?"

She twirled a strand of hair around her finger and pictured Lysander's glorious face. The desire he'd leveled at her while she'd sucked him dry had been miraculous. *You don't want to talk about him, remember?* "Yes. It was terrible." Terribly wonderful.

"You bringing him to Buda for the wedding?"

The words were sneered, clearly a joke, but Bianka found herself shouting, "No!" before she could stop herself. A Harpy dating an angel? Unacceptable!

And anyway, allowing the demon-possessed Lords of the Underworld to surround a warrior straight from heaven would be stupid. Not that she feared for Lysander. Guy could handle himself, no problem. The way he formed a sword of fire from nothing but air was proof of that. But if something were to happen to Gwennie's precious Sabin, like, oh, decapitation, the festivities would be somewhat dimmed.

"I'll be there, though," she added in a calmer tone. "I kinda have to, you know. Since I'm the maid of honor and all."

"Oh, hell, no. I am, remember?"

She grinned slowly. "You told me you'd rather be hit by a bus than be a bridesmaid."

"Yeah, but I want to have a bigger part than you, so… here I am, in Budapest, helping little Gwennie plan the ceremony. Not that she's taking my suggestions. Would it kill her to at least *consider* making everyone come naked?"

They shared a laugh.

"Well, you and I can attend naked," Bianka said. "It'll certainly liven things up."

"Done!"

There was a pause.

Kaia pushed out a breath. "So you're fine?" she

asked, a twinge of concern finally appearing in her voice.

"Yeah." And she was. Or would be. Soon, she hoped. All she had to do was figure out what to do about Lysander. Not that he'd tried to stick around, the jerk. He hadn't been able to get away from her fast enough. Sure, she'd pushed him away. But dude could have fought for her attention after what she'd done for him.

"You're gonna make the angel pay for taking you without permission, right? Who am I kidding? Of course you are. If you wait till after the wedding, I can help. Please, please let me help. I have a few ideas and I think you'll like them. Picture this. It's midnight, your angel is strapped to your bed, and we each rip off one of his wings."

Nice. But because she didn't know whether Lysander was watching and listening or not—was he? It was possible, and just the thought had her skin heating—she said, "Don't worry about it. I'm done with him."

"Wait, what?" Kaia gasped out. "You can't be done with him. He abducted you. Held you prisoner. Yeah, he oil-wrestled Paris and I'm pissed I didn't get to see, but that doesn't excuse his behavior. If you let him off without punishment, he'll think it's okay. He'll think you're weak. He'll come after you again."

Yes. Yes, he would, she thought, suddenly trying not to grin. "No, he won't," she lied. *Are you listening, Lysander, baby?*

"Bianka, tell me you don't like him. Tell me you aren't lusting for an angel."

Abruptly her smile faded. This was exactly the line of questioning she'd hoped to avoid. "I'm not lusting for an angel." Another lie.

Another pause. "I don't believe you."

"Too bad."

"Mom thought Gwen's dad was an angel and she regretted sleeping with him all these years. They're too good. Too…different from us. Angels and Harpies are not meant to mix. Tell me you know that."

"Of course I know it. Now, I've gotta go. Tell the bridezilla to go easy on you. Love you and see you soon," she replied and hung up before Kaia could say anything else.

Despite her fear of what Lysander made her feel, Bianka wasn't done with him. Not even close. But she'd been on his turf before and therefore at a disadvantage. If he wasn't here, she needed to get him here. Willingly.

She'd told him to leave her alone, she thought, and that could be a problem. Except…

With a whoop, she jumped up and spun around. That wouldn't be a problem at all. That was actually a blessing and she was smarter than she'd realized. By telling him to stay away from her, she'd surely become the forbidden fruit. Of course he was here, watching her.

Men never could do what they were told. Not even angels.

So. Easy.

Even better, she'd given him a little taste of what it was like to be with her. He would crave more. But also, she hadn't allowed him to pleasure her. His pride would not allow her to remain in this unsatisfied state for long, while he had enjoyed such sweet completion.

And if that wasn't the case, he wasn't the virile warrior she thought he was and he therefore wouldn't deserve her.

How long till he made an actual appearance? They'd only been apart half a day, but she already missed him.

Missed him. Ugh. She'd never missed a man before. Especially one who wanted to change her. One who despised what she was. One who could only be labeled *enemy*.

You have to avoid him. You want to sleep in his arms. You were protective of him while he fought Paris. He angered you but you didn't kill him. And now you're missing him? You know what this means, don't you?

Her eyes widened, and her excitement drained. Oh, gods. She should have realized…should at least have suspected. Especially when she'd protected him, defended him.

Lysander, a goody-goody angel, was her consort.

Her knees gave out and she flopped onto the floor. As long as she'd been alive, she'd never thought to find one. Because, well, a consort was a meant-to-be husband. Some nights she'd dreamed of finding hers, yes, but she hadn't thought it would actually happen.

Her consort. Wow.

Her family was going to flip. Not because Lysander had abducted her—they'd come to respect that—but because of what he was. More than that, she didn't trust Lysander, would never trust him, and so could never do any actual sleeping with him.

Sex, though, she could allow. Often. Yes, yes, she could make this work, she thought, brightening. She could lure him to the dark side without letting her family know she was spending time with him. Humiliation averted!

Decided, she nodded. Lysander would be hers. In secret. And there was no better time to begin. If he was watching as she suspected, there was only one way to get him to reveal himself.

She dressed in a lacy red halter and her favorite skinny jeans and drove into town. Only reason she owned a car was because it made her appear more human. Flying kind of gave her away. Though her arms and navel were exposed, the frigid wind didn't bother her. Chilled her, yes, but that she could deal with. She wanted Lysander to see as much of her as possible.

She parked in front of The Moose Lodge, a local diner, and strode to the front door. Because it was so early and so cold, no one was nearby. A few streetlamps illuminated her, but she wasn't worried. She unlocked the door—she'd stolen the key from the owner months ago—and disabled the alarm.

Inside, she claimed a pecan pie from the glassed refrigerator, grabbed a fork and dug in while walking to her favorite booth. She'd done this a thousand times before.

Come out, come out, wherever you are. He wouldn't have just left her to her evil ways without thinking to protect the world from her. Right? She wished she could feel him, at least sense him in some way. His scent perhaps, that wild, night-sky scent. But as she breathed deeply, she smelled only pecans and sugar. Still. She hadn't sensed him when he'd snatched her from mid-free fall, so it stood to reason she wouldn't sense him now.

Once the pie was polished off, the pan discarded and her fork licked clean, she filled a cup with Dr. Pepper. She placed a few quarters in the old jukebox and soon an erratic beat was echoing from the walls. Bianka danced around one of the tables, thrusting her hips forward and back, arching, sliding around, hands roving over her entire body.

For a moment, only a brief, sultry moment, she thought she felt hot hands replace her own, exploring her breasts, her stomach. Thought she felt soft feathered wings envelop her, closing her in. She stilled, heart drumming in her chest. So badly she wanted to say his name, but she didn't want to scare him away. So…what should she do? How should she—

The feeling of being surrounded evaporated completely.

Damn him!

Teeth grinding, not knowing what else to do, she exited the diner the same way she'd entered. Through the front door, as if she hadn't a care. That door slammed behind her, the force of it nearly shaking the walls.

"You should lock up after yourself."

He was here; he'd been watching. She'd known it! Trying not to grin, she spun around to face Lysander. The sight of him stole her breath. He was as beautiful as she remembered. His pale hair whipped in the wind, little snow crystals flying around him. His golden wings were extended and glowing. But his dark eyes were not blank, as when she'd first met him. They were as turbulent as an ocean—just as they'd been when she'd left him.

"I thought I told you to stay away from me," she said, doing her best to sound angry rather than aroused.

He frowned. "And I told you to behave. Yet here you are, full of stolen pie."

"What do you want me to do? Return it?"

"Don't be crass. I want you to pay for it."

"Moment I do, I'll start to vomit." She crossed her

arms over her middle. *Close the distance. Kiss me.*
"That would ruin my lipstick, so I have to decline."

He, too, crossed his arms over his middle. "You can
also earn your food."

"Yeah, but where's the fun in that?"

A moment passed in silence. Then, "Do you have no
morals?" he gritted out.

"No." *No sexual boundaries, either. So freaking kiss
me already!* "I don't."

He popped his jaw in frustration and disappeared.

Bianka's arms dropped to her sides and she gazed
around in astonishment. He'd left? Left? Without touching her? Without kissing her? Bastard! She stomped to
her car.

LYSANDER WATCHED AS Bianka drove away. He was hard
as a rock, had been that way since she'd paraded around
her cabin naked, had lingered in a bubble bath and then
changed into that wicked shirt. His shaft was desperate for her.

Why couldn't she be an angel? Why couldn't she
abhor sin? Why did she have to embrace it?

And why was the fact that she did these things—
steal, curse, lie—still exciting him?

Because that was the way of things, he supposed,
and had been since the beginning of time. Temptation
seeped past your defenses, changed you, made you long
for things you shouldn't.

There had to be a way to end this madness. He
couldn't destroy her, he'd already proven that. But what
if he could change *her?* He hadn't truly tried before,
so it *could* work. And if she embraced his way of life,

they could be together. He could have her. Have more of her kisses, touch more of her body.

Yes, he thought. Yes. He would help her become a woman he could be proud to walk beside. A woman he could happily claim as his own. A woman who would not be his downfall.

CHAPTER NINE

As Lysander had never had a…girlfriend, as the humans would say, he had no idea how to train one. He knew only how to train his soldiers. Without emotion, maintaining distance and taking nothing personally. His soldiers, however, *wanted* to learn. They were eager, his every word welcomed. Bianka would resist him at every turn. That much he knew.

So. The first day, he followed her, simply observing. Planning.

She, of course, stole every meal, even snacks, drank too much at a bar, danced too closely with a man she obviously did not know, then broke that man's nose when he cupped her bottom. Lysander wanted to do damage of his own, but restrained himself. Barely. At bedtime, Bianka merely paced the confines of her cabin, cursing his name. Not for a minute did she rest.

How lovely she was, dark hair streaming down her back. Red lips pursed. Skin glowing like a rainbow in the moonlight. So badly he wanted to touch her, to surround her with his wings, making them the only two people alive, and simply enjoy her.

Soon, he promised himself.

She'd given him release, yet he had not done the same for her. The more he thought about that—and think about it he did, all the time—the more that did not sit well with him. The more he thought about it, in fact, the more embarrassed he was.

He didn't know how to touch her to bring her release, but he was willing to try, to learn. First, though, he had to train her as planned. How, though? he wondered again. She seemed to respond well to his kisses—his chest puffed up with pride at that. He'd never rewarded his soldiers for a job well done, but perhaps he could do so for Bianka. Reward her with a kiss every time she pleased him.

A failproof plan. He hoped.

The second day, he was practically humming with anticipation. When she entered a clothing store and stuffed a beaded scarf into her purse, he materialized in front of her, ready to begin.

She stilled, gaze lifting and meeting his. Rather than bow her head in contrition, she grinned. "Fancy meeting you here."

"Put that back," he told her. "You do not need to steal clothing to survive."

She crossed her arms over her middle, a stubborn stance he knew well. "Yeah, but it's fun."

A human woman who stood off to the side eyed Bianka strangely. "Uh, can I help you?"

Bianka never looked away from him. "Nope. I'm fine."

"She cannot see me," Lysander told her. "Only you can."

"So I look insane for talking with you?"

He nodded.

She laughed, surprising him. And even though her amusement was misplaced, he loved the sound of her laughter. It was magical, like the strum of a harp. He loved the way her mirth softened her expression and lit her magnificent skin.

Have to touch her, he thought, suddenly dazed. He took a step closer, intending to do just that. *Have to experience that softness again.* And in doing so, she could begin to know the delights of his rewards.

She gulped. "Wh-what are you—"

"Are you sure I can't help you?" the woman asked, cutting her off.

Bianka remained in place, trembling, but tossed her a glare. "I'm sure. Now shut it before I sew your lips together."

The woman backed away, spun and raced to help someone else.

Lysander froze.

"You may continue," Bianka said to him.

How could he reward her for such rudeness? That would defeat the purpose of her training. "Do you not care what people think of you?" he asked, head tilting to the side.

Her eyes narrowed, and she stopped trembling. "No. Why should I? In a few years, these people will be dead but I'll still be alive and kicking." As she spoke, she stuffed another scarf in her purse.

Now she was simply taunting him. "Put it back, and I'll give you a kiss," he gritted out.

"Wh-what?"

Stuttering again. He was affecting her. "You heard me." He would not repeat the words. Having said them, all he wanted to do was mesh their lips together, thrust his tongue into her mouth and taste her. Hear her moan. Feel her clutch at him.

"You would willingly kiss me?" she rasped.

Willingly. Desperately. He nodded.

She licked her lips, leaving a sheen of moisture behind. The sight of that pink tongue sent blood rushing into his shaft. His hands clenched at his sides. Anything to keep from grabbing her and jerking her against him.

"I—I—" She shook her head, as if clearing her thoughts. Her eyes narrowed again, those long, dark lashes fusing together. "Why would you do that? You, who have tried to resist me at every turn?"

"Because."

"Why?"

"Just put the scarves back." *So the kissing can begin.*

She arched a brow. "Are you trying to bribe me? Because you should know, that won't work with me."

Rather than answer—and lie—he remained silent, chin jutting in the air. Blood…heating.

Still watching him, she reached out, palmed a belt and stuffed it in her purse, as well. "So what do you plan to do to me if I keep stealing? Give me a severe tongue-lashing? Too bad. I *don't* accept."

Fire slid the length of his spine even as his anger spiked. He closed the distance until the warmth of her breath was fanning over his neck and chest. "You could not get enough of me in the heavens, yet now that you are here, you want nothing to do with me. Tell me. Was your every word and action up there a lie?"

"Of course my every word and action was a lie. That's what I do. I thought you knew that."

So…did she desire him or not? Two days ago she'd told her sister, Kaia, that she wanted nothing to do with him. At the time, he'd thought she was merely saying that for Kaia's benefit. Now, he wasn't so sure.

"You could be lying now," he said. At least, that's

what he hoped. And who would have thought he'd ever wish for a lie?

Excitement sparked in her eyes and spread to the rest of her features. She patted his cheek, then flattened her palm on his chest. "You're learning, angel."

He sucked in a breath. So hot. So soft.

"Here's a proposition for you. Steal something from this store and *I'll* kiss *you*."

Wait. Her words from a moment ago drifted through his head. *You're learning, angel. He* was learning? "No," he croaked out. He would not do such a thing. Not even for her. "These people need the money their goods provide. Do you care nothing for their welfare?"

A flash of guilt joined the excitement. "No," she said.

Another lie? Probably. That guilt...it gave him hope. "Why do you need to steal like this, anyway?"

"Foreplay," she said with a shrug.

Blood...heating...again.

"Ma'am, I need you to come with me."

At the unexpected intrusion, they both stiffened. Bianka's gaze pulled from his; together they eyed the policeman now standing beside her.

She frowned. "Can't you see that I'm in the middle of a conversation?"

"Doesn't matter if you're talking to God Himself." The grim-faced officer latched onto her wrist. "I need you to come with me."

"I don't think so. Lysander," she said, clearly expecting him to do something.

Instinct demanded he save her. He wanted her safe and happy, but this would be good for her. "I told you to put the items back."

Her jaw dropped as the officer led her away. And, if Lysander wasn't mistaken, there was pride in her gaze.

ARRESTED FOR SHOPLIFTING, Bianka thought with disgust. Again. Her third time that year. Lysander had watched the policeman usher her in back, empty her purse and cuff her. All without a word. His disapproval had said plenty, though.

She hadn't let it upset her. He'd stood his ground, and she admired that. Was turned on by it. This wouldn't be an easy victory, as she'd assumed. Besides, for the first time in their relationship, he'd offered to kiss her. *Willingly* kiss her.

But only if she replaced her stolen goods, she reminded herself darkly. Didn't take a genius to figure out that he wanted to change her. To condition her to his way of life.

It was exactly what she wanted to do to him. Which meant he wanted her as desperately as she wanted him.

It also meant it was time to take this game to the next level. She, however, would not be the one to cave. The six hours she'd spent behind bars had given her time to think. To form a strategy.

She was whistling as she meandered down the station steps. Lysander had finally posted her bail, but he hadn't hung around to speak with her. Well, he hadn't needed to. She knew he was following her.

At home, she showered, lingering under the hot spray, soaping herself more slowly than necessary and caressing her breasts and playing between her legs. Unfortunately, he never appeared. But no matter.

Just in case her shower hadn't gotten him in the mood, she read a few passages from her favorite romance novel. And just in case *that* hadn't gotten him in the mood, she decorated her navel with her favorite dangling diamond, dressed in a skintight tank and skirt and knee-high boots, and drove to the closest strip club.

"I only have a few days left. Then I'm traveling to Budapest for Gwen's wedding and you are not invited. Do you hear me? Try and come and I'll make your life hell. So, if you want a go at me, now's the time," she said as she got out of the car.

Again, he didn't appear.

She almost screeched in frustration. So far, her strategy sucked. What was he doing?

The night was cold yet the inside of the club was hot and stuffy, the seats packed with men. Onstage, a redhead—clearly not a natural redhead—swung around a pole. The lights were dimmed, and smoke clung to the air.

"You gonna dance, darling?" someone asked Bianka.

"Nope. Got better things to do." She did, however, steal the stranger's wallet, sneak a beer from the bar and settle into a table in the back corner. Alone. "Enjoy," she whispered to Lysander, toasting him with the bottle.

"Have you no shame?" he suddenly growled from behind her.

Finally! Every muscle in her body relaxed, even as her blood heated with awareness. But she didn't turn to face him. He would have seen the triumph in her eyes. "You have enough shame for both of us."

He snorted. "That does not seem to be the case."

"Really? Well, then, let's loosen you up. Do you want a lap dance?" She held up the cash she'd taken. "I'm sure the redhead onstage would love to rub against you."

His big hands settled on her shoulders, squeezing.

"Or maybe you'd like a beer?"

"I would indeed," the stranger she'd stolen from said, now in front of her table. He reached into his back pocket. Frowned. "Hey, my wallet's gone." His gaze settled on the small brown leather case resting on her tabletop. His frown deepened. "That looks like mine."

"How odd," she said innocently. "So do you want me to buy you a beer or not?"

Lysander's grip tightened. "Give him back his wallet and I'll kiss you."

Her breath caught in her throat. Gods, she wanted his kiss. More than she'd ever wanted anything. His lips were soft, his taste decadent. And if she allowed him to kiss her, well, she knew she could convince him to do other things.

But she said, "Steal his watch and I'll kiss you."

"What are you talking about?" the guy asked, brow furrowed. "Steal whose watch?"

She rolled her eyes, wishing she could shoo him away.

Lysander leaned down and cupped her breasts. A tremor moved through her, her nipples beading, reaching for him. Sweet heaven. Her stomach quivered, jealous of her breasts, wanting the touch lower.

"Give him back the wallet."

Suddenly she wanted to do just that. Anything for more of Lysander and this sultry side of him. She didn't need the money, anyway. Wait. *What are you doing? Caving?* She straightened her spine. "No, I—"

"I'll kiss you all over your body," Lysander added.

Oh… Hell. He'd decided to take their game to the next level, as well.

Damn, damn, damn. She couldn't lose. If she did,

he would control her with sex. He would expect her to be good like him. All the damn time. There would be no more stealing, no more cursing, no more *fun*. Well, except when they were in bed—but would he expect her to be good there, too?

Life would become boring and sinless, everything a Harpy was taught to fight against.

She stood to shaky legs and turned, finally facing him. His hands fell away from her. She tried not to moan in disappointment. His expression was blank.

She blanked hers, as well, reached out and cupped *him*. Though he showed no emotion, he couldn't hide his hardness. "Steal something, anything at all, and I'll kiss *you* all over." Her voice dipped huskily. "Remember last time? You came in my mouth, and I loved every moment of it."

His nostrils flared.

"Yes!" the guy behind her exclaimed. "Give me five minutes and I'll have stolen something."

"You aren't trainable, are you?" Lysander asked stiffly.

"No," she said, but suddenly she didn't feel like smiling. There'd been resignation in his tone. Had she pushed him too far again? Was he going to leave her? Never return? "That doesn't mean you should stop trying, though."

"Wait. Trying what?" the stranger asked, confused.

Gods, when would he leave?

"Lysander," she prompted.

"That's not my name."

"Get lost," she growled.

Lysander's gaze lifted, narrowed on the human. Then Bianka heard footsteps. Her angel hadn't said anything, hadn't revealed himself, but had somehow managed to make the human leave. He had powers she hadn't known about, then. Why was that even more exciting?

"If you won't give the wallet back and I won't steal anything, where does that leave us?" he asked.

"At war. I don't know about you, but I do my best fighting in bed," she said, and then threw her arms around his neck.

CHAPTER TEN

WIND WHIPPED THROUGH Bianka's hair, and she knew that Lysander was flying her somewhere with those majestic wings. She had her eyes closed, too busy enjoying him—finally!—to care where he took her. His tongue made love to hers. His hands clutched her hips, fingers digging sharply. Then she was tipping over, a cool, soft mattress pressing into her back. His weight pinned her deliciously.

And it shouldn't have been delicious. This was not a position she allowed. Ever. It caged her wings, and her wings were the source of her strength. Without them, she was almost as weak as a human. But this was Lysander, honest to a fault, and she'd wanted him forever, it seemed. And as wary as he'd been about this sort of thing, she was afraid any type of rebuke would send him flying away.

Besides, he could do anything he wanted to her like this…

"No one is to enter," he said roughly.

Moaning, she wound her legs around his waist, tilted her head to receive his newest kiss and enjoyed a deeper thrust of his tongue. White lightning, the man was a fast learner. Very fast. He was now an expert at kissing. The best she'd ever had. By the time she finished with him, he'd be an expert at *everything* carnal.

His cock, hard and long and thick, rode the apex of her thighs. She could feel every inch of him through the softness of his robe. His arms enveloped her, and when she opened her eyes—they were inside his cloud, she realized—she saw his golden wings were spread, forming a blanket over them.

She tangled her hands in his hair and pulled from the kiss. "Are you going to get into trouble for this?" she asked, panting. Wait. What? Where had that thought come from?

His eyes narrowed. "Do you care?"

"No," she lied, forcing a grin. No, no, no. That wasn't a lie. "But that adds a little extra danger, don't you think?" There. Better. That was more like her normal self. She didn't like his goodness, didn't want to preserve it and keep him safe.

Did she?

"Well, I will not get into trouble." He flattened his palms at her temples, boxing her in and taking the bulk of his own weight. "If that is the only reason you are here, you can leave."

How fierce he appeared. "So sensitive, angel." She hooked her fingers at the neck of his robe and tugged. The material ripped easily. But as she held it, it began to weave itself back together. Frowning, she ripped again, harder this time, until there was a big enough gap to shove the clothing from his shoulders and off his arms. "I was only teasing."

His chest was magnificent. A work of art. Muscled and sun-kissed and devoid of any hair. She lifted her head and licked the pulse at the base of his neck, then traced his collarbone, then circled one of his nipples. "Do you like?"

"Hot. Wet," he rasped, lids squeezed tight.

"Yeah, but do you like?"

"Yes."

She sucked a peak until he gasped, then kissed away the sting. A tremor of pleasure rocked him, which caused a lance of pride to work through her. "Why do you desire me, angel? Why do you care if I'm good or not?"

A pause. A tortured, "Your skin…"

Every muscle in her body stiffened, and she glared up at him. "So any Harpy will do?" She tried to hide her insult, but didn't quite manage it. The thought of another Harpy—hell, any other woman, immortal or not—enjoying him roused her most vicious instincts. Her nails lengthened, and her teeth sharpened. A red haze dotted her line of vision. *Mine,* she thought. She would kill anyone who touched him. "We all have this skin, you know?" The words were guttural, scraping her throat.

His lashes separated as his eyes opened. His pupils were dilated, his expression tightening with…an emotion she didn't recognize. "Yes, but only yours tempts me. Why is that?"

"Oh," was all she could first think to say, her anger draining completely. But she needed to respond, had to think of something light, easy. "To answer your question, you want me because I'm made of awesome. And guess what? I will make you so happy you said that, warrior."

Warrior, rather than angel. She'd never called him that before. Why? And why now?

"No. I will make *you* happy." He ripped her shirt just as she had done his robe. She wasn't wearing a bra, and her breasts sprang free. Another tremor moved through him as he lowered his head.

He licked and sucked one nipple, as she had done to him, then the other, feasting. Savoring. Soon she was arching and writhing against him, craving his mouth elsewhere. Her skin was sensitized, her body desperate for release. Yet she didn't want to rush him. She was still afraid of scaring him away. But damn him, if he didn't hurry, didn't touch her between her legs, she was going to die.

"Lysander," she said on a trembling breath.

His wings brushed both her arms, up and down, tickling, caressing, raising goosebumps on her flesh. Holy hell, that was good. So damn good.

He lifted from her completely.

"Wh-what are you doing? I wasn't going to tell you to leave," she screeched, bracing her weight on her elbows.

"I do not want anything between us." He shoved the robe down his legs until he was gloriously naked. Moisture gleamed at the head of his cock, and her mouth watered. Reaching out, he gripped her boots and tore them off. Her jeans quickly followed. She, of course, was not wearing any panties.

His gaze drank her in, and she knew what he saw. Her flushed, glowing skin. The aching juncture between her legs. Her rose-tinted nipples.

"I want to touch and taste every inch," he said and just kind of fell on her, as if his will to resist had abandoned him completely.

"Touch and taste every inch next time." Please let there be a next time. She tried to hook her legs around his waist again. "I need release *now*."

He grabbed her by the knees and spread her. Her head fell back, her hair tangling around her, and he kissed a path to her breasts, then to her stomach. He lingered at her navel until she was moaning.

"Lysander," she said again. Fine. She'd jump on this grenade if she had to; if he wanted to taste, he could taste. "More. I need more."

Rather than give it to her, he stilled. "I…took care of myself before following you this day," he admitted, cheeks pinkening. "I thought that would give me resistance against you."

Her eyes widened, shock pouring through her. "You pleasured yourself?"

A stiff nod.

"Did you think of me?"

Another nod.

"Oh, baby. That's good. I can picture it, and I love what I see." His hand on his cock, stroking up and down, eyes closed, features tight with arousal, body straining toward release. Wings spread as he fell to his knees, the pleasure too much. Her, naked in his mind. "What did you think about doing?"

Another pause. A hesitant response. "Licking. Between your legs. Tasting you, as I said."

She arched her back, hands skimming down her middle to her thighs. Although he already held her open, she pushed her legs farther apart. "Then do it. Lick me. I want it so bad. Want your tongue on me. See how wet I am?"

He hissed in a breath. "Yes. Yes." Leaning down, he started at her ankles and kissed his way up, lingering at the back of her knees, at the crease of her legs.

"Please," she said, so on edge she was ready to scream. "Please. Do it."

"Yes," he whispered again. "Yes." Finally he settled over her, mouth poised, ready. His tongue flicked out. Then, sweet contact.

She expected the touch, but nothing could have prepared her for the perfection of it. She did scream, shivered. Begged for more. "Yes, yes, yes. Please, please, please."

At first, he merely lapped at her, humming his approval at her taste. Thank the gods. Or God. Or whoever was responsible for this man. If he hadn't liked her in that way, she wasn't sure what she would have done. In that moment, she wanted—needed—to be everything *he* wanted—needed. She wanted him to crave every part of her, as she craved every part of him.

Even his goodness?

Yes, she thought, finally admitting it. Yes. Just then, she had no defenses; she'd been stripped to her soul. His goodness somehow balanced her out. She'd fought against it—and still had no plans to change—but they were two extremes and actually complemented each other, each giving the other what he or she lacked. In her case, the knowledge that some things were worth taking seriously. In his, that it wasn't a crime to have fun.

"Bianka," he moaned. "Tell me how...what..."

"More. Don't stop."

Soon his tongue was darting in and out of her, mimicking the act of sex. She grasped at the sheets, fisting them. She writhed, meeting his every thrust. She screamed again, moaned and begged some more.

Finally, she splintered apart. Bit down on her bottom

lip until she tasted blood. White lights danced over her eyes—from her skin, she realized. Her skin was so bright it was almost blinding, glowing like a lamp, something that had never happened before.

Then Lysander was looming above her. "You are not fertile," he rasped. Sweat beaded him.

That gave her fuzzy mind pause. "I know." Her words were as labored as his. Harpies were only fertile once a year and this wasn't her time. "But how do you know that?"

"Sense it. Always know that kind of thing. So…are you ready?" he asked, and she could hear the uncertainty in his voice.

He must not know proper etiquette, the darling virgin. He would learn. With her, there was no etiquette. Doing what felt good was the only thing that drove her.

"Not yet." She flattened her hands on his shoulders and pushed him to his back, careful of his wings. He didn't protest or fight her as she straddled his waist and gripped his cock by the base. Her wings fluttered in joy at their freedom. "Better?"

He licked his lips, nodded. *His* wings lifted, enveloped her, caressing her. Her head fell, the long length of her hair tickling his thighs. He trembled.

Would he regret this? she suddenly wondered. She didn't want him to hate her for supposedly ruining him.

"Are *you* ready?" she asked. "There's no taking it back once it's done." If he wasn't ready, well, she would…wait, she realized. Yes, she would wait until he *was* ready. Only he would do. No other. Her body only wanted him.

"Do not stop," he commanded, mimicking her.

A grin bloomed. "I'll be careful with you," she assured him. "I won't hurt you."

His fingers circled her hips and lifted her until she was poised at his tip. "The only thing that could hurt me is if you leave me like this."

"No chance of that," she said, and sank all the way to the hilt.

He arched up to meet her, feeding her his length, his eyes squeezing shut, his teeth nearly chewing their way through his bottom lip. He stretched her perfectly, hit her in just the right spot, and she found herself desperate for release once more. But she paused, his enjoyment more important than her own. For whatever reason.

"Tell me when you're ready for me to—"

"Move!" he shouted, hips thrusting so high he raised her knees from the mattress.

Groaning at the pleasure, she moved, up and down, slipping and sliding over his erection. He was wild beneath her, as if he'd kept his passion bottled up all these years and it had suddenly exploded from him, unstoppable.

Soon, even that wasn't enough for him. He began hammering inside her, and she loved it. Loved his intensity. All she could do was hold on for the ride, slamming down on him, gasping. Her nails dug into his chest, her moans blended with his. And when her second orgasm hit, Lysander was right there with her, roaring, muscles stiffening.

He grabbed her by the neck and jerked her down, meshing their lips together. Their teeth scraped as he primitively, savagely kissed her. It was a kiss that stripped her once more to her soul, left her raw, agonized. Reeling.

He was indeed her consort, she thought, dazed. There was no denying it now. He was it for her. Her one and only. Necessary. Angel or not. She laughed, and was surprised by how carefree it sounded. Tamed by great sex. It figured. After this, no other man would do. Ever. She knew it, sensed it.

She collapsed atop him, panting, sweating. Scared. Suddenly vulnerable. How did he feel about her? He didn't approve of her, yet he had gifted her with his virginity. Surely that meant he liked her, just as she was. Surely that meant he wanted her around.

His heart thundered in his chest, and she grinned. Surely.

"Bianka," he said shakily.

She yawned, more replete than she'd ever been. *My consort.* Her eyelids closed, her lashes suddenly too heavy to hold up. Fatigue washed through her, so intense she couldn't fight it.

"Talk…later," she replied, and drifted into the most peaceful sleep of her life.

CHAPTER ELEVEN

FOR HOURS LYSANDER HELD Bianka in the crook of his arm while she slept, marveling—this was what she'd craved most in the world and *he* had given it to her—and yet, he was also worrying. He knew what that meant, knew how difficult it was for a Harpy to let down her guard and sleep in front of another. It meant she trusted him to protect her, to keep her safe. And he was glad. He *wanted* to protect her. Even from herself.

But could he? He didn't know. They were so different.

Until they got into bed, that is.

He could not believe what had just happened. He had become a creature of sensation, his baser urges all that mattered. The pleasure...unlike anything he'd ever experienced. Her taste was like honey, her skin so soft he wanted it against him for the rest of eternity. Her breathy moans—even her screams—had been a caress inside his ears. He'd loved every moment of it.

Had he been called to battle, he wasn't sure he would have been able to leave her.

Why her, though? Why had *she* been the one to captivate him?

She lied to him at every opportunity. She embodied everything he despised. Yet he did not despise her. For every moment with her, he only wanted more. Everything she did excited him. The pleasure she'd found in his arms…she had been unashamed, uninhibited, demanding everything he had to give.

Would he have been as enthralled by her if she had led a blameless life? If she had been more demure? He didn't think so. He liked her exactly as she was.

Why? he wondered again.

By the time she stretched lazily, sensually against him, he still did not have the answers. Nor did he know what to do with her. He'd already proven he could not leave her alone. And now that he knew all of her, she would be even more impossible to resist.

"Lysander," she said, voice husky from her rest.

"I am here."

She blinked open her eyes, jolted upright. "I fell asleep."

"I know."

"Yeah, but I feel asleep." She scrubbed a hand down her beautiful face, twisted and peered down at him with vulnerable astonishment. "I should be ashamed of myself, but I'm not. What's wrong with me?"

He reached up and traced a fingertip over her swollen lips. How hard had he kissed her? "I'm…sorry," he said. "I lost control for a moment. I shouldn't have taken you so—"

She nipped at his finger, her self-recrimination seeming to melt away in favor of amusement. "Do you hear me complaining about that?"

He relaxed. No, he did not hear her complaining. In fact, she appeared utterly sated. And he had done that. He had given her pleasure. Pride filled him. Pride—a foolish emotion that often led to a man's downfall. Was that how Bianka would make him fall? For as his temptation, she *would* make him fall.

With a sigh, she flopped back against him. "You turned serious all of the sudden. Want to talk about it?"

"No."

"Do you want to talk about *anything?*"

"No."

"Well, too bad," she grumbled, but he heard a layer of satisfaction in her tone. Did she enjoy making him do things he didn't want to do—or didn't think he wanted to do? "Because you're going to talk. A lot. You can start with why you first abducted me. I know you wanted to change me, but why me? I still don't know."

He shouldn't tell her; she already had enough power over him, and knowing the truth would only increase that power. But he also wanted her to understand how desperate he'd been. Was. "At the heart of my duties, I am a peacekeeper, and as such, I must peek into the lives of the Lords of the Underworld every so often, making sure they are obeying heavenly laws. I…saw you with them. And as I have proven with my actions this day, I realized you are my one temptation. The one thing that can tear me from my righteous path."

She sat up again, faced him again. Her eyes were wide with…pleasure? "Really? I alone can ruin you?"

He frowned. "That does not mean you should try and do so."

Laughing, she leaned down and kissed him. Her breasts pressed against his chest, once again heating his blood in that way only she could do. But he was done fighting it, done resisting it. "That's not what I meant. I just like being important to you, I guess." Her cheeks suddenly bloomed with color. "Wait. That's not what I meant, either. What I'm trying to say is that you're for-given for whisking me to your palace in the sky. I would have done the same thing to you had the situation been reversed."

He had not expected forgiveness to come so easily. Not from her. Frown intensifying, he cupped her cheeks and forced her to meet his gaze. "Why were *you* with *me?* I know I am not what your kind views as accept-able."

She shrugged, the action a little stiff. "I guess you're my temptation."

Now he understood why she'd grinned over his proc-lamation. He wanted to whoop with satisfied laughter.

"If we're going to be together—" She stopped, wait-ing. When he nodded, she relaxed and continued, "Then I guess I could only steal from the wicked."

It was a concession. A concession he'd never thought she would make. She truly must like him. Must want more time with him.

"So listen," she said. "My sister is getting married in a week, as I told you before. Do you want to, like, come with me? As my guest? I know, I know. It's short no-tice. But I didn't intend to invite you. I mean, you're an angel." There was disgust in her voice. "But you make love like a demon so I guess I should, I don't know, show you off or something."

He opened his mouth to reply. What he would say, he didn't know. They could not tell others of their rela-tionship. Ever. But a voice stopped him.

"Lysander. Are you home?"

Lysander recognized the speaker immediately. Ra-phael, the warrior angel. Panic nearly choked him. He couldn't let the man see him like this. Couldn't let any of his kind see him with the Harpy.

"We must discuss Olivia," Raphael called. "May I enter your abode? There is some sort of block preventing me from doing so."

"Not yet," he called. Was his panic in his voice? He'd never experienced it before, so didn't know how to combat it. "Wait for me. I will emerge." He sat up and slipped from the bed, from Bianka. He grabbed his robe, or rather, the pieces of it, from the floor and wrapped it around himself. Immediately it wove back together to fit his frame. The material even cleaned him, wiping away Bianka's scent.

The latter, he inwardly cursed. *For the best.*

"Let him in," Bianka said, fitting the sheet around her, oblivious. "I don't mind."

Lysander kept his back to her. "I do not want him to see you."

"Don't worry. I've covered my naughty nakedness."

He gave no reply. Unlike her, he would not lie. And if he did not lie to her, he would hurt her. He did not want to do that, either.

"So call him in already," she said with a laugh. "I want to see if all angels look like sin but act like saints."

"No. I don't want him inside right now. I will go out to meet him. You will stay here," he said. Still he couldn't face her.

"Wait. Are you jealous?"

He gave no reply.

"Lysander?"

"Stay silent. Please. Cloud walls are thin."

"Stay…silent?" A moment passed in the very silence he'd requested. Only, he didn't like it. He heard the rustle of fabric, a sharp intake of breath. "You don't want him to know I'm here, do you? You're ashamed of me," she said, clearly shocked. "You don't want your friend to know you've been with me."

"Bianka."

"No. You don't get to speak right now." With every word, her voice rose. "I was willing to take you to my sister's wedding. Even though I knew my family would laugh at me or view me with disgust. I was willing to give you a chance. Give *us* a chance. But not you. You were going to hide me away. As if *I'm* something shameful."

He whirled on her, fury burning through him. At her, at himself. "You *are* something shameful. I kill beings like you. I do not fall in love with them."

She didn't say anything. Just looked up at him with wide, hurt-filled eyes. So much hurt he actually stumbled back. A sharp pain lanced *his* chest. But as he watched, her hurt mutated into a fury that far surpassed his.

"Kill me, then," she growled.

"You know I will not."

"Why?"

"Because!"

"Let me guess. Because deep down you still think you can change me. You think that I will become the pure, virtuous woman you want me to be. Well, who are you to say what's virtuous and what isn't?"

He merely arched a brow. The answer was obvious and didn't need to be stated.

"I told you that from now on I'd only hurt the wicked, right? Well, surprise! That's what I've done since the beginning. The pie you watched me eat? The owner of that restaurant cheats at cards, takes money that doesn't belong to him. The wallet I stole? I took it from a man cheating on his wife."

He blinked down at her, unsure he'd heard correctly. "Why would you have kept that from me?"

"Why should it change how you feel about me?" She tossed back the cover and stood, glorious in her nakedness. Her skin was still aglow, multihued light reflecting off it—he'd touched that skin. Dark hair cascaded around her—he'd fisted that hair.

"I want to be with you," he said. "I do. But it has to be in secret."

"I thought the same. Until what we just did," she said as she hastily dressed. Her clothes were not like his, did not repair on their own, and so that ripped shirt revealed more than it hid.

He tried again. Tried to make her understand. "You are everything my kind stands against, Bianka. I train warriors to hunt and kill demons. What would it say to them were I to take you as my companion?"

"Here's a better question. What does it say to them that you hide your sin? Because that's how you view me, isn't it? Your sin. You are such a hypocrite." She stormed past him, careful not to touch him. "And I will not be with a hypocrite. That's worse than being an angel."

He thought she meant to race to Raphael and flaunt her presence. Shockingly enough, she didn't. And because he hadn't commanded her to stay, when she said, "I want to leave," the cloud opened up at her feet.

She disappeared, falling through the sky.

"Bianka," he shouted. Lysander spread his wings and jumped after her. He passed Raphael, but at that point, he didn't care. He only wanted Bianka safe—and that hurt and fury wiped away from her expression.

She'd turned facedown to increase her momentum. He had to tuck his wings into his back to increase his own. Finally, he caught her halfway and wrapped his arms around her, her back pressed into his stomach. She didn't flail, didn't order him to release her, which he'd been prepared for.

When they reached her cabin, he straightened them, spread his wings and slowed. Snow still covered the ground and crunched when they landed. She didn't pull away. Didn't run. Something else he'd been prepared for.

Clearly he knew very little about her.

"It's probably best this way, you know," she said flatly, keeping her back to him. The wind slapped her hair against his cheeks. "That was my afterglow talking earlier, anyway. I never should have invited you to the wedding. We're too different to make anything work."

"I was willing to try," he said through gritted teeth. *Don't do this,* he projected. *Don't end us.*

She laughed without humor, and he marveled at the difference between this laugh and the one she'd given inside his cloud. Marveled and mourned. "No, you were willing to hide me away."

"Yes. Therefore I was *trying* to make something work. I want to be with you, Bianka. Otherwise I would not have followed you. I would have left you alone from the first. I would not have tried to show you the light."

"You are such a pompous ass," she spat. "Show me the light? Please! You want me to be perfect. Blameless. But what happens when I fail? And I will, you know? Perfection just isn't in me. One day I will curse. Like now. Fuck you. One day I will take something just because it's pretty and I want it. Would that ruin me in your eyes?"

"It hasn't so far," he spat back.

She laughed again, this one bleaker, grim. "The scarves I took were made by child laborers. So I haven't really done anything too terrible yet. But I will. And you know what? If you were to do something nauseatingly righteous, I wouldn't have cared. I would still have wanted to take you to the wedding. That's the difference between us. Evil or not, good or not, I wanted you."

"I want you, too. But that was not always the case, and you know it. You *would* care." He tightened his grip on her. "Bianka. We can work this out."

"No, we can't." Finally, she twisted to face him. "That would require giving you a second chance, and I don't do second chances."

"I don't need a second chance. I just need you to think about this. To realize our relationship must stay hidden."

"I'm not going to be your secret shame, Lysander."

His eyes narrowed. She was trying to force his hand, and he didn't like it. "You steal in secret. You sleep in secret. Why not this?"

"That you don't know the answer proves you aren't the warrior I thought you were. Have a nice life, Lysander," she said, jerking from his hold and walking away without a backward glance.

CHAPTER TWELVE

LYSANDER SAT IN THE BACK of the Budapest chapel, undetectable, watching Bianka help her sisters and their friends decorate for the wedding. She was currently hanging flowers from the vaulted ceiling. Without a ladder.

He'd been following her for days, unable to stay away. One thing he'd noticed: she talked and laughed as if she was fine, normal, but the sparkle was gone from her eyes, her skin.

And he had done that to her. Worse, not once had she cursed, lied or stolen. Again, his fault. He'd told her she was unworthy of him. He'd been—*was,* right?—too embarrassed of her to tell his people about her.

But he couldn't deny that he missed her. Missed everything about her. That much he knew. She excited him, challenged him, frustrated him, consumed him, drew him, made him *feel.* He did not want to be without her.

Something soft brushed his shoulder. He barely managed to tear his gaze from Bianka to turn and see that Olivia was now sitting beside him.

What was wrong with him? He hadn't heard her arrive. Normally his senses were tuned, alert.

"Why did you summon me here?" she asked. She

glanced around nervously. Her dark curls framed her face, rosebuds dripping from a few of the strands.

"To Budapest? Because you are always here anyway."

"As are you these days," she replied dryly.

He shrugged. "Did you just come from Aeron's room?"

She gave a reluctant nod.

"Raphael came to me," he said. The day he'd lost Bianka. The worst day of his existence.

"Those flowers aren't centered, B," the redheaded Kaia called, claiming his attention and stopping the rest of his speech to his charge. "Shift them a little to the left."

Bianka expelled a frustrated sigh. "Like this?"

"No. *My* left, dummy."

Grumbling, Bianka obeyed.

"Perfect." Kaia beamed up at her.

Bianka flipped her off, and Lysander grinned. Thank the One True Deity he had not killed all of her spirit.

"I think they're perfect, too," her youngest sister, Gwendolyn, said.

Bianka released the ceiling panels and dropped to the floor. When she landed, she straightened as if the jolt had not affected her in any way. "Glad the princess is finally happy with something," she muttered. Then, more loudly, "I don't understand why you can't get married in a tree like a civilized Harpy."

Gwen anchored her hands on her fists. "Because my dream has always been to be wed in a chapel like any other normal person. Now, will someone please remove the naked portraits of Sabin from the walls? Please."

"Why would you want to get rid of them when I just

spent all that time hanging them?" Anya, goddess of Anarchy and companion to Lucien, keeper of Death, asked, clearly offended. "They add a little something extra to what would otherwise be very boring proceedings. *My* wedding will have strippers. Live ones."

"Boring? Boring!" Fury passed over Gwen's features, black bleeding into her eyes, her teeth sharpening.

Lysander had watched this same change overtake her multiple times already. In the past hour alone.

"It won't be boring," Ashlyn, companion to Maddox, the keeper of Violence, said soothingly. "It'll be beautiful."

The pregnant woman rubbed her rounded belly. That belly was larger than it should have been, given the early state of her pregnancy. No one seemed to realize it, though. They would soon enough, he supposed. He just hoped they were ready for what she carried.

What would a child of Bianka's be like? he suddenly wondered. Harpy, like her? Angel, like him? Or a mix of both?

A pang took root and flourished in his chest.

"Boring?" Gwen snarled again, clearly not ready to let the insult slide.

"Great!" Bianka threw up her arms. "Someone get Sabin before Gwennie kills us all in a rage."

A Harpy in a rage could hurt even other Harpies, Lysander knew. As Gwen's consort, Sabin, keeper of Doubt, was the only one who could calm her.

With that thought, Lysander's head tilted to the side. He had never seen Bianka erupt, he realized. She'd viewed everything as a game. Well, not true. Once, she had gotten mad. The time Paris had punched him.

Lysander had been her enemy, but she'd still gotten mad over his mistreatment.

Lysander had calmed her.

The pang grew in intensity, and he rubbed his breastbone. Was he Bianka's consort? Did he want to be?

"No need to search me out. I'm here." Sabin strode through the double doors. "As if I'd be more than a few feet away when she's so sensitiv—uh, just in case she needed my help. Gwen, baby." There at the end, his tone had lowered, gentled. He reached her and pulled her into his arms; she snuggled against him. "The most important thing tomorrow is that we'll be together. Right?"

"Lysander," Olivia said, drawing his attention from the now-cooing couple. "The wait is difficult. Raphael came to you and…what?"

Lysander sighed, forcing himself to concentrate. "Answer a few questions for me first."

"All right," she said after a brief hesitation.

"Why do you like Aeron when he is so different from you?"

She twisted the fabric of her robe. "I think I like him *because* he is so different from me. He has thrived amid darkness, managing to retain a spark of light in his soul. He is not perfect, is not blameless, but he could have given in to his demon long ago and yet still he fights. He protects those he loves. His passion for life is…" She shivered. "Amazing. And really, he only hurts people when his demon overtakes him—and only if they are wicked, at that. Innocents, he leaves alone."

It was the same with Bianka. Yet Lysander had tried to make her ashamed of herself. Ashamed when she should only be proud of what she had accomplished, thriving amid darkness, as Olivia had said. "And you are not embarrassed for our kind to know of your affection for him?"

"Embarrassed of Aeron?" Olivia laughed. "When he is stronger, fiercer, more alive than anyone I know? Of course not. I would be proud to be called his woman. Not that it could ever happen," she added sadly.

Proud. There was that word again. And this time, something clicked in his mind. *I'm not going to be your secret shame, Lysander,* Bianka had said. He'd reminded her that she committed all her other sins in secret. Why not him? She hadn't told him the answer, but it came to him now. Because she'd been proud of him. Because she'd wanted to show him off.

As he should have wanted to show *her* off.

Any other man would have been proud to stand beside her. She was beautiful, intelligent, witty, passionate and lived by her own moral code. Her laughter was more lovely than the song of a harp, her kiss as sweet as a prayer.

He'd considered her the spawn of Lucifer, yet she was a gift from the One True Deity. He was such a fool.

"Have I answered your questions sufficiently?" Olivia asked.

"Yes." He was surprised by the rawness of his voice. Had he ruined things irreparably between them?

"So answer a few now for me."

Unable to find his voice, he nodded. He had to make this right. Had to try, at least.

"Bianka. The Harpy you watch. Do you love her?"

Love. He found her among the crowd and the pang in his chest grew unbearable. She was currently adding a magic marker mustache to one of Sabin's portraits while Kaia added...other things down below. Kaia was giggling; Bianka looked like she was just going through the motions, taking no joy.

He wanted her happy. Wanted her the way she'd been.

"You think you are embarrassed of her," Olivia continued when he gave no response.

"How do you know?" He forced the words to leave him.

"I am—or was—a joy-bringer, Lysander. It was my job to know what people were feeling and then help them see the truth. Because only in truth can one find real joy. You were never embarrassed of her. I know you. You are embarrassed by nothing. You were simply scared. Scared that *you* were not what *she* needs."

His eyes widened. Could that be true? He'd tried to change her. Had tried to make her what he was so that she, in turn, would *like* what he was? Yes. Yes, that made sense, and for the second time in his existence, he hated himself.

He had let Bianka get away from him. When he should have sung her praises to all of the heavens, he had cast her aside. No man was more foolish. Irreparable damage or not, he had to try and win her back.

He jumped to his feet. "I do," he said. "I love her." He wanted to throw his arms around her. Wanted to shout to all the world that she belonged to him. That she had chosen him as her man.

His shoulders slumped. Chosen. Key word. Past tense. She would not choose him again. She did not give second chances, she'd said.

She often lies...

For the first time, the thought that his woman liked to lie caused him to smile. Perhaps she had lied about that. Perhaps she would give him a second chance. A chance to prove his love.

If he had to grovel, he would. She was his temptation, but that did not have to be a bad thing. That could be his salvation. After all, his life would mean nothing without her. Same for her. She had told him that he was her own temptation. He could be *her* salvation.

"Thank you," he told Olivia. "Thank you for showing me the truth."

"Always my pleasure."

How should he approach Bianka? When? Urgency flooded him. He wanted to do so now. As a warrior, though, he knew some battles required planning. And as this was the most important battle of his existence, plan his attack he would.

If she forgave him and decided to be with him, they would still have a tough road ahead. Where would they live? His duties were in the heavens. She thrived on earth, with her family nearby. Plus, Olivia was destined to kill Aeron, who would essentially be Bianka's brother-in-law after tomorrow. And if Olivia decided not to, another angel would be chosen to do the job.

Most likely, that would be Lysander.

One thing his Deity had taught him, however, was that love truly could conquer all. Nothing was stronger. They could make this work.

"I've lost you again," Olivia said with a laugh. "Before you rush off, you must tell me why you summoned me. What Raphael said to you."

Some of his good mood evaporated. While Olivia had just given him hope and helped him find the right path, he was about to dash any hopes of a happily-ever-after for her.

"Raphael came to me," he repeated. *Just do it; just say it.* "He told me of the council's unhappiness with you. He told me they grow weary of your continued defiance."

Her smile fell away. "I know," she whispered. "I just…I haven't been able to bring myself to hurt him. Watching him gives me joy. And I deserve to experience joy after so many centuries of devoted service, do I not?"

"Of course."

"And if he is dead, I will never be able to do the things I now dream about."

His brow furrowed. "What things?"

"Touching him. Curling into his arms." A pause. "Kissing him."

Dangerous desires indeed. Oh, did he know their power. "If you never experience them," he offered, "they are easier to resist." But he hated to think of this wonderful female being without something she wanted.

He could petition the council for Aeron's forgiveness, but that would do no good. A decree was a decree. A law had been broken and someone had to pay. "Very soon, the council will be forced to offer you a choice. Your duty or your downfall."

She gazed down at her hands, once again twisting the fabric of her robe. "I know. I don't know why I hesitate. He would never desire me, anyway. The women here, they are exciting, dangerous. As fierce as he is. And I am—"

"Precious," he said. "You are precious. Never think otherwise."

She offered him a shaky smile.

"I have always loved you, Olivia. I would hate to

see you give up everything you are for a man who has threatened to kill you. You do know what you would be losing, yes?"

That smile fell away as she nodded.

"You would fall straight into hell. The demons there will go for your wings. They always go for the wings first. No longer will you be impervious to pain. You will hurt, yet you will have to dig your way free of the underground—or die there. Your strength will be depleted. Your body will not regenerate on its own. You will be more fragile than a human because you were not raised among them."

While he thought he could survive such a thing, he did not think Olivia would. She was too delicate. Too... sheltered. Until this point, every facet of her life had dealt with joy and happiness. She had known nothing else.

The demons of hell would be crueler to her than they would be even to him, the man they feared more than any other. She was all they despised. Wholly good. Destroying such innocence and purity would delight them.

"Why are you telling me this?" Her voice trembled. Tears streaked down her cheeks.

"Because I do not want you to make the wrong decision. Because I want you to know what you're up against."

A moment passed in silence, then she jumped up and threw her arms around his neck. "I love you, you know."

He squeezed her tightly, sensing that this was her way of saying goodbye. Sensing that this would be the last time they were offered such a reprieve. But he would not stop her, whatever path she chose.

She pulled back and smoothed her trembling hands down her glistening white robe. "You have given me much to consider. So now I will leave you to your female. May love always follow you, Lysander." As she spoke, her wings expanded. Up, up she flew, misting through the ceiling—and Bianka's flowers—before disappearing.

He hoped she'd choose her faith, her immortality, over the keeper of Wrath, but feared she would not. His gaze strayed to Bianka, now walking down the aisle toward the exit. She paused at his row, frowned, before shaking her head and leaving. If he'd been forced to pick between her and his reputation and lifestyle, he would have picked her, he realized.

And now it was time to prove it to her.

CHAPTER THIRTEEN

I'VE GOT TO PULL MYSELF from this funk, Bianka thought. This was her youngest sister's wedding day. She should be happy. Delighted. If she were honest, though, she was a tiny bit—aka a *lot*—jealous. Gwen's man, a demon, loved her. Was proud of her.

Lysander considered Bianka unworthy.

She'd thought about proving herself to him, but had quickly discarded the idea. Proving herself worthy—his idea of worthy, that is—would entail nothing more than a lie. And Lysander hated lies. So, according to him, she would never be good enough for him. Which meant he was stupid, and she didn't date stupid men. Plus, he didn't deserve her.

He deserved to rot in his unhappiness. And that's what he'd be without her. Unhappy. Or so she hoped.

"So much for our plan to go naked," Kaia muttered beside her. "Gwen saw me leave my room that way and almost sliced my throat."

"Did not," the bride in question said from behind them.

They turned in unison. Bianka's breath caught as it had every time she'd seen her youngest sister in her gown. It was a princess cut, which was fitting, the straps thin, the beautiful white lace cinching just under her breasts before flowing to her ankles. The material covering her legs was sheer, allowing glimpses of thigh and those gorgeous red heels.

Her strawberry curls were half up, half down, diamonds glittering through the strands. There was so much love and excitement in her gold-gray eyes it was almost blinding.

"I almost pushed you out a window," Gwen added.

They laughed. Even stoic Taliyah, their oldest sister, who had her arm wrapped through Gwen's. Since it turned out Gwen's father was the Lords' greatest enemy, and Gwen's mom had disowned her years ago, Taliyah was escorting Gwen down the aisle.

"Hence the reason I'm now wearing this." Kaia motioned to her own gown, an exact match to Bianka's. A buttercup-yellow creation with more ribbons, bows and sequined rose appliqués than anyone should wear in an entire lifetime. They even wore hats with orange streamers.

Gwen shrugged, unrepentant. "I didn't want you looking prettier than me, so sue me."

"Weddings suck," Bianka said. "You should have just had Sabin tattoo your name on his ass and called it good." That's what she would have done. Not that Lysander ever would have agreed to such a thing. Whether they were together or not.

Which they never would be. Bastard.

"I did. Have him tattoo my name on his ass," Gwen said. "And his arm. And his chest. And his back. But then I casually mentioned how much I'd always wanted a big wedding, and well, he told me I had four weeks to plan it or he'd take over and do it himself. And everyone knows men can't plan shit. So…" She shrugged again, though the excitement and love on her face had intensified. "Are they ready for us yet?"

Bianka and Kaia turned back to the chapel, peeking through the crack in the closed doors.

"Not yet," Bianka said. "Paris is missing."

Paris, who had gotten ordained over the internet, would be presiding over the nuptials.

"He better hurry," she added grumpily. "Or I'll find a way to make him oil-wrestle again."

"You've been so depressed lately. Missing your angel?" Kaia asked her, pinkie-waving to Amun, who stood in the line of groomsmen beside Sabin at the altar.

Amun shouldn't have been able to see her, but somehow he did. He nodded, a smile twitching at the corners of his lips.

"Of course not. I hate him." A lie. She hadn't told her sisters why she and Lysander had parted, only that they had. Forever. If they knew the truth, they'd want to kill him. And as all but Gwen were paid killers, immensely good at their job, she'd find herself the proud owner of Lysander's head.

Which she didn't want.

She just wanted him. Stupid girl.

"I only would have teased you for a few years, you know," Kaia said. "You should have kept him around. It might have been fun to corrupt him."

He didn't want to be corrupted any more than she wanted to be purified. They were too different. Could never make anything work. Their separation was for the best. So why couldn't she get over it? Why did she feel his gaze on her, every minute of every day? Even now, when she looked like a Southern belle on crack?

"So Sabin doesn't have a last name," she said to

Gwen, drawing attention away from herself. "Are you going to call yourself Gwen Sabin?"

"No, nothing like that. I'm going to call myself Gwen Lord."

"What's Anya plan to call herself? Anya Underworld?" Kaia asked with a laugh.

"Knowing our goddess, she'll demand Lucien take *her* last name. Trouble. Or is that her middle name?"

"I here, I here," a voice suddenly screeched. Legion pushed her way in front of Bianka and Kaia. She was wearing a yellow dress, as well. Only hers had more ribbons, bows and sequins. A basket of flowers was clutched in her hands, her too-long nails curling around the handle. Best of all, she wore a tiara. Because she didn't have hair, it had had to be glued to her scaled head. "We begin now."

She didn't wait for permission but shouldered her way through the door. The crowd—which consisted of the Lords of the Underworld, their companions and some gods and goddesses Anya knew—turned and gasped when they saw her. Well, except for Gideon. He'd recently been captured and tortured by Hunters, the Lords' nemeses, and was currently missing his hands. (His feet weren't in the best of shape, either.) Because of his injuries, he was beyond weak, so he lay in his gurney, barely conscious. He'd insisted on coming, though.

From his pew, Aeron smiled indulgently as Legion tossed pink petals in every direction. Just as she reached the front, Paris raced to the podium. He looked harried, pale, and Sabin punched him in the shoulder.

Sabin looked amazing. He wore a black tux, his hair slicked back, and when he turned to face the door, watching for Gwen, his entire face lit. With love. With pride. Bianka's jealousy increased. She wanted that. Wanted her man to find her perfect in every way.

Was that too much to ask?

Apparently so. Stupid Lysander.

"Go, go, go," Gwen ordered, giving them a little push.

Bianka kicked into motion, heading toward Strider, her appointed groomsman. He smiled at her when she reached him. He would be proud to call her his woman, she thought. She tried to make herself return the gesture, but her eyes were too busy filling with tears. She looked around, trying to distract herself.

The chapel really was beautiful. The glittery white flowers she'd hung from the ceiling were thick and lush and offered a canopy, a haven. They were the best part of the decor, if you asked her. Candles flickered with golden light, twining with shadows.

Kaia approached her side, and everyone except for Gideon stood. The music changed, slowing down to the bridal march. Gwen and Taliyah appeared. Sabin's breath caught. Yes, that was the way a man should react to the sight of his woman.

What makes you think you were ever Lysander's woman?

Because she was his one temptation. Because of the reverent way he had touched her. Because she liked how he made her feel. Because they balanced each other. Because he completed her in a way she hadn't known she needed. He was the light to her darkness.

He was willing to show you that light. Over and over again.

Perhaps she should have fought for him. That's what

she was, after all. A fighter. Yet she'd given in as if he meant nothing to her when he had somehow become the most important thing in her life.

Bianka didn't mean to, but she tuned out as Paris gave his speech and the happy couple recited their vows, her thoughts remaining focused on Lysander. Should she try and fight for him now? If so, how would she go about it?

Only when the crowd cheered did she snap out of her haze, watching as Sabin and Gwen kissed. Then they were marching down the aisle and out the doors together. The rest of the bridal party made their way out, as well.

"Shall we?" Strider asked, holding out his arm for her.

"She can't." Paris grabbed her arm. "You're needed in that room." With his free hand, he pointed.

"Why?" Was he planning revenge against her for forcing him to oil-wrestle Lysander? He hadn't mentioned it in the days since her return to Buda, but he couldn't be happy with her. He should be thanking her, for gods' sake. He'd gotten to touch all of Lysander's hawtness.

Paris rolled his eyes. "Just go before your boyfriend decides he's tired of waiting and comes out here."

Her boyfriend. Lysander? Couldn't be. Could it? But why would he have come? Heart drumming in her chest, she walked forward. She didn't allow herself to run, though she wanted to soooo badly. She reached the door. Her hand shook as she turned the knob.

Hinges creaked. Then she was staring into—an empty room. Her teeth ground together. Paris's revenge, just as she'd figured. Of course. That rat bastard piece of shit was going to pay. She wasn't just going to make him oil-wrestle. She was going to—

"Hello, Bianka."

Lysander.

Gasping, she whipped around. Her eyes widened. In an instant, the chapel had been transformed. No longer were her sisters and friends inside. Lysander and his kind occupied every spare inch. Angels were everywhere, light surrounding them and putting Gwen's candles to shame.

"What are you doing here?" she demanded, not daring to hope.

"I came to beg your forgiveness." His arms spread. "I came to tell you that I am proud to be your man. I brought my friends and brethren to bear witness to my proclamation."

She swallowed, still not letting hope take over. "But I'm evil and that's not going to change. I'm your temptation. You could, I don't know, lose everything by being with me." The thought hit her, and she wanted to wilt. He could lose everything. No wonder he had wanted to destroy her. No wonder he had wanted to hide her.

"No, you are not evil. And I don't want you to change. You are beautiful and intelligent and brave. But more than that, you are my everything. I am nothing without you. Not good, not right, not complete. And do not worry. I will not lose everything as you said. You have not committed an unpardonable sin."

She gulped. "And if I do?"

"I will fall."

Okay. A small kernel of hope managed to seep inside her. But no way would she let him fall. Ever. He loved being an angel. "What brought this on?"

"I finally pulled my head out of my ass," he said dryly.

He'd said *ass*. Lysander had just said the word *ass*. More hope beat its way inside and she had to press her lips together to keep from smiling. And crying! Tears were springing in her eyes, burning.

Could they actually make their relationship work? Just a little bit ago, she'd been grateful—or pretending to be grateful—that they were apart, since so many obstacles existed.

"I only hope you can love so foolish a man. I am willing to live wherever you desire. I am willing to do anything you need to win you back." He dropped to his knees. "I love you, Bianka Skyhawk. I would be proud to be yours."

He was proud of her. He wanted her. He loved her. It was everything she'd secretly dreamed about this past week. Yes, they could make this work. They would be together, and that was the most important thing. But she told him none of that.

"Now?" she screeched instead. "You decided to introduce me to your friends now? When I look like this?" Scowling, she peeked over his shoulder at them and saw their stunned expressions. "I usually look better than this, you know. You should have seen me the other day. When I was naked."

Lysander stood. "That's all you have to say to me?"

She focused back on him. His eyes were as wide as hers had been, his arms crossed over his middle. "No. There's more," she grumbled. "But I will never live this yellow gown thing down, you know."

"Bianka."

"Yes, I love you, too. But if you ever decide I'm unworthy again, I'll show you just how demonic I can be."

"Deal. But you don't have to worry, love," he said, a slow smile lifting those delectable lips. "It is I who am unworthy. I only pray you never learn of this."

"Oh, I know it already," she said, and his grin spread. "Now c'mere, you." She cupped the back of his neck and jerked him down for a kiss.

His arms banded around her, holding her close. She'd never thought to be paired with an angel, but she couldn't regret it now. Not when Lysander was the angel in question.

"Are you sure you're ready for me?" she asked him when they came up for air.

He nipped at her chin. "I've been ready for you my entire life. I just didn't know it until now."

"Good." With a whoop, she jumped up and wound her legs around his waist. A wave of gasps circled the room. They were still here? "Ditch your friends, I'll blow off my sister's reception and we'll go oil-wrestle."

"Funny," he said, wings enveloping her as he flew her up, up and into his cloud. "That's exactly what I was thinking."

* * * * *

THE AMAZON'S CURSE

CHAPTER ONE

NOLA STOOD IN THE CENTER of the battle tent, watching as her sisters-by-race lined up. Each shifted eagerly from one foot to the other, clutching their weapon of choice. She spotted several axes, a few spears, but mostly swords. Anticipation thickened the air.

Mating season had officially begun.

Soon the females would break into groups, fighting each other for the right to whichever stolen slave they desired. Those slaves, eight in number, were currently chained to the far wall at the end of the spacious enclosure. Three dragon shifters, two centaurs, two male sirens and a vampire. All eight were muscled, beautiful…and all but one was grinning. The vampire.

Her vampire. Zane.

The men would be bedded this night and for several weeks to come. Then they would be freed, never to return. That was the way of the Amazons. Capture, breed and abandon. Of course the males were happy about this. All but Zane. His fury was palpable.

Despite that fury, her gaze drank him in. Zane had dark hair, equally dark eyes and a body made for war. And sex. He had muscle stacked upon muscle and scars that laced his corded chest.

He also had the fiercest temper she'd ever encountered. He didn't like to be touched and had actually in-

jured many Amazons—not an easy feat—in his quest
for freedom. Finally, in an effort to tame him, they had
stopped feeding him the blood he needed for strength.
Now he was physically weakened, only able to lean
against the wall and wait for his mistress to be declared.

However, nothing could weaken his hatred—or the
promised retribution that radiated from him.

Nola had met him what seemed an eternity but had
actually only been four months ago. He'd desired her,
for whatever reason, and had tried to win her affections—and she'd tried to kill him.

With the memory, guilt filled her. But in her defense,
she hadn't known him then. Had only been concerned
with her own survival. The gods had swept them to a
remote island, along with several other creatures, and
pitted them against each other, forcing them to fight.
Worse, forcing them to watch helplessly as their friends
were executed.

More than that, she'd spent her entire life hating men
and the pain they brought with them. As a young child,
she'd been sold by her own mother to male after male;
she'd been used, hurt, taunted…ruined. Zane's desire
had frightened her, and she had lashed out.

And now, she was paying for that.

No one could see her. No one could hear her. Though
she was encircled by the bright, golden light seeping
through the tent's apex, no one knew she was there, that
she'd been among them, month after month. The gods
had cursed her with invisibility when she'd been elimi-
nated from their impossible contest—and then chained
her to this camp as surely as Zane was now chained.

The gods had seen to Zane's captivity, as well, gifting
the vampire to the Amazons to use as they saw fit. And

use him they would—and had already. Because mating season had not begun until today, they had forced him to work their land, hauling boulder after boulder for the building of more tents. He'd had to find sticks and sharpen them into weapons. They'd even forced him to feed many of the women by hand. Of course, he'd tried to escape, time after time, so they'd resorted to starving him. That starvation had caused him to weaken unbearably, rendering him useless. Lately all he'd been able to do was lie in place and curse.

She hated seeing him like this. Maybe because she no longer viewed him as an enemy. How could she? He suffered as she suffered. But now, they would never have a chance to explore their…feelings for each other. Yes, feelings, she thought. On her part anyway. Finally, she *felt*. A need to protect. A need to defend.

Yet she could do neither. And after the way she had treated him, rejecting his advances, he might not want her to try.

What did he see in me, anyway? She'd never understood. That dislike of another's touch…he'd possessed it even on the island. Even with his own king, Layel. Except with her.

Her, he had welcomed. Again, why? What made her so different?

And why had she not reveled in him while she'd had the chance?

Foolish girl. That's what her mother had called her every time she'd complained about her abuse. Nola had never agreed. Until now.

"It is time," a commanding female voice suddenly boomed. "Stand before the slave you wish to claim."

A royal decree the warrioresses rushed to obey, breaking apart, rushing forward.

Kreja, the Amazon queen, stood at the edge of her royal dais, her gaze scanning, expectant. She was a lovely woman, with pale hair and light eyes, both of which gave her the appearance of fragility. But she possessed an iron core, a vicious nature. Which was why Nola had always served her well. She cherished order and had truly enjoyed being led by a woman who thought battles were to be won at any cost.

Now? Not so much.

Finally, the women were crowded around the males that tempted them.

Nineteen of the thirty-two females chose Zane.

Shocking. She had thought their aversion to biting and blood would deter them. She should have known better. Strength was prized among the Amazons, and Zane had nearly won his freedom. Twice. They wanted that strength for their offspring, which was the entire point of mating season.

Her hands curled into fists. Fists that would remain useless, for they could make contact with no one but herself.

"Excellent," Kreja said with a grin. She nodded to the ones standing in front of Zane. "You have chosen well. Though the vampire is a parasite, his daughters will be stalwart."

His daughters.

They should have been mine. Amazons only gave birth to girls. Nola didn't know why or how, only that it was so. And she wanted to kill anyone who would accept this man's seed.

"And if our goddess is shining upon us," Kreja continued, "we will be able to train those daughters to consume something besides blood. If not…" She shrugged, but Nola knew what she implied.

The daughters would be killed.

Zane snarled.

That delighted the women around him, edging them to a new level of eagerness.

Nola fought a wave of anger, of helplessness. *He knows what Kreja plans, and does not like it. He wants to protect his children, even though none have yet been conceived.* No, she should not have feared Zane. She should have enjoyed him, maybe run away with him.

Like him, she did not like being touched. Except by him. His was the first touch in the entire span of her life that had not filled her with disgust. There had been something almost…reverent in his every gentle caress. If she'd welcomed him, he might have helped purge the demons of her past. He might have saved her from herself.

Now, she would never know.

Just as she'd wondered what made her so different to him, she wondered what made him so different to her. That they were so alike? That they sensed, on a bone-deep level, the other's hurt? Because yes, every time she neared him, her heart squeezed and shuddered. Pain always rested in his eyes.

"Fight for me if you wish," he said through sharp, gritted teeth, drawing her thoughts back to the tent, "but know that I will slay the winner with my bare hands."

He was not a man given to boasting, Nola knew. He promised—and he followed through.

"So vengeful," someone twittered happily.

"So mine," another snapped.

"It is *I* who will win his seed," still another growled. "I who will give birth to his offspring."

"No one will bear my child," he roared. "I will die first."

He could not die!

He is not meant to be a slave, Nola longed to shout. He was too proud, too defiant. Traits she also possessed. Which was why she had finally risen up and slain her own mother. Which in turn was why she sometimes cried herself to sleep, wishing she could claw the bloody images from her mind.

Scowling, Nola strode forward and reached out, hoping that, for once, her fingers would do more than ghost through as she tried to shove the Amazons aside. As always, her hand slipped through their bodies as if she were nothing more substantial than mist.

A cry of frustration escaped her.

Still, no one paid her any heed.

"Those of you who desire the vampire will now enter the arena." Kreja's hard voice silenced their arguments. Together they did as commanded, bypassing Nola, even stepping through her. "He shall be the first prize."

"Damn you!" she shouted. "Hear me!"

Of course, they did not.

Shoulders slumping, she closed the distance between herself and Zane and sank beside him. Like the others, he did not act as if he noticed. But she could almost—almost—feel his warmth, and goose bumps broke out over her skin.

"Lily," Kreja called with a wave of her hand.

Lily, the child-princess who would one day rule this clan, stood from her throne atop the dais and walked to her mother's side, her little body draped in velvet robes rather than the leather straps and skirts worn by the warrioresses.

She had changed much in the past few months. No longer was this queen-in-training giddy and innocent. Once having run from camp to prove herself worthy of her people—thereby inadvertently beginning a war between the Amazons and the dragons, a war she'd once thought had caused the deaths of Nola and another Amazon, Delilah—she was now solemn. She'd even relinquished her right to claim Brand the dragon shifter, another of the gods' exiles, as her personal servant, and had offered him up to her people. He now sat among the other slaves.

"You will not fight to the death," Lily proclaimed in her soft voice. "But you will continue to engage each other until only one of you is left standing. It is she who will earn the right to bed the vampire."

And when that winner tired of him, she could pass him on to her friends if she so chose. Increasing Zane's humiliation.

Mating season had never bothered Nola before, but it bothered her now.

Leave. After Nola's own experience with the gods' cruel contest, she had no desire to watch another. For Zane, however, she would watch. And she would wish.

Every female in the ring assumed the battle stance.

There was only a slight pause before Kreja said, "You may begin."

Immediately the women leapt into action. Metal clanged against metal, grunts abounded, and sand was flung in every direction. Seconds bled into minutes. Minutes to what seemed hours. An eternity. Bodies began collapsing, cries of pain echoing, one pink-haired female savagely working her way through the masses.

Soon, she was the only one standing.

Over. Done.

Nola wanted to vomit.

"And so we have a winner," Kreja decreed proudly. She motioned to Zane with a wave of her hand. "Claim your prize, beloved. Know that we are pleased with the strength and tenacity you have demonstrated this day."

As the female approached, Zane trembled. In rage. Perhaps in fear.

I'm so sorry, vampire. "I won't let her have you," Nola vowed, though she knew there was nothing she could do to stop what was to come.

CHAPTER TWO

THE FEMALE WAS GOING to kill him, Zane thought dazedly, dispassionately.

She'd won him, however long ago she'd fought for him—one day? Two? Weak as he was, he'd lost track of time. All he knew was that she'd tried multiple times to bed him. But she needed a hard cock for that, and he hadn't given it to her.

Denying her had delighted him. Still did.

Now two of those wretched Amazons stood around him, staring down at his naked body. If he hadn't been half-starved and teetering on the brink of total collapse, those stares would have sent him into a killing rage. He hated being looked at as much as he hated being touched.

He'd spent too many centuries as the demon queen's whore, hers to use, hers to hurt. And hurt him she had.

Many times, she'd forced him to drop to his knees and "worship" her with his mouth. Many times, she had forced him to clean each and every one of the horns covering her body. Again, with his mouth. Many times, she had forced him to do the same to others while she watched.

But the worst… He shuddered, hating to remember. But just then, his memories were all he had. They filled him up, consumed him, eating him bite by rancid bite. She'd blindfolded him and bound him to her bed. He had not known who kissed and touched him. Male, female. Demon, another slave. He *hadn't known*.

He hated, *hated* that there were people in Atlantis who knew of his humiliation and subjugation. He hated that those people had seen him naked, tasted him, brought him to climax in terrible ways, yet he did not know who they were.

Bile rose from his stomach into his throat. *Demon whore.* That's what he was, all he would ever be. *Demon whore, demon whore.* He squeezed his eyes shut. He wanted to cover his ears, but could not. His arms were tied, true, but even if he had been free, he was too weak to move.

Demon whore.

How could he have allowed such things? And he had. Allowed them. He could have walked away at any time. Yet he hadn't.

All for the love of a woman. A slave, as he was supposed to be now. Marina, that detestable queen, had promised to set his beloved free if Zane pleased her until she grew tired of him. But she'd never grown tired of him, and Cassandra, his chosen mate, had begun to hate him as a result. For all he knew, she could have been forced to watch him with the queen.

Demon whore.

Yet still he'd stayed, determined to finally win his prize. His Cassandra. If he couldn't have her as a mate, he'd at least wanted her to be happy. And as he well knew, no one could be happy without freedom.

But then, his actions hadn't mattered. Layel, the vampire king, had done the impossible—what Zane had craved but had not yet had the strength to do—and drained the demon queen, finally freeing both Zane and Cassandra. He'd thought to earn back her love. However necessary. After all, everything he had done had been for her. Every hated touch, every blinded session. Only, she'd fled him. For another man.

Demon whore.

Perhaps that had been for the best.

Zane was not the man he'd once been. He eschewed females and wanted no part of them. Wanted no part of sex. He shuddered at even the thought of it, and sickness once again churned in his stomach. Had he eaten that day, he would have vomited.

One bright light. Remember your one bright light.

Nola.

Finally, his stomach calmed.

Nola had walked into his life, chasing away the darkness. Beautiful, passionate, fierce Nola. A woman who hadn't wanted him, who had rebuffed him. A woman he'd craved with every ounce of his being despite what had been done to him. A woman the gods had taken from him. Why did he want her so damned passionately? He hadn't known then, and he didn't know now. Yet still he craved her. As if she were necessary to him. To his survival. As if, the first moment their eyes had met, hers as haunted as he knew his were, she had become a part of him.

Would he ever see her again?

He did not know if she'd survived their island game or if the gods had set her free, but sometimes he would swear that he smelled her sweet scent, felt the gentle glide of her hands on him. A touch he still did not mind.

A touch he needed. She…soothed him.

And, actually, the first time he'd seen her, he'd thought her a gift from the gods. For why else would he have been able to endure—no, enjoy—her touch and no other? Now, he thought that perhaps she'd been another curse. He craved her still, yet like Cassandra he could never have her.

What did I do to deserve this?

Demon whore.

"I'm strong," his owner said now, drawing his attention, "so of course he desires me. I mean, look at what I did to my competitors! Eighteen against one, yet I *owned* that arena. But he's too weak to be claimed. That's the problem here. Surely."

"You're right. Clearly he needs blood," another said.

"Yes, but if he's given blood, he'll be able to raise his head and bite me."

Both of the females shuddered.

Did these Amazons—who abhorred the biting of flesh and the drinking of blood and who thought to rape him to steal a child from him—not realize the child of a vampire would *not* be trainable, as the Amazon queen had said? A vampire needed blood. Blood was nourishment. Life. That was not something that could be "trained" away.

And so, any child of his would be killed. That's what the foolish queen had implied.

His baby. Killed. Even through the haze of weakness, rage sparked inside his chest. He would kill them first, he thought, once again struggling against his bonds.

They expected him to leave his child behind, to be raised by them. Abused by them. Something he would never do. What was his, was *his*. He did not share. He did not abandon.

"Weak, but still fighting," the pink-haired Amazon said with awe.

"Yet still no hardened shaft," the other tsked.

Calm. Or they will stop feeding you altogether.

Though every bone in his body screamed for him to do otherwise, he relaxed against his pallet.

"You're going to have to feed him."

"I know. But even now, I think he would bite me if I got too close. What is to happen when he's stronger?"

Before his last escape attempt, they'd kept him nourished by allowing him three small cups of blood a day. Who had donated the blood, he didn't know. Didn't care. He didn't like to take from a living source, only from those he'd slain. So he'd pretended the blood came from one of his victims.

"Let's think this through, then. Perhaps there is another way. Did you try manipulating his rod?"

"Of course. He's not my first slave, you know."

"Well, give him blood, then...bind his mouth. Yes, that might work. That way, he'll be strong enough to bed but unable to nibble on you."

"Oh, excellent idea! Grab a goblet." The pink-haired woman—he hadn't cared to remember her name— palmed one of her daggers, sliced a groove in her wrist and held the wound over the offered cup.

His mouth watered at the sight and smell of that crimson nectar; his fangs elongated. She was not dead, he couldn't pretend otherwise, but he would still take from her. Sacrifices must be made in times of adversity.

She approached him and held the cup to his lips. Thankfully, her skin did not brush his. "Drink."

As though in a trance, he obeyed, swallowing three precious mouthfuls. Instantly, warmth spread through him, followed on its heels by strength. So good...

"It's working. His color is returning." The goblet was removed from his mouth, and he found his gaze locked with that of his captor. She was pretty, if he cared for such things.

He didn't. He only cared that she had pink hair rather than black, brown eyes rather than turquoise, and she did not smell like Nola. Like sea and storms and flowers.

There was a pause, then a purr of agreement. "He's beautiful, isn't he?"

"Don't forget he's mine," was the snapped reply.

"Well, his cock is still flaccid, so you won't be claiming him any time soon," the other Amazon lashed back.

As the blood continued to work through him, the lethargy that had plagued him all these many days dissolved, leaving energy in his muscles, a sizzle in his bones. *Escape,* he thought, a growl working its way past his throat.

Both Amazons jumped away from him with a yelp. "Hurry! Let's bind his mouth."

"Don't touch me!" Growls intensifying, Zane jerked at the chains circling his wrists and ankles. He hissed and snapped, kicking as much as he was able as the Amazons maneuvered around him. "No touching! Do you hear me? I'll kill you."

Metal cut past his flesh, hitting those sizzling bones. Still he fought, imagining his blade slicing through both of these women. More blood would spill. He would lap it up. Strengthen even more. He would tear through their camp. No mercy.

Suddenly a golden ray of light spilled inside the tent, and he would have sworn he caught a glimpse of…no, surely not. Couldn't be. Yet…there she was. His Nola.

"No—" He stilled, his heart slamming against his ribs. Couldn't be, he thought again. Unless…was she a hallucination? He'd had them before, yet they never ceased to shock him.

His captor moved, reaching for his neck, blocking the vision.

"Out of my way!" he shouted, bumping his hip against hers and sending her toppling to her face. He'd imagined Nola before, there in the battle tent. Sadly, that glimpse had lasted only a few heart-stopping seconds. How long would this one last?

Had his captor already dispelled it?

If she had...

No. There Nola was again, a shimmering outline of long black hair, a glow of turquoise eyes. She was trying—ineffectually—to tug his captor away from him. He lost his breath. *So lovely.* His shaft hardened quickly and painfully. Nola. His sweetest tormentor.

Then the vision wavered, the air dabbled...gone. She was gone.

He wanted to scream and hurt and maim. To kill and be killed. The desire came too late, though, his stunned immobility costing him. The Amazon was able to leap to her feet and easily hook a thick strap of material around his useless mouth.

"Finally." Sighing with satisfaction, she leaned away from him, crouching on her haunches and smiling smugly. "And just as I suspected, your rod is—" Her words halted and her smile faded as his cock withered before her eyes. "But...you were...why..."

He had only imagined Nola; he knew that, but he couldn't stop his gaze from searching for another glimpse of her. To his dismay, he saw only furs, carved furniture and weapons.

Even as his captor and her friend attempted to arouse him once more, stripping for him, caressing him, he did not stop searching.

Finally, exasperated with him, the Amazons dressed and stormed from the tent, leaving him alone with his insanity.

CHAPTER THREE

As MANY TIMES AS NOLA had been chained and used in her life, she knew the humiliation, frustration and helplessness Zane was now feeling. He must want to kill Amelia, his new owner. *She* did.

Hurting another Amazon went against every instinct Nola possessed, every rule she'd ever been taught—after she'd escaped her mother, that is—but she would have sliced the warrioress to pieces if she'd been able to grip a blade. Exactly as she'd done to her mother. Zane's eyes had been so wild, his snarls so desperate. And she'd been unable to aid him, had only been able to watch in horror.

"I will take his place," she shouted to the ceiling, not knowing if the gods were listening. Or if they even cared. But she had to try. Zane didn't deserve this. No one did. At least she had endured servitude before. She could do so again. And were she to actually take Zane's place, the women wouldn't rape her, of course, but they *would* work her and beat her. Neither of which would break her. Because she would know she had helped her man.

"Please," she shouted. "Switch us!"

No response. But suddenly air was sucked through Zane's nostrils, and his body jerked. Then he began struggling against his bonds again. Her attention whipped to him. He was staring directly at her, his dark gaze boring into her.

"Zane," she said, rushing to his side and kneeling. "Shh, now. Shh. You'll only injure your wrists and ankles further." Already he was bleeding, losing the blood he'd just been given.

He tracked her every movement.

Could he…no. Not possible. No matter how many times she'd wished otherwise, she'd remained as unnoticeable as the air he breathed. Besides, if he knew she was here, he would be fighting her as he'd fought Amelia. Perhaps even more violently. She had not only rebuked his advances, she had tried to hurt him, too. Had called him vile names he had not deserved. All because she'd been too frightened of her feelings.

I am not worthy of being an Amazon warrioress.

Frantic, Zane rubbed his jaw against his shoulder until the material fell away from his mouth. "Nola," he rasped. "Nola, Nola, Nola. You are here."

He *could* see her. Oh, gods. Oh, gods! Could she touch him? Her arm shook as she reached out, meaning to brush his hair from his face, but as always, her hand ghosted through him. She moaned in frustration.

He laughed, the sound full of sweet satisfaction. "I've finally slipped over the edge of sanity and I don't care." He relaxed against the blankets spread out beneath him. "My Nola, here to comfort me. As beautiful as ever."

His Nola? A shiver moved through her. Oh, if only… "You aren't imagining me, Zane. I'm truly here. I've been here since the day of your arrival."

Zane didn't seem to hear her. His gaze was too busy drinking her in. "Of course I would imagine you like this, soft and lush, but still not mine to possess."

"Listen to me. The gods cursed me, as they cursed you, only I am not to be seen, heard or felt." Until now. Why, why, *why* could she now be seen and heard but still not felt?

Finally, her words seemed to take root. His eyelids narrowed and his lips pulled tight against his teeth, revealing the tips of those deadly fangs. "How is that possible?"

"Need I remind you of the gods' powers?"

His cheeks flushed. "How can I see you now, then?" he asked, mirroring her thoughts. "What has changed?"

"I wish I knew," she said on a sigh. Would others be able to see her, as well?

He laughed without humor. "So. Another curse is to be heaped upon me. To see, but never to touch the only one I desire." He turned his head from her, as if he couldn't bear to look at her another second.

That was the treatment she'd expected from him, but it still hurt. *You deserve it. Take it like a warrior.*

At least he no longer thought himself crazy.

"You…still wish to touch me?"

A pause, heavy, laden with tension. "Why aren't you with Brand?" he demanded rather than answer her.

Brand, the dragon shape-shifter who had been cursed right alongside them. "I don't…" What? She liked Brand, but she wasn't concerned with his treatment. He had not fought his captivity like Zane. He had embraced the thought of a temporary Amazon owner.

Other than Lily, that is. Lily had been too young for him, and he'd been nothing more than a maid for her. Since she'd released him into the *tender* care of the other Amazons, though, he'd looked nothing but content.

But even if he had not been enjoying himself, Nola

still would have chosen to watch over Zane. His strength and determination, and even his wildness, drew her. Maybe because that wildness had never truly extended to her. Even when she'd stabbed both of his shoulders with spears, he had not attempted to hurt her. He had cried out for her, wanting to be with her.

I hate myself for rejecting him.

"Why haven't you used your…gift to help you escape?" she asked, ignoring his question as he'd ignored hers. Much as this man had to hate her, despite the desire he'd professed—or had she imagined that?—she wasn't ready to voice her softer feelings. Even she didn't understand her change from tormentor to tormented. And what if *he* were to reject *her?* Her already bruised and battered heart would not survive.

His cheeks heated in embarrassment, but still he did not face her.

He'd once used that gift on her. Had slipped inside her dreams and showed her how good it would be between them. How he would kiss and taste every inch of her body, enjoy her, help her enjoy him.

"You can show the Amazons the destruction you will unleash if they fail to release you."

"The gods stripped me of the ability when they sent me here," he finally admitted. "I can no longer enter dreams. Or create nightmares. They also stripped me of my ability to transport myself to other locations with only a thought."

Damn them! "There has to be a way to free you. I wish I could leave camp and visit your king. Word has spread through Atlantis that he is wed now to my sister, Delilah. They would help you, I know it. And maybe, like you, they would be able to see and hear me. But I am bound to this camp, as surely as if I were shackled. I cannot leave its boundaries."

Or perhaps she could, now that part of her curse seemed to be lifted. She wanted to check, but couldn't force herself to move away.

Zane shifted even further away from her, his chains rattling. It was another stark reminder of their doomed circumstances. "Why would you help me?"

"Because I—" She peered down at her hands. Her fingers were twined together and twisting the leather of her skirt. They wanted to be on Zane's body, learning his every nuance. What would make him gasp in pleasure? What would make him moan? "I owe you. I hurt you, and I'm sorry for that. Sorrier than I can ever express. I want—"

"Enough," he growled, cutting her off. "I don't want your apology. I never did."

Rejection. Even though she had not professed her new feelings. As she'd suspected, her heart stopped. Literally stopped. Tears burned her eyes. She had not cried in years. Not since she was a little girl, huddled in bed, dreading the monsters who would visit her.

"I've always wanted you…your body," he added in a croak. "Still do."

"Wh-what?"

"I want you."

Shocking. Need trembled through her. Welcome need. Beloved need. "Yes." *Yes.* "I would rather give myself to you than give the apology, for I want you, too." There. Admission. Not as scary as she had thought. Freeing, actually. "But you can't touch me, and I cannot touch you. How…" Hated need, she thought next. A craving that could never be satisfied.

"We will figure it out." Huskily said, softening expression.

How? she wanted to ask again, but didn't. No telling when Amelia would return. Their privacy was limited, and she did not want to spend it grasping for solutions they would never find.

Apparently, Zane did not either.

"Climb on top of me," he beseeched. "I want to see you there. Want to imagine."

To her surprise, she obeyed without hesitation, eager, straddling his waist. His eyes closed, and he arched up. Imagine, he'd said. He was imagining sinking inside her.

Yes, she thought. Yes. She would like that. Wanted that. She imagined his hard shaft entering inch by inch and moaned. A few times, the act had felt pleasurable rather than painful, but those times had left her wallowing in shame. How could she have liked being bedded by those disgusting males, even for a moment?

This time, however, there was no shame. Only acceptance. *More.*

"Zane, I—"

"Feel good?"

"Yes."

"I'm glad. Would you like me to—"

The entrance to the tent flapped, and Amelia strode inside. "Well, vampire. I have decided—" Her eyes widened, and she stopped. "Nola? What are you doing here?"

Nola jumped up as though burned. She wanted to scream in frustration, but held her tongue. One question had been answered, at least. Others *could* see her.

"Hello, Amelia." Did she sound as breathless to the warrioress as she did to herself?

"We thought you were dead."

"You thought wrong."

Amelia's dark gaze swung to Zane, then back to Nola. "Either way, you will move away from my slave. If you wanted him for yourself, you should have been brave enough to return and fight for him."

"I do want him for myself."

"Too late."

No. It wasn't. She refused to believe that.

"Nola," Zane said, and there was a warning in his tone.

A warning of what? Nola didn't face him, but squared her shoulders and forced her expression to harden. "Well, I am here now. Amelia, I challenge you for the vampire."

CHAPTER FOUR

"HURRY! SHE'LL RETURN any moment, and she'll have others with her. Perhaps the entire army."

Zane watched as Nola tried and failed to jerk the head of his chains from the iron pole they were attached to, a pole that was anchored deep in the earth. As before, her fingers merely passed through the object.

His shock had yet to diminish. Nola was here; Nola wanted him; Nola thought to help him. After her announcement—*I challenge you for the vampire*—his captor had stormed out of the tent with every intention of speaking to the Amazon queen. And having Nola imprisoned.

No. He would not allow that.

She was his.

Earlier when she'd apologized to him, it had not been remorse thickening her voice. It had been desire. Then she'd climbed on top of him without any uncertainty, had moaned when he'd arched into her. He hadn't been able to feel her, but oh, just the thought of doing so had been enough for him. He'd never craved a female more.

"How do you propose to fight her?" he demanded. "You cannot hurt her, and she cannot hurt you." Thank the gods. He would rather endure an eternity of slavery than watch this woman bleed.

"I didn't want to fight her. Well, I did, do, but know

I can't. I just wanted time. And why are you just lying there?" She peered down at him, hands on her hips, dark hair streaming wildly around her delicate face. "Fight free!"

So lovely. Everything he'd craved these many months of his captivity—Nola, freedom, a chance to be together—was now being offered to him. No longer did he feel cursed. Never had he been so blessed.

He couldn't feel her? So what. Being with her was more important.

"You will come with me? If I escape?" he asked.

"If I can, yes. I want that more than anything," she added in a fierce whisper.

Again, there was no uncertainty. There was even a flicker of hope in her magnificent eyes. She truly did not hate him.

What had brought about this change in her?

Would she change her mind if she knew of his past?

Demon whore.

He squeezed his eyes closed, wishing once again that he could cover his ears.

"Zane, darling. What's wrong?"

Don't tell her. Don't ever tell her. "Nothing." She would run from him as Cassandra had.

"You're hurting," Nola said. She tapped on his chest, just above his heart. "Here. Tell me why."

"I will escape," he said instead. "You will come with me."

He was suddenly fueled with a fervor he had never experienced before. He wanted this. Would have this. Just as…soon as…he broke…free. For what seemed an eternity, he pulled hard at his wrists and ankles, straining so forcefully his bones eventually gave way.

Out came both his ankles; out came both his wrists. The pain of it nearly bowled him over as he sat up, then stood to trembling legs. He didn't care about the pain, though. He was free at last.

Together. They could be together.

"I hear them," Nola gasped. "Come on." She made to grab him, but her hand misted through his body. "Damn this!"

There was no sensation, no chill, but the knowledge that she had tried to touch him caused him to shiver rather than shudder. From the very first, it had been that way. Others he ran from. Others he abhorred. Her, he only yearned for more of. Why? he wondered again.

"This way." She raced to the far end of the tent. "Raise the flap."

He lumbered to her, stumbling constantly, and did as commanded. All the while, his battered body screamed in agony, black winking over his vision, stomach threatening to heave. Vampires were fast healers, but he'd been without blood too long, the few sips he'd had earlier already used up.

Outside, light poured from the crystal dome surrounding all of Atlantis, heating and stinging his now-sensitive skin and making his eyes water. This kind of reaction had only happened once before. On that cursed island of the gods.

The reminder of his time there infuriated him and that fury gave him strength. He could do this. Tent after tent dotted the surrounding land. Amazons were scattered throughout. Some were bent over a fire and hammering at weapons; some were hanging animal hides.

"Walk behind me," Nola said, "as if you are my slave."

Without waiting for his agreement, she moved forward, head held high. Behind him, he could hear a murmur of voices inside his captor's tent. Amelia had returned, and she had indeed brought an army with her. Zane kicked into motion. Thankfully, no one paid them any heed—until a horn blasted. The Amazons around him straightened, a few even reaching for weapons.

"Run!" Nola shouted, picking up speed. "Run!"

No longer content to remain behind her, he matched her pace. A forest loomed a few yards ahead, thick trees promising cover.

"Nola!" someone shouted. "Stop!"

"Vampire," his captor screamed. "Not another step. I *will* punish you."

Zane tripped over a rock. He lurched forward, his broken ankles unable to support him. When he hit the ground, he hit hard and lost every bit of oxygen in his lungs. Grimacing, he lumbered back up. Started running again.

All the while, Nola encouraged him. "You can do it. I know you can. That's the way. Just a little farther. You're so strong. You're so brave. I'm so proud of you."

Sweeter words had never been spoken. Such encouragement… No one, not even his king, had offered it. He soaked it up, bloomed under it. His speed increased, his steps firmed.

But when they reached the trees, Nola stopped and screeched. "No! No, no, no."

He, too, stopped and faced her. He tried to grab her, but as before, encountered only air. "Come. Now. We'll enter the forest and disappear." Together, he thought again, satisfaction filling him.

"I can't. It's like a wall is blocking me." Frantic, she

tossed a glance over her shoulder at the scowling Amazon warrioresses bearing down on them. "Go. Please. Just go."

Still she could not leave the camp's boundary?

He remained in place, the screams in his head no longer for his bodily pain. He couldn't leave this woman behind. But he couldn't stay here, broken as he was. He was no good to either of them.

Damn the gods to Hades!

Demon whore. To think, even for a moment, that he'd felt blessed. Foolish.

"Will they attempt to punish you?" he asked. He had to know. He would stay here, even broken as he was, even helpless as he was. Anything to protect her.

"They can't hurt me. They might be able to see me, but I'm untouchable, remember?" She smiled, but it didn't quite reach her eyes. "Now go, before they take you. They will not be as gentle with you this time."

"Nola…" *She is mine. I keep what is mine.*

"Zane. Go. *Please.* Save yourself. You are not meant to be any woman's slave. Not even mine."

A muscle ticked below his eye. "I will come back for you. Soon as I'm healed, I will come back." As he spoke, he walked backward.

"I will think and dream of you always."

A goodbye? Oh, no. "I will come back," he repeated. "Watch for me." Only when she was blocked from his view did he spin and run.

CHAPTER FIVE

NOLA FACED OFF WITH HER sisters. They formed a menacing half-circle around her, each glaring at her.

"You freed my slave," Amelia growled, and several warrioresses booed and hissed at Nola.

She had always been something of a tribe outsider, so she wasn't surprised at the cold welcome. "He isn't yours, but yes," she said proudly. "I freed him." And she would do so again. Anything for Zane.

I will come back, he'd said. Twice. She shivered.

A frowning Kreja stepped forward, separating herself from the masses and placing herself nose to nose with Nola. "I want five of my elite armed and hunting the vampire within the next five minutes."

Footsteps echoed as the warrioresses complied. They could look, but they wouldn't find him. He was too determined. *I will come back.*

"And you," the queen continued, "you know the punishment for stealing your sister's slave?"

"Yes," Nola repeated. The punishment—a savage, wish-you-were-dead whipping. Not that they could administer it. But even if she'd been tangible, she would have risked it. Zane's freedom was worth losing the skin on her back. At the very least.

"Delilah returned and told us you lived still, but that did not stop our worry for you. And now I find you here, working against us. Why would you do such a thing?" the queen asked, sounding genuinely curious, slightly sad, rather than fully enraged.

"The vampire had endured enough at the hands of the Amazons. Like us, he is a living being with feelings. He is courageous, wild as the animals in this forest and fierce beyond imagining. We would have broken him." Or tried to.

"Wise words." Kreja arched a brow. "And yet, he left you here to endure punishment, even though you aided him. Do you find that a worthy trait?"

I will come back.

And he would. She had no doubt. Never before had she trusted a man, but she trusted Zane. Having watched him these past few months, she knew he was not the kind of man who made vows lightly. She knew he did not say things simply to placate his audience. Oh, yes. He would return.

What they would do when he reached her, she didn't know. She only knew that she needed to be with him. To see his face and hear his voice. She could live with any curse, as long as he was alive and well and with her.

"I find *him* worthy," she finally replied.

Kreja sighed. "That does not change what you have done. Not only did you free a slave, you freed your *sister's* slave. For that, you will deal with Amelia in the battle arena. She will be armed. You will not. Afterward, if you survive, you will be whipped, as is our custom."

The queen reached out—and wrapped her fingers around Nola's suddenly solid forearm, dragging her toward the arena, Amelia marching close on her heels.

Nola gasped in shock. *What...why...how was it possible?* She could be touched now.

"I will not go easy on you," Amelia snarled at her.

They can touch me. Which means they can *hurt me,* Nola realized, dread sweeping through her.

Would she be alive when Zane returned?

ZANE REACHED THE VAMPIRE stronghold and collapsed at its gates. His strength—gone. His wounds—unhealed. Followed as he'd been, he hadn't been able to hunt for food. Broken as he was, he wouldn't have been able to capture a single animal and feed himself.

Thankfully the guards recognized him. He was hefted over a shoulder and carted inside the palace. The touch disturbed him, but he didn't fight it. He was in too much of a hurry and knew this was the best way. By the time they reached his personal chamber, there was a buzz of activity, his name being whispered from everyone's lips.

"Blood," he rasped as the guard lay him down on the bed.

That guard tilted his head, offering his own neck.

Zane shook his head and closed his eyes. "Glass." He would not take from a living source. Still couldn't stomach the thought—unless that living source was Nola. Once, when he'd ensured she would welcome him by invading her dreams, he had tasted her. The sweetness of her blood...the decadence of her moans...he'd reveled in every nuance of her. He would not overshadow that precious memory by taking from someone else, even in his desperation.

How did she affect him this way?

Would he always be forced to wonder?

Perhaps he did not mind her hands on him because he saw himself in her eyes. Every damned time he looked at her. He saw vulnerability and pain, fear and yearning.

Perhaps they shared a similar past; she'd alluded to such a thing once before, when they'd been pitted against each other on the island. Back then, he had been too wrapped in his newfound desire to pay much attention to her words. Never again, he vowed. What she said came first. Always. As did protecting her, defending her.

And maybe she would feel the same about him.

He suddenly wanted to hug her close and tell her everything that had happened to him. Admit that he'd once been the demon queen's willing sexual toy. She might…she might understand rather than run.

Demon whore.

How could anyone understand?

But for once, the taunt did not drive him to distraction. *She* might, and for now, that was enough.

Warm hands settled on his shoulders and shook him.

His eyelids fluttered open, a growl in his throat. When he saw that Layel loomed above him, glass in hand, he forced himself to relax against the feathered mattress. "My king, I—"

"No talking just yet. Drink," Layel said, placing the glass to his lips. Tall and leanly muscled, with white hair and blue eyes, he was an eerily beautiful sight that reminded Zane of both his rescue from the demon queen and the horrors he'd later endured at the hands of the gods. "Drink."

Zane opened his mouth, and the sweet nectar of life poured down his throat. He swallowed greedily.

Once again, warmth spread through him. Warmth and strength and determination.

He had not lied to Nola. He was going back for her. He would conquer that damn camp and everyone inside it.

Nola will not like that. Those women are her sisters.

Well, they damn well should not have tried to enslave him, he thought darkly. But he knew deep down that he wouldn't hurt them. Not really. For Nola, he would simply send them on their way, claiming the camp as his own and remaining there until she could leave it. And if she could never leave it, he would never leave it.

"Good now?" Layel asked.

"More," he said when the supply ran out. He'd need every ounce of his strength to conquer the Amazons.

Layel cut his wrist, filled the glass with his own life force, and offered it up. This time, Zane was able to hold the glass on his own. Again, he drained every drop. When he finished, he licked his lips and faced the king.

"I am ready to talk," he said.

"Good. I have questions."

"Answer mine first. You escaped the gods and their island." He grunted as his wrists and ankles popped back into place. "Did you win their game?"

The king's lips slowly lifted in a grin. "Delilah did. She saved us both. We have been searching for you since the moment of our return, but the Amazons hid you well. We knew you were there, but we could find no sign of you."

"Have you news of my sister?" a female voice asked.

Zane looked past his king and saw Delilah standing in the doorway. She was petite in appearance, but as fierce as Nola on a battlefield. Her blue hair was falling around her shoulders, and worry was etched in the violet depths of her eyes.

"She is alive," he told her, and she expelled a relieved breath. "And she is mine."

A pause.

"And does she agree with that statement?" Delilah's head tilted to the side as she rubbed at her slightly rounded belly. There was barely contained fury in her tone. She would slay him without mercy if he hurt Nola, that much was obvious.

Rather than plead his case, he focused on that belly. Slightly rounded. A baby? Layel was to become a father? An ache bloomed in Zane's chest. He'd wanted children with Cassandra. Had dreamed of them. Yet that, too, had been denied him. Until…now?

With Nola… *You cannot truly touch her, you fool. That dream is still dead.* He couldn't make himself care, however. As long as he had Nola, nothing else mattered.

"Well?" Delilah insisted.

Did Nola wish to belong to him? she'd asked. He thought so, yes. She had helped him. She had even wanted to go with him. But she was also a warrior to her core, an *Amazon* warrior at that, and they only tolerated men during mating season. He wanted far more than that. No matter the circumstances. He wanted what Layel and Delilah clearly had.

"We will see," Zane said, kicking his legs over the bed.

"You only just returned," Layel said. "Where are you going?"

"To get my woman." This one, he wouldn't let get away.

CHAPTER SIX

GRUNTS, GROANS AND THE CLANG of metal against metal roused Nola from her troubled sleep. She wanted to rise, to see what was happening, but could not force her body into action. Her back was a mass of agony, the skin flayed completely. The rest of her, well, it had not fared much better during her battle with Amelia. Nola had won, her determination stronger than any weapon, but she had not emerged unscathed. There were deep sword slices all down her arms, stomach and legs.

She lay on her bed, her stomach pressed into soft blankets. Alone, always alone. No one was allowed to help her. Not in any way. Amazons healed as slowly as humans, so she knew she would suffer like this for many weeks to come.

Outside, a scream echoed. Her muscles were heavy as stones, and she didn't have the strength to drag herself upright. Or gather food. Not that she even had the strength to eat. She wanted to help her sisters, though. Despite what had been done to her, she loved them.

They had welcomed her into their fold when she'd had nowhere else to go. They had despised her mother for what the woman had done to her.

"You will die for this, vampires!" someone shouted.

"Not by your hand," she heard a male voice say. The

vampire king? That had sounded like his rough, cocky timbre.

Despite her pain, Nola grinned. Relaxed.

Zane was here.

For hours, the battle continued to rage. Nola didn't want her sisters injured, but neither did she want Zane to lose, and waiting proved difficult. She chewed at her cheeks, dug her nails into her palms and broke into a sweat, which caused her back to burn as if it had been set on fire as well as flayed.

Finally, the tent flap rose and light flooded inside. And then he was there, standing in front of her. Her vampire. Zane. Her heart knocked against her ribs.

"Knew you'd come," she said, her voice barely audible. She hadn't screamed during her whipping, hadn't made a sound, but holding her cries inside had scraped her throat raw.

"Nola…sweet…" He approached her slowly, as if she were a trapped animal. "What did they do to you?" There was horror in his tone. He crouched beside her, reached out and smoothed her hair from her damp forehead. Then he froze. "How is this possible? I'm touching you. Feeling your warmth."

"Yes. Happened just after you'd left." Any other time, she would have been mortified for him to see her like this: broken, helpless, naked but for a sheet covering her lower half. Her relief at seeing him alive and well, however, was simply too great.

"I will destroy the gods for this. How dare they do this to you! Allow you to feel only when you will be injured. The cruelty such an act requires… I will find a way to raid the heavens and I will—"

"No, no. This is a blessing. I've had time to think,

and I believe I know what's happening. Each time I admit something about you, like the fact that you did not deserve what was done to you, and that I trust you, I've been given back a piece of my life."

His brows furrowed together, and a spark of hope entered his eyes. "Can you pass the camp boundary now?"

"No. My sisters carried me there, meaning to toss me out after my whipping, but that invisible wall blocked them."

Fury replaced the hope. "We didn't hurt your sisters—I knew you would hate it if we did, but now I wish I'd sliced each and every one of them to pieces. They abandoned camp or I would see to it now."

"You're here now. That's all that matters." And it was. "But…how long will you be able to stay?" Her nervousness returned. His king would want him back. And the Amazons would one day come back. This was not the first time their camp had been taken. They always came back. Angrier. Far more brutal. "You can't remain forever, and I can't leave. We'll be forced to separate again and—"

"It's all right. It's all right, sweet. Do not worry yourself. Think only of healing. I'm here, and I'm not leaving without you. No matter what. You freed me. I will find a way to free you."

The burst of strength her nervousness had given her drained, and she expelled a breath. "As long as I have you, I'll be all right." The words flowed freely. Talking about her feelings was becoming easier.

"Yes, you will." He stretched out beside her and angled his head, displaying his neck to her. The scent of him filled her nose. Dark spice and tree dew. She inhaled deeply, savoring. "Drink," he said.

"Wh-what?" Even when they'd been trapped on that island, he had not let anyone drink from him. Not from his wrist, and certainly not from his neck.

"*Drink.* I know biting and blood are distasteful to your kind, but you will heal faster if my blood flows inside your veins. I have watched others of my kind do this for their mates who were not vampires."

"No, you don't understand. I don't mind drinking from you. I just don't want to disgust *you.* I know you do not like such things being done to you."

Precious little lights flickered in his eyes. "I want to give you everything, Nola. Even this. With you and no other. I need this, so please. Please."

Please, this proud, strong man had said. How could she deny him? She cried out as she edged toward him—pain, so much pain—and sank her teeth into his neck, hard as she could, cutting past skin and hitting vein. Blood instantly trickled down her throat.

Once, the thought of doing this would have been distasteful to her, as he'd claimed. But this was Zane. She wanted him inside her. Any part of him that she could get. And like him, she wanted him to have everything she had to give.

"I never thought to allow someone to take from me again," he said, petting her head. "I—I have to tell you something. Something that may make you hate me. But you deserve to know."

Nothing could make her hate him. Nothing.

He did not give her time to tell him that. "The demon queen," he continued. "I was her slave for many centuries. Her...bedmate. Willingly. She took from me whenever and however she desired. Her methods sickened me, but I allowed them because she had something— someone—my compliance was supposed to purchase."

Nola released his neck. "I—"

"No. Do not speak. Keep drinking. There is more I must tell you, but my courage will abandon me if your mouth is gone from me."

She sank her teeth back into his neck, the warmth of his blood spinning through her, lighting her up from the inside out.

"When she died and I was freed, I thought to never endure such things again. You, though, I think I would allow to do anything to me. It has been that way from the first. I don't understand it, either. Your presence doesn't drown out the memories or take away my revulsion for this act. My...need for you simply overrides it. Even though I fear you will find me, a dirty demon whore, unworthy of you. I *am* unworthy of you."

"No," she said, wrenching away. Blood trickled from the side of her mouth. "You are perfect. Wonderful." She snuggled into his waiting embrace, head cradled in the hollow of his neck. The action pained her, but only a little. She could feel the flesh weaving together on her back. "Never say otherwise."

"You...you do not wish to leave me now?" So hesitant. So unsure.

"If you are a demon whore, then I am an Amazon whore. When I was a child, my mother mated with a man and left the Amazon camp to live with him. They had no money and so they...sold me, time and time again," she said, heat spreading over her cheeks. "I know the desire to never again be touched by another. Except you."

"Oh, sweet. I am so sorry for what you endured. And you are not a whore. Never say such a thing."

That gentle tone brought tears to her eyes. "If I cannot, you cannot."

"Agreed." He wrapped his arm around her, careful of her injuries. "You once told me your family had destroyed you, that you had killed them for it, but until now, I had no idea they'd done such things to you."

She flattened her palm against his chest, exactly as she'd wanted to do all these months while watching him. His heart beat fast and hard. "Maybe we remind each other of what we were like, before. Unafraid, untainted. Maybe we see the future in each other and the past ceases to matter."

He didn't reply, which disappointed her. Instead, he settled her onto the blankets and sat up. Old fears surfaced. Did he not want a future with her? Was that what his silence signified? Did he—

He traced a fingertip along her spine, and she shivered. "All healed," he said huskily. "And now, all mine."

Thank the gods. She wasn't sure what she would have done if he'd rebuffed her as she'd once done him. *You should not have doubted him. Even for a moment.*

She wouldn't. Not ever again.

"Make love to me, Zane." She'd never been with a man of her choosing. Never given herself completely. She was suddenly desperate to know what that was like. With this man. Only this man, who was surely a gift from the heavens, even amid her curse. "Please. Let us join."

"Forever."

"Forever."

CHAPTER SEVEN

ZANE FLIPPED NOLA TO HER back so that she was peering up at him. A gasp escaped her, but she didn't try to scramble away, even though he loomed above her, dressed in his blood-splattered battle clothes while she was naked.

Her breasts were small but firm, perfectly tipped with hard pink nipples. Her stomach was flat, her skin sun-kissed and smooth. He could see every ridge of her ribs and knew she hadn't eaten since his departure six days ago. Damn her sisters! Had she not already been through enough torment, without her tribe adding to it?

He was going to burn away the images of what they'd done to her. Burn away the memories of the men who had used her. He would replace both with thoughts of himself. He didn't care what he had to do to accomplish it.

"Have you ever experienced pleasure in the act?" he asked.

Up and down her chest rose with the force of her breathing. "A few times. Perhaps a little. But it was…"

"Say no more. I understand." And he did. Even when you hated the person you were bedding, your body sometimes reacted.

"You?" Nola asked.

"Long, long ago." He only prayed he remembered

how to please his woman. With the demon queen, he hadn't cared to try. He'd simply endured. Never had a female's enjoyment been more important to him. "If I scare you, do something you don't like, tell me."

She nodded, nervously licked her lips. "You tell me, as well."

It was his turn to nod. Rather than suck on her nipples as he desired, he lifted himself off her, reached behind him and tugged off his shirt. He tossed the material aside. His boots and pants quickly followed, leaving him as bare as she was.

Nola's gaze traveled the length of him, and fire leapt inside her turquoise eyes. "Zane…"

"Afraid?"

"No. You won't hurt me. I just wanted you to know I like what I see. You are beautiful. So pale and strong."

Her trust emboldened him, as did her praise. Gently he eased atop her. Skin against skin, hardness against softness. They moaned in unison. Contact with anyone else, even his king, was hell. Contact with Nola was heaven. Her legs opened, allowing him a deep cradle.

So soft.

"I want to kiss you now," he rasped.

Only when she whispered her consent did he lean down and press his lips against hers. Softly at first, barely even a touch. But the sweet scent of her was in his nose, her nipples hard against his chest, her thighs pliant against his, and soon he had to have more. He licked at her, and her lips eagerly parted. His tongue glided past teeth to intertwine with hers.

He'd had her blood, but he'd never had her mouth. To his delight, this was even better. Sweeter, headier, not for living or healing or even to relieve hunger, but simply for pleasure. It was addictive, and he wondered how he'd gone without this for so long.

Tentatively, she tangled her hands in his hair. And at first, her tongue was hesitant against his. Seeking, as if she wasn't sure what to do with it. But the more he explored her mouth, the bolder she became. Soon their teeth were banging together, their bodies writhing against each other. Sweat was beading over his skin, his blood heating as though lava flowed in his veins.

"Going to…suck your…breasts now," he managed to say between pants. "Like that?"

"Yes. Yes." She, too, was panting. She, too, was sweating. Her eyes were closed and her head was thrashing from side to side.

I did that. Pride filled him as he lowered his head, fitting his lips around one tight little pearl. He laved it with attention before turning to the other one—careful, so careful to deliver pleasure without any sting.

When he kissed his way down her stomach, she quivered and gasped his name.

"Stop?" he asked. It would be difficult, but he would find a way.

"More."

Thank the gods. Never had he been more determined in his life. He would know this woman, every inch of her. Nothing would be prohibited. Body, mind…soul. Mouth watering, he licked between her legs. Wet, wild, wanton.

A memory of doing this very thing to the demon queen slipped into his mind. *Do not think about the demon. She has no place in this wondrous moment.* He'd once hated this act—until he'd tried it on Nola on that island. Oh, how he had enjoyed doing so, which had shocked him. Since then, he'd craved it—another shock. He wanted this to last forever. Nola was precious, a treasure, her cries a drug for his ears.

"Like?" *Please, please, please.*

"Mmm, yes. Before, they just ripped at my clothes and shoved their way—"

"No, no. None of that." As she'd spoken, she'd stopped writhing. Had released her death grip on his hair. "That does not belong between us. It's just you and me in this bed. You and me."

Her eyes were luminous as she nodded. "Bite me, then. Take my blood and remind me that my vampire is claiming me."

"No. No, I can't."

"Because you do not take from living beings?" she asked hesitantly.

"You, I would gladly take from. Anytime you would have me." It was the truth. "But as I told you, I know your kind abhors that, and I will never ask you to do anything you do not want to do. I will find my nourishment elsewhere."

"No!" she shouted, and it was a soldier's cry. She might appear delicate, but she truly had the soul of a warrior. "You will only ever take from me."

A possessive warrior, he realized, wanting to grin. He crawled up her body, fit his cock against her moist entrance. "I will only ever crave you, sweet. That much is true. Are you ready for me?"

"Yes. I need you inside me. I need to feel you, as deep as you can go. Your shaft—and your teeth. Take all of me. Please."

Oh, that please... He'd seen the way her expression

softened when he'd uttered that word. Now she thought to use it against *him,* bless her.

Inch by inch, he sank inside her, careful, meticulous. Never had he exercised such exquisite care. Finally, though, he was in her to the hilt. They were joined; they were one. She surrounded him, hot and tight and wet, and it was better than he'd anticipated.

Tenderly he cupped her face. Her beautiful face. His thumbs brushed over her lips. He would care for her all the days of his life. He would ensure no one ever hurt her again.

"Ready for more?"

"With you? Always."

He withdrew from her, almost all the way out, before sinking back in and groaning at the bliss. Her back arched, and her perfect white teeth nibbled on her bottom lip. Her head fell to the side, revealing the delicious plane of her neck. Still he did not bite her. He wouldn't. Wouldn't do that to her.

In and out he moved, in and out he savored her. He stared into her eyes the entire time, and she stared into his. It was as if they were each other's anchor. As if seeing each other kept them here, locked in the moment, just the two of them, safe and cherished. There was nothing else, no one else, the fruition of every secret yearning he'd ever possessed.

"Bite," she commanded.

"No. You are still healing."

"No, I *am* healed. You told me so. Bite me. I want it. I need it. Don't deny me this. Please, don't deny me this."

"Nola—"

"Please, Zane. Please. With you, nothing seems wrong. Don't make me beg."

He could not stand the thought of this strong woman begging for anything. He bit, fangs drilling into her neck. The sweetness of her taste exploded on his tongue, through his body, making his muscles quiver and his bones vibrate.

"Zane," she cried as her inner walls spasmed around his shaft. "Zane, Zane." Her hands clutched at his back, her nails digging into his muscles. "Yes, yes, yes."

"Nola!" That was all his body needed to propel into its own release. He roared, shooting inside her, filling her up with everything that he was. In that moment, his entire existence made sense. He'd been born to be this woman's mate. He'd given himself to a demon to better understand this precious woman's pain. He'd been chosen for the gods' cruel game to ensure this woman's survival.

He loved her. Would always love her.

And now, he thought, an idea springing to life, he would save her.

CHAPTER EIGHT

NOLA CUDDLED AGAINST Zane's body, happier than she'd
ever been in her life. She'd just made love. Truly made
love. And it had been amazing. Her body had hummed
with pleasure, and her mind had soared to the heavens.

Only once had she considered her past, and Zane
had quickly defeated the memories, as only a strong,
fierce warrior could. No one had ever made her feel as
protected or as prized as this man had.

She hadn't thought such feelings possible, actually.

"Zane," she said, grinning. She was buzzing with
joy, drunk with it, and just might smile for the rest of
her life. "Thank you."

"I did do a good job, didn't I?"

It was the first time he'd ever teased her, and she
liked it. A laugh bubbled from her; she couldn't hold it
back. Soon she was laughing so hard, tears were streaming down her cheeks. Laughter.

Shocking.

Zane's lips were twitching. "Some men would take
this as a criticism of their performance."

Only when her giggles subsided did she say, "But as
you know you did a good job…"

"I'm not one of them," he agreed.

They shared a grin. What a tranquil, amazing moment. The first she'd ever had. But she knew it would be the first of many.

His arms tightened around her. "You said every time you admitted something about me, you were freed from some part of your curse."

"Yes." Reminded of her plight, some of the happiness drained from her.

He arched a brow. "Then do you have something else to admit to me?"

"Oh. Well… I—" Nola sat up and peered down at him. No longer did he appear so confident and joyous. His expression was blank. No, not blank. Fear was sparking in the depths of his eyes. For some reason, seeing it gave her courage. "I love you. I love you so much I ache with it." The words tumbled from her; she couldn't stop them. "I can't imagine my life without you in it. I want to make love to you every night and wake up to you every morning. And I don't want you to think I'm saying this only because I wish to lift the curse. I'm not."

"You are too honest for such a trick." He grabbed her and rolled her under him. "And just so you know, I love you, too. So much I would die without you. You are my life, my heart, my everything. Wherever you are, that's where I want to be."

She hadn't dared dream of having a man like him, or a life like they would surely lead, not even as a child. It had seemed too much to ask, too unattainable, and she had preferred to wallow in her sorrows rather than risk hope.

"The gods didn't take your ability from you, you know," she said. "Not completely. You can still create dreams. For the first time in my life, I see joy in my future."

"Oh, Nola. *You* are my joy."

With another laugh, she threw her arms around him and rolled him to *his* back. Her dark hair fell around him, forming a curtain that left only the two of them—just the way she liked it.

They made love twice more and spent several hours simply talking and getting to know each other better, before dressing and emerging from the tent. Night had fallen, but vampire warriors still patrolled the area.

She froze in place. "Zane. I don't know about this."

"We must speak with Layel," he said, remaining beside her. "Inform him that you will be coming with us."

"*If* I can."

"You can."

He sounded confident. "How do you know?"

"You admitted you loved me."

"Yes, but that might not be the admission needed to free me from this camp."

He ignored her, perhaps sensing there was nothing he could say to assuage her fears. "Now, where is that king of mine?"

Distraction. He did know her well. Nola spotted the king and her sister in front of the fire, and gulped. There was no love lost between herself and Delilah. Nola had once tried to murder Layel, after all. "Will they...what if..."

Zane captured her hand with his own and squeezed. "They will love and welcome you or we will find somewhere else to live."

She shook her head. "I don't want you to lose everything you hold dear because of me."

"Nola," he said, forcing her to look up at him. "*You* are all that I hold dear. Nothing else matters to me."

Tears burned her eyes. "What did I ever do to deserve you?"

"It is I who is undeserving. But you have my word, I will do everything in my power to prove myself worthy of you."

She pressed a soft kiss to his lips. "You already have."

"Nola," she heard Delilah call.

Zane wrapped his arms around her, keeping her in the protection of his embrace as they started forward. The blue-haired warrioress was walking toward her, expression blank. Layel stayed close on her heels, a blade in his hand, as protective of his woman as Zane was of Nola.

"You are well?" Delilah said, looking her over.

"Yes. And you?"

"Yes." And then Delilah was there, grinning, pushing Zane aside to hug her tightly. "I've been so worried about you."

Nola glanced at Zane and he gave her a nod of encouragement. Biting her lip, Nola hugged her sister back. *Shocking,* she thought again.

"I thought I was going to have to burst into that tent and give Zane a stern talking-to," Delilah said, pulling back, grin widening. "But the moans were of pleasure rather than rebuke, so Layel was able to hold me back."

Nola's cheeks heated.

So did Zane's, she noticed. And for some reason, that eased her own embarrassment. They were in this together.

Layel slapped him on the back. Zane stiffened for a

moment, then relaxed against Nola. "Good man," the king said with a laugh. "Doing our people proud."

"Well, shall we go home?" Delilah asked. She rubbed her belly, which Nola suddenly realized was not quite as flat as she remembered. "As protector of this little hellion, I am not the soldier I once was and prefer the comfort of my own bed."

A baby. Nola again glanced at Zane. He offered a soft smile—one that promised they, too, would one day experience such a joy. "Congratulations, Delilah. I am so happy for you."

Delilah beamed. "Thank you."

The warrioress and her husband shared a tender smile before Layel escorted her a few feet away, to where the horses were chewing on grass. "Zane? Will you be joining us?"

"Is Nola welcome?"

"She is." No hesitation.

"Then, yes. We shall try."

Whether the king understood or not, he merely nodded. "Back to the palace, men," he called.

Zane helped Nola atop his horse, then swooped up behind her. Nervousness skidded through her when they began moving. First Layel and Delilah disappeared beyond the trees, then the vampire troops. Soon their turn would come…soon she would know if she was still bound to the camp.

"Zane," she said, unable to keep the tremor from her voice.

He didn't say a word, just urged the horse into a quicker pace. And then they were past the trees, just like everyone else. They were in the forest, foliage surrounding them, heading away from their captivity.

"We did it! We're free! We're really free!"

"As I knew we would be." He kissed the top of her head. "The gods are not the cruel monsters I imagined. How can they be, when they paired us together?"

Thank you, she mouthed to the top of the dome. Not once did she look back. There was too much to look forward to. "I love you, Zane. So much."

"And I love you. It will be my pleasure to prove it to you, over and over again."

"Even when mating season ends?" she teased.

He squeezed her tight. "I have a feeling our mating season will last for eternity, sweet."

So did she. Oh, yes, so did she.

* * * * *

THE DARKEST PRISON

PROLOGUE

Reyes, once an immortal warrior for the gods, now possessed by the demon of Pain and living in Budapest, entered his bedroom. He was drenched in sweat and panting from the force of his workout. Because he could not experience pleasure without physical suffering, the burn in his muscles had excited him. *Was* exciting him.

As always, his gaze sought out his woman, and he palmed the blade they preferred to use during their love-play. She was sitting at the edge of their big bed, lovely features drawn tight as she studied the canvas in front of her. A canvas she'd propped on an easel and lowered so that she had a direct view. Blond hair fell to her shoulders in wild disarray, as if she'd tangled her fingers through the thick mass multiple times, and she was chewing on her bottom lip.

Sex could wait, he decided then. She was troubled, and he would be unable to think of anything else until he'd solved this dilemma for her. Whatever it was. He sheathed the blade.

"Something wrong, angel?"

Her eyes lifted and landed on him, worry in their emerald depths. She offered him a small smile. "I'm not sure."

"Well, why don't I help you figure it out?" Anything that bothered her, he would dispatch. No hesitation. For her happiness, he would do anything, kill anyone.

"I would like that, thank you."

"Shall I shower before I join you?"

"No. I like you just how you are."

Darling woman. But he didn't like the thought of dirtying her pretty clothes. He quickly grabbed a towel from the bathroom and rubbed himself dry. Only then did he settle behind his woman, his legs encasing hers, his arms wrapping around her waist. Breathing deeply of her wild storm scent, he rested his chin in the hollow of her neck and followed the direction of her gaze.

What he saw surprised him.

It shouldn't have. Her paintings were always vivid. As the All-Seeing Eye, an oracle of the gods and one of their most cherished aides, she could peer into heaven and Hell. And did, every night, though she had no control over what she witnessed. Past, present, future, it didn't matter. Every morning, she painted what she'd seen.

This one was of a man. A warrior, clearly. With that muscle mass, he had to be. A gold collar circled his neck, cinching tight. He was on his knees, legs spread. His arms rested on his thighs, palms raised. His dark head was thrown back, and he was roaring up at a domed ceiling. In pain, perhaps. Maybe even fury. There was blood smeared all over his chest, seeping from multiple wounds. Wounds that looked as if his skin had been carved away.

"Who is he?" Reyes asked.

"I don't know. I've never seen him before."

Then they would reason this out as best they were able. "Was he from heaven or Hell?"

"Heaven. Definitely. I think he's in Cronus's throne room."

A god, then? A few months ago, Titans had overthrown the Greeks and seized control of the divine throne. So, if this man was in Cronus's throne room, chained up, hurt, and Cronus was leader of the Titans, that must mean the warrior was a Greek. A slave who had been punished, perhaps?

"You saw only this image?" Reyes asked. "Not what got him to this point?"

"Correct," Danika said with a nod. "I heard him scream, though. It was…" She shuddered, and his arms squeezed her in comfort. "I felt so sorry for him. Never have I heard so much rage and helplessness."

"We can summon Cronus." Cronus wasn't too fond of Reyes and his fellow Lords of the Underworld—the very men who had opened Pandora's box, unleashing the evil from inside. The men who had then been cursed to carry that evil inside themselves. But the god king hated their enemy, the Hunters, more, because Danika had seen Galen, the leader of the Hunters, chop off Cronus's head in a vision. Now the god king was determined to kill Galen before Galen could kill him. Even if that meant soliciting the aid of the Lords. "We can ask him if he knows this man."

A moment passed while Danika pondered his suggestion. Finally, she sighed, nodded. "Yes. I'd like that." Then she surprised him by turning to him and offering the sweetest smile he'd ever seen. Well, all of her smiles were that way. "But it's too early in the morning to summon anyone, and besides, I think you had other things on your mind when you entered the room. Why don't you tell me about them?" she suggested huskily.

He was rock hard in seconds—that's what she did to him. "That would be my pleasure, angel."

She pushed him to his back, smile widening. "And mine."

CHAPTER ONE

"BE STILL, NIKE. YOU'RE ONLY making this worse for yourself." Atlas, Titan god of Strength, stared down at the bane of his existence. Nike, *Greek* goddess of Strength. And Victory, he inwardly sneered. She loved to remind him that many called her the goddess of Strength *and* Victory. As if she were better than him. In reality, she was his godly counterpart. His equal. His enemy. And an all-around grade-A bitch.

Two of his best men held her arms and two held her legs. They should have been able to pin her without incident. She was collared, after all, and that collar prevented her from using any of her immortal powers. Even her legendary strength—strength that was *not* on par with his, thank you. But never had a female been more stubborn—or more determined to fell him. She continually struggled against their hold, punching, kicking and biting like a cornered animal.

"I will kill you for this," she growled at him.

"Why? I'm not doing anything to you that you didn't once have done to me." Motions clipped, Atlas tore his shirt over his head and tossed the material aside, revealing his chest, the ropes of his stomach. There, in the center, in big black letters spanning from one tiny brown nipple to the other, was her name, spelled out for all the world to see. N-I-K-E.

She'd branded him, reduced him to her property.

Had he deserved it? Maybe. Once, he'd been a prisoner in this bleak realm. In Tartarus, a divine dungeon. He'd been a god overthrown and locked away, forgotten, no better than rubbish. He'd wanted out, and he had been willing to do anything to see it done. *Anything.* So he had seduced Nike, one of his guards, using her amorous feelings for him against her.

Though she would deny it now, she truly had fallen a little in love with him. The proof: she'd arranged his escape, a crime punishable by death. Yet she'd been willing to risk it. For him. Only, just before she could remove his collar, allowing him to flash himself away—moving from one place to another with only a thought—she discovered that he had also seduced several *other* female guards.

Why rely on one to get the job done when four could serve him better?

He'd counted on the fact that none of the Greek females would want their affair with an enslaved Titan known. He'd counted on their silence.

What he should have done was count on their jealousy. *Women.*

Nike had realized she'd been used, that his emotions had never really been engaged. Rather than throw him back into his cell and pretend he did not exist, rather than have him beaten, she'd had him held down and marked permanently.

For years he'd dreamed of returning the favor. Sometimes he thought the desire was the only thing that kept him sane as he whiled away century after century in this hellhole. Alone, darkness his only companion.

Imagine his delight when the prison walls began to

crack. When the defenses began to crumble. When their collars fell away. It had taken a while, but he and his brethren had finally managed to work their way free. They'd attacked the Greeks, brutally and without mercy.

In a matter of days, they had won.

The Greeks were defeated and now locked exactly where they'd locked the Titans. Atlas had volunteered to oversee the realm and had thankfully been placed in charge. Finally, his day of vengeance had arrived. Nike would forever bear *his* mark.

"You should be grateful you're alive," he told her.

"Fuck you."

He smiled slowly, evilly. "You've done that, remember?"

Her struggles increased. Increased so viciously she was soon panting and sweating right alongside his men. "You bastard! I will flay you alive. I will torch you to ash. Bastard!"

"Flip her over," he ordered the guards over her curses. No mercy. Atlas didn't have the patience to wait until she tired. "And a warning to you, Nike. You had best be still. I'll just keep tattooing until my name is clear enough to satisfy me."

With a frustrated, infuriated screech, she finally settled down. She knew he spoke true. He always spoke true. Threats were not something he wasted his breath uttering. Only promises.

"Bastard," she rasped again.

He'd been called worse. And by her, no less. "That's a good girl." Atlas strode forward and ripped the cloth from her back. The skin was tanned, smooth. Flawless. Once, he'd caressed this back. Once, he'd kissed and licked it. And yes, being with her had been more satisfying than being with any of the others, because she'd looked at him with such adoration, such hope and awe. He'd felt…humbled. Lucky to be there, touching her. But he would not be ruled by his dick and release her before branding her, all in the hopes that he could get her into bed again.

He *would* do this.

"Ready?" he asked her.

"That's not what I did to you," Nike growled. "I didn't mark your back."

"You would rather I brand your lovely breasts?"

At that, she held her tongue.

Good. He didn't want to mar her chest. Her breasts were a work of art, surely the world's finest creation. "No need to thank me," he muttered. He held out his hand and someone slapped the needed supplies in his palm. "At least you won't have to look at my name every day of your too-long life." As he had to do. "Everyone else will, though. They'll see." *And they'll know who mastered her at last.*

"Every lover I choose, you mean."

He popped his jaw. "Not another word from you. It is time."

"Don't do this," she suddenly cried. "Please. *Don't.*" She turned her head and there were tears in her brown eyes.

She wasn't a beautiful woman. Could barely be called pretty. Her nose was a little too long, and her cheeks a little too sharp. She had ordinary brown hair cut to hit her too-wide shoulders, and no true curves to speak of. Besides her breasts. No, she had the body of a warrior. But there was something about her that had always drawn him.

"Please, Atlas. Please."

He rolled his eyes. "Dry the fake tears, Nike." And he knew they were fake. She wasn't prone to displays of emotion. "They don't affect me and they certainly don't become you."

Instantly her eyelids narrowed, the tears miraculously gone. "Fine. But I *will* make you regret this. I vow it."

"I'm looking forward to your attempts." Truth. Sparring with her had always excited him. She should know that by now.

Without a single beat of hesitation, he pressed the ink gun just below her shoulder blade. His grip was steady as he etched the outline of the first letter. *A.* Not once did she flinch. Not once did she act as if she felt a single ounce of pain. He knew it hurt, though. Oh, did he know. To permanently mark an immortal, ambrosia had to be mixed into the colored liquid and that ambrosia burned like acid.

She remained silent as he finished each of the outlines. Silent, still, as he filled in the letters. When he finished, he sat back on his haunches and surveyed his work: A-T-L-A-S.

He expected satisfaction to overtake him, so long had he waited for this moment. It didn't. He expected relief to overwhelm him; finally vengeance had been achieved. It didn't. What he didn't expect was a white-hot sweep of possessiveness, but that's exactly what he experienced. *Mine.*

Nike now belonged to him. Forever. And all the world would know it.

CHAPTER TWO

NIKE PACED THE CONFINES of her cell. A cell she shared with several others. Knowing her temper as intimately as they did, they were careful to stay out of her way. Still. Roommates sucked. She could feel their eyes boring into her robe-clad back, as if they could see the name now branded there.

A-T-L-A-S.

If they dared say a single word about it... *I will kill them!*

There hadn't been enough cells to contain all of the Greeks, so they'd been crammed into each chamber in groups. Male, female, it hadn't mattered. Maybe the Titans hadn't cared about the mixing of the sexes, or maybe they'd done it to increase the torment of each prisoner. The latter was probably the case. Husbands had not been paired with wives and friend had not been paired with friend. No, rival had been paired with rival.

For her, that rival was Erebos, the minor god of Darkness. Once, Erebos had treated her like a queen. Once, she'd really liked him. Had even considered marrying him. But then she'd fallen in love with Atlas—that womanizing, lying bastard Atlas—so she'd cut Erebos loose. *Then* she'd discovered that Atlas had never really wanted her, that Atlas had only been using her.

Love had quickly morphed into rage.

The rage, though, had eventually cooled. She'd forgotten him. For the most part. *Liar.* Now, with his name decorating her back, she hated him with every fiber of her being.

Maybe—*maybe*—she'd overreacted when she'd done the same to him. Branded him forever. Impulsiveness had always been her downfall. For years, she'd even regretted her decision. Not that she would ever admit such a thing to him. Regret was not what she felt now, however.

She hadn't lied to him. She *would* kill him for this.

First, she would have to find a way to remove the stupid collar around her neck. As long as she wore it, she was powerless. The thick gold did not remove her god-given abilities, but merely muted them. Substantially. Too substantially. Second, she would have to find a way to escape this realm.

The first, in theory, should have been easy. Yet she'd already tried clawing and beating at it, and had even attempted to melt it from her neck. All she'd done was cut her skin, bruise her tender flesh and singe her hair off. She should have known that's what would happen. How many times had she watched Titan prisoners try the same things? The second, in theory *and* reality, seemed impossible.

Her gaze circled her surroundings. After the Titans had escaped, they'd reinforced everything. How, she didn't know. The prison was supposedly bound to Tartarus, the Greek god of Confinement who'd once kept guard over the Titans, and when he'd begun to weaken for no apparent reason, the realm had weakened, as well. Everything in it became structurally unsound. But now, Tartarus was missing. The Titans didn't have him and no one knew where he was. There was no reason the realm should be as strong as it was in his absence.

The walls and floor were comprised of godly stone, something only special godly tools—tools she didn't have—could break through. And yet, even without Tartarus's presence, there was not a crack in sight.

The thick silver bars that allowed a glimpse of the guard's station below had been constructed by Hephaistos, and only Hephaistos could melt such a metal. Unfortunately, he resided somewhere else. As with Tartarus, no one knew where. Still, without Tartarus, she should have been able to bend that metal. She couldn't; she'd already tried.

"Could you settle the hell down?" Erebos grumbled from one of the cots.

Nike flicked him a glance. From his dark hair to his dark skin, from his handsome features to his strong body, he was the picture of unhappy male, and all of that unhappiness was directed at her.

"No," she replied. "I can't."

"We're trying to plan an escape here."

They were always planning an escape.

"Besides," he continued, "your ugly face is giving me a headache."

"Go suck yourself," she replied. Though she'd been the one to hurt him all those centuries ago—*unintentionally*—he'd repaid her a thousand times over. Purposely. Not emotionally, but physically. He liked nothing better than to "accidentally" trip her, bump into her and send her flying, as well as to eat what little portion of food was meant for her before she could fight her way to the front of the line, starving her.

If she hadn't been wearing the collar, he never would

have been able to do those things. She would have been too strong. And he would have been too scared. Another reason to despise her captivity.

"Sucking myself would probably elicit better results than when you did it," he retorted.

The handful of gods and goddesses around him snickered.

"Whatever," she said, as if the taunt didn't bother her. Except, her cheeks did flush. She was the epitome of Strength—or she was supposed to be—and she'd always been more mannish than feminine. That was why Atlas's attentions had so surprised and delighted her. That gorgeous man could have won anyone, yet he'd chosen her. Or so she'd thought. And she'd fallen for his act because he'd somehow made her feel like a delicate, beautiful woman.

Stupid. I was so stupid.

From the corner of her eye, she saw a black-clad male stride into the guard's station. She didn't have to see him to know who it was. Atlas. She *felt* him. Always she felt his heat.

When her gaze found him, she discovered that he had his arm wrapped around a leggy blonde. A blonde who cuddled herself into his side as if she belonged there—and had rested there many times before.

The thought angered Nike. It shouldn't have; she despised Atlas with all of her being and didn't care who he slept with. Didn't care who he pleasured. And yes, he would have pleasured the blonde with those talented hands and seeking lips. He was an amazing lover whose touch still haunted Nike's dreams. But there it was. Anger.

She didn't mean to, but found herself striding to

the bars and gripping them for a better, closer look at him. Three other guards stood around him, all talking and laughing. While prisoners wore white, guards wore black, and he wore that darkness well. It was the perfect complement to his dark, chopped hair and sea-colored eyes.

His face had been chiseled by a master artist, everything about him perfectly proportioned. His eyes were the perfect distance apart, his nose the perfect length, his cheeks the perfect sharpness, his lips the perfect shape and color and his chin a perfect, stubborn square.

He was perfect while she was nothing but flaws.

She should have known he was playing her the moment he'd turned those dangerous eyes on her and they lit with "interest." Men just didn't look at her like that. Not even Erebos had, and he had loved her.

"Bastard," she muttered, the curse for both the men in her past.

As if he heard her, Atlas lifted his gaze. The moment their eyes met, she wanted to release the bars. She wanted to step away, out of sight. But she didn't allow herself that luxury. That would have been cowardly, and this man had seen her weak one too many times.

Just to taunt him, and hopefully make him feel as out of control as he always made her feel, she allowed her attention to fall to his chest, exactly where her name rested. She smiled smugly before raising her gaze and arching a brow.

Score. A muscle ticked in his jaw.

What does your lover think of your mark? she wanted to shout. *What does the blonde think of my name on your body?*

He jerked the stupid blonde deeper into his side and,

without breaking eye contact with Nike, planted a lush, wet kiss on her mouth. Of course, the bitch reacted as any other woman would have. She wrapped her arms around him and held on for dear life. As Nike well knew, that man could make a woman come with the expertise of his kiss.

Nike's anger intensified. Had she been able, she would have stomped down there and ripped them apart. Then she would have killed them both. Not because she wanted Atlas for herself—she didn't—but because he was clearly using yet another woman. Passion did not glow from his expression. Only determination did.

Nike would be doing the female population a favor by snuffing him out.

"Erebos," she called. "Come here. I want to kiss you."

"What?" he gasped out, his shock clear.

"Do you want a kiss or not? Get over here. Quickly."

There was a rustling of clothing behind her and then her former lover was beside her. He was a prisoner, and sex was a rarity. He would take what he could get, even from someone he loathed. That much she knew.

Nike turned to him; he was already leaning down. Like the blonde, she wrapped her arms around her companion's neck and held on tight. Only, she didn't enjoy the kiss, familiar as it was. Erebos's taste was too…what? Different from Atlas's, she realized, and that ratcheted her anger another notch. No man should have that much power over her.

Still. She let Erebos continue. Atlas needed to realize that she no longer desired him. He needed to realize that he would never, *never* play her emotions again. She was not an idealistic little girl anymore.

He'd made sure of that.

CHAPTER THREE

RAGE. ABSOLUTE RAGE FILLED Atlas. He released his companion—he couldn't recall her name—and she gasped in protest at the abruptness of his actions. He didn't bother explaining what he was about as he stomped away from her. The rage continued to spread as he climbed the stairs that led to the prisoners' cages and to the cell holding Nike.

His name was on her back. How dare she allow another man to put his lips on her?

When he reached his destination, he raised his arm, and the sensor he'd had embedded in his wrist caused the bars to slide open. Several prisoners were seated against the far wall. Rapturous longing colored their faces as they watched the minor god of Darkness and the goddess of Strength clean each other's tonsils. So absorbed were they, in fact, that they didn't rush Atlas and try to escape. Or maybe that had something to do with the pain they would feel if they did so. He had only to press a button, and their collars would ravage their brains.

Nike moaned, as if she really liked what was being done to her. Red flickered through Atlas's vision. How. Dare. She. Teeth grinding, he grabbed Nike by the collar of her robe and jerked her into the hard line of his body, away from Erebos.

A gasp escaped her. Unlike when the blonde had gasped, he did not remain unaffected. He wanted to swallow the sound—and do something, anything, to cause Nike to make it again.

What's wrong with me?

"Hey," Erebos snapped, foolishly reaching for her to finish what had been started. "We were busy."

Scowling, Atlas kicked him in the chest. The smaller man flew backward, slamming into his fellow prisoners. The minor god jumped to his feet to attack, saw who had rendered the blow and stilled, nostrils flaring, hands fisting.

"Touch her again," Atlas said calmly, though he was gritting the words out as if they were being pushed through a meat grinder, "and I'll remove your collar. Right along with your head."

The god paled, perhaps even whimpered. "I won't go near her. She wasn't worth it, anyway."

Atlas might kill him for such an insult, as well. Her kisses were heaven, damn it.

"What the hell do you think you're doing?" Nike demanded, suddenly coming to life and drawing his attention. She whirled on him, glaring up at him. "I can sleep with whoever I want. And hey, guess what? I might even pick one of your friends. What do you think of that?"

Despite her heated claims, she wasn't breathless as she would have been if Atlas had been the one kissing her, and her cheeks weren't flushed. Her nipples weren't even hard.

Finally, something cooled the hottest flames of his rage.

"Just zip your mouth." He latched on to Nike's upper

arm and dragged her out of the cell with him. Automatically, the bars closed behind him.

"What the hell do you think you're doing?" she said again, tugging against his hold. She'd never been one to obey him.

"What the hell did you think *you* were doing?" he countered. When he reached the bottom of the steps, he stopped. The blonde, who just happened to be the goddess of Memory—damn it, what was her name? Kneemah? No, but close. Nee Nee? Closer. Mnemosyne. Yes, that was it—Mnemosyne, as well as the three other warriors chosen to guard Tartarus today, were gaping at him.

"What?" he snapped. At least Nike stopped resisting him. She stilled at his side, attention darting from him to the others, the others to him.

"You can't just remove a prisoner," Hyperion, god of Light, said. He was a handsome man, though as pale as his title suggested, and Nike had better not be eyeing him as a possible bedmate.

"I'm not removing her," Atlas replied stiffly. "I'm relocating her." To a cell of her own, where no one could put their dirty, disgusting lips on her. Where no one could put their roving hands on her body. There was nothing…possessive about this decision, either. He simply didn't want her experiencing any type of pleasure. She didn't deserve it.

"Why?" Mnemosyne regarded him curiously, not a single thread of upset or jealousy in her expression.

Why? he wondered himself. Mnemosyne been eager to date him for months, summoning him constantly. Last night, she'd even shown up at his home naked. She was beautiful, yes, and he'd almost given in and slept with her. His body had been worked into a frenzy after what had transpired with Nike, after all, and he'd been desperate for release. But before he sealed the deal, he'd sent the determined goddess away. He'd felt too guilty to continue. As if he were cheating on Nike. Which was ridiculous. The only relationship he had with Nike was one of hate.

Besides, who wanted to spend time with a female who would never forget your mistakes? A female who would remember your every transgression? A female who could spin new, false memories into your mind, making you believe whatever she wished. Not him. Yet he'd flashed to Mnemosyne's home this morning and asked her to spend the day with him, just so he could bring her to the prison this morning. He'd been strangely jubilant at the thought of parading her in front of Nike.

So again, he wondered why Mnemosyne did not feel as if Nike were a threat. Most females didn't, he knew. He'd heard them talk. Nike was too tall, too muscled, they said. She was too hard, and too coarse. But those were the things that had first sparked his interest in her. She could handle his strength. She gave as good as she got. She would never wither under his glare. She would never run from his anger. She would always face him head-on. And he liked that. A lot. No other female he'd ever encountered had that kind of courage.

And she *was* pretty, he thought. Yes, only yesterday he'd thought her barely so, but, just now, that seemed wrong on every level. Only a short while ago, when he'd first walked into the prison, he'd felt her gaze on him and had looked up. For a second, only a second, her defenses had been lowered. She hadn't known he'd been watching her, so she hadn't guarded her expression. An expression that had been soft, wistful, her eyes luminous.

The sight of her had heated his blood as if he'd been caught on fire.

That still didn't mean he desired her, his enemy. The fact that his name was spelled across her back was simply playing havoc with his mind, he was sure.

"Well," Mnemosyne prompted.

"Yeah," Nike said. "We're waiting for an answer."

"Shut up, prisoner," Mnemosyne snapped. She was sister to Rhea, the god queen, and an elitist. Always had been. She loved power and strength above all else, and viewed most people as beneath her.

He wanted to scold her for using that tone with Nike, but didn't. They were waiting for an answer to what? he wondered, thinking back over the conversation. Oh, yeah. Why was he moving Nike? He raised his chin, refusing to look down at her. Not that he would have had to look far. At six feet, she was nearly as tall as he was. "I don't need a reason. I'm responsible for this prison and everyone in it. Therefore, if I want to move you, I can."

The last was meant for the Titans. They would do well not to question him.

Without another word, he dragged Nike away.

"But Atlas," Mnemosyne called.

He ignored her. Where should he take Nike? There were not many private places in this doomed structure. All of the cells were filled to capacity. That left—his office, he decided.

"You're lucky I don't have that bastard slain," he said

when they snaked a corner and he was sure the others couldn't hear him.

Nike didn't have to ask who "that bastard" was. "What for? He did nothing wrong."

Nothing wrong? *He touched what's mine.* "He didn't have permission to consort with you." There. An answer to pacify. Truthful, yet misleading. Atlas snaked another corner, and there at the end of the hallway was his door.

"Consort with me?" She laughed without humor. "Oh, wait. I get it. You can screw anyone you want, but I can't."

Good. They were on the same page. "That's right." He pushed his way inside, kicked the door shut and finally released her. His hands itched to return to her, but he kept them at his sides. Rather than settle behind his desk, he faced her, placing them nose to nose. "You are to suffer in solitude." Gods, she smelled good. Like passion. Pure, white-hot passion.

"As if. I have more fun with myself, anyway."

The image those words evoked nearly sent him to his knees. He should back away from her. Before he did something foolish.

Her eyes narrowed. "You haven't changed, you know. You're as much of an ass now as you were years ago."

"However," he continued, as if she hadn't just insulted him. Foolishness be damned. She was here, and they were alone. "If you need to be kissed, I'll take care of it."

And, godsdamn it, that was the absolute truth.

CHAPTER FOUR

THERE WAS NO TIME to protest. In less time than it took to blink, Nike found herself smashed into the wall, Atlas pressing against her, solid chest to soft breasts, his hands pinning her temples, his mouth slamming into hers. His tongue thrust deep, without warning, forcing its way past her teeth.

She could have bitten him. Wanted to bite him, actually, and not in affection. She wanted to draw blood, pain. Instead, her body instantly became his slave, as if centuries of hatred hadn't passed, and she welcomed him inside. She wound her arms around him and arched into his erection. Erection? Oh, yes. He was hard. Hard and long and thick. Just as she remembered.

His taste was decadent, wild and burning, like dark spices. His muscles were tensed under her palms. Up she moved them, until her fingers were tangled in his hair. The short spikes abraded deliciously, causing her to shiver.

Touch me, she wanted to shout. It had been so long, so damned long, since she'd experienced this. Oh, she'd been with other men since giving herself so foolishly to Atlas, because she'd been searching for something as intense as what they had shared. Something to soothe her, heal her even. But each experience had left her hollow and unsatisfied. She'd actually felt worse. And then she had been captured—by Atlas himself—and unceremoniously stuffed into this prison.

With the lack of privacy, there'd been no opportunities to find companionship. Not that she would have wanted to or had even tried. No one drew her anymore. No one but Atlas, damn him.

Yes, damn him. *Him.* The man who had held her down only yesterday and etched his name into her flesh. What was she doing, allowing this? He would think she still cared for him. He would think she still pined for him, dreamed of him…craved him. That might be true, curse it, but she would never allow him to know it.

Panting, she tore her mouth away. *How dare you stop,* her body cried. "I don't want you," she lied. "Let me go. Now." *Hold me forever.*

A low growl erupted from his throat. "I don't want you, either." Once, twice, he rubbed his shaft against her. "But I'm not letting you go."

Thank you.

Stupid body.

Tremors slid the length of her spine. Sweet heaven. He'd hit her sweet spot, and sensation rocketed through her. Then one of his hands lowered and cupped her breast, and her knees almost buckled.

"Why?" The word was a mere whimper. And why was she allowing him the choice? Why wasn't she ripping away from him? *You are Strength. Act like it.*

"Why won't I let you go?" He rolled her hardened nipple between his fingers.

That was why she remained as she was, she thought, dazed. The pleasure was building, flowing through her veins, burning her up, recreating her into a new being. Someone who lived for satisfaction alone. Someone who didn't care that the one responsible for her desire was an enemy.

"Yes."

"I just...I..." Those fingers tightened, stinging her a little. "Just shut up and kiss me again."

"Yes," she replied before she could stop herself.

Their mouths met again, and this time she rose on her tiptoes to meet him. As their tongues clashed and warred, he cupped her ass and lifted her feet off the floor. So strong he was. Forcing him to hold her weight would have been fun, but not nearly as pleasurable as winding her legs around his waist and pressing her needy core against his shaft.

Clever girl.

With her braced against the wall, he was able to tunnel both of his hands under her robe. Their bodies were too close together for him to reach her slick center, where she wanted him most, but having his hands on her cheeks, wanting skin against fiery skin, was almost as welcome. He was hotter than she remembered.

His lips left hers, but before she could moan her disappointment, he was kissing and licking his way down her neck.

"Yes," she gasped. "Yes. Like that."

"More?" His nose nuzzled the golden slave collar as if it were a trinket rather than a device that could kill her. For once, *she* even liked the collar.

"Yes." More. At the moment, that was the only word she was capable of. Unless...did he think to make her beg?

Fury suddenly blended with desire. Well, she would show him. She would beg for nothing. Not even this. Especially this. Not for him.

"Then more you shall have," he said, shocking her. She had not begged, yet he was giving her what she wanted. He tugged the fabric of her robe down, revealing her breasts. Air hissed through his teeth. "So lovely. So perfect." His tongue flicked out and circled the nipple he'd pinched just a short while ago. "So mine."

Her head fell back, and her nails scratched at his back. So *good*. The heat...the wetness...the— "Yes!" The suction. He was sucking at her so forcefully, her stomach muscles were quivering. No one else had been physically powerful enough to suit her. Their caresses had felt like whispers, barely there, utterly unsatisfying. "Atlas," she groaned. "Don't stop." A command, not a plea.

"I won't. I can't." He straightened, his narrowed gaze suddenly pinning her in place far more effectively than his body. "I want you. All of you."

She struggled to regain her breath. Her senses. "You mean sex?" *Yes, yes, yes.* Here, now.

A clipped nod was the only answer she received. She opened her mouth to reply, but somehow found the strength to stop herself. She drank in the sight of him—a sight that delighted her almost as much as it angered her. Angered? Why? Her delight should be all-consuming. His nostrils were flared, his lips pulled tight. He looked as if he barely had himself under control. Nothing like he'd looked with Mnemosyne.

He truly wants me.

But...why? she wondered. Or was he merely that good an actor?

Yes, she mused darkly. He was that good an actor. And that was where the anger sprang from. He'd looked at her like that once before, the last time they'd had sex.

That look had been the catalyst to her decision to free him, despite the consequences to herself. Consequences that could have resulted in a death sentence. *But,* she'd thought, *he truly loves me with the same intensity that I love him.* She'd thought *anything* worth the risk of freeing him. Of possibly being with him for eternity.

How they would have managed that, she hadn't known. But she'd wanted to try. He had not.

Thank the gods she'd encountered one of the members of his skank parade mere minutes after escorting him from the building and into the clouds outside, where he would have been able to flash away. He'd still had his collar on—she hadn't wanted to remove it until they'd bypassed every single guard. That way, everyone who saw them walking together would have assumed she was simply moving a prisoner.

But outside, they'd been seen. No one could flash out of or into the prison itself, so everyone had to walk through the front door. Aergia, the goddess of Laziness, of all things, had decided to come to work early, surprise, surprise—just to be with Atlas again. She'd stopped Nike to question where he was being taken.

I'm taunting him with what he can never have again, Nike had claimed.

The goddess had frowned. *Well, take him to my office when you're done.*

Why?

The frown became a slow, sensual smile. *So I can dish my brand of...punishment to him.*

Dread had sparked inside her. *And how do you punish him?*

How do you think? But don't worry. I'll leave him begging for more. I always do.

Atlas had tried to run then, mowing right over them both, but with his collar still in place, he hadn't gotten far. Nike had locked him back up and, suspicious, questioned all the female guards. Nearly every single one of them had had a go at him. And he'd told them all the same thing: *You are beautiful. I want to spend my life with you. All I need is my freedom, and I will be your slave for eternity.*

So, have sex with him again? "Hell, no."

"You want me," he snapped. His grip tightened on her, his fingers digging deep, bruising. "I know you do."

Just like that, she knew what this little make-out session was about. He planned to sleep with her, make her fall in love with him all over again, and then dump her. He'd grind up her pride, spit it out and stomp all over it. Again. All to punish her, she was sure, for daring to tattoo him as she had. Marking her with his name clearly wasn't enough.

"Wanting you dead and wanting your body aren't the same things." With a sugar-sweet grin, she patted his cheek. "And I can promise you that while I do want the first, I was only teasing you about the second." Now who was playing who? "So…if we're done here…? I believe there is a minor god awaiting my return."

Atlas ran his tongue over his teeth. His arms fell away from her, and he stepped back. She nearly collapsed, but managed to shift her legs and absorb her own weight. Unaffected. That's how she had to appear.

"We're done," he said, his tone clipped. "We are definitely done."

Good, she thought. So why did she suddenly want to cry for real?

CHAPTER FIVE

ATLAS HAD TO EMPTY A CELL of its seven occupants and place those gods and goddesses within other, already cramped cells to make a place for Nike. The time and effort was worth it, though. He couldn't tolerate the thought of her with that bastard Erebos, doing the same things to him that she'd once done to Atlas.

Not. Going. To. Happen.

Ever.

And maybe, perhaps, there was a slight chance it had nothing to do with punishing her and everything to do with the pleasure he'd earlier denied. In her arms, he'd come alive. That had happened last time, too, but he'd written it off as prisoner insanity. Now, he couldn't write it off. He wasn't a prisoner; he was a warden. He'd come alive, and he needed more. Of her, only her. Yet she claimed she'd merely been playing him.

Fucking *playing* him. He wanted that to be a lie more than he wanted to take his next breath. Which he really wanted to take. He didn't understand this. She was doomed to spend eternity hidden away, which meant they could not have any kind of life together. Not even if he freed her. *He* would then be locked away or put to death. Unlike her, that was not something he was willing to risk.

But that she had been, all those centuries ago…it was *humbling.* He still could not get over the emotion.

Surely she still wanted him.

For a week, Atlas lamented his plight and pondered what to do. All the while, he stayed away from Nike's new cell. That didn't stop him from thinking about her, however. What was she doing? Did *she* think of *him?* Did she dream of him and that shattering kiss?

He did. Every time he closed his eyes, he saw the passion glowing from her face. A face that was exquisite. From barely passable, to pretty, to exquisite, all in a week's time. He shook his head in wonder. But she deserved the praise. Her lashes were long and as rich as black velvet. Velvet that framed sensual chocolate eyes. Her cheeks were smooth, perfect for caressing, and her lush, red lips were sweeter than ambrosia. And all that strength…his shaft filled and lengthened just remembering it. She'd gripped and scratched him with savage abandon. He still bore the marks.

Fine. He had lied to her. They definitely weren't done. Not even close. He had to experience that again.

Finally, he could stand the separation no longer. Thankfully, his shift was over. A shift that had consisted of walking the prison halls, watching the prisoners inside their cells and ensuring everyone remained calm.

That should have bored him. After all, he was a warrior. But bore him it didn't. And *that* should have irritated him. After all, he'd spent countless centuries in this place and had sworn never to return once he'd escaped. But again, irritation was not what he felt. He'd wanted this job to be close to Nike. To have his vengeance, he'd once told himself. Now, he wasn't so sure.

Today, and all week really, he'd walked the halls invigorated, knowing all he had to do to catch sight of her was turn a corner.

He hadn't allowed himself to do so. Until now. Finally, he would see her.

The moment she came into view, his blood heated, blistering. His breath followed suit, flaming his lungs to ash. She sat atop her cot, arms gripping the rail, knees drawn up while she leaned slightly forward. Her hair was finger-combed to perfection, and her eyes were narrowed, shielding her irises and the emotion banked there, but at least he could see the shadows her lashes cast over her cheeks. Shadows he might trace with a fingertip. Or his tongue.

Oh, yes. She was exquisite.

"Where's your girlfriend?" Her voice was smooth as silk. Just beneath that silk, however, he thought he caught a tendril of fury.

Was she mad that he'd come? Or mad that he'd stayed away so long?

"I don't have a girlfriend." Though Mnemosyne was still trying to change that.

Even though he pushed her away every damn time.

Nike shrugged. "Too bad for you that whores never commit."

He knew he was the whore that she spoke of, and popped his jaw. But he deserved that, he supposed. "I did what I had to do to escape, Nike. That doesn't mean I didn't feel—" No. Oh, no. He would not go down that road. He hadn't wanted to feel anything for her, but he had. That hadn't stopped him from using her, so she'd never like what he had to say about the matter. "I'm sure you'd do anything to escape, as well."

Her expression darkened, but she did not refute his words. "So, did you come to free me?"

"Hardly."

"Then why are you here? We have nothing more to say to each other."

Because you're all I think about anymore. He never should have marked her. This might have been avoided. Or not. He might have slept with others all those years ago because he'd been desperate to flee this place, but it had been her face he'd imagined when he'd done so.

Without looking away from her, he leaned back against the bar behind him and crossed his arms over his chest. "There's plenty to say. About the kiss."

She yawned, patting her beautiful mouth. A mouth he wanted all over his body. "I'd rather sleep."

So. She still wanted him to think she had been unaffected. Part of him believed it. An insecure part of him that had never really known how to deal with her, his equal in every way. Yes, even strength, though he often liked to deny it. The other part of him, the masculine part, knew she had liked everything he'd done. She'd shouted his name, for gods' sake, and he hadn't even made her climax.

"You're saying you don't want me?" he asked as silkily as she had.

"Not even a little."

"Really?" He rested his fingers at the waist of his pants, twisting the button, and her eyes followed the movement. His cock was already hard, already straining, rising over the top. Moisture glistened there. "Not even a tiny, tiny bit?"

She gulped. "N-no." The word was croaked. "But you are. Tiny, that is."

Liar. She did. She wanted him. And he was huge, thank you very much. He stretched her. The sense of possessiveness returned, all the more intense because it was joined by satisfaction.

"I'll have you yet, Nike. That I promise you."

"Just…go away," she said, suddenly sounding almost…dejected. She eased to her side, then rolled to her back, facing away from him. "We're done with each other. Remember?"

Wrong move. Seeing her back, even covered by that baggy robe, reminded him of what he'd done and that set fire to his blood anew. Whatever he had to do, he *was* going to have this woman.

"I guess we'll find out," he told her before walking away.

To think. To plan.

CHAPTER SIX

ATLAS PUSHED PAST the double doors that led into Cronus's throne room. Armed guards, immortal warriors Cronus himself had created, were stationed along the edges of the walls. Each held a spear, and swords swung from the sheaths at their waists. They stood at attention, waiting for an order or a threat. They would spring into action for both.

Of course, there were also warriors lining both sides of the purple lamb's fleece carpet that led to the bejeweled dais, crowding Atlas as he made his way forward. His weapons had already been removed, but they were taking no chances, eyeing his every movement with distrust.

He wondered if, when she had been a free woman, Nike had ever been summoned to this room, albeit to meet with Zeus, *her* king. And if she had, had it been for a reward or a punishment?

Stop thinking about her. Concentrate on Cronus. He's wily, that one. The god king was not the same man he'd been before his incarceration. The thousands of years inside Tartarus had changed him; he was harder, harsher. Utterly unforgiving. Any weakness, he pounced upon.

Nowadays, Cronus refused to stay in the heavens without an army to shield him. But then, a man at war with his own wife couldn't be too careful. Especially when that wife was a queen with powerful abilities and allies of her own. A wife who—

Dizziness spun through Atlas's head, fragmenting his thoughts, and he frowned. Frowned but didn't stop until he reached the end of the fleece. He kept his attention, foggy as it was, fixed on Cronus. What was wrong with him?

The king was seated atop a throne of solid gold. Dark strands were threaded through his silver hair, and his beard had thinned since the last time Atlas had seen him. Some of the age lines had even disappeared from his weathered features. He wore a long white robe, much like the prisoners of Tartarus. Why? Atlas had often wondered.

Only two explanations made any sense. Cronus had worn the garment for centuries and now felt most comfortable in it. Or he did not want to forget what he'd once been—and could be again if he weren't careful. Atlas had been more than happy to shed his own robe. Would Nike do the same, if ever she gained her freedom? Not that she would.

You're thinking about her again.

A woman stood beside the throne. She possessed one of the plainest faces Atlas had ever seen, and had pale, freckled skin. She was reed thin, with dark, curling hair and delicate shoulders. Power did not hum from her. Rather, she seemed...insubstantial. Ethereal, as he imagined a ghost might look. There, but see-through. There, but wavering. Her eyes were shadowy, vacant, as if no one was home.

When she reached up and brushed a lock of hair from her brow, he could only gape. The elegance of the movement was awe inspiring. More graceful than a dancer, more delicate than a butterfly wing. Someone was indeed home, she just didn't care about what was happening around her.

Atlas pulled his attention from the female and studied the chamber. There were thousands of chandeliers overhead, each dripping with glistening teardrops. Multihued glitter sparkled in the air. Odd, he thought, head tilting to the side for a better view. That air was even sweetly scented with—he inhaled deeply—ambrosia. Ah. Now he understood the dizziness *and* the glitter. Dried ambrosia was being pumped through the room. To keep him docile?

"Atlas, god of Strength," Cronus said with a nod of greeting, drawing him from his musings.

Atlas bowed, as was proper. "My king. It's an honor to have this audience with you."

Cronus leaned forward, silver eyes bright with anxiety. "All is well in Tartarus, yes?"

"Most assuredly."

Relief instantly replaced the anxiety. "Why, then, did you request this meeting?"

There was no one who hated the Greeks more than this man, this Titan sovereign, and with very good reason. They'd stripped him of his power, humiliated him in front of his people. Even Nike had been a participant. *Just tell him. Get this over with.* "I want to remove a woman from the prison and set her up—"

"Stop. Stop there." Scowling, Cronus raised a hand. "There will be no removing *anyone* from Tartarus. It is too dangerous."

He'd expected that answer. However, he persevered. "Perhaps the reward is worth the danger. I would keep her locked inside my home, Majesty. I would never re-move her collar—" well, except to whisk her to his home, for she couldn't be flashed out of Tartarus with it on, but he would recollar her the moment they reached their destination "—and she would be my personal slave. I would ensure her misery." His first lie of the day, but probably not his last. He only wanted to give Nike pleasure.

Had he forgiven her for what she'd done to him? He wasn't sure. All he knew was that he no longer wanted to kill her when he thought about it. He would tire of her eventually, and he looked forward to the day. Until then, this was his only recourse.

The king ran his tongue over his teeth. "Of which *her* do you speak?"

"Nike. Greek goddess of Strength." He did not allow a single bit of affection to lace his tone.

The king's eyes widened. "The one who…" Now those eyes dropped to Atlas's chest, where his shirt covered his tattoos.

"Yes. The very one." *Hear my anger, only my anger.* Except, what she'd done no longer angered him. The marks were as much a part of him now as his were a part of her.

"Interesting." Cronus leaned back in the throne, the picture of contemplation. "Do you not think she is being made to suffer enough inside Tartarus?"

Time for his second lie. "No. I do not." In truth, as dejected as she'd sounded at their last meeting, the god-dess was suffering. And he didn't like it.

"And what will you do to *increase* her suffering?"

"Much as she hates me—" desires me, he added in-side his head, so that he wouldn't reveal the depths of irritation thoughts of her possible loathing elicited "—she will take particular displeasure in cleaning my home, preparing my food and warming my bed."

The king smiled up at the ghostly girl. "What you'd like to do to your Paris, eh, my Sienna? Make him your slave."

Her expression never changed. She offered no response, either.

Paris, the demon-possessed immortal who used to haul new prisoners into Tartarus? Atlas wondered, and then shrugged. He didn't care. Nike was his only concern at the moment.

"My king?" Atlas prompted. "I lack only your permission to begin Nike's torment. My determination is unparalleled. You will not be disappointed in the results."

Cronus faced him once again, his smile falling away. A minute passed in silence, then another. Then the king sighed. "I'm afraid my answer has to be no. While I like the thought of Nike's anguish intensified at your hands, I'm unwilling to risk the removal of her collar, even for the few seconds required to flash her. She is Strength, and were she to somehow escape you and free her brethren, another heavenly war would erupt. I cannot afford to have my attention divided now. Well, not any more than it already is. I find I spend most of my time observing the Lords of the Underworld."

The Lords of the Underworld. So. The girl named Sienna *did* wish to enslave the immortal Paris. Atlas had never dealt with the man or any of his friends, as they'd been his enemy and he'd already been incarcerated before Zeus created them.

But he'd heard stories and knew they were vicious…
brutal.

"My king. If you will just—"

"I have declared my answer, Strength. I do not understand why you are still here."

Atlas's own sense of dejection—and fury—bloomed. He wanted to stalk up that dais, grab the king and shake him. How dare his request be denied? How dare his desires be discarded? Instead, he said, "Very well, my king. I thank you for your time," and pivoted on his heel. To do otherwise would have invited punishment.

He strode from the chamber, his determination overshadowing all else. He'd already decided that nothing would keep him from claiming Nike. Now he realized that not even this would do so. The king's will be damned. He would have his woman, just as he wanted.

CHAPTER SEVEN

"COME WITH ME."

Nike's heart raced at the sound of that deep voice. Hesitant, she rolled over on her cot. Sure enough, her skin tingled when her gaze found Atlas. Gorgeous as ever, he stood at the bars—bars that were now open. His hand was extended, and he was waving her over. There was fury in his too-tight expression.

What had she done this time?

She'd tried to ignore him. She'd tried to pretend that she felt nothing for him. Anything to stop the madness. But gods, she couldn't stop thinking about their kiss. She couldn't stop wishing she'd allowed him to take her all the way. That she'd have experienced *everything* before being taken back to nothing.

So what if he would have tired of her afterward? So what if he would have been smug about her capitulation? So what if he found someone else and paraded her before Nike? For a few blessed hours—who was she kidding?—for a few blessed minutes, because it wasn't as if either one of them would last beyond that, she would have known the joy of being with him again. Of simply feeling, giving, taking, sharing…loving.

Have all the rest, common sense piped up, *but deny the love.*

That would be my pleasure. But I have to get him to

offer *me the rest first*. She still would not beg. A girl had her pride, after all.

Pride will not make you come.

"Come," he repeated.

What did he have planned? Did it matter? Anything was better than this monotony.

Slowly she sat up. Her hair was in desperate need of a brush, and gods, the rest of her needed a shower. How long since she'd had one? Prisoners were given a bowl of water each day and that was it.

"Why?"

A muscle twitched in his jaw. "Do you want to spend a few hours outside the prison or not?"

Wait. What? *Leave* Tartarus? She was on her feet before her brain could process what she was doing. Her knees almost buckled, she'd spent so much time prone, bored, but she managed to stay upright. She even reached out and twined their fingers together. The heat of his skin should not have shocked her, but it did. The calluses should not have ignited a fire in her blood, but they did.

"You're taking me outside?"

"Yes. But do not say a word when we reach the guard's station. Understand?"

"Yes." This could be a trick. A trick to build up her hopes only to dash them cruelly, but she didn't care. If there was a chance, slight though it was, that he would actually stay true to his word, she would do anything he asked.

Without a word, he led her from the cell and down the hall. Other prisoners spotted her and gasped. Some began to murmur amongst themselves, gossiping as they'd once enjoyed doing in the heavens. Some gripped their bars and simply watched her through wistful eyes.

Erebos even shouted, "Hey, where are you going with her now?"

Atlas ignored him, and Nike followed suit. A sense of urgency pounded through her. If Atlas did this, took her outside, even for a few hours… Why would he do such a thing?

"Did you get permission for this?" she asked. "And we're not at the guard's station yet, so it's okay that I'm talking."

"No. I didn't get permission." His words were curt, clearly meant to end the conversation.

As if she'd ever done what was expected of her. "Then why are you—"

"Just be quiet."

"Or what?"

"Or I'll shut you up my favorite way."

Her mouth fell open. Did he mean he'd shut her up with a kiss? Or by pushing a button on her collar and shooting painful lances through her brain? It was fifty-fifty, she thought. His proclamation had the desired results, however. She was too busy pondering his meaning to talk.

In the guard's station, two Titans were laughingly making bets about the prisoners. They looked up at Atlas and nodded politely in greeting—only to freeze when they spotted her. As promised, she remained quiet.

"She try to escape?" one demanded, obviously ready to beat her for doing so.

"No. But I'm taking her out for a bit," Atlas replied.

"Why?" the other gasped out. "There's nothing out there."

"Her viper's tongue offends me. Therefore, she deserves a new punishment. To that end, I plan to taunt her with what she cannot have."

The very words she'd once offered Aergia, the goddess of Laziness. He'd remembered.

Still the guard persisted. "Has this been cleared with—"

"*I'm* in charge of this prison and the people inside it. Now shut up and do your job." With that, Atlas ushered her out of the building and into the daylight. No one else tried to stop him.

As the first ray hit her skin, she jerked free of his hold and stopped, simply basking in the moment. Clouds. Sun. She closed her eyes, head thrown back, arms splayed. The warmth, followed by a cooling breeze… the brightness—her skin soaked them up greedily. Oh, how she'd missed them. She would have loved to have seen temples and golden streets and people, as well, but she would take what she could get without complaint.

Strong arms suddenly banded around her. "You're beautiful," Atlas whispered, his nose nuzzling her ear, practically purring. "Do you know that?"

"I know what I look like." Her lashes fluttered open. The clouds enveloped him, creating a dream haze. Her heart was hammering against her ribs, and she couldn't have stopped herself from flattening her hands on his chest to save her life. His own heart was racing, she realized with astonishment. Was he…could he be as affected by her as she was by him? "And beautiful is not a word that describes me."

His head lifted, and he gazed down at her. Tenderness softened his expression, and she thought he'd never been more appealing. "Then you don't see yourself as I do."

How did he see her? As much as he hated her—but did he hate her still? How could he, when he'd just escorted her to paradise?—she would have guessed he pictured her with horns, fangs and a tail.

She cleared her throat, too afraid to ask. "Why did you do this for me?" A much easier question, with an answer that probably wouldn't destroy what little was left of her feminine pride.

"I have my reasons," was all he said. "Now, as much as I'd love to stay in this exact spot with you, we only have a short amount of time. Do you want to spend it here or eating the food I've prepared, as well as bathing? I know those are the two things I missed most during my tenure here."

"Eat…eating. Bathing." Was this really happening? Or was she merely dreaming about him again? Nothing else explained this change in him, in her situation.

He kissed the tip of her nose. "Then food and a bath you shall have. Come. Since I can't flash you outside of this realm, and there are no homes, inns or shops here, I've set up camp a mile north, out of view of the prison."

Dreaming, surely. Perhaps a trick, as she'd first supposed. But she allowed him to lead her through the clouds without protest.

CHAPTER EIGHT

BY THE TIME THEY REACHED the camp he'd set up, Atlas was hard and aching. Nike had been pressed against his side the entire mile, her female scent in his nose, her heat radiating into his body.

When she spied the tent he'd erected, she gasped. Wide brown eyes flicked up to him with wonder before she raced forward, not slowing as she barreled through the front flap. He heard another gasp.

Grinning, Atlas followed her inside. He liked this softer side of her. She stood in the center, twirling, clearly trying to take everything in at once. He'd spread furs on the floor and had even carted a small round table here and piled it high with her favorite foods. There was a porcelain tub already filled with steaming water, rose petals floating on the surface.

Never let it be said that the Titan god of Strength did not know how to romance a woman.

Nike's hand fluttered over her heart, her gaze glued to the plate of strawberries and feta. "How did you know I liked those?"

Because he'd always been hyperaware of her every action. He'd watched her from his cell while she'd eaten them with her friends and he'd fumed that he was not the one with her, basking in her good humor. That was not something he'd admit to, however.

"Good guess," he finally said.

She peered down at the rug and kicked out her bare, dirty foot. "I don't understand why you're doing this, Atlas."

"That makes two of us," he replied gruffly.

"But—"

"Just enjoy it, Nike. It's all I can give you."

Her lashes fluttered up, and her gaze pinned him. "But why would you want to give me anything?"

"Stop analyzing my reasons. This isn't a ploy or a punishment, I promise you. And the food is not poisoned, if that's what you're thinking." He closed the distance between them, placed his hands on her shoulders and urged her to the table.

There, they ate in silence. The rapture on her face, rapture that increased with every bite, delighted him. The wine she savored sip by sip, moaning with every swallow.

Bringing her here was worth the risk of Cronus's wrath, he thought.

Although, to get technical, Cronus had merely ordered him to keep her in Tartarus. Which he had done. The clouds around the prison were part of the realm. So really, he had not broken any rules. Cronus, though, being Cronus, would not see it that way.

Still, Atlas couldn't regret it. He had never seen this joyful, eager side of the Greek goddess, and he found that he liked it just as much as he liked everything else about her. Which was way more than he should have.

When every crumb had been consumed, she turned her attention to the bath. "That's for me?" Utter longing radiated from her, yet she didn't move toward it.

"Yes. But I can't leave you. You know that, right?"

She chewed on her bottom lip and nodded. "What you're saying is, I can bathe with you watching or not at all."

"Exactly."

He expected her to fight him on that. Hell, she could have refused outright. What he did not expect was for her to push to her feet and discard her robe without hesitation. At the sight of her nakedness, he hissed in a breath. Already he'd thought her exquisite…but now, now… Holy gods. She was the finest creature the gods had ever produced.

Her skin, so golden and smooth, covered lean muscle and succulent breasts. Those breasts were soft, perfect for his hands, and her nipples were as pretty a pink as he remembered. His mouth watered for them.

She walked to the tub and stepped inside. Her ass, her back…his name. He was on his feet before he realized what he'd done. He wanted to kiss those tattoos, something she would probably fight him over. He wouldn't apologize for having given them to her, though. Hell, no. He liked them too much.

Nike pivoted slowly, and her gaze met his as she sank into the water. There was no hiding the desire he felt—it consumed him, ate him up and left him as bare as she was. Her expression, however, was blank.

Slowly, she worked the bar of soap he'd brought her over her entire body. She seemed completely unabashed as the suds danced over her, sliding down those magnificent breasts hiding beneath the rose petals. She washed her hair, too, and soon the locks were dripping down her face and shoulders.

With every move she made, he inched a little closer to her. He just couldn't help himself. Finally she finished and stood. Another feast for his eyes. All the strength he craved more than anything else in the world was now wet, and he wanted to lick away every drop.

"What are you thinking about?" she asked, stepping from the tub. Her voice was as devoid of emotion as her expression. Why?

"I need you," he managed to croak past the lump in his throat.

Finally. A reaction. Relief and desire, such intense desire, claimed her, and she grinned a siren's smile. "Then have me you shall."

They were a mimic of his earlier words, and completely unexpected. Why the change in her? *Doesn't matter.* As he'd told her earlier, there was no good reason to analyze a change of heart. Not in either of them. Not now.

He had the distance between them defeated a split second later. Had his arms wrapped around her, jerking her into him, a second after that. Their lips met in a wild tangle, their tongues seeking, rolling together. On and on the kiss continued, drowning him in all that she was.

He hated to stop, even for a moment, but he had to remove his clothes. If he didn't experience skin-to-skin contact soon, he was going to ignite into flames. Panting, he tore away his shirt, his boots, then his pants.

She moaned. "Atlas."

He pulled her back into his embrace. Finally. Blessedly. Skin to skin. Both of them groaned at the headiness. Her nipples rubbed against his chest, his tattoos, while their lower bodies thrust together. Then she was bending down, tracing those letters with her tongue—and gods, he had never been happier that he had them.

After she'd traced the last one, she kissed her way down his stomach. She dropped to her knees.

Was she going to—*please, please, please*—but she didn't like him enough to do it. Did she? "What are you—"

She sucked his cock deep into her mouth.

His head fell back, and he roared. All that wet heat was ecstasy, surely the first he'd ever truly known, for nothing had ever felt this damned good. Except her, that first time he claimed her. Up and down she moved, allowing him to hit the back of her throat.

"Gods! Don't make me come."

She laughed, pulled off and licked his sac. "When have I ever listened to you?"

"Vixen."

"Why can't I make you come?"

"Because I want inside you." With a growl, he dropped to his knees, as well. She could taste his seed. Later. He hadn't lied to her. More than anything, even more of that ecstasy, he wanted inside her, and he didn't want to have to wait for it. "Spread your legs for me."

The moment she obeyed, he had two fingers buried deep. More wet heat. And to his delight… "You're ready for me." Never had he been more proud that he'd brought a female to this point. And that he'd done so with kisses, only kisses….

She trembled, had to grip his shoulders to remain upright. "I'm ready for you every damn time I see you."

And she didn't like it, he could tell from her tone, but he could only bask in the admission. "It's the same for me."

At first, she blinked, as if she couldn't allow herself to believe him. So vulnerable she appeared, so—dare he wish?—hopeful. Then she placed a sweet kiss on his lips and breathed him in. "Don't say things like that," she whispered.

"Why not? I spoke true."

"Because they affect me."

Headier words had never been spoken. "Let's finish this before I combust, sweetheart."

"Please."

He was sweating, panting, as he settled back on his ass, reached out and cupped hers. He jerked her onto his lap, forcing her to wrap her thighs around his waist. As her hands tangled in his hair, he lifted her, placing her eager core at the tip of his erection.

"Ready?" he asked hoarsely. This was it. The moment he felt he'd been waiting forever for.

"Ready."

He thrust up and she pushed down, and then he was all the way in, surrounded by the very thing he had defied his king, his sovereign, to possess. It was better than he remembered, better than he could have imagined. He couldn't pause, couldn't give her time to adjust. Over and over he pushed in, pulled out, too overwhelmed by pleasure to do anything but ride out the storm. Perhaps it was the same for her. Her nails scored his back, and her moans rang in his ears.

Gods, he was close. On fire. Burning. Desperate. He reached between their bodies and pressed his thumb against his new favorite place.

"Atlas!" she shouted, her inner walls suddenly milking him.

She was climaxing, lost to all that he was, and the thought drove him over the last bit of the edge, as well.

He jetted inside her, lost to all that *she* was, the most intense orgasm of his life claiming him.

An eternity later, his spasms stopped. Together, they fell backward, onto the softness of the fur. He kept his arms around her, unwilling to let her go. Now…always?

Yes, always, he thought, and his eyes widened. He wanted her always. Wanted more of this. *Had* to have more of this. When he'd forgiven her completely, he didn't know. When he'd softened, he didn't know, either. He only knew that she'd become an important part of his life. Perhaps she always had been; he'd just been too foolish to realize it.

What the hell was he going to do?

They could be together each night after his shift, but they'd never have privacy, and her pride would soon chafe at his amorous attentions, all while he refused to set her free. It would have been the same for him when the situation had been reversed. Besides, she was too precious to hurt in that way. But the problem was, he couldn't be without her. He'd proven that already.

Damn, he thought next, suddenly sick to his stomach. Damn!

He'd finally found the one woman for him, but they were doomed.

CHAPTER NINE

SHE LOVED HIM, NIKE THOUGHT. Again. *I'm hopeless.*

He'd just…he'd been so amazing. He'd whisked her away, given her everything she'd craved: food, water and his body. Gods, had he given her that delectable body. She'd savored every moment. Savored his taste, his touch, the feel of him pounding inside her.

Four days had since passed, but she craved more. Always she craved more. She'd spent the time locked inside her cell, pacing, trying to think of ways for them to be together. If he still wanted her, that is. Atlas had come by at least once a day to make sure she was properly fed and that her basin of water was filled, but he'd never said a word to her. Actually, they hadn't spoken since leaving the tent.

At the time, she'd felt too raw, too exposed. She'd feared her feelings for him had been shining in her eyes. He was everything she'd ever wanted in a mate. His strength matched hers. She would never have to worry about hurting him. He was witty and charming. He was a protector, a warrior. He was deliciously vengeful, she knew firsthand.

She smiled, wishing she could reach between her shoulder blades and feel his name. She was certain the letters would be as hot as the man himself. But…

Why hadn't he spoken to her?

Why didn't you speak to him?

Because she hadn't known what to say. Did he still want her? Did he feel anything for her? How would she react if he didn't, which was most likely the case? Part of her wanted to take anything he would give her. The other part of her knew her pride wouldn't allow her to do such a thing. But there at the end, when they'd returned to Tartarus and he'd closed the bars to her cell, she had thought she'd glimpsed regret. Regret that he had to seal her inside. Regret that they couldn't spend more time together—in bed and out.

Nike tugged at her collar and screeched. Damn this. She was the epitome of strength, yet was as helpless as a babe. How could she win a man's heart when she couldn't even win her own freedom?

ATLAS HEARD A SCREECH of frustration and knew immediately who had uttered it. Nike. His Nike. His beautiful Nike. He'd deliberated about what to do, how they could be together, for four days. Well, the time for thinking was over, it seemed. She was close to her breaking point. She'd tasted freedom; being sequestered now had to be a thousand times worse than before.

He hated that she was locked up, and he knew they could never be together while she was. He also knew they could not be together if he released her. She would most likely run, and he would most definitely be punished.

Maybe she loved him, maybe she didn't. Maybe she'd stay with him. Or try to. She liked him and was attracted to him, he would go so far as to say. After everything that had transpired between them, she wouldn't have slept with him otherwise. But love? He wasn't sure.

And it didn't matter, really. *He* loved *her.* Perhaps he always had. He'd never felt so strongly about a woman. He'd never wanted to spend his every waking minute with someone before, had never wanted to cuddle someone into his side for every sleeping minute. He'd never wanted to eat every meal together. To talk and laugh about their days. To spar, verbally and physically. But he did with her.

And since they couldn't be together, no matter what way things panned out, there was only one thing to do.

Dread. That's what he felt as he pounded up the stairs and to her cell. Also...relief. She was banging a fist into the wall, plumes of dust forming around her. The sight of her nearly undid him. He wanted to kiss her, put his fingers all over her, sink inside her. *Harden your heart. Do what is needed.* His hand was shaking as he lifted the sensor.

She heard the slide of the bars and turned. A gasp parted her beautiful lips. Without a word, he held out his palm.

"What—"

"Just take it."

She frowned as she accepted.

Still silent, he pulled her along the same path he had just taken. The same path they'd taken those four days ago. No one tried to stop him this time. In fact, as he passed the guard's station, the two gods on duty rolled their eyes.

Outside, with the clouds all around him, he whirled on Nike. He still wanted to kiss her, but knew that if he did so, he would not be able to let her go. And he had to let her go.

"Atlas," she said with a seductive grin. She tried to

wrap her arms around his neck. "Another outing? I'm glad."

He shook his head and placed his fingers on the designated indentations in the collar. Cool metal met his touch. Then he leaned down and fit his lips over the center.

Her grin fell away. A tremor moved through her. "Wh-what are you doing?"

"Be still." He drew in a deep breath, held it…held it…and then slowly released it. As that breath slithered through the inside of the collar, the metal loosened… finally splitting down the center and tumbling to the ground. Such a simple thing, the removal. Touch and breath. Yet only an uncollared god could do so, a fact that had to taunt the incarcerated. Perhaps that's why the bands had been designed as they had.

Eyes wide, she reached up, felt her bare neck. "I don't understand what's happening," she said. They were the same words she'd spoken before. He hadn't had an answer then. He did now. He loved her, but he could never tell her that.

"Go," he said. "Flash somewhere. Maybe earth. And whatever you do, stay hidden. Do you understand me?"

"Atlas…no." She shook her head violently, even fisted his shirt. "No, I can't. When they discover I'm gone for good, and they will, you'll be charged with a crime. You'll be locked away, placed with the Greeks who hate you. Or, if you're lucky, you'll be killed."

She felt, he realized, both amazed and saddened. She cared for him, which meant she would suffer without him. If anything, that only increased his determination to save her. She did not deserve a life behind bars.

He forced his expression to harden. Forced himself

to jerk away from her. "I can't stand to look at you anymore. I've had you, and now I'm bored with you."

Her arms dropped to her sides as if weighed down by rocks, but she quickly pulled them around her middle. "Then keep me locked up and stay away from me. You don't want to do this."

Still willing to give up her freedom to be near him? Damn her. He fell a little more in love with her. "Go! Did you not hear me? I can't stand the sight of you anymore. Don't you get it? You make me sick, Nike."

"Shut up." Tears filled her eyes. Real godsdamned tears. "You don't mean that. You *can't* mean that." The last was whispered brokenly.

His heart constricted painfully. *Do it. Finish it.* "I'd rather be killed or locked away than look at you another moment. Because every time I look at you, I'm reminded of what we did and I—I want to vomit. I was using you, wanting to punish you, but I took things too far. Even for me." Hating himself, he turned away from her. "So do us both a favor and go."

For a long while, she didn't speak. He knew she didn't flash away, either, for he heard no rustle of clothing. But then, he *did* hear a whimper. A sob. More of those tears must be falling.

Gods, he couldn't do it. He couldn't send her away like this. He spun, meaning to grab on to her and tell her the truth, to force her to listen. To make her leave another way. But she was gone before their eyes could meet and his hands encountered only air.

"You insolent fool!"

Atlas peered up at the fuming Cronus. Not like he could do anything else. His wrists were chained to poles, forcing him to remain on his knees. The very collar he'd removed from Nike was now wrapped around his own neck.

He'd known this would happen, but he hadn't cared. He still didn't. Nike was free, and that was all that mattered.

"Have you nothing to say for yourself?"

"No."

"One Greek can raise an army. That army can attack us. Ruin us. I told you that, and still you defied me."

"Nike won't do that," he said confidently. He trusted her to disappear. Even as angry as she had to be with him, she would not endanger herself to save people she had never truly liked.

Cronus slammed his fist against the arm of his throne, ever the petulant child. "You can't know that! You aren't my All-Seeing Eye."

Atlas arched a brow, refusing to be cowed. "Would you risk being imprisoned again to help your fellow Titans? I may not be able to see all the secrets of the heavens and Hell, yet I know you would not. She will not, either."

The king had no response to that, but that didn't stop him from growling. "You disobeyed a direct order, and for that you will be punished."

"I understand." He offered the statement without hesitation. It was the truth. He understood that the god king had to make an example out of him. Otherwise, others would see Cronus as weak. They would disobey him as Atlas had.

"I think you actually do." Some of Cronus's fury abated. "Only this morning I saw a portrait of you. A portrait painted by my Eye. With it, she showed me exactly how to punish you." The king smiled evilly and looked to the ghostlike girl still standing at his side. "You know what to do, sweet Sienna."

Sienna strode forward, a knife appearing in her hand. She stopped in front of Atlas and dropped to her knees, placing them eye to eye. So this was it, he thought. The end. As an immortal, he'd never thought to reach this point. Still. He found he only regretted that he hadn't had more time with Nike, that he hadn't gotten the chance to apologize for his harsh words the last time they were together and that he would never have the chance to confess his love.

With absolutely no emotion on her face, the girl dug the tip of the blade into his wrist and cut out his sensor, rather than chop off his head. That's when he realized Cronus meant to lock him away rather than kill him. Good. More time to think about Nike and what could have been.

But then Sienna moved the blade to his chest and pressed, slicing. It stung, but that was not what made him struggle against her ministrations. No, it was the fact that she began carving away Nike's name. He roared loud and long, fighting for all he was worth. Guards were called over and hard hands settled over him, pressing him down, holding him steady. Still he fought, but in the end, they managed to remove all four letters.

As each person walked away from him, he glanced down at himself through burning, watery eyes. Blood poured down his chest and four open wounds stared up at him, the muscles torn, the skin completely gone. He might have hated that brand at one point in his life, but he'd grown to love it as much as the woman who'd given it to him. More than that, it had been the last remaining evidence of her presence.

His hands fisted, and his back straightened. Blood and sweat mingled, stinging further. Another roar burst from his lips, and he tossed it to the domed ceiling. He didn't stop until his throat was shredded from the strain.

"Are you quite finished?" Cronus asked him.

His gaze fell to the dais, narrowing. "I will destroy you for this," his vowed brokenly. "One day you will die by my hand."

"Not likely. Take him to Tartarus," the king told his guards, unconcerned. "Where he will rot for all eternity."

CHAPTER TEN

IT TOOK HER TWO DAYS, but Nike finally located Atlas's home, a sprawling estate in Olympus. Or Titania, as Cronus had renamed the city. The amount of wealth Atlas had needed to acquire such a place astonished her—and she knew exactly how much he'd paid because *she* had once owned it. But then, she supposed he'd considered every cent worth it. After living in a tiny cell for thousands of years, he'd most likely wanted every bit of space he could get. And every amenity.

There was a swimming pool, more than thirty bedrooms, two winding, marble staircases and four fireplaces, and all the walls were comprised of solid gold. None of that interested her, however. Only his bedroom did.

There, she discovered more about the man who had sent her on her way. A man who would not have risked *this* just to avoid her face, as he'd claimed. A man who would not have risked his life for anything other than love.

Nearly everything was as she'd left it. A huge bed covered with black silk sheets. The walls were painted with murals of the sun and sky, and the furniture smelled of rich mahogany. There were multiple bookcases, each filled with leather-bound books. Her books. Beaded pillows were strategically placed along the floor. Places for him to lounge and read, as she had done.

What held her attention, however, was the only difference. A portrait hung above the hearth. A portrait of *her*.

He must have commissioned it after their time inside that tent, for she was reclined in a porcelain tub, bubbles sliding over her shoulders and chest, her hair soaked. She would have looked as plain and masculine as always, except he'd had the artist add a sensual light to her dark eyes and a come-and-get-me curve to her lips.

Finally she knew how he saw her. As someone beautiful. He'd once told her so, but she'd had trouble believing him. Now...

Only a man in love would do such a thing. Only a man in love would keep such a thing in such a prominent place. Only a man in love would want to see a woman's portrait every night before he fell asleep, then wake up looking at it.

Oh, yes. He loved her. As she loved him.

There, outside of Tartarus, she'd thought, hoped, that he did so, but she had let his words scrape against her already low self-esteem. How could so beautiful and sensual a man want her? she'd wondered. But he did. He loved her. Proof: he'd risked everything for her.

She could do no less for him.

Nike strode through the bedroom, knowing her lover would have a weapons case stashed somewhere—and knowing exactly what to do with it.

ATLAS WAS NOT GIVEN A CELL of his own—not at first. Still bleeding and frantic, fighting, he had been thrust into a cell with Erebos. Of course, that's who had been chosen as his cell mate, he'd thought, rage filling him. A male who had once thought to claim his Nike. A male who had then stolen food from her, pushed her around and called her terrible names.

Atlas had seen it happen on numerous occasions. He hadn't done anything about it then, telling himself she deserved what she got, but he'd wanted to. And there was no better time than now.

Even with his strength corralled by the collar and half his blood dried to his chest, even with his still-seeping wounds splitting open with every move he made, Atlas managed to defeat Erebos in record time. He punched, he kicked, he did not play fair, kneeing the god in the balls while he was down. In the end, a broken, bloody Erebos lay crying on the dirty floor, right alongside everyone who had tried to save him.

That's when Atlas was moved to the empty cell Nike had occupied. He stretched out on the cot, simply breathing in her lingering essence. His sweet, sweet Nike. He would have to spend eternity without her. Without even her brand. Once again, he roared.

What was she doing now? If she sought solace in the arms of another man, even in the years to come, he would tear this prison apart stone by stone and kill the bastard. *As if. You sent her on her way to do just that. You want her happy.*

"What's all the racket? Seriously."

Gods, he was hearing her voice now. Locked up two days, and he was already headed into insanity.

His bars rattled, slid open. He rolled to his side, determined to send whoever it was away. When he caught sight of his beloved Nike, he blinked. Oh, yes, he was indeed going insane. She stood before him, clad in a black leather bra top and black leather pants. Her hair was slicked back in a smooth ponytail. Blood splattered her cheeks. Never had she looked more beautiful, her strength there for all to see.

She was holding someone's arm. Without their body. For the sensor in the wrist?

His hallucinations were certainly detailed.

"Well?" she said, clearly impatient. She tossed the arm aside. "Aren't you going to say anything?"

Slowly he sat up. He didn't want this moment to end. Didn't want to lose sight of her. "I missed you. So much."

"And I wanted an apology. Stupid me. I much prefer this." She grinned, practically beaming. "I missed you, too, but we'll have to catch up later." Her gaze fell to his chest, and she gaped in astonishment. Then she growled. "Did the god king cut my name off you?"

"Yes."

She was holding a knife, he saw, and her knuckles bleached of color. "I. Will. Kill. Him."

"Already promised to do so."

"We'll do it together, then. After we get out of here." Her attention flicked behind her, urgent, before returning to him. "Come on. We have to go before someone realizes what I've done."

"Just let me look at you. Just let me enjoy this moment. Let me apologize for what I said to you. You said you wanted an apology, yes? I didn't mean it, not a word I said that last day, but I—"

She closed the distance between them and slapped him. Hard. The blow knocked him back against the cot and caused stars to wink over his vision.

Once more, he blinked at her. "You hit me."

"Yeah, and I'll do it again if you don't get your ass in gear."

"You're real."

"Yes."

"But you're *real*." He sat up, saying the words but not truly absorbing them. This couldn't be happening.

She dropped to her knees so that they were eye to eye. "Again, yes." Just as he'd once done to her, she placed her fingers over his collar and blew into the center. As the metal softened, he finally understood what his brain had been trying to tell him. Nike was here. She was really here. And she was saving his life.

With a scowl, he jumped to his feet. "I told you to go to earth, damn it."

"Okay, not the reaction I expected." She stood and pressed a swift kiss to his lips. "Good thing I never listen to you. Now let's go. I've already taken out the guards below. And no, I didn't kill your friends. Just made them wish they were dead." As she spoke, she latched on to his hand and dragged him out of the cell. "Cronus could realize what's going down at any moment and appear, and then we'll both be in trouble. As long as we're here, we're easy pickings."

True. Nike was a fugitive now; he wanted her out of this prison, out of this realm, as soon as possible. "You risked your life to save me, you fool."

"Well, you risked your life to save *me*."

Down the stairs they pounded and, sure enough, all three of the guards were flat on their faces, motionless. One of them was missing an arm—and he knew exactly where to find it. Not that he'd take the time to tell. The arm, lost or not, would grow back. "But you were free. You had what you wanted."

"Not everything," she threw over her shoulder.

Okay, wow. She'd just admitted she wanted him more than freedom. Atlas couldn't help himself. He gave a tug, propelling her backward, into his arms. "I love you," he finally proclaimed, and mashed their lips together. His tongue thrust deep, tasting, demanding. "I mean it. I love you more than anything. Anyone."

She only allowed the kiss for a few seconds, her hands fisting his hair and taking everything he had to give, before she pulled away, panting. "I love you, too. But let's get the hell out of here. I need your pretty head connected to your amazing body."

Once again, they surged forward. Still, he almost couldn't believe this was happening. It was so much like a dream. "I'm going to spend the rest of eternity making up for what I did to you."

"Good. I think I'll like seeing you grovel. But just for the record, I love my tattoo and I know why you said those nasty things. Sure, I would have found a better way to get you to safety, but then, I'm smarter than you are, so really, I can't blame you."

He laughed. Gods, he loved this woman. "Vixen."

"Your vixen."

"Mine. Always. You'll mark me again just as soon as my skin heals."

"Already planned on it."

Good. He wouldn't feel complete until she did. "So where are we going to live?" he asked. "We can't stay in the heavens."

"You ordered me to hide on earth. I thought we could

do so—together. Though I hate that you have to give up your amazing house."

"You've been there?" He found he really liked the thought of her there, surrounded by his things, breathing in his essence. "You know where I chose to live?"

"Yes. Why did you? Choose there, I mean."

"To feel closer to you."

"Well, you're about to be a *lot* closer to me."

A laugh boomed from him. There was no woman more perfect for him. "The only thing I'll miss from that house is the portrait of you. But now I have the real thing." He placed a swift kiss on her lips. "Back to our new living arrangements. There are other gods out there, Greeks like you, who are in hiding. Cronus has never been able to find them. That means there are places he can't see."

"Maybe we'll find them and join them. We are Strength, after all. And Victory."

"Yes. Victory."

"We can succeed where he has failed."

"In the meantime, we might even try to find the Lords of the Underworld. Cronus mentioned being distracted by them. If they are his enemies, they might be good friends for us to have."

Her eyes widened. "I know of whom you speak. They were Zeus's immortal warriors long ago, but now they house the demons once locked inside Pandora's box. Cronus will have his hands tied for a long, *long* time with them. They would be *very* good friends to have."

They reached the door and burst outside, all without incident. Clouds instantly enveloped them, the sun shining brightly. Nike whirled and threw herself in his arms, placing nips and kisses all over his face.

"We did it. Now take us somewhere. Anywhere. As long as we can be together."

"I love you," he said again, then did exactly as his woman had ordered.

* * * * *

nocturne™

COMING NEXT MONTH

Available SEPTEMBER 27, 2011

#121 LORD OF RAGE
Royal House of Shadows
Jill Monroe

#122 THE VAMPIRE'S SEDUCTION
Cynthia Cooke

You can find more information on upcoming
Harlequin® titles, free excerpts and more at
www.HarlequinInsideRomance.com.

HNCNM0911